The Horus Heresy series

Book 1 – HORUS RISING
Dan Abnett

Book 2 – FALSE GODS
Graham McNeill

Book 3 – GALAXY IN FLAMES
Ben Counter

Book 4 – THE FLIGHT OF THE EISENSTEIN
James Swallow

Book 5 – FULGRIM
Graham McNeill

Book 6 – DESCENT OF ANGELS
Mitchel Scanlon

Book 7 – LEGION
Dan Abnett

Book 8 – BATTLE FOR THE ABYSS
Ben Counter

Book 9 – MECHANICUM
Graham McNeill

THE HORUS HERESY

TALES OF HERESY

Edited by Nick Kyme
& Lindsey Priestley

A BLACK LIBRARY PUBLICATION

First published in Great Britain in 2009 by
BL Publishing,
Games Workshop Ltd.,
Willow Road, Nottingham,
NG7 2WS, UK.

10 9 8 7 6 5 4 3 2 1

Cover and page 1 illustration by Neil Roberts.

A CIP record for this book is available from the British Library.

ISBN 13: 978 1 84416 683 1
ISBN 10: 1 84416 683 X

See the Black Library on the Internet at
www.blacklibrary.com

Find out more about Games Workshop
and the world of Warhammer 40,000 at
www.games-workshop.com

Printed in the UK by CPI Bookmarque, Croydon, CR0 4TD

THE HORUS HERESY

It is a time of legend.

Mighty heroes battle for the right to rule the galaxy. The vast armies of the Emperor of Earth have conquered the galaxy in a Great Crusade – the myriad alien races have been smashed by the Emperor's elite warriors and wiped from the face of history.

The dawn of a new age of supremacy for humanity beckons.

Gleaming citadels of marble and gold celebrate the many victories of the Emperor. Triumphs are raised on a million worlds to record the epic deeds of his most powerful and deadly warriors.

First and foremost amongst these are the primarchs, superheroic beings who have led the Emperor's armies of Space Marines in victory after victory. They are unstoppable and magnificent, the pinnacle of the Emperor's genetic experimentation. The Space Marines are the mightiest human warriors the galaxy has ever known, each capable of besting a hundred normal men or more in combat.

Organised into vast armies of tens of thousands called Legions, the Space Marines and their primarch leaders conquer the galaxy in the name of the Emperor.

Chief amongst the primarchs is Horus, called the Glorious, the Brightest Star, favourite of the Emperor, and like a son unto him. He is the Warmaster, the commander-in-chief of the Emperor's military might, subjugator of a thousand thousand worlds and conqueror of the galaxy. He is a warrior without peer, a diplomat supreme.

As the flames of war spread through the Imperium, mankind's champions will all be put to the ultimate test.

CONTENTS

Blood Games   *by Dan Abnett*   9

Wolf at the Door   *by Mike Lee*   61

Scions of the Storm *by Anthony Reynolds* 159

The Voice   *by James Swallow*   211

Call of the Lion   *by Gav Thorpe*   275

The Last Church   *by Graham McNeill*   323

After Desh'ea   *by Matthew Farrer*   375

BLOOD GAMES

Dan Abnett

quis custodiet ipsos custodes?

HE HAD BEEN circling for ten months. Ten months, and eighteen identities, most of them so authentic they had fooled Unified Biometric Verification. He'd faked out three blind trails to throw them off his scent, one into the Slovakian fiefs, one to Kaspia and the Nord Reaches, and the other a meandering route down through the Tirol to the Dolomite Shrines overlooking the Pit of Venezia. He'd overwintered in Boocuresti Hive, and crossed the Black Sea Basin by cargo spinner during the first week of ice-ebb. At Bilhorod, he had turned back on himself to lose an unwanted tail. He had spent three weeks hiding in a disused manufactory in Mesopotamia, preparing his next move.

Ten months; a little long for a blood game, but then he was playing it out carefully, synchronising his movements with global patterns, following trade routes, inter-provincial traffic and seasonal labour migrations. He was one hundred per cent certain they didn't have an orbital grid fix for him, and he was fairly confident they didn't even have an approximate. There'd been no one on his heels since Bilhorod.

He trekked up-country through Baluchistan, mostly on foot, sometimes stealing a lift on transports, and crossed the border into the Imperial Territory three hundred and three days after he had set out.

THE TOP OF the world had changed in ten months. An entire peak had disappeared from the blinding skyline, a gap at odds with his memories, nagging like a missing tooth. The high-altitude air smelled of pitch, molten alloys and shaved stone. Primarch Dorn's warrior-engineers were crafting their poliorcetics, armouring the highest and most robust steeples of the Earth.

The smell of pitch, alloy and stone was the smell of approaching war. Its fragmented notes hung on the bright air of the old Himalazia.

THE SCENERY WAS SO white it scorched his eyes, and he was glad of his glare-goggles. A few degrees below zero, the air was like glass, and the sun like a fusion torch in the blue sky. Perfect snows coated the peaks and the ascents, painfully white, achingly empty.

He had considered the south his best option, Kath Mandau and the towering central Precinct, but as he approached he realised how much things had changed. Security, which had never been less than rigorous, had cinched up as tight as a penitent's cilice. The coming war had trebled the guards on the gates, quadrupled the gun-nests and automated weapon blisters, and multiplied the biometric sensors a hundredfold.

Vast workcrews of migrant labourers, serving the orders of the Masonic Guilds, had gathered around the Palace: their camps, their workings, their very bodies staining the high snows green and black and red like algae growth.

Security is tighter, but there are millions more faces to watch.

He observed the labour hosts for six days, eschewing his plans for the south and turning north instead, following the high pastures and walking trails over onto the plateau, keeping the toiling hosts in view. Constant streams flowed down the snowy valleys and passes from Kunlun: columns of fresh workers, and convoys of cargo and building materials from the Xizang mines. The columns looked like rivers of slow, dark meltwater, or racing black glaciers. Where the influx streams met the worker armies, temporary cities sprouted in the shadows of the immense walls, habitent towns and canvas metropoli, accommodating the migrants, corralling their pack animals and servitors, seeing to their needs of food and water and medicine. The unloaded materials: timber, pig alloy, mule steel, ores and ballast, stacked up around the camp cities like slag heaps. Hoist cranes and magnificent derricks lifted pallets of materials up over the walls. Horns snorted and echoed around the high valleys.

Sometimes, he just sat and looked at the Palace as if it was the most wonderful thing in creation. It probably wasn't. There were undoubtedly feats of ancient, inhuman architecture on forgotten, scattered worlds that dwarfed it, or eclipsed it in stupendous scale or awe-inspiring scope. The architecture was not the point. It was the *idea* of the Palace that made it the most wonderful thing. It was the inner notion, the concept that it made flesh.

The Palace was vast, beautiful, the greatest mountain range on Terra refashioned into a residence and a capital, and now, belatedly, a fortress.

The missing Himalazian peak had been levelled for building materials. The recognition of that feat made him smile. These days, the schemes of man were never modest.

Adopting rags and dirty leg armour, he spent three days labouring with the genestock ogres from Nei Monggol. Nicknamed the *migou*, they slogged up and down the passes, carrying sheets of zurlite and huge panniers of nephrite and Egyptian pebble. They dug embankments and earthworks with massive shovels made from the blade-bones of giant grox, and formed hammer gangs to rhythmically sink the iron stakes that would support the concertinaed spools of flay-wire.

At night, in the work camps, the massive genestock stoked their over-muscled bodies with *qash*, a resin derived from the venom of a Gobi Waste nematode. The substance made their veins bulge, and their eyes roll white. It made them speak in tongues.

He watched the effects, and made estimates of dosage and systemic duration.

The genestock were prepared to work with him, but they treated him with general suspicion. He tried to be just another Caucasian broadback, keen to earn a stipend and a bonus from the Masonic Guilds. His papers were in order. When he tried to purchase a little *qash*, however, they turned sour, fearing him to be a genewhip sent into the camps to keep the workforce clean.

They tried to kill him.

Under the pretence of a quiet sale, three genestock migou drew him apart from the main camp, and led him to a rock pasture where fire stone and cacholong spoil had been heaped up by porter gangs. They unwrapped a cloth roll with slices of brown resin in it to show him. Then one drew a punch-dagger and tried to insert it into his liver.

He sighed – a complication.

He took hold of the migou's wrist, folded the arm around and broke it against itself with his elbow. The joint went the wrong way, and the arm went so slack, he simply peeled the punch-dagger out of the dead fingers. The genestock uttered no expression of pain. He simply blinked in surprise.

All three of them were titanic creatures, corded and slabby with unnatural, hard-cut muscle definition. It had not occurred to any of them that the

Caucasian, though extremely large and well made, would offer them a moment's problem.

One threw a punch, a blow driven with huge force but desultory effort, as if he was aggrieved that they should be put to such trouble. The punch was designed to finish matters, to put the Caucasian down, his jaw pulped, his head slack on the column of his spine.

The blow did not connect with any part of the Caucasian. Instead, it encountered the punch-dagger, which had suddenly been angled to face it. The impact shaved flesh and muscle away from bone. This produced a pain response. The genestock howled, and tried to gather in his shredded hand and forearm. The Caucasian shut him up by jabbing the punch-dagger into his heavy forehead. It cracked in through the bone like the tip of a rock-breaker's pick.

The genestock toppled backwards, wearing the grip of the punch-dagger above his eyes like some curious tiara.

The third migou grabbed him from behind in an ursine hug. The genestock with the broken arm tried to claw at his face. It was all tiresome now. He broke free of the embrace with a shrug of his shoulders, turned and drove his right hand into the genestock's chest. The sternum split. When the Caucasian wrenched his hand out again, it looked as if it was wearing a red glove. Most of the migou's heart was clenched in his steaming fist.

The genestock with the broken arm, now the only one of the trio left alive, murmured in fear and started to run away across the rock pasture.

He bore the wounded genestock no especial malice, but he couldn't let him go. With bloody fingers, he bent down, selected a small piece of fire stone, weighed it in his hand and launched it with a snap of his wrist.

It made a *pokk!* noise as it penetrated the back of the fleeing ogre's head like a bullet. He fell heavily, and his hefty corpse slithered down the litter of a spoil heap on its face.

He disposed of the three bodies in a fathomless gorge, washed his hands with snow and took the roll of *qash* resin.

The confluence of workers gathered around the skirts of the Palace had brought, as any great body of humanity always did, lice and vermin and scavengers with it. Rad-wolves had followed the workers down off the plateau, and gathered at night, red eyes in the dark catching the flicker of the campfire rings. Thousands of war hounds patrolled the camp perimeters at night, or lingered on the escarpments before the Palace. The night was regularly interrupted by sudden gales of howling and barking, the growl and shiver of animals mauling one another as the faithful hounds drove off wolves that had become too inquisitive.

In the darkness, it was hard to tell the difference between hounds and wolves.

He had received regular physiological testing his entire life, and he had memorised all the results in forensic detail so as to best judge his limitations.

He cut the *qash* resin into sample measures, weighing each on a set of fine scales that he'd borrowed from a gem cutter.

The reinforcement of the Annapurna Gate was half done. Every day, the mouth of the huge gate bustled with thousands of labourers, and the towering hoist cranes swung cradles of ceramite plating, rebar and reinforced rockcrete up over the cyclopean arch. It was too intensive a task for the sentries to scan each labourer in and out individually: the labour gangs would snarl up, and the work would run slow. Instead, the entire gate zone was covered by a biometric reader field, projected by slowly rotating vanes in the eaves of the primary arch.

At dawn, he secured himself under the tarps of one of the payloads due to be taken in over the gate by hoist crane. He huddled down between sheets of mule steel and bundles of ironwood.

He had prepared a four-gram dose of *qash*, an overdose by migou standards. Its efficacy was such, he would be insensible less than a minute after ingesting it.

He waited for two hours until he felt the jolt of the lift crews securing the payload's chains. He heard the steel cables of the hoist crane whining. He felt the heavy sway as the pallet he was hiding on left the ground.

He swallowed the *qash*.

Observation had shown him that it took the hoist crane mechanism forty-three seconds to bring a payload up to clearance height, and a further sixty-six seconds to traverse it in over the gate top. Twenty-four seconds into that second time period, the moving pay-load would enter the biometric reader field.

The *qash* did its work. He was stiff and dead twelve seconds before he entered the field. The field read nothing except a payload of inert building materials.

HE WOKE. THE pallet had set down, and some of the tarps had been pulled back. Riggers and roof-gangers were beginning to unload the mule steel.

His body ached. Most of his muscles were cramping. He focused and performed some purging exercises to throw off the vestiges of the somatic rigour that the *qash* had induced. Death to most mortal men, near-death to a being like him; a brief, death-like fugue to allow him to slip in through the Palace biometrics.

He slid off the pallet, sore and woozy. Enormous gunboxes and shielded fighting platforms were being constructed around the upper ramparts, and thick dura-plating and adamantium were being bonded to the walls. Workers milled around on scaffolds and gantries, some suspended like mountaineers over the edge of the wall's sheer drop. The air was filled with noises of hammering and cutting. Powered tools shrilled. Fusion torches buzzed and flickered with arc-tic blue light.

Phantoms fought behind his eyes, the ghost flares of fusion cutters. There was blood in his throat. He scooped up a box of rivets and a concussion mallet, and blended with the workforce.

HE PENETRATED THE outer levels of the Palace. This process took a further three days. He stopped being a masonic labourer and became a shadow, then a footman polishing brasswork, then a lamp-lighter with a spark-pole, and then a doorkeeper, wearing a livery he had purloined from a laundry room and a concealed displacer field to disguise his height and bulk.

He followed hallways that were dressed in diaspore and agate, and descended stairwells planed from solid pieces of onyx. He watched his reflection cross polished marble floors, and his shadow chase along walls carved from quartz and sardonyx. He waited in the ivory gloom of huge processionals while warbands passed by in marching time. He lingered in doorways while almost endless trains of servitors brought past trays of raw meats and hydroponic vegetables for the high table.

He became a footman again, then a carpet beater, then a beadle, and then a messenger man with an attaché box full of blank papers, hunching to disguise his build and height. Every once in a while, he stopped to get his bearings. The Palace was bigger than many cities. Its levels and byways took a lifetime to learn. From the rails of high balconies, he looked down into artificial ravines five hundred storeys deep, filled with lights and teeming with people. Some of the great domes in the Precinct, especially the Hegemon, were so vast, they contained their own miniature weather systems. Microclimate clouds drifted under painted vaults. Rain in the Hegemon was said to be a portent of good fortune.

As far as he knew, it had not rained in the Hegemon for three years.

THE CUSTODES WERE abroad, watching over the inner reaches of the Precinct, majestic in their ornate golden armour. Their plume crests were crimson, like sprays of arterial blood frozen in the air. The pre-Unity symbol of the lightning bolt was blazoned on their armour. They lurked in the gloomy halls and shadowed cloisters of the Palace, their Guardian spears upright, frighteningly vigilant.

They were impassive, silent, and they guarded their secrets solemnly, but in their very presence there was a truth to be unpicked.

He noted their deployment. Two custodes were watching the Southern Circuit that snaked like silver braid towards the Hegemon. Two more stood at the Jade Bailey, and another three patrolled beneath the fretted ironwork and malachite of the Congressional. A lone custodes, almost invisible, held position under the waxy emerald leaves of the Qokang Oasis, watching the outfall of the crystal-clear pleasure lake thunder down into the turbine gulf in misty cascades. Four more prowled the upper platforms of the Taxonomic Towers.

There were, however, none on the Northern Circuit, and none on the western limits of the lake, and none near the Investiary. It was so telling. They were like visible moons betraying the position of an invisible planet, bright astral bodies pushed into a certain pattern by the gravitational ministrations of an unseen star. By noting where they were, and where they weren't, he could determine the location of his prey.

The Hall of Leng seemed most likely. From the disposition of the steadfast custodes, his prey had to be somewhere in the western hemispheric portion of the Precinct, which meant the Hall of Leng, the House of Weapons, the Great Observatory, or the private apartments adjoining the latter two, but he knew the Hall of Leng was a favourite place. When he wasn't sequestered in secret toil in the deep, private crypts of the Palace, his prey was known to spend a great deal of time in the Hall, measuring the angles of space and time.

It was said that past and future co-mingled at that site, and had done so since primordial times, before the place had owned the name Leng, before his prey had been born, before a roof had been raised above it, or human eyes had seen it. The Hall of Leng, long-beamed and dark, was simply a domestication of one of the materium's anomalies, a pulled thread in the fabric of time, a scab on the skin of space.

He had never felt comfortable in the Hall. It was filled with a tangible darkness, which seemed to exhale softly, like the respiration of a slumbering god, but it was a fitting place, and it would serve.

HE APPROACHED THE Hall from the south-west, following an ouslite walkway that had been laid along an avenue of sycamore and silver birch. He no longer wore a guise of any kind, no more fake lamp-lighters or pretender carpet-beaters, no more displacer field to mask his stature. He had unfolded the cobweb-thin falsehood out of its tiny silver box and wrapped himself in it. It felt as cold and light as snowflakes on his shoulders, back and scalp. Light ignored him, as if he no longer merited notice. It bent around him, twisted away, avoided his form and, in avoiding him, robbed him of shadows and colours too.

As inconsequential as a whisper, he walked the avenue of trees, and crossed the lawns behind the Hall. He could smell oblative incense, and hear the gentle creak and moan of the Hall's unnatural harmonics.

His weapon was ready: a Nei Monggol punch-dagger, sharpened to a refined keenness of edge that no genestock knife grinder could have matched. The blade was laced in catastrophically lethal nematode venom distilled and refined from *qash* resin.

Enough to slay a demigod? He believed so. Enough to finish a blood game, certainly.

THERE WERE NO locks. He had memorised the traceries of the quantum alarms, and the lumin sensors simply disdained to read his falsehood. He gripped the blade in his left hand.

The light in the outer portico seemed opaque, as if stained brown by smoke. He padded forwards across black tiles that had been worn dull by centuries of visitors. Pure meltwater dripped into a stone basin beside the inner doors. Above the doorframe, in bas relief, the architrave showed the tribulations of the first pilgrims to visit Leng.

The inner doors were heavy and older than the
Palace, framed panels of ancient mountain oak, half
a metre thick, worn and handmade, none of the
angles quite true. He lifted the black iron latch, and
pushed one of the doors open. Air hushed out at
him. It smelled of cold stone.

The immense Hall was starlight-dark and
midnight-silent. Every now and then, a sound
breathed through the black space, a sound that was
almost the gust of a Himalazian wind and almost the
crush of breakers on an ocean coast, but not in fact
either of those things. Small orange sparks danced
under the high roof, like fireflies, like *ignis fatui.*

He watched them, adapting his eyes to darkness.
He began to pick up the silver outlines of objects in
the hall: columns, ancient statuary, and the assayers
and binding apparatus set up by antiquarians of previous epochs and never removed. The devices stood
like giant metal insects in the gloom, probe arms
raised like mantis limbs, metal wingcases marked
with arcane, abstruse symbols for settings and
degrees. They were gathering dust.

He slipped between them. Somewhere ahead of
him, somewhere close by, a presence lingered. It was
distracted, its mind detained by other things. It had
not noticed him. It had not even felt him.

He moved around a column, its cold flutes against
his back, and set eyes on his prey.

In the centre of the Hall's broad, open floor, his
prey was kneeling, engrossed, turning the pages of a
massive leather-bound codex. The codex was open
on the stone floor like a spread-eagled bird, its spine

a metre and a half long. Beautiful hands slowly turned the pages. They were sculptor's hands, artisan's hands.

His prey had his back to him. His prey was wearing a hooded white cloak. It would show the blood.

A common assassin might creep forwards, to steal up on his target stealthily from behind, but this prey was far too dangerous and aware for such timid techniques. Now he was in striking distance, he had no option but to pounce. After ten months, one chance was all he was going to get.

He surged forwards, his arm rising.

Halfway there, with the tip of his punch-dagger just a moment away from the centre of his prey's broad back, a shadow came the other way to meet him.

Fluid darkness intercepted his blade. The punch-dagger was wrenched aside, and his strike was shorn of its momentum. He turned.

He could barely see his assailant. Another falsehood was defying the light. The attacker drove in at him, a shadow against a shadow. He glimpsed the long, straight blade of a spatha.

He deflected one sword-blow over-hand, and another under-hand, swinging the punch-dagger around. Each impact rang out with a sharp clang of metal on metal. Sparks flew. He backed hastily across the black tiles as the falsehooded swordsman moved against him.

Their blades clashed again. The punch-dagger afforded him no reach. The advantage was entirely with the swordsman. The clatter of metal against metal seemed atrociously sharp in the breathy silence of the Hall.

Despite the nuance of his grip, the spatha flicked the punch-dagger clean out of his hand. It embedded itself, quivering, in a nearby stone column. He went in with his bare hands, banging aside the rising sword blade with the back of his right hand and locking his fingers around the wrist of his attacker's sword arm. He hooked his foot out to sweep the swordsman's legs out from under him, but the swordsman leapt the sweeping calf and tried to snatch his wrist free.

He smashed his left hand in, and caught the false-hooded swordsman across the side of the head. There was enough weight in the punch to stagger the man backwards. He blundered into one of the old assaying machines, scraping its metal feet across the stone tiles and buckling one of its insectile legs.

The swordsman recovered his balance, and discovered he was no longer a swordsman. The spatha had been ripped from his hand.

The Caucasian weighed the captured sword in his right hand. He snapped it around, and put the flat of it across his adversary's cranium, knocking him down.

The Caucasian turned from his fallen foe, the spatha in a low, defensive grip. Two more false-hooded opponents were oozing out of the Hall's shadows to confront him.

He blocked both their blades at once, and rallied against them in a series of dazzling, turning cuts and thrusts. The percussive clash of swords rang through

the gloom. More sparks shot out, bright and brief, as
if the three sword blades were made of flint.

He wrong-footed one of his opponents, and
clubbed him down to his knees with a blow of his
spatha's pommel. The other swordsman came at
him, thrusting his blade, but he turned it aside deftly
so that the stroke ran out harmlessly under his arm,
and drove the heel of his left hand into the man's
face, cracking him backwards onto the floor.

He started to run as the pair of them struggled to
rise again. The game was done. Escape was the only
acceptable conclusion remaining to him. He ran for
the doors, threw them open and sprinted through
the thick gloom of the portico towards the lawns
outside the Hall.

They were waiting for him. Five custodes, fully
armoured, their faces hidden by their golden,
hawked visors, stood in a semicircle around the
mouth of the portico. They had their Guardian
spears, those great, gilded hybrids of halberd and
firearm, aimed at his chest.

'Yield!' one of them ordered.

He raised his stolen sword for the last time.

HE WAS NOT the first occupant of the cell, and he
would not be the last. The stone walls, floor and ceiling of the cell had been painted in a bluish-white
gloss, like the skin of a glacier. Fingernails and other
sharp edges had scored away the paint over the years,
inscribing the walls with scraped frescoes of men
and eagles, of armoured giants and lightning bolts,
of ancient victories and long shadows. They were

simple, elemental marks that reminded him of primordial cave paintings showing hunters and bison.

He added his own.

After a night and a day, the cell door rumbled open. Constantin entered. The master of the custodes wore a simple monastic robe of dark brown wool over a black bodyglove. He leaned his huge back against the cell wall, folded his mighty arms and regarded the prisoner on the cot.

'Trust you, Amon,' he said. 'Trust you to get closer than anyone else.'

'Amon' was the start of his name, the earliest part of it. The second part was 'Tauromachian' and, together, these two words served most circumstances in which his name was used or spoken. He was Amon Tauromachian, custodes, first circle.

Violent obliteration notwithstanding, custodes lived long lives, far longer than mortal men, and they accumulated long names in those lifetimes. Following 'Tauromachian', which was not a family name but at least one that described the occupation of the bloodline that had provided his gene-source, there came 'Xigaze', the site of his organic birth, then 'Lepron', the house of his formative study, and then 'Cairn Hedrossa', the place where he was first tutored in weapon use. 'Pyrope', seventeen words into his nomenclature sequence, remembered his first live combat, deployed on an orbital of that name. So on, and so on, each new piece of his name honouring an action or a life landmark. Each was awarded him formally, by the masters of the first circle. 'Leng' would now become part of his name, the latest ultimate part, recognising his feat in the blood game.

A custodes's name was engraved inside the chest plate of his gold armour. The name began at the collar, on the right side, just the first element exposed, and then wound like a tight, secret snake around the inside of the plate. For some custodes like Constantin, the oldest veterans, accumulated names had filled up the linings of their torso plates, and the tails of their snakes now ran out around the bellies of the plates, looping like incised belts through the abdominal decorations. Constantin Valdor's name was nineteen hundred and thirty-two elements long.

Amon's custodes armour and armaments had been stored in the House of Weapons during his absence. As he walked along the Southern Circuit with Constantin to reclaim them, he asked about the progress of other blood games.

'Zerin?'

'Apprehended before he had even crossed into the Imperial Territories. He brushed a gene-sniffer in Irkutsk.'

'Haedo?'

'Detected by sweeps in the Papuan Deserts four months ago. He made it as far as Cebu City by dust yacht, but we had a scoop team waiting for him.'

Amon nodded. 'Brokur?'

Constantin smiled. 'He got into the Hegemon in the guise of a Panpacific delegate before he was spotted. An impressive feat, one that we did not expect to be bettered.'

Amon shrugged. Blood games were a fundamental element of Palace security and a duty of the custodes. It was a matter of honour for them to play blood games out to the very best of their abilities. Using their ingenuity and comprehensive inside knowledge of the Palace and, indeed, Terra itself, the custodes volunteered to test and probe Imperial security, to expose any weakness or chink in Terran defences. They would play wolf to test the hounds. At any given time, at least half a dozen custodes were loose, operating secretly and autonomously, devising and executing methods of penetrating the great Palace.

There would be scrupulous debriefings and extensive interviews, examining Amon's strategies and dismantling his techniques. Every scrap of information, every morsel of advantage, had to be extracted from the blood game. He had penetrated the Palace. He had got further than anyone else. He had come within striking distance.

'I wonder if I have caused offence?' he mentioned to Constantin. 'I raised my hand against him.'

Constantin shook his head. He was a giant of a man, bigger even than Amon, like one of the overscaled statues in the Investiary brought to life. 'He forgives you. Besides, you would not have hurt him.'

'My blow was blocked.'

'Even if it hadn't been, he would have stopped you.'

'He knew I was there.'

Constantin scratched at his chin. 'He won't tell me how long he knew. He wanted to see how long it would take the rest of us to notice you.'

Amon paused before replying. 'In the past, he has not seen much sense in blood games. He considered them worthless.'

'That was the past,' Constantin replied. 'Things have changed since you were last among us, Amon.'

IN THE HOUSE of Weapons, he and Constantin armoured themselves. Amon felt the old familiarity of the handmade plate sections, the buckles and clasps and the magnetised seams. The weight settled on him reassuringly.

In arming chambers on the lower levels of the House of Weapons, servitors and slaves were ritually plating a squad of proud Astartes of the Imperial Fists, anointing them with oils and whispers as they locked each piece of armour in place. The squad was preparing for a long patrol shift on the southern ramparts.

Such was the custom of most Astartes: the ritual, the gloving, the blessing. They were beings wrought for war, their mindsets particular. Ritual aided their singularity of focus. It refined their purpose.

They were not like custodes at all. Like cousins, perhaps, like kin from the same bloodline, the custodes and the Astartes were similar but distinct. The custodes were the product of an older, formative process, a process, some said, that had been refined and simplified to produce the Astartes en masse. Generally, custodes were larger and more powerful than Astartes, but the differences were only notice-ably significant in a few specific cases. No one would be foolish enough to predict the outcome of a con-test between an Astartes and a custodes.

The greatest differences lay in the mind. Though custodes shared a familial bond through the circles of their order, it was nothing like the keen brother-hood that cemented the Legions of the Astartes. Custodes were far more solitary beings: sentinels, watchmen, destined to stand forever, alone.

Custodes did not surround themselves with slaves and servitors, aides and handservants. They armoured themselves, alone, pragmatically, without ceremony.

'Dorn armours the Palace for war,' Amon said, as more of an observation than a question. Only a cus-todes of the first circle would refer to a primarch so bluntly.

'War is expected.'

'Now it is expected,' said Amon. 'Before, it was not expected, never, not from ourselves.'

Constantin did not reply.

'How did this happen?' Amon asked.

'It is not possible to say,' replied the master of the custodes. 'As one who knew the Warmaster well, I cannot believe it is overweening pride or ambition that has inspired this infamy, nor resentment. I believe–'

'What?' asked Amon, buckling his abdominal plates tight.

'I believe Horus Lupercal is unsound,' said Con-stantin. 'Unsound of mind or of humour. Something has unseated his rational thought, and the good council of those around him.'

'Are you suggesting Horus Lupercal is mad?' asked Amon.

'Perhaps. Mad, or sick, or both. Something has happened to him that cannot be explained by the scheme of the galaxy as we have come to understand it.' Constantin looked out through the high windows of the House of Weapons, and studied the line of the Western Ramparts, newly reinforced and obese with additional shield plating and gun platforms. 'We must prepare for the unthinkable. War will come to us, war from within. Sides are drawn, choices made.'

'You make it sound matter-of-fact,' Amon said.

'It is,' replied Constantin. 'The Emperor is threatened. We are his protectors. We will stand against the threat. There is nothing else for us to speculate upon, not even the madness of those we once loved.'

Amon nodded. 'The Palace is becoming a fortress. I approve. Dorn has done superlative work.'

'It was ever his skill, and the skill of his Astartes. Defence and protection. At this, the Imperial Fists excel.'

'But we remain the last line,' said Amon.

'We do.'

'This will require more than strong walls and battlements.'

WITH THEIR CRESTED helmets held under their arms, they walked across the inner courts of the Palace from the House of Weapons to a tower of the Hegemon where the custodes kept their office of watch.

Custodes had gathered to greet Amon at the entrance of the tower. Heads bowed, they struck the shafts of their Guardian spears against the flagstones, a clattering murmur of welcome and approval.

HAEDO STEPPED FORWARDS, his features hidden by the shadows of his visor. 'Amon Tauromachian, good that you return,' he said, clasping Amon's right hand.

'You have cut deeper than any of us,' Emankon said.

They entered the tower through high-arched rooms where the murals were so old and faded they looked like the pencil sketches and cartoons the artist had made in preparation for his work. Information streams from the vast data looms in the sub-levels of the Palace pulsed in the conduits under their feet. Cyber-drones floated under the high vaults, clusters of them moving like shoals of fish, dragged and gusted as if by the wafts of deep marine currents.

The Watchroom was bathed in violet light from the vast overhead hololithic emitters. Data freckled and danced across this smoky dome of light. The comparison/contrast programs running in the central cogitation consoles speared beams of gold and red up into the violet gloom, and roped divergent data elements in lassos of light. The global data sea and the Unified Biometric Verification System were being trawled and panned by the Watchroom's codifier assembly, and disparate elements were being grouped together, connections

made, traces followed. An anti-Unity cell in Baktria
had been betrayed by some restricted treatise they
had tried to access from a library in Delta Nilus. Pro-
Panpacific terrorists had been eradicated in
Archangelus, traced by a weapons-buy they had tried
to pull off in some backwater Nordafrik shanty.
Every day, a billion clues and a million secrets were
analysed and examined by the custodes watch, sifted
with acute, painstaking precision through the ever-
shifting, fluid levels of Terra's information sphere.

'What is the chief matter of the hour?' Constantin
asked.

Every sixty minutes, the Watchroom prioritised a
dozen of the most sensitive findings for special
attention.

'Lord Sichar,' replied the custodian of the watch.

HE HAD NOT hefted a Guardian spear in ten months.
He went to the practice chambers in the subter-
ranean levels beneath the tower, and cued up a
dozen blade-limbed servitors to oppose him. The
spear swung and looped in his hands, his muscles
remembering the old skills and training. When the
exercise ended, and the servitors were broken and
dismembered on the mat around him, he called up
fresh units for a second round.

How much of our lives are spent in rehearsal, he
considered. The blood games, the training, all of it
just pantomime coaching in preparation for the real
thing.

Amon hated himself for the tiny thrill of exhilara-
tion that he felt. The real thing was coming. No

matter the infamy and outrage of it, the custodes would at last be called from rehearsal to perform the duty they had been created to perform.

To relish the imminent war was unseemly. As he closed out the second round of practice, Amon focused his mind instead on the case of Lord Sichar.

'The matter is already under inspection, Amon,' Constantin had told him.

'I have been out ten months,' Amon had replied, 'I am rusty and idle, and eager for a proper puzzle to divert me. I ask your favour.'

Constantin had nodded. The matter of Lord Sichar had been passed to Amon Tauromachian for review.

LORD PHEROM SICHAR had always been a person of interest to the custodes. Hereditary lord of Hy Brasil, the most powerful of all the Sud Merican cantons, Sichar had often been vocal in his criticism of Imperial policies. His dynastic links, through bloodline and marriage, to the Navis Nobilite provided him with a considerable trade empire off Terra. Sichar was reckoned to be one of the fifty most powerful feudal lords of the colonies. Only the most careful political gamesmanship by Malcador the Sigillite had prevented Sichar's elevation to the Council of Terra. Of greater concern was the fact that Sichar was a direct descendant of Dalmoth Kyn, one of the last tyrants to hold out against the Emperor's forces in the dying days of the Unification Wars. It was understood that the

Emperor tolerated Sichar's rule of Hy Brasil – and his barracking and sniping in the Hegemon – in order to heal the old wounds left by the Wars of Unification and encourage ethnic settlement. Sichar was a powerful man, and an articulate, outspoken statesman. He often spoke tolerable sense, in Amon's opinion, and his policies were pragmatic and robust.

His opposition to Imperial directives was not so fierce it required him to be placed under house arrest, like Lady Kalhoon of Lanark, or be removed from office entirely and charged with treason to the Imperial state, like Hans Gargetton, chancellor of the Atlantic Platforms, but Sichar was always to be handled with caution.

AFTER HIS TRAINING session, Amon changed into a simple robe and bodyglove, and went to one of the consultation suites on the floor above the Watchroom, where a strategically stationed Sister of Silence maintained an aura of absolute discretion. He laid out all the key intelligence on the screens of a stochastic processor, and began to assess them using the noetic and retrocognitive techniques taught to all custodes.

Sichar, already under permanent surveillance by the custodes Watchroom, had become a security priority thanks to particular scrutiny of his communication patterns.

His off-world holdings were considerable. His greatest possession was Cajetan in 61 Isthmus, a colonial world rich in resources that provided him with a gateway to the lucrative mineral zones of Albedo Crucis. Sichar's trade worth was so considerable, junior houses and minor grandees of the Sud Merican aristocracy were flocking to him, and strengthening his support base. If a seat fell open on the Council of Terra, it would be hard to deny it to Lord Sichar.

The threads of connection were vague, but their lines could be traced. Sichar was in direct and regular communication, via astropathic link, with the Governor of Cajetan, and the viceroys of Albedo Crucis II and Sempion Magnix. His correspondence with them, all of the clients he had effectively installed, was conducted in a private cipher that the custodes had not yet broken. It appeared to be a variation of Ansprak Tripattern, one of the few wartime codes used by the anti-unionists that had never been unravelled.

Further threads of connection could be traced, via diplomatic back-channels, to elements of the 1102nd and 45th Imperial Expedition Fleets, and through them to minor colonial holdings, and two service and supply fleets operating out of the Chirog Nebula. Intel suggested that the service fleets, amongst other duties, supplied materiel to the Imperial Army deployed forces on the Butan Group.

There lay the question mark. Five months previously, several sections of the Imperial Army in the Butan Group were rumoured to have declared for the Warmaster. There was a distinct possibility that Lord Sichar, through a lengthy and deliberately complex chain of correspondence, was in communication with the heretics.

Lord Sichar of Hy Brasil, in all likelihood, was trafficking intelligence between Terra and Horus Lupercal.

As IT TURNED, the craft caught the sun across its silver fuselage and shone like a brief star in the mauve reaches of the upper atmosphere. A civilian-pattern Hawkwing, registered to Fancile et Cie, operating out of the Zeon-Ind orbital, it was just another transport coming in along the signal pulse of the Planalto Central traffic beacon.

The flying machine, an orbit-capable bird, wore a burnished metallic skin, and was a wide, elegant shape, like a giant ray or a skate, with broad, triangular wings and a slender dart of a tail. As it skimmed in towards the four high towers of the Planalto Central landing spire, its retarding burners lit with hot jets of green-yellow flame in the lazy evening light, and trailing edge spoilers lifted along the wings like bent feathers. The great towers, dust-brown against the indigo heavens, blinked out powerful white lights from their masts. Two kilometres below, the vast sprawl of urbanised Hy Brasil stretched out, a trillion lights in the dark.

As the Hawkwing adjusted for its final approach, its transponders broadcast its identity packets at the request of Planalto Administratum.

The packets informed Planalto Administratum that the craft was carrying Elod Galt, a senior negotiator for Fancile et Cie, who was visiting Hy Brasil to

conduct exploratory talks with representatives of
several Albedo mining congloms.

According to Unified Biometric Verification, Elod
Galt's idents were entirely in order.

NOT A BLOOD game this time, the real thing.

He would have preferred to work alone, at least to
begin with, but there was a role to play. To seem the
part, he needed servitors, an astropath and, most
likely, a pilot and a lifeguard too. Haedo, in a simple grey bodyglove and slave-mask, doubled in the
last two roles. His biometric declared him to be
Zuhba, no family name, a genestock migou bought
on the Gangetic bodymarket.

As Elod Galt, Amon was obliged to wear sheensilk
robes that appeared wet and iridescent, like oil on
water, as well as a wolf-pelt mantle, a formless hat
with too many brims, and an ornamental sabre of
considerable size that was nothing more than an
ostentatious, theatrical prop and would be precisely
useless in an actual combat situation. Most aggra-
vating of all, he was obliged to wear another
displacer field to visibly diminish and disguise his
build.

His six attending servitors – one for voxcasting,
one for medical duties and food tasting, one for
environmental surveying, one for translation, one
for recording and rubrication, and one for general
service – were fine creations of polished blue steel
and were, apparently, exactly the sort of suite of service units that would be expected to accompany a
senior industrial negotiator.

A scallop-shell platform carried the Hawkwing
down into the landing spire, down a vast flue lit by
tracking lights of red and blue that lit in series. Other
platforms were raising and lowering aircraft to and
from the landing berths. Arriving at the designated
berth-level, the platform shivered, halted and then
swung sideways, delivering the cooling Hawkwing
into the waiting embrace of the berth's landing cradle.
The cradle closed its digits and clamps around the
craft like a carnivorous plant grasping an insect, and
withdrew it into the steamy alcove of the berth, where
grubby servitors, cargo shamblers and deck crewmen
were waiting with hoists and blocks, and fuel umbili-
cals.

Haedo glanced at Amon as the internal cabin lights
changed from cold white to a muted yellow standby.

'Shall we begin?' he asked.

Amon nodded. He looked over at the vox servitor.
'Anything from control?' he asked.

The servitor dipped its head and issued an apolo-
getic tone.

'Inform me as soon as they connect,' Amon said.

He put on his hat. Haedo fixed his slave-mask – a
screaming cockerel, for some reason of custom and
protocol – to his face, and buckled on his sidearm.
Interlocks clattered as the craft's hatches linked to the
berth's air gate, and then the boarding hatch opened.

As HE TOOK the pre-arranged meetings with the agents
of the mineral congloms, he thought of decomposi-
tion, of worms boring into a bloated carcass. His own
worms were at work. False cowlings behind the

Hawkwing's afterburners had folded back during berthing, and the sterile compartments within had released sacks of vermicular probes. Sixteen thousand in all, each one an autonomous rope of articulated chrome no bigger than a chopstick. With every passing minute, they were crawling deeper into the fabric of Hy Brasil, spreading wider, chewing their way into data ducts and system trunking, gnawing their way into memory vaults, record banks and datastacks. Some would be found, some flushed by automated security systems, some would follow dead leads and abort when their power cells failed, but some would feast, and transmit their diet back to him.

He sat in a stateroom panelled with Kirgizian fretscreens, and feigned interest in the boasts of gross tonnage and silicate purity made by the agents of the mineral congloms. He thought about the risks. With Constantin's permission, they had deployed into Hy Brasil to conduct covert inspection, but they still awaited authority to move, in any open way, against Lord Sichar. If they were discovered, they could claim reasonable cause, but the worms were a breach of their legal parameters. If the burgraves of Hy Brasil discovered that the custodes had entered their canton without a warrant and riddled their systems with a swarm of probe worms, there would be uproar. It was an egregious violation of Hy Brasilean sovereignty. Even now, unity was a fragile thing, like a sculpture made of glass or ice: beautiful, precise, solid, but so very easy to break. In the shadow of Horus Lupercal's great and spreading treason, the last thing the Palace needed was a continental uprising on Terra.

'It is a great risk,' Haedo had said in transit from the orbital.

'It is,' Amon had agreed, 'but if Pherom Sichar is what we think he is, waiting to act is a far greater risk.'

Servitors brought them refreshments. The fashion in Hy Brasil seemed to be for mannequins finished in varnished dark wood with brass articulation. They looked like naked nursery dolls: dolls with porcelain faces and hands rendered to seem utterly lifelike, yet whose bodies, beneath their clothes, were crude wood with no effort of realism at all. The servitors whirred around the stateroom, offering infusions of mint and green tea.

The stateroom, high in a tower in the Sao Paol division of the Planalto, overlooked the vast and luminous landscape of the Winter Fields. Hy Brasil drew its power from a series of vast reactors buried in the heart of the main conurbation. The reactors required monumental heat-exchange processes to keep them running within safety tolerances, and as a consequence, the surface levels of the reactor district were caked in thick sheet-ice all year round, forming a gigantic frost park thirty kilometres square in the centre of the Planalto that the hive populations used for recreation. From his vantage point, Amon could see the tiny shapes of skaters near the frozen shore, and children on the banks and ice walks with kites and slithering mechanical toys. Further out, in the yellow haze of the open fields, ice yachts skimmed silently under coloured sails, and powered rakers raced one another around the lighted masts of the speed circuit, spraying up wakes of ice spume.

Negotiations resumed. Amon checked his data-slate, which was discreetly monitoring all infeed to his vox servitor. Authority had still not been sent through from the Palace.

THE NEXT MEETING took place in a monolithic tower on the far side of the Winter Fields. For amusement's sake, proud of their frozen landscape, the agents of the congloms conveyed Elod Galt to the meeting aboard an ice yacht. Amon tried to look impressed.

Their host was waiting for them on the quay below the tower, a tall man dressed in furs.

'I am Sichar,' he announced, bowing to Galt.

Ptolem Sichar was the fourth brother of Lord Sichar, but used the name unqualified for effect. Lord Sichar had installed Ptolem as the chief executive officer of Cajetan Imports, the trade consortium and shipping line he had founded to service his immense mineral resources.

Ptolem Sichar had dark green eyes that suggested to Amon an overuse of sabenweed. Though a large man, with duelling scars proudly displayed on his cheek, he was no threat. His body was soft, and out of the habit of regular exercise. His mind was soft too. A few minutes' conversation with him assured Amon that Ptolem Sichar was a superficial dolt.

His retinue was otherwise. He was flanked by the usual servitors, and a quartet of houseguards in scaled green armour. They were warriors of Hy Brasil's military wing, a body known as the Dracos, competent and efficient soldiers. Amon was certain that the Dracos detailed to guard the ruler's brother would be members of the specialist veteran squads.

Another figure accompanied the brother, a figure in a coal-black velvet coat and jet body plate. Ptolem introduced him as Ibn Norn, and he was one of the infamous and almost extinct Lucifer Blacks. Such was Lord Sichar's power and wealth, he had provided every member of his blood family with a bodyguard from the ancient and elite Ischian brigade of Lucifers.

Trailed by Haedo in his cockerel mask, and his string of blue-metal servitors, Amon walked with Ptolem Sichar up the quay and into the tower. They spoke of ice sports, of the coming war, of the effect on trade. Amon was aware that the Lucifer Black was studying him closely.

As they stepped onto a grav platform to be lifted up into the upper decks of the tower, Amon realised, with absolute certainty, that Ibn Norn knew he was wearing a displacer field. He had no idea what subtle thing had given it away. The Lucifer Blacks were as famous for their perception and their razor-sharp minds as for their fighting prowess. Ibn Norn knew that Elod Galt was, at the very least, disguising something or, at the very worst, concealing a dangerous lie.

IT WAS TOO late to disengage. Waiting and hoping for a confirmation from control, Amon began his meeting with Ptolem Sichar. They sat at a mahogany table on a radial platform high in the tower's skylight levels. Sichar was easily distracted, and Amon

encouraged this foible to buy time, leading the
man off on discursive ruminations of such random
topics as orbital viticulture, gerontological break-
throughs, genethliacal provenances and the
wisdom of studying extinct religions to extract
viable ethical value systems.

All the while, Amon thought of the probes,
squirming through the dark recesses and cybernetic
cavities of the Planalto like mealworms. He thought
of the views that he and Haedo had seen en route to
Hy Brasil: hive cities closing their meteoritic shields;
conurbations reigniting field bulwarks and auto
defences left over from the last Terran conflicts;
oceanic platforms rigging for submarine function
and slowly submerging into the protective bosom
of the waters. The homeworld was bracing itself for
the traitors' onslaught, an event that would be, perhaps, the single greatest holocaust mankind would
ever have to endure. There was too much at stake to
disengage.

At a break in the meeting, Amon checked the
infeed of his communication servitor. Nothing had
been received from control. Using the data-slate, he
also ascertained that nothing of any consequence
had so far been received from the probes. In particular, no progress had been made elucidating the
version of Ansprak Tripattern used in the question-
able transmissions.

A bell rang, and Amon assumed it was supposed
to signal them back to the table for the next round
of discussions. The atmosphere had changed, however. Ptolem Sichar and his staff hung back, in quiet

and solemn discussion. Certain data displays on the radial platform had been masked.

Be ready, Amon signalled to Haedo.

'My lord Galt,' said one of the Dracos, striding over to attend them. 'I'm afraid there's been an incident. We must suspend talks for the day while it is dealt with. My master expressly apologises for the delay.'

'What manner of incident?' Amon asked.

'A breach of data confidence,' the Draco replied indirectly.

'How so?'

'An outrage. An act that impugns this canton's—' The Draco cut himself short. 'Forgive me, I'm not at liberty to discuss it. It is a sovereign matter.'

'It sounds grave indeed,' said Elod Galt with apparently genuine concern. 'Should I arrange to return to my orbital?'

'No, sir.'

They turned. Ibn Norn, the Lucifer Black, had joined them. 'Security issues are under review across the Planalto. Transit would be an unnecessary complication, and you would be greatly inconvenienced by delays and searches. We have arranged a suite in this tower where you can relax in comfort until the present circumstances are over.'

Where you can watch us, Amon thought. Elod Galt nodded graciously.

THE SUITE LAY on the sixtieth level. Once the escort had departed, Haedo swept the rooms for surveillance devices using scanners concealed in the torso of the food-tasting servitor.

'I would ask you to respect our integrity measures and refrain from using your vox servitor,' Ibn Norn had remarked cordially before leaving them. The servitor's function displays showed that vox channels were being jammed anyway.

Haedo opened the back of the rubrication servitor and initialised the compact cogito-analyser hidden behind the ribs. Using invasive programs so acutely coded that no Hy Brasilean systems would even notice them, Haedo linked the unit to the Planalto's data-sphere.

'The probes have been discovered in the memory cores of the Planalto Administratum,' he reported. 'There is...' He scanned the data rapidly. 'There is a palpable sense of outrage. Security across the Planalto has been raised to level amber six. The canton parliament is calling an emergency session to discuss the incident. There is furious debate in the intelligence communities as to whether the data invasion is the work of a foreign power or industrial espionage.'

'If Sichar is guilty as charged,' said Amon, 'he'll know the probable cause and the probable origin. How long will it take them to analyse and trace the vermicular probes?'

'They were sterile and trace-free until they were launched,' said Haedo, 'but they would collect specific particulates during transit. A decent forensic examiner should be able to trace them back to our craft in a few hours.'

'We are already suspected,' Amon said.

'Already?'

'That Lucifer Black knows we're not what we seem to be. I believe they are just looking for evidential confirmation before they confront us.'

'And we still have no authority,' said Haedo.

Amon nodded, slowly.

'But they don't know that,' he said.

Haedo didn't respond. He was studying the cogito-analyser intently.

'What is it?' Amon asked.

'Parliament has initiated a system-wide purge to flush out and destroy the probes,' Haedo replied. 'The order was countersigned by Pherom Sichar, presiding over the parliament. But that's not it... I'm getting feedback from the probes. Seven of them have penetrated the Planalto's communication archive, and one has sourced Lord Sichar's archive log for the last seven months.'

'Translations?'

Haedo shook his head. 'No, the code is still a wall to us. But the sender and receiver header codes on each message form are not encrypted. They're stored in binaric. I'm running the entire list against comparative data. Wait... wait...'

Tight lines of script began to flow up the small screen of the compact device.

'Four confirmed matches,' Haedo whispered. 'Four, you see? Each one is quite clearly the operative reception code for the *Vengeful Spirit*.'

The Lupercal's flagship. Amon nodded. 'That's just cause. That's all we need. We move.'

Strike teams summoned from the Palace could be in the heart of the Planalto in less than twenty-five

minutes, but Amon judged that course to be coun-
terproductive. An open shooting war would just
make matters worse. He and Haedo had to secure
the person of Sichar immediately, and then let a sys-
tematic investigation pick Sichar's network of
conspirators apart.

He took a trigger unit from the pocket of his robes
and pressed it.

'Brace for apport,' he said. There was a loud, double-
bang of over-stressed air pressure as the site-to-site
teleport delivered two heavy, metal caskets into the
suite directly from the Hawkwing. They appeared,
fuming with vapour, in the centre of the carpet. The
overpressure cracked two of the suite's windows.
Alarms, set off by the violent apport and its energy
signature, started to pulse.

Haedo and Amon threw open the metal caskets.
Inside each one, carefully packed, lay their golden
custodes armour and the disengaged segments of
their Guardian spears.

DRILL TEAMS OF the Draco elite, led by Ibn Norn, burst
into the holding suite less than four minutes later.
The chambers were empty. A fierce wind blew in
through a section of reinforced window that had been
entirely cut out.

Ibn Norn glanced at the open, empty apport caskets, and the discarded clothes on the floor beside
them. He saw the cockerel mask, the decorative sabre,
and the wires of a displacer field hastily torn off.

He crossed to the window, and looked down into
the streaming wind. The towers and street scheme of

the Planalto spread out below him, far away. In the middle distance, on the shore overlooking the wide and gleaming edges of the Winter Fields, he saw Parliament House.

Ibn Norn activated his grav arrestor and leapt through the window.

PARLIAMENT HOUSE WAS a splendid structure built from filaments of silvered steel and pylons of a pale stone that looked like buffed ivory. Bells were ringing, urgently advising the delegates, burgraves and grandees to shelter or seek the protection of their bodyguards. Thousands of Dracos were gathering around the building's various entrances, especially the broad main steps that led in a magnificent sweep up from the state quays of the Winter Fields.

Haedo and Amon landed on the roof of the largest quay house, disturbing ice powder that had been driven in off the fields. They killed their jump packs and surveyed the scene ahead.

'We've roused them like a colony of angry ants,' Haedo murmured.

Amon touched his arm and nodded.

A black figure flew in out of the winter sky, rebounded with agile grace off the spire of the gatehouse and landed in the midst of the milling Draco troops on the main steps.

'Scanners!' they heard Ibn Norn order. 'They're right here! Secure this precinct and find them!'

Haedo and Amon leapt down off the quay house roof and walked towards the steps side by side.

Dracos bustled around them, checking handheld monitors or breaking heavier scanning equipment out of carry boxes. Voices were chattering urgently. Gun crews were setting up tripod weapons along the shore to watch the ice fields. Packs of gunships purred low overhead.

The two custodes calmly walked up the steps through the anxious soldiers. They came within three metres of the Lucifer Black. Norn was barking commands, and trying to organise a perimeter.

They entered Parliament House unopposed. The echoey main chamber was emptying. The grandees of Hy Brasil were filing off the banked seating and flowing towards the exits, under the dutiful watch of armed Dracos.

Lord Sichar was still in his seat, a canopied throne of dark wood that presided over the upper and lower houses. He was a noble-looking man in red and green robes, a little younger than Amon had imagined. Sichar's own Lucifer Black was waiting to hurry his lord to a place of safety, but Sichar was busy signing some last documents brought to him by delegates and scribes, and conferring urgently with the master of parliamentary protocol.

'Try not to harm his person,' Amon instructed Haedo. 'We need him viable for interview.'

'We'll probably have to kill his Lucifer,' Haedo replied.

'Agreed, but only if he resists. One clean shot. I don't want a fight in here.'

Thirty metres from the canopied throne, they threw aside their falsehoods.

'Sichar of Hy Brasil,' Amon announced. 'You are sanctioned by the Adeptus Custodes as an enemy of Terra. Do not attempt to resist us.'

Sichar, the delegates, the scribes and the master of protocol turned and gazed at them in astonishment. One of the scribes broke and ran for the exit in terror. The twin golden giants in their crested armour exuded nothing but ferocious menace.

The Lucifer Black seemed to reach for his weapon.

'One excuse,' Haedo snarled, aiming his spear in the direction of the Lucifer.

Sichar rose to his feet, retaining more composure than the underlings around him. He gazed down from his podium at the two gleaming custodes.

'This is inexcusable,' he began. Despite his defiance, he could not keep a tremor of fear out of his voice. No one faced the might of the custodes without faltering. 'This is utterly inexcusable. This dishonours the sovereignty of Hy Brasil. I will demand a full apology from your master when–'

'He's your master too,' declared Amon.

Sichar blinked. 'I... What?'

'He's supposed to be your master too,' Amon repeated. 'You will accompany us now and answer to a list of issues that brand you a traitor. Step down from the podium.'

A bright flash of light burst across the main chamber, swiftly followed by another and another. For a second, Amon thought grenades had been detonated, but he revised that idea quickly. The light blooms were teleport flares.

There were suddenly seven figures standing between the custodes and their target. Six of them were Adeptus Astartes in full battle armour, instantly recognisable as huscarls of the Imperial Fists. As the teleport flares dissipated, the six Astartes took one step forwards in perfect unison and aimed their bolt-guns at the custodes with a clatter.

The seventh figure stood in their midst, tall and mantled in a cloak of gold thread and red velvet. His hair was white and cropped short, and his noble face seemed weathered and tired.

'My lord,' said Amon, bowing his head to the primarch.

'This must stop,' said Rogal Dorn.

DORN STEPPED FORWARDS, through the ranks of his Astartes.

'Put up your weapons,' he said gently.

The Imperial Fists smartly raised the boltguns to their shoulders.

'I meant everyone,' added Dorn, looking at the custodes.

Amon and Haedo kept their spears aimed at the canopied throne.

'My lord, Pherom Sichar is a traitor and spy,' replied Amon carefully. 'He is using the networks of his extensive mercantile empire to communicate with the Warmaster and his benighted rebels. We have just cause and evidence enough to hold him and interrogate him. He will come with us.'

'Or?' asked Dorn with a soft, almost amused smile.

'He will come with us, my lord,' Amon insisted.

Dorn nodded.

'An object lesson in determination and loyalty, eh, Archamus?' he said.

'Indeed, my lord,' replied the commander of the huscarls.

'They would fight six Astartes and a primarch in order to accomplish their duty,' Dorn said.

'My lord,' Amon said, 'please stand aside.'

'I'm half-tempted to let you attempt to go through me,' said Dorn. 'I would, of course, hurt you both.'

'You would try,' replied Haedo. 'My lord,' he added.

'Enough,' said Dorn. 'Archamus?'

The retinue commander stepped forwards.

'Lord Sichar of Hy Brasil is a spy,' he announced, quite matter-of-factly. 'Lord Sichar of Hy Brasil has been in regular communication with Horus Lupercal, and has exchanged with the traitor a great deal of intelligence.'

'You admit it?' asked Amon.

'He's *our* spy,' said Dorn. The primarch came up to Amon face to face. They were the tallest beings in the room.

'I am fortifying Terra as best I can for the coming war,' said Dorn. 'That means more than walls and shields and gun platforms. That means information. Viable, solid data. Proper intelligence. Lord Sichar is as loyal as you or I, but his reputation as an opponent of Imperial policy made him a credible defector to the traitor's camp. Horus thinks he has friends on Terra, friends and allies, who will rise up and turn to fight with him when his host arrives.'

'I see,' said Amon.

'Sadly,' said Dorn, 'this great fuss may have compromised him. I may have to develop other spies now.'

'My lord,' said Amon, 'we are custodes. We guard Terra and the Emperor as surely as you. Would it not have made sense to tell us of Lord Sichar's involvement?'

Dorn exhaled and did not reply.

'Do you know what a blood game is, my lord?' asked Haedo.

'Of course,' replied Dorn. 'You hounds play wolves and test the Emperor's defences for the slightest flaw or vulnerability. I have reviewed many of your reports, and accommodated their findings into my reinforcements.'

'Then perhaps,' suggested Amon, 'we could consider this a blood game? The weakness revealed being that all those who seek to serve and protect the Emperor must work with unified purpose and shared information.'

THE RAKER SPED away from the landing quay in a blizzard of ice crystals. It was a powerful, two-seater recreational model, painted cobalt-blue, with an upturned nose and hefty ice-blade. Aft of its stabiliser vanes, its ion engines burned with green fury. It lit off across the Winter Fields, making a sound like a knife being dragged across glass.

Cheth, or whatever his real name was, hadn't even bothered to unslip the mooring lines. He'd gunned down the two wharfmen on the quay who had

come to see what the commotion was about, and
then leapt into the raker's cockpit and slammed the
sliding canopy.

Amon crashed down onto the quay just as the
raker pulled away. The impact of his huge,
armoured bulk cracked several flagstones. The
mooring lines, dragged tight, were snapping with
pistol-shot cracks. Amon managed to seize one of
the lines before it parted, and held on as it broke.
Dragged by the line, he was whipped off the edge of
the quay and hit the ice on his belly, slithering and
ripping along like an unseated rider pulled behind
his steed. Ice chips blinded him. The vibration and
friction was almost too much to bear. As the raker
increased its velocity, Amon felt his armour dent
and buckle. He was rolling and bouncing, spinning
from side to side on the end of the trailing line. His
grip was failing.

Amon let go, and slid clear in a long, wide arc
across the ice. He dug in his heavy boots to try and
arrest his slide, and as he slowed to a halt, he began
to rise.

The raker was accelerating away across the fields.
Skaters and ice yachts veered in panic to get out of
its headlong path. It ploughed through the flag-
lines of a speed-skate course.

Behind him, Amon heard another explosion.
Another gout of flame and smoke bellied into the
sky from Parliament House.

'Amon! Amon!' Haedo's voice yelled over the vox.

'Go.'

'Where are you?'

'In pursuit. The assassin is heading out across the ice lake. Is the primarch safe?'

'I have confirmation from the Imperial Fists,' Haedo replied. 'Primarch Dorn had left Parliament House before the first bomb.'

'Lord Sichar?'

'Dead, along with eight members of the legislature. Amon, stand by. I'm securing a 'thopter. I'll be en route to you in–'

'No time,' Amon replied. He rose and triggered his jump pack. The launch impact threw him high into the air. Climbing, he saw the raker turning ahead of him, below. It was swinging west over the Winter Fields, cutting through a yacht formation.

Lord Sichar had been murdered by his own Lucifer Black, his bodyguard, a man called Gen Cheth. Ibn Norn had introduced him to Amon. Whoever had been wearing the black armoured suit when Amon had nodded to him, his name hadn't been Gen Cheth. Or, a darker possibility, Gen Cheth hadn't ever been the man his closest comrades thought he was.

It seemed that the Lupercal had spies of his own. Hounds were wolves and wolves were hounds. Primarch Dorn had been obliged to compromise Lord Sichar's position as a double-agent for Amon's benefit. The Lucifer Black had been right there. *Horus's man* had been right there. Lord Sichar's secret had been revealed. Lord Sichar was suddenly a vulnerability to be expunged and an enemy to be punished.

The concussion bomb had seen to that. It had vaporised the centre of the Parliament chamber, and brought down the roof. Haedo and Amon had been thrown backwards through wooden partitions into the consular voting room. Amon had been first on his feet.

The assassin had run. Leaving at least one more bomb behind him, he had fled for the fields. Amon wondered why. Assassins were focused beings. Execution or suicide was the usual conclusion of their efforts. Did this man think he could escape?

Surely not. Then what was he trying to accomplish?

Amon swooped down at the racing craft. Arms across his face, he struck it like a lightning bolt, shearing the canopy clean away. Glass splinters and pieces of window strut billowed away in the rushing wind. Amon tried to hold on. The black-armoured figure struggled to maintain control of the raker one-handed while he fumbled for his weapon. The craft bucked. Amon slid, and ended up clinging to the raker's upturned nose.

He dug his fingers into the metal skin of the fuselage, making his own handholds, and dragged himself forwards. The assassin had found his weapon. He fired at Amon over the dashboard hump, and a bolt round shrieked past the custodes's ear. The raker began to approach maximum velocity. Amon clawed on and reached the torn-open cockpit. The assassin fired again, blasting up at the custodes looming over him. The bolt punched through Amon's left shoulder and blood sprayed into the slipstream.

Amon punched down with his right fist. The blow crushed the black metal helmet and pulped the head inside it.

The raker veered wildly as the assassin's corpse lolled sideways from the controls. Clinging on, Amon tried to reach in to cut the engines.

He saw what was in the pillion seat behind the driver.

Another bomb, the largest and most destructive of all. Now Amon understood. The assassin had been planning suicide all along. He had been planning to finish his work by riding the raker out into the middle of the Winter Fields and detonating the device. The bomb would take out Hy Brasil's vast reactors, buried under the fields. The reactors would annihilate the Planalto. Terra would understand, with a sick jolt, the wrath and influence of Horus Lupercal.

Almost shaken off by the savage vibration of the uncontrolled raker, Amon could see a light-beat countdown. There was no way of telling how much longer was left on the timer.

In sheer desperation, Amon tore out his trigger unit. There was no time for complex readjustment or re-calibration, no time to punch in an alternate set of coordinates. Amon simply managed to reset the altitude, adding two kilometres. Then he hit the actuator stud and hurled the unit into the cockpit.

He leapt clear. The site-to-site teleport vanished most of the speeding raker before Amon had even hit the ice. He landed with a bone-jarring crunch, and tumbled for thirty or forty metres in a flurry of ice. A stabiliser vane and part of the raker's tail assembly, severed by the teleport beam's tight focus, clattered and cartwheeled past him, shedding debris, the cut edges glowing and molten.

On his back, half-conscious, Amon slid in circles and slowly, slowly, came to a halt. He looked up into the mauve Sud Merican sky.

Two kilometres above him, there was a bright flash, followed by a blinding, surging, expanding blossom of white light. Then the noise and the shockwave hit him and stamped him down into the ice.

BY THE WALLS of the Palace, in the Himalazian dusk, the loyal hound rose from the ice and shook itself. It was hurt, but most of the blood on its snout and flanks belonged to the wolf it had just driven, braying, into the dark with its throat torn open.

It plodded back towards the gates, limping, and leaving spots of blood on the snow behind it. Its breath steamed in the cold evening air.

Behind it, out in the blackness, more wolves were gathering and coming ever closer.

WOLF AT THE DOOR

Mike Lee

Dawn was still two hours from breaking when the armoured column made its way from the still-burning city and rumbled westwards, along the great causeway that once supplied the Tyrants of Kernunnos with the plundered riches of a dozen worlds. The procession stretched for more than a kilometre, winding out along the western plains like a sinuous, steel-clad dragon. Heavy tanks of the Imperial Army took the lead, their armoured hulls still scarred and smoke-stained from the bitter fighting inside the planetary capital, followed by low-slung Chimera armoured personnel carriers containing the veteran troops of the Arcturan Dragoons. It had been the Dragoons who had spearheaded the attack on the Tyrants' capital and had fought their way first to the battered palace at the centre of the city. By virtue of blood and valour, they had earned their place in the procession and the ceremonies to follow.

The column set a slow, purposeful pace through the fire-lit darkness, following the causeway past vast landing fields now littered with the burnt-out hulls of great treasure ships. One of the landing fields was little more than a gaping crater, its insides still glowing like molten glass. A treasure ship had tried to escape the doom of Kernunnos and been caught in the opening salvoes of the orbital bombardment. The flare of its exploding reactors had engulfed the multitudes of terrified refugees fleeing along the causeway and flung smaller craft like toys into the flanks of their larger brethren, leaving a swathe of melted wreckage for kilometres in every direction.

Past the debris-strewn landing fields the terrain gave way to broad, rolling plains dominated by the sprawling agri-combines that had once provided the capital with much of its food. Now the fields of wheat, corn and salix were cratered by artillery shells and littered with the hulks of burnt-out tanks. Packs of scavengers slinked about the charred hulls, drawn by the scent of the cooked flesh within. Here and there amid the tanks lay the broken bodies of the Tyrants' bipedal war engines, their limbs riddled by lascannon fire and their chests burst open like jagged metal flowers. Tank commanders swept the fields with their heavy stubbers as they rode past, their auspex goggles picking out the furtive figures of refugees – men, women and children – fleeing across the ruined fields away from the column.

Thirty kilometres from the city the road began to climb into smoke-wreathed foothills that lay at the foot of a low mountain range that the locals called the Elysians. From time out of mind the region had been the playground of the Tyrants and their supporters in the Senate, but six hours of constant bombardment from orbital batteries and planetside artillery had turned the hills and the mountainsides into a splintered, smouldering wasteland. The villas of the great and powerful had been incinerated, along with the villages that supported them and huge tracts of the surrounding forestland.

It was into these mountains that the Tyrants had fled, following word that the last of their much-vaunted battlefleet had been destroyed in a pitched battle near Kernunnos's primary moon. There was a refuge deep within the Elysians, a vault bored into the heart of one of the largest peaks that had been built during the Age of Strife, when Old Night had reared up and swallowed mankind's first interstellar civilisation. The vault had been built to protect the planetary elite from the warp-spawned horrors that had walked the land, and over the centuries its formidable construction had become legendary. It was the ultimate fastness, a citadel that could withstand the fires of Armageddon itself.

The column rumbled on through the foothills, occasionally grinding its way over fallen trees and wrecked vehicles strewn in its path. Navigating by orbital maps, the procession passed through the ruined and deserted villages, past the splintered villas and up a series of cracked and pitted roads that led towards the fortress. The mountain had been hacked and riven by searing beams and bombardment cannons, its flanks scoured clean and split by massive blasts. Deep craters in the mountain slope contained the wreckage of orbital laser batteries that had attempted to contest the arrival of the Imperial invasion fleet.

Two-thirds of the way up the mountain the road emptied out onto a broad, artificial plateau, carved like a shelf into the side of the mountain and paved over with ferrocrete. The wreckage of more than a half-dozen military ornithopters lay scattered across the landing field, surrounded by the burnt corpses of their aircrew. On the western end of the expanse, sheltered beneath a massive brow of scorched and splintered granite, stood a towering, featureless metal door.

The armoured vehicles spread across the plateau in a carefully orchestrated routine. APCs halted and lowered their rear ramps, disgorging platoons of battle-hardened Dragoons. Sergeants barked orders and shouted streams of leathery curses, and soon the troops were dragging away the bodies of the enemy and battle tanks were carefully nosing the wrecked ornithopters to the far edges of the plateau. Within thirty minutes the field was clear, and the troops had assembled by companies into two large formations to the far left and far right of the plateau. Off to the east, the great city built by the Tyrants flickered and glowed like a bed of dying embers.

Fifteen minutes before dawn there came a brassy growl of thunder from over the horizon, a steady, building drumbeat that drew nearer and nearer through the overcast sky. The heavy, leaden clouds seemed to roil over the plateau, lit from within by a rising, blue-white glow. Finally the smoke-stained overcast was rent by the rakish noses of a trio of Stormbird assault craft, their landing gear deployed like grasping talons as the pilots flared their engines and brought the huge craft down in a three-point tactical deployment, right in the midst of the waiting Imperial troops.

No sooner had the transports touched down than the heavy assault ramps lowered with a hiss of hydraulics. The crimson glow of battle-lanterns shone from the depths of the crouching Stormbirds, silhouetting the armoured giants waiting within.

Sergeants shouted along the ranks. The Arcturan Dragoons snapped to attention with a crash of hob-nailed boots as the Emperor's Wolves set foot on the blasted earth of Kernunnos.

The assault ramps on two of the transports rang with swift footfalls as grey-armoured warriors dashed out onto the plateau, their huge boltguns held at the ready. They were Space Wolves, gene-engineered supermen of the Emperor's VI Legion and the pinnacle of the Imperium's military might, yet their appearance was a study in contrasts between the advanced and the archaic. Servos whined beneath the overlapping plates of their Mark II Crusader-pattern power armour; helmeted heads swept left and right, scanning the landing zone with augmetic optical systems that perceived wavelengths from the infrared to the ultraviolet. Yet their broad shoulders were framed with heavy cloaks of wolf or bear skin, and strange fetishes of iron, wood or bone were affixed to their scarred breastplates. Every one of the warriors carried a sword or a battle-axe at their hip, and many boasted gruesome battle-trophies, like gilt skulls or exotic weapons slung from equipment hooks at their waists. Even the hardest veteran among the Arcturan Dragoons lowered their eyes as the Emperor's Wolves went by.

The Space Wolves fanned out in a tight arc, advancing past the lead Stormbird and forming up by squads a few yards ahead of the transport's assault ramp. They continued to scan the plateau for a few moments more, then the warriors raised their weapons to port arms and a silent signal was relayed to the lead ship. At precisely the appointed time, just as dawn began to stain the overcast sky to the east, Bulveye, Wolf Lord of the Space Wolves' Thirteenth Great Company and commander of the 954th Expeditionary Fleet, descended the ramp of the lead Stormbird with his senior lieutenants and the champions of his Wolf Guard in tow.

The Wolf Lord and his chosen men were resplendent, their power armour polished to a mirror sheen and adorned with tokens of honour and courage earned in the crucible of war. Gold wolf's head medallions glittered from their grey pauldrons, each one bearing a frayed strip of parchment inscribed with war-oaths or invocations to the Allfather. Their breastplates were decorated with medals of silver or plaques of rune-etched iron, each one representing an act of valour against humanity's many foes. They wore their best cloaks of wolf or ice-bear hide, and at their belts hung their most prized battle-trophies: gilded fangs, cracked skulls or ivory finger bones taken from enemy champions slain in single combat. Bulveye's armour was more ornate still: fashioned by the master-artificers on distant Mars, the edges of his pauldrons were chased in gold, and the curved surfaces were inscribed with ornate scenes of battle. Trophies from scores of hard-fought campaigns hung from his cuirass and his war-belt of adamantine plates, and a circlet of hammered gold rested upon his brow. A heavy, single-bladed battle axe was clenched in the Wolf Lord's gauntleted hand; the steel haft was wrapped in strips of cured sealskin, and the casing of the power weapon's field generator was etched with runes of victory and death.

His expression grim, Bulveye strode past the waiting squads of his honour guard and approached the fortress entrance. Two warriors fell into step behind him, eyeing the massive doors warily.

'They're late,' Halvdan Bale-eye grumbled. Bulveye's chief lieutenant was a grim, brooding figure even at the best of times, more at home on the battlefield than in the mead-hall. His wiry copper hair, streaked with grey, hung in two heavy braids that draped across his breastplate, and a bristling beard covered the lower part of his face. He had a nose like an axe blade, and sharp-edged cheekbones crisscrossed with dozens of old scars. His eyes were mismatched, shining from deep-set sockets beneath a craggy brow. Halvdan's left eye socket was seamed and uneven, the bone broken by a sword stroke that had put out the eye as well. He'd survived the terrible wound and had disdained an eye-patch afterwards, using the empty socket to unnerve foes and shipmates alike during his raiding days on Fenris. Now the unblinking lens of an augmetic eye shone from its depths, its focusing elements clicking softly as the warrior surveyed the entrance and its splintered overhang. Halvdan growled deep in his throat. 'The damned fools might have changed their minds. They could be planning treachery at this very moment.'

To that, the warrior beside Halvdan let out a derisive snort. 'Can't get those big doors open, more like,' Jurgen replied. He was lean and rangy, his skin drawn taut over the bones of his face and showing the cable-like muscles cording his neck above the rim of his breastplate. His black hair, speckled with grey, was cropped short; lately he'd adopted the Terran tradition of shaving his chin, earning no small amount of jibes from his pack-mates. 'After six hours of bombardment it's a wonder they weren't all buried alive.' He gave his lord a sidelong look, his dark eyes glittering with raven-like mirth. 'Did anybody think to bring shovels?'

Bulveye gave Jurgen a look of brotherly irritation. They were all old men by the standards of the Astartes, having been reavers and sword-brothers to Leman, King of the Rus, for many years before the Allfather had come to Fenris. When the truth of Leman's heritage was finally revealed, every warrior in the king's mead-hall had drawn their iron blades and clamoured to fight at his side, as sword-brothers ought. But they were all too old, the Allfather told them; not a man among them was younger than twenty years. The trials they would have to endure would very likely kill them, no matter how courageous and strong-willed they were. Yet the men of Leman's mead-hall were mighty warriors, each man a hero in his own right, and they would not be dissuaded by thoughts of suffering or death. Leman, the king, was moved by their devotion, and could not find it in his heart to refuse them. And so his loyal thanes undertook the Trials of the Wolf, and true to the Allfather's word, the vast majority of them died.

Out of hundreds, almost two score survived, a number that amazed even the Allfather himself. In honour of their courage, Leman – no longer king now, but Primarch of the VI Legion – formed a new company around the survivors. Ever since, the other warriors of the Legion referred to the Thirteenth as the Greybeards. The members of the company, however, called themselves the Wolf Brothers.

'If they won't come out, we'll use the Stormbirds and the battle tanks to get those doors open and go in after them,' Bulveye said grimly. 'One way or another, the campaign ends here.'

Jurgen grinned and made to reply, but the expression on the Wolf Lord's face made him think better of it. Bulveye had a square-jawed, sharp-nosed face that appeared stubborn and unyielding even in the best of times. Though of an age with Jurgen and Halvdan, his head was bald, and there was no hint of grey in his close-cropped blond beard. His eyes were pale blue, as sharp and deadly as glacial ice. Bulveye had sworn an oath to the primarch to bring the entirety of the Lammas subsector into compliance, and his lieutenants knew that when the Wolf Lord gave his word on a thing, he was as relentless and implacable as a winter storm.

Halvdan chuckled at Jurgen's discomfort. The bare-chinned lieutenant shot the warrior a hard look, but before he could reply a deep rumble reverberated from the scarred mountainside and with a grating of metal and stone the huge doors of the fortress began to slide open.

A stir went through the Dragoons. Sergeants shouted down the murmurs spreading through the ranks. Clouds of dirt gusted through the widening gap between the doors, and a handful of men in tattered uniforms staggered out into the cool mountain air. Their jackets were stained with sweat and mud, and the scabbards of their dress sabres were dented and scarred. Several of the men fell to their knees, gasping in exhaustion, while others simply stared in shock at the Space Wolves and the men assembled behind them.

Moments later an officer appeared, his dress uniform no less filthy than the rest but his spirit still intact despite the ordeal he and his men had suffered. He barked a series of orders, and the men responded as best they could, straightening their jackets and forming into a rough group beside their leader. More men clambered through the gap into the open air, joining the rest, until almost a full platoon of battered soldiers stood at attention facing the Wolves. From their uniforms, Bulveye could tell they were members of the Companions, the Tyrants' elite bodyguards. At the beginning of the campaign the Companions had been six thousand strong, a thousand fanatical defenders for each of the empire's overlords.

The commander of the bodyguards looked over his men one last time, then gave a curt nod. Backs straight, the soldiers marched the short distance to the waiting Space Wolves, and one by one they unbuckled their sabres and laid them at the giants' feet. When the last soldier had turned over his weapon, their commander approached the Wolf Lord and, with a hollow look in his eyes, he added his weapons to the pile. Bulveye studied the man dispassionately, taking note of the rank tabs on his uniform. 'Where is your commanding officer, subaltern?' the Wolf Lord asked.

The junior officer straightened, his arms stiff at his sides. 'With his ancestors,' the young man replied with as much dignity as he could muster. 'He shot himself this morning, shortly after the surrender terms were accepted.'

Bulveye considered this, and nodded gravely. The subaltern lowered his eyes, turned about and rejoined his men. The young man took a deep breath, snapped an order, and the surviving Companions sank to their knees, pressing their foreheads to the ferrocrete as the surrender ceremony began.

The slaves came first, clad in torn and bloodied robes and staggering beneath the burden of heavy metal chests. Their faces were dull and dirt-stained, worn down by the twin scourges of exhaustion and starvation. One after another they approached the fearsome, armoured giants, laid the chests at their feet and pulled the lids open to reveal the wealth contained within. Raw gemstones and precious metals gleamed dully in the diffuse morning light: the ransom of six Tyrants, plundered from the length and breadth of their petty empire. It piled up around the Space Wolves like a dragon's hoard, drawing avaricious murmurs from the soldiers of the Imperial Army. When their task was complete, the slaves knelt beside the vast treasure, their expressions vacant and uncaring.

Next came the daughters and wives of the Tyrants, a wailing procession clad in white robes of mourning, their coiffed hair undone and their pale faces smeared with ash. The youngest ones recoiled and cried out in fear as they saw the fearsome giants and the leering Dragoons; no doubt they had spent a sleepless night imagining the terrible abuses that awaited them. The women fell to their knees a few yards in front of the Wolves; some wept inconsolably, while others kept their faces expressionless, evidently resigned to their fate.

Last of all came the Tyrants themselves. They emerged from the fortress one at a time, taking short steps beneath the weight of their heavy gilt robes and jewelled chains of state. The self-styled masters of the Lammas subsector were small, pale-skinned men, their faces blotched and saggy from a lifetime of debauchery and excess. Two of the men had to be helped along by a cluster of slaves. Their eyes were glassy and unfocused; either they had chosen to face their ruin through a haze of drugs, or their spirits had simply shattered under the weight of their defeat.

A new chorus of wails rose from the women as the Tyrants approached the Space Wolves. Trembling hands grasped at the hem of their robes as the former rulers passed by their loved ones and came to stand before their foes. Slowly, haltingly, they knelt before the conquerors, and in the tradition of their people, they bared their necks and prepared to die.

Halvdan and Jurgen shared a brief look and shook their heads in disgust. Bulveye studied the Tyrants for a long moment, then stepped forwards, his axe held loosely in his right hand. He towered over the kneeling men like a vengeful god, glaring coldly at each man in turn.

'And so we meet again,' the Wolf Lord said, 'just as I told you we would, seven years ago. Back then, I stood in your palace of crystal and steel and brought you glad tidings from our Allfather, the Emperor of Mankind. I bore a message of welcome, and promises of peace and order. I gave you this –' Bulveye said, holding out his open left hand – 'and you spat upon my palm. You scorned the gifts of my lord and sent me into the streets like a beggar, threatening to kill me if we met again.'

The Wolf Lord glowered at the Tyrants and showed them his axe. 'Before I left, I swore to you that this day would come. Now your fleets have

been broken and your armies scattered.' Bulveye
gestured eastwards. 'Your palace of steel and crystal
is no more. Your sons are dead, and your cities lie
in ruins.' His voice lowered to a throaty growl, and
his lips drew back in a snarl, revealing prominent,
wolf-like canines. 'You are Tyrants no longer. You
have been cast down, and I've seen to it that neither
you nor your kind will *ever* rise again.'

Bulveye gestured to his lieutenants. Halvdan and
Jurgen stepped forwards, their expressions grim.
Groans went up from the fallen Tyrants, and their
wives cried out in misery. But instead of drawing
their blades, the two Space Wolves took the chains
of state from the trembling men and tossed them
onto the treasure-pile, then grabbed hold of their
rich robes and tore them away as well.

'Had it been left up to me, you would have never
emerged from those tunnels,' Bulveye snarled. 'I
would have turned this entire mountain into your
tomb. But the Allfather in his wisdom has decided
otherwise.' The Wolf Lord gestured to the heaps of
treasure. 'This wealth belongs to the many worlds
you have despoiled – planets that became battlefields thanks to your arrogance and greed. You will
use this fortune to begin rebuilding what was lost,
and ensure that the worlds of this subsector
become prosperous and stable members of the
Imperium. Each planet will soon have an Imperial
governor to oversee their reconstruction, and they
will send me regular reports of your efforts.' He
glared down at the naked and shivering men. 'Do
not give me reason to return here ever again.'

Slowly and deliberately, Bulveye lowered his axe. The former Tyrants and their families fell silent, unable to contemplate at first that their lives and their virtue were to be spared. The Wolf Lord turned on his heel and strode back towards the waiting Stormbird. As he picked his way through the treasure trove he gazed sternly at the kneeling slaves. 'Get up,' he commanded. 'You are slaves no longer. From this day forwards, you are citizens of the Imperium, and so long as the Allfather lives, you will never bow your knee to another master.'

For the first time, a hint of life returned to the beleaguered faces of the former servants, and slowly, tentatively, they started to climb to their feet. Among the nobles, one young woman let out a hysterical cry of relief and half-crawled, half-stumbled to the side of her father, who tried to cover his nakedness with trembling hands and stared hatefully at the retreating backs of the Space Wolves.

The three warriors passed through the cordon established by their waiting battle-brothers and continued on to the Stormbird's ramp. Halvdan stole a look behind him at the fallen Tyrants and growled deep in his throat. 'We should have killed every last one of them,' he grumbled. 'They won't learn. You can be sure of that. In another ten or twenty years we'll have to come back here and finish the job.'

But Jurgen shook his head. 'The Lammas subsector will still be a shadow of its former self a *hundred* years from now, much less twenty,' he replied. 'We were very thorough, brother. Every city, every industrial centre, every starport will have to be rebuilt.'

'A damned waste,' the Wolf Lord murmured, surprising both men. 'So much destruction. So many lives thrown away, all for the sake of six arrogant fools.'

Halvdan shrugged. 'Such is the price of resistance. It's ever been thus, my lord, even back in the old days on Fenris. How many petty kings did we lay low at the command of King Leman? How many villages burned, how many longboats smashed to kindling? It's the way of things. Empires are built with broken bones and rivers of blood.'

'Aye, that's so,' Bulveye agreed. 'I don't deny it. And the Allfather's cause is a just one: mankind *must* be made whole again if we're to reclaim what is rightfully ours. This galaxy belongs to us, and it's our duty to reclaim it, regardless of the cost. Otherwise, everything humanity has suffered up to this point will have been for naught.'

'And we'd be no better than all the xenos filth that came before us,' Jurgen added. He clapped Bulveye on the shoulder. 'It's been a long, hard-fought campaign, my lord. You've broken the Tyrants and reclaimed the entirety of the Lammas subsector. Take pride in the knowledge that you've fulfilled your oaths to the Allfather, and be content.'

Just then, a wiry, older man wearing the dark grey tunic of a Legion bondsman descended the dropship's ramp and hurried to meet the oncoming Wolf Lord. He was Johann, one of Bulveye's own huscarls, and the Wolf Lord frowned at the tense expression on the bondsman's face.

'What's happened?' he asked quietly as Johann drew near.

'Two ships arrived in system a few hours ago,' the huscarl said gravely. 'One was a courier, bearing a priority message from Leman Russ himself. We're to conclude all operations immediately and rendezvous with the primarch at Telkara in five months' time.'

The Wolf Lord's eyes widened. 'The entire company?'

Johann shook his head. 'No, lord. The entire *Legion*. Orders have reached the primarch from the Allfather himself. We're bound for Prospero.'

'Prospero?' Halvdan interjected. 'That's madness! Where did you hear such a thing?'

'It says so in the message,' the huscarl replied. 'Though no reason is given. No doubt we will learn more when we reach Telkara.'

'Five months,' Jurgen echoed. He shook his head. 'We've got warriors and ships scattered all over the subsector, hunting down the last of the Tyrants' supporters. It could take months just to assemble everyone and see that they're supplied for the journey.'

Bulveye nodded. Telkara was far to the galactic north, more than two sectors away. Withdrawing the company from combat and preparing them for such a trip was no small task. 'Despatch couriers with orders for the company to marshal at Kernunnos at once,' he said to Johann. With much of the Imperial fleet orbiting the Tyrants' former throne world, it would be the logical place to resupply the ships of the Great Company before they made way for Telkara. The Wolf Lord paused. 'One moment. You said two ships arrived in system. What was the other one?'

'One of the long-range scout ships, my lord,' Johann replied. 'You instructed Admiral Jandine to continue probing the region along the eastern edge of the subsector.'

'I know what I instructed Admiral Jandine,' Bulveye snapped. 'Did they find anything?'

'Yes, lord,' the huscarl said. 'The scouts report that the warp storms continue to diminish throughout the region, opening more and more of the area to safe navigation.' He started to say more, but hesitated.

The Wolf Lord's eyes narrowed. 'What else?'

'One of the ships managed to reach a star system in the region, one previously cut off by the storms,' he said. 'It's listed on our older charts, though there's no indication that a colony was ever established there.'

'But?'

Johann took a deep breath and plunged ahead. 'But the scout ship detected vox transmissions at standard frequencies emanating from the fourth planet in the system,' the huscarl reported.

Bulveye's expression darkened. Halvdan shot a sidelong glance at Jurgen and shook his head. 'Leave it,' he said to the Wolf Lord. 'It's just one world. Let the Army have a look. We've got new orders, haven't we?'

'Halvdan is right, my lord,' Jurgen added. 'We've reclaimed every settled world in this subsector. What more can we do?'

Bulveye was silent for a moment more. 'What more? Our duty to mankind, of course,' he said, then focused his attention on the huscarl.

'Tell me of this world,' the Wolf Lord commanded.

THE BATTLE-BARGE IRONWOLF hung like a poised blade above the green-and-ochre surface of the battered world. Light from the system's distant yellow sun glinted coldly on the warship's cathedral-like superstructure and highlighted the raw battle-scars along its armoured hide. The *Ironwolf* had seen hard fighting in the last seven years of the Great Crusade, and the great battle-barge bore its wounds proudly. She was the flagship of the 954th Expeditionary Fleet, and her honour rolls bore testament to the battles she'd fought and the wayward worlds she'd reclaimed in the name of the Emperor of Man.

Bulveye felt the leaden weight of acceleration press his armoured form against its restraining cradle as the Stormbird flared its engines and launched from one of the *Ironwolf's* cavernous launch bays. The thunder of the assault ship's massive engines deadened abruptly as the Stormbird streaked across the gleaming curve of the planet's upper stratosphere and began a gradual descent towards the surface. A hololith installed in the bulkhead in front of the Wolf Lord's acceleration cradle displayed the Stormbird's trajectory, along with status icons detailing everything from the craft's airspeed and angle of attack to its weapons' status, fuel consumption and turbine pressure. Interfacing with the Stormbird's onboard systems via his armour's vox-unit, Bulveye called up the high-altitude reconnaissance images taken of the planet over the past twenty-four hours and began to study the picts with a steely, blue-eyed stare.

The planet had no name, according to the *Ironwolf's* star charts; given their position, far to the galactic south, it had likely been one of the last human colonies, settled sometime in the Eighth Diaspora prior to the Age of Strife. The colonists had been very lucky, or very brave, or both, Bulveye reckoned. Few such colonies had survived the centuries of isolation that had followed; the Lammas subsector alone was strewn with the skeletal ruins of settlements that hadn't been strong enough to endure the warp storms and the horrors they spawned.

And this world had suffered greatly, the Wolf Lord saw. Much of its landmass was barren and lifeless. Thousands of kilometres of wasteland stretched all the way to the planet's polar ice caps, leaving perhaps a score of green and vibrant regions strung like a chain of emeralds around the world's equator. He could see the outlines of great lakes and inland seas that had been transformed into cracked and broken plains, and broad mountain slopes scoured down to bare, unyielding stone. According to the auspex arrays aboard the *Ironwolf*, much of the lifeless terrain was dangerously radioactive.

Bulveye froze the pict-feed on a single image. 'Magnify by ten,' he murmured into his vox-bead. The pict blurred as it expanded; cogitators in the base of the hololith clattered as the enhancement algorithms refined the smear of tan, ochre and dark grey into low, rounded hills surrounding a gently sloping basin some eighty kilometres across. The grey line of a dry riverbed wound like a serpent's track across the centre of the basin, its borders smudged in places by drifts of choking dust. A broad expanse of broken stone and jagged, black girders rose from the dust along one broad bend of the riverbank. A small city had thrived there once, hundreds of years past.

Metal and military-grade plas creaked loudly behind the Wolf Lord. 'Must've been quite a war,' Halvdan said admiringly, squinting at the pict over Bulveye's shoulder.

Bulveye reached down and disengaged the swivel lock on his acceleration cradle so he could turn to face the interior of the transport's forward troop compartment. A dozen Marines of his Wolf Guard filled the cramped space, locked into their own cradles along the chamber's outer bulkheads. Their wargear had been cleaned of the grit and gore from the fighting on Kernunnos, and their armour polished to a mirror sheen. It was a small honour guard for so important a mission, but the Wolf Lord had been loath to withdraw any more warriors from vital combat duties on the Tyrants' former throne world. Time was short, and Bulveye was resolved to make do with the men he had available. The Allfather expected no less of his Legions.

The Wolf Lord considered the hololith a moment more, then shook his head dubiously. 'If it was a war, it was a damned strange one,' he replied. He indicated the lifeless plains outside the ruined city. 'No craters. No ruined vehicles. No signs of abandoned fortifications or other field positions. And the devastation extends for thousands of kilometres, into northern and southern latitudes that would have been hostile to human life under *normal* conditions, much less something like this.'

Halvdan's expression darkened. 'Psykers, then,' he grumbled, reaching up to finger an iron charm hung from a leather cord about his thick neck. Psykers – more commonly called warlocks by the primitive folk on Fenris – had spontaneously emerged on countless human worlds just before the Age of Strife. Their unnatural powers caused widespread chaos and destruction; the most powerful psykers could warp the very fabric of reality itself. More than once during the course of the Crusade, the Expeditionary Fleets had come upon colonies that had fallen under the sway of these nightmarish beings. The Allfather had ordered the planets burnt to ash and the coordinates of the systems stricken from the star charts.

'Perhaps,' Bulveye allowed, 'but if so, the people here must have found a way to stop them.'

Across the troop compartment, Jurgen shifted in his acceleration cradle to get a better view of the hololith. 'I've yet to see a psyker survive an atomic blast,' he muttered. 'It would explain all that radiation, and the scale of the devastation. They nuked three-quarters of their own planet to wipe them out.'

'Except that we've seen no indication of any military forces at all, much less atomic weapons,' Bulveye pointed out. 'And then there's this.'

The Wolf Lord turned back to the hololith and transmitted a command. The pict of the ruined city dissolved into a polychromatic fog. Cogitators whirred and clicked. Moments later another image resolved from the mist.

A city appeared in the foreground, built of solid slabs of glistening white stone and fitted cunningly into the slopes of forested hills at the base of a tall, cloud-swept mountain range. Streets made from stone or some local composite connected the terraced buildings and teemed with hundreds of people and small, dome-shaped vehicles going about their daily business. There was little in the way of detail, but something about the scene suggested frenetic – almost harried – activity.

Halvdan's augmetic eye clicked softly as he focused on the image. 'Seems pleasant enough,' he said.

'Not the city,' Bulveye said. He leaned against the restraints and jabbed a finger at a faint, dark object in the background of the image. 'I'm talking about *that.*'

The Wolf Lord pointed to a thin, dark line, straight as a knife-edge and rising above the hills a long way away from the city. Halvdan scowled, peering intently at the image. 'Well, it's big, whatever it is,' he said.

'Big?' Jurgen echoed. 'Judging by the scale, it must be *huge.*'

Bulveye nodded. The image vanished, replaced by another showing a closer look at the object. It was a spire, narrower at the tips and bulging slightly in the middle, like a dart balanced precariously on the palm of a man's hand. The surface was a matt black, so dark it seemed to swallow the light around it. Only vague irregularities in the spire's silhouette suggested that it wasn't perfectly smooth, but possessed hundreds of small ledges and narrow alcoves.

'It's more than five thousand metres high,' the Wolf Lord declared. 'No one on the *Ironwolf* can tell me how old it is, or what it's made of. About the only thing the Iron Priests can agree on was that no human hand could possibly have made it. And there's one like it in each of the twenty habitable zones left on the planet.'

Jurgen scowled at the strange image. 'And you're certain there aren't any psykers down there?'

'Any psyker arrogant enough to build something like that isn't the sort to hide in the shadows,' Bulveye countered. 'Our recon flights intercepted a large number of civilian vox transmissions over the last few days – news broadcasts and the like. There's no hint of psyker activity anywhere on the planet.'

'And yet,' Halvdan said, stroking the charm around his neck, 'the spires are only found in close proximity to people. That can't be a coincidence.'

'My thoughts exactly,' Bulveye agreed. 'Needless to say, I've got a number of questions for the Planetary Senate once we've finished with the important business of the day.'

'I don't like this at all,' Jurgen grumbled. 'And it's not as though we've no more important work to do, my lord. The primarch has summoned us; why do we dally here?' He waved a gauntleted hand at the hololith. 'This is a minor world on the very fringe of human space. As best we can tell, there're perhaps a hundred and twenty million people on the entire planet: there were *cities* on Kernunnos that were larger than that! And that's nothing compared to what awaits us at Prospero.'

Halvdan clenched his bearded jaw, but nodded as well. 'For once, I agree with Jurgen,' he said. 'Our destiny lies far to the galactic north. What is to be gained here, of all places?'

The Wolf Lord's eyebrows rose at the question. 'What is there to be gained? A hundred and twenty million lost souls to begin with,' he replied. 'Not to mention the honour of our company! The primarch sent us here to bring the worlds of the subsector into compliance – *all* of them – and that's exactly what I mean to do. It will take another eight weeks at least to marshal the rest of the company at Kernunnos; in the meantime, we have a job to perform.'

Jurgen did not reply at once. Instead, he studied his lord for several long moments. 'My lord, you and I have fought together for almost three hundred years now,' he said. 'I know you better than most men know their own brothers, and I can't help but wonder if there's more to this little expedition than simply fulfilling your duty.'

Bulveye gave his lieutenant a hard look, which Jurgen bore without remark. Finally the Wolf Lord sighed and turned back to the hololith. 'Since when was our duty ever simple?' he growled underneath his breath.

* * *

THE STORMBIRD ENTERED the planet's atmosphere on
a plume of fire and descended in a long arc over the
world's equator. Within an hour the drop-ship was
swooping low over cloud-wreathed mountains and
green, forested hills as they approached the sprawling city of Oneiros. The low, white structures
clustered against the hills like colonies of toadstools,
surrounding a concentrated metropolitan area more
in keeping with a modern Imperial city. Bulveye
reckoned that the tall buildings and stately
amphitheatres were made for public use, given that
Oneiros was also the seat of the planetary govern-
ment. The Wolf Lord also noted terraced vineyards
skirting a number of the smaller hills, and other
lands set aside for growing crops or grazing livestock. Bulveye could see that most of the herds were
small and relatively young, and that the fields were
swarming with farmhands hurriedly taking in the
harvest.

They had to circle the city twice to find any traces
of the former starport. The huge landing fields that
once serviced massive cargo shuttles or smaller
tramp freighters were now grassy meadows, their
precise, man-made edges still visible from the air. A
white flock of beasts that could have been goats or
sheep bolted for a nearby stand of trees as the huge
ship passed overhead and came in for a vertical
landing on the sward. The heat from the transport's
thrusters set alight broad swathes of the field's
greenish-blue grass as it touched down.

By the time the drop-ship's assault ramp had lowered to the smouldering ground there were close to a

score of the dome-shaped local vehicles approaching the Stormbird from the edge of the landing field. They stopped at a discreet distance and a number of men and women climbed out just as the first of Bulveye's Wolf Guard rushed out into the sunlight and established a security cordon around the ship.

Bulveye reached the bottom of the ramp in enough time to witness the reaction of the locals at the sight of the towering Astartes. Fear and surprise were etched clearly on their youthful faces; the young men goggled at the size and power of the Astartes, while the women stared worriedly at the massive boltguns in the warriors' hands.

The Wolf Lord surveyed the broad field slowly, somewhat bemused at the lack of spectators. Even on Kernunnos, a world that thought itself superior to ancient Terra and hostile to the servants of the Imperium, the starport and the roads leading to the palace had been jammed with people, all eager to see the 'barbarians' from beyond the stars. Had their visit to Oneiros been kept secret from the populace?

'Stand down, brothers,' he subvocalised over his vox-bead, and his bodyguards lowered their weapons at once. With Jurgen and Halvdan in tow, he approached the welcoming party and quickly took their measure. Not one of them had to be older than twenty-one, he thought. They dressed expensively, favouring gold ornaments on their leather doublets and jewelled beading on their flared trousers. None of them bore a weapon, but they carried themselves with confidence and a kind of supple grace that came from physical conditioning and hard training.

Without thinking, Bulveye sized them up from a predator's standpoint, identifying who led the pack and who followed. Like all Space Wolves, Bulveye's senses were superhumanly keen. He could smell the fear emanating from each person in the group, but also the acrid tang of challenge as well. The Wolf Lord turned to a young man in the forefront of the group and nodded his head respectfully. 'I am Bulveye, Lord of the Thirteenth Great Company and sword-brother to Leman Russ, Primarch of the VI Legion.'

The young man was startled at being addressed so directly. He was tall and lithe for a normal human, with dark hair and a sombre, bearded face. 'I am Andras Santanno. My father, Javren, is the Speaker of the Planetary Senate.' Santanno's leather doublet creaked as he sketched a deep bow. 'Welcome to Antimon, lord.'

Bulveye studied the young man carefully. 'Your voice is familiar,' he said. 'Were you the person I spoke to when we tried to contact your Senate?'

This time Andras attempted to conceal his surprise. 'I – yes, that's correct,' he stammered. 'My father – that is, the Speaker of the Senate – has been informed of your arrival. Fortunately, they're currently in session, discussing –' he paused, suddenly wary – 'important business. They've agreed to see you, though,' the young man added quickly. 'I relayed to them everything that you told me, and they would like to hear more. I've come to take you to the Senate chambers.'

Bulveye nodded as if he expected no less, though his mind was working furiously, considering the implications of everything Andras had told him. 'Let us go then,' he said carefully. I have a great deal to discuss with your father and his colleagues, and I fear that time is short.'

Andras frowned slightly at Bulveye's answer, but quickly regained his composure. He turned, gesturing towards the waiting vehicles. 'Follow me,' he said.

Bulveye was dubious that the flimsy-looking Antimonan vehicles could hold a fully armoured Astartes, much less carry one at any decent speed, but the ground cars' interiors could be almost entirely rearranged to suit any occasion, and were made of sterner stuff than they appeared. Soon the Wolf Lord and his men were being transported along a bewildering array of narrow, curving roads that wound among the city's tall hills. They passed dozens of low-slung, rounded stone buildings; up close, Bulveye could not help but notice the thickness of the walls and the sturdiness of their construction; in many ways they were more like bunkers than homes. People were coming and going from each house in a steady procession, carrying in bags of supplies and leaving empty-handed. The Antimonans paid little attention to the ground cars as they sped quietly past; when they did notice, it was with furtive, almost forbidding stares.

Andras sat in the car's front compartment, alongside the driver; Bulveye expected a stream of questions from the Antimonans, but they sat quietly for nearly the entire trip. When they spoke at all it was to one another, in a dialect of accented High Gothic that the Wolf Lord found difficult to follow.

Bulveye did not mistake the tense sound of their voices, however, or the hunched, apprehensive set of their shoulders. As they rode deeper into the city, the Wolf Lord kept himself composed and outwardly calm, but his sense of unease steadily grew.

The Antimonans were preparing for something dire. That much was clear. Had the *Ironwolf's* arrival in orbit caused this? Until he knew more, Bulveye resolved to keep his observations to himself. He knew that his men were doubtless forming their own impressions of the city and its inhabitants. Later, when the opportunity arose, he would take his lieutenants aside and see if their thoughts matched his. For the first time, he began to doubt the wisdom of this journey. Jurgen was right: he'd been too impetuous, haring off to an unknown world in the hope of a joyful welcome and a triumphal end to years of brutal, merciless warfare. He had been too eager to scrub the cruelties of the Lammas Campaign from his soul.

It took more than an hour for the long line of vehicles to reach the city centre, and the transition from the low structures in the hills to the towers of the city proper was jarring. Though made from the same white stone, the style of the tall structures was entirely different, built more for aesthetics and func-tion than security. Bulveye had little doubt that the towers dated back to the earliest days of the colony.

The Senate building was a curious, spiral-like affair, with a wide, conical base and grand terraces connected by spiral ramps that climbed the outside of the structure. There were few people about, and those that were seemed to be busy with official duties; Bulveye noted that a number of the bureaucrats carried hololith slates and portable vox-units that were smaller and more sophisticated than anything available in the Imperium, which he knew would interest the Iron Priests aboard the *Ironwolf*. It appeared that Antimon had managed to retain at least some of the technological capabilities that existed prior to the Age of Strife. Like Andras and his fellows, the bureaucrats were startled by the size and demeanour of the Astartes – in one case, an older man took one look at Halvdan and went white as a sheet before quickly turning about and dashing into the building from where he came. The bearded lieutenant seemed not to notice, but the Wolf Lord knew better. From the surreptitious looks passing between the members of the Wolf Guard, it was clear that everyone was well aware of the strange reception and the mood of the Antimonans in general.

Andras alone led the Wolf Lord and his men inside the Senate building, through a wide, open entranceway and into an echoing foyer decorated in elegant green marble. Niches surrounding the circular chamber contained hand-chiselled statuary of remarkable quality: the first example of art or culture he'd seen anywhere in the city, Bulveye realised. The pieces were ancient, possibly made during the Age of Strife or even earlier. The figures were clothed in archaic styles of dress similar to what Andras and his fellows wore, and seemed to depict Antimonans from many walks of life: artists, scholars, scientists, statesmen and entertainers. Two figures near the entrance were particularly noteworthy: one was clearly a spacer, clad in a shipboard utility suit. The other caught the Wolf Lord's eye because of the long-sleeved hauberk he wore, and the long, slim sword held at his side. Two sleek, almost frail-looking pistols were tucked in the warrior's wide belt, and the man's face was concealed by a veil-like covering made of fine mail.

Jurgen took a few steps towards the statue of the swordsman and studied it for a long moment. 'It would appear you Antimonans knew a thing or two about warfare, once upon a time,' he said lightly. 'How fortunate you were able to leave such barbaric pursuits behind.'

An edge in the Space Wolf's tone made the off-hand comment sound like an accusation. Andras, who had been about to lead the delegation through the ornate doors at the opposite end of the foyer, froze in mid-step. After a moment, he replied in a cold voice. 'The armigers were the young sons and daughters of Antimon's noble houses, an hon-ourable tradition that kept our planet safe for millennia. Were it not for the will of the Senate, those customs would still be practised today.'

'Ah, I see,' the lieutenant said, as casually as before. 'Forgive me then, if I spoke out of turn. I didn't realise you were a member of Antimon's noble class.'

Andras glanced back over his shoulder at Jurgen and nodded stiffly. 'No apologies are necessary,' he replied. 'The law–' Suddenly, the young man paused, clamping his mouth shut against the rest of

his response. 'Please, come with me,' he said quietly,
and continued across the room. When the young
Antimonan's back was turned, Bulveye glanced over
at Jurgen and caught the speculative look in the warrior's dark eyes.

The young noble paused a moment before the
entrance to regain his composure, then placed his
hands against the ornate wooden doors and pushed
them open. At once, a flood of raucous noise washed
over Bulveye and his men. Judging by the sound, the
entire Senate was engaged in a furious debate.

Halvdan stepped close to his lord. 'Should I have
the men ready their weapons?' he said quietly. The
warrior's tone was half-jesting, half-hopeful. Bulveye
shook his head, squared his shoulders and followed
Andras into the chamber.

The interior of the Senate building was
breathtaking – an immense, open space that rose for
twelve storeys on graceful, vaulted arches of super-
tensile steel. Glowing shafts of sunlight penetrated
the lofty space through the spiral of terraces that
wound around the outside of the building, allowing
those on the ground floor to observe a series of
historical murals laser-etched into the curved
ceiling. The great space was humbling even to the
Astartes in its cathedral-like grandeur. The effect was
marred only by the shouted curses echoing back and
forth just above their heads.

The Senate conducted its business from a semicircular balcony suspended half a storey above the
floor of the chamber, accessed by a central staircase
that climbed to the feet of the Speaker's tall, wooden

chair. Each senator had his own throne-like chair, carved from a rich, honey-coloured wood, but at the moment the men and women were on their feet, shaking their fists and shouting over one another as they tried to bully their opposition into surrender. Their High Gothic was even more accented and technical than what Bulveye had heard previously: he caught the words 'lottery' and 'quota', but little else before the Speaker noticed the arrival of the delegation and began shouting for silence. As soon as the senators were aware of the armoured figures in their midst, the chamber fell silent at once. Many of the older statesmen sank back into their chairs with shocked expressions and faint murmurs of surprise. Others eyed the Astartes with an equal mix of shock, distrust and outright hostility.

Bulveye had seen such expressions before, back on Kernunnos. A feeling of dread settled into his gut.

Javren Santanno, Speaker of the Senate, directed his hostile stares more towards his own peers than the wary Astartes. He was a tall, bent-shouldered man well into old age, with a beak-like nose and loose, wattle-like flesh around his scrawny neck. Like the other senators, he wore a green velvet robe over his richly appointed doublet, and a wide chain of gold links dimpled the thick fabric over his chest. A soft felt hat slouched over his bald head, emphasising the Speaker's large, hairy ears. With a final, warning scowl aimed at his peers, the Speaker glared down at Bulveye and his warriors.

'Let me begin this farce by stating for the record that my son, Andras, is a fool,' Javren said in a querulous voice. 'He's barely twenty years and five, and despite all that he has seen of beasts such as yourselves, he is still stubbornly ignorant of the ways of the universe.' The Speaker levelled a gnarled finger at Andras. 'He had no authority to respond to your broadcasts, much less invite you to meet with us in this august chamber.'

Javren scanned the assembled Marines coldly, his lip curling in distaste as he took in their fur cloaks, and the gilded skulls hanging from their belts. 'The only reason I agreed to this meeting was to make it absolutely clear that while this child may be credulous, *we* are most certainly not.' The Speaker addressed Bulveye directly. 'Judging by the weight of the baubles hanging from your chest, I assume you're the leader of this pack of wolves. Who are you, then?'

The contempt in Javren's voice left Bulveye speechless. For a moment the Wolf Lord was left struggling to maintain his composure. On Fenris, such sneering talk would have led to spilled wine and bared blades at the very least. Clans had fought bloody feuds for generations over lesser slights. Bulveye could sense the tension rising in his warriors as the silence stretched, and he knew that if he didn't speak soon, Jurgen or Halvdan would take matters into their own hands.

Forcing himself to relax, Bulveye inclined his head respectfully. 'I am Bulveye, Lord of the Thirteenth Great Company of the Imperium's Sixth Legion–'

Javren cut the Wolf Lord off with a wave of his hand. 'We do not need a recitation of your petty titles,' he said. 'Make your demands, Bulveye, and then get out.'

'Now listen,' Halvdan growled, taking a step towards the Speaker. The warrior's hand drifted towards the sword at his hip.

'If there is a misapprehension here, I believe it is on your part, honoured Speaker, not ours,' Bulveye said quickly. There was an iron tone of command in his voice that brought Halvdan up short. The bearded lieutenant glanced back at his lord, and the look on Bulveye's face brought the man back to the Wolf Lord's side.

'We are not here to make demands of you or your people,' Bulveye said calmly. 'Nor are we the beasts you imagine us to be. We are Astartes, servants of the Allfather, Lord of Terra and Emperor of Mankind.' At the mention of the Allfather, Bulveye felt his resolve surging like the tide, and he raised his head and addressed the Senate as a whole. 'We have journeyed across the stars to bring you glad tidings: the storms that divided us have subsided at last, and Terra reaches out once more to embrace all her lost children. That which was broken will soon be re-forged, and a new civilisation will arise to reclaim our rightful place as masters of the galaxy.'

Bulveye was no skald, but his voice was clear and strong, and the words were as familiar to him as the weapons at his side. Consternation warred with mistrust on the faces of the assembled senators, while Andras's face was lit with joy. As though in battle, Bulveye sensed the tide against him start to shift; he pressed ahead without pause.

'No doubt your oldest legends speak of the days when our people crossed the stars and found new homes upon foreign stars,' the Wolf Lord said. 'Much has changed since those days; I'm no storyteller, but let me share the news of all that has passed since Antimon was lost to us.'

And so he began to tell the tale, of the rise of Old Night and the collapse of galactic civilisation, of the wrack and ruin of worlds. He told the story as best he could, begging his audience's forgiveness when the tale grew muddled and confused; so much time had passed, so much knowledge lost or distorted, that no man would ever know the truth of all that had transpired over the last few millennia.

None of the listeners chose to interrupt Bulveye, much less gainsay his story. Long was the telling of it: the Wolf Lord spoke nearly without ceasing as the afternoon progressed to evening, and one by one the shafts of light arcing above the Senate chamber went from yellow to mellow gold, from gold to dusky orange, and then went out altogether. Globes of pale light winked into being from metal sconces that ringed the senators' balcony, plunging the statesmen into shadow.

Finally, Bulveye told the tale of the Allfather's conquest of Terra, and the creation of the first Astartes to fill the ranks of his armies. From there he recounted the beginnings of the Great Crusade, and the reunion of the Allfather with his children, the primarchs. Bulveye concluded his epic with the first meeting between Leman Russ and the Allfather on Fenris, a tale he knew very well.

'And so we have served him faithfully ever since, reclaiming lost worlds in the Allfather's name,' Bulveye said. 'That is what brings us here today, honoured Speaker. Your people's isolation is at an end.'

The Wolf Lord strode forwards, climbing partway up the stair towards the Speaker's throne. The senators looked on, their expressions rapt, as Bulveye held out his left hand. 'I greet you in the name of the Allfather,' he said. 'Take my hand, and be at peace. The Imperium welcomes you.'

Like the rest of the statesmen, the Speaker of the Senate had retreated to his throne over the course of Bulveye's tale, but his rheumy stare had never wavered as the long hours passed. He did not reply to the Wolf Lord at first, and much of his face was hidden in shadow. Slowly, awkwardly, he rose from his seat and set his feet upon the stair. One step at a time he descended towards Bulveye, until perhaps a third of the staircase was all that remained between them.

Javren Santanno leaned forwards, staring down at the Wolf Lord's open hand.

'Lies,' he hissed. 'Damned lies, every word of it.'

Bulveye rocked back as though struck. Halvdan let out an outraged shout and Jurgen joined in. The senators sprang to their feet, shaking their fists and shouting, though it was unclear whom exactly they were shouting at.

Black rage gripped the Wolf Lord. No man, however exalted, called a Space Wolf a liar and lived to tell of it. Bulveye fought to maintain his self-control;

better to endure a fool's slander and hope for reason to prevail than to draw steel and bring ruin to another human world. He opened his mouth to shout for silence – when suddenly the bedlam was drowned out by the sharp crackle of thunder.

No, not thunder. After two hundred years of campaigning, Bulveye knew that sound all too well.

The senators had heard it, too. They froze, their jaws agape, and then, out in the city, came the low, mournful wail of sirens. One of the senators, an older woman, pressed her hands to her face and screamed. 'They're here!' she cried. 'Blessed Ishtar, they've come early! We're not ready!'

'Who is here?' Jurgen snapped. He knew as well as Bulveye that the sound they heard wasn't thunder; it was high-yield ordnance being deployed in the upper atmosphere. 'What's going on?'

Snarling, Bulveye keyed his vox-bead. '*Ironwolf*, this is Fenris. Do you read me?' There was a squeal of static, and the Wolf Lord thought he heard a faint voice trying to reply, but it was too garbled to make out.

The senators were racing for the stairs, their robes flapping like the wings of panicked birds. Javren's face was a mask of rage as he swept down the stairs towards Bulveye. 'I see your plan now!' he yelled. 'You meant to distract us – maybe lure us out into the open – while your soulless cronies swept down on us! I knew you couldn't be trusted! I knew it! Get back to your damned ship and never return, barbarian! We want no part of your Imperium, or your so-called Allfather!'

Bulveye wanted to grab the Speaker and shake the insolence out of him, but now was not the time. As the statesmen fled from the building, he turned to his men. 'Condition Sigma,' he snapped, and weapons sprang into the Wolf Guards' hands. 'We need to get to high ground and try to re-establish contact with the *Ironwolf*,' he said to Halvdan and Jurgen. 'Contact the drop-ship and tell the pilot to prep for launch. If we have to, we'll hold here until they can extract us.'

The two lieutenants nodded curtly, and Jurgen began speaking into his vox-bead. A crowd of Anti-monans rushed into the room from outside; the Wolf Guard brought up their boltguns, but Bulveye recognised them as Andras's friends. The young men and women stopped short at the sight of the levelled weapons, their faces white with fear. Bulveye quickly scanned the room and saw Andras nearby, still right where he'd been when they had first entered the chamber.

'What's happening?' Bulveye demanded of the young noble.

Andras had a stricken expression on his face, a look of shattered innocence that the Wolf Lord had seen all too often on the battlefields of Fenris. The nobleman turned to Bulveye as though in the depths of a nightmare.

'It's the Harrowers,' he said fearfully. 'They've returned.'

THE BATTLE IN orbit lit the night sky with stuttering flashes of light and the thin, almost metallic crackle of thunder. Lines of ruby and sapphire light criss-crossed through the darkness, leaving razor-edged afterimages dancing in Bulveye's vision. There was no way to be certain who was shooting at whom, but it was clear to the Astartes that a large number of ships were involved and that the *Ironwolf* was in the thick of it.

The Space Wolves ascended the spiral ramps ringing the Senate building at a full run, climbing as high as they could to improve their vox transmissions amid the surrounding hills. Jurgen, charging along beside Bulveye, let out an angry curse. 'I can't raise the Stormbird,' he reported. 'It could be atmospheric ionisation from the battle overhead or some kind of wide-spectrum jamming.'

Bulveye nodded and keyed his own vox-bead once more, hoping that the battle barge's more powerful communications systems would be able to punch through the interference. '*Ironwolf*, this is Fenris, come in! What is your status?'

A howl of static clawed at Bulveye's ears – and then a voice, faint but audible, replied:

'Fenris, this is *Ironwolf* – we are heavily engaged by xenos warships! At least twenty, possibly thirty cruiser-sized vessels and dozens of escorts! They caught us completely by surprise – some kind of cloaking field that defeats long-range auspex sweeps–' The transmission dissolved into another wail of static, then resolved again. '–reports engine damage, and we have enemy boarders on the hangar deck!'

The Wolf Lord bared his teeth as he envisioned the tactical situation unfolding high above the planet. Against such odds, there was only one feasible course of action. '*Ironwolf*, this is Fenris – break orbit and disengage at once! Repeat, break orbit and disengage–'

He was cut off by another discordant howl of static. A voice – possibly the officer on the battle-barge, but it was too faint to tell – shouted something, then the frequency broke up in jagged bursts of atonal noise.

'Morkai's black teeth!' Bulveye cursed. 'We're definitely being jammed now.' He skidded to a halt on the smooth ramp, and his Wolf Guard formed up around him.

'How bad is it?' Halvdan asked. The calm, businesslike tone of his voice belied the fierce expression on the warrior's face.

Bulveye stared up at the battle raging overhead, his expression grim. 'As it stands, the *Ironwolf* doesn't have a chance,' he said. 'If they can escape orbit and get some manoeuvring room, perhaps they can break contact with the enemy and disengage–'

For a brief instant a red flash lit the night sky, throwing long shadows against the walls of the Senate building. The sight stunned the Space Marines into silence; somewhere out in the city, Bulveye heard a woman's terrified scream. Seconds later came the rumble of the explosion, a heavy, bass drumbeat that sent tremors through the stone beneath the Wolf Lord's feet.

The warriors looked skywards as the flare diminished. A shower of long, glittering streaks etched

WOLF AT THE DOOR   103

their way across the sky like shooting stars as debris from the explosion burnt up in Antimon's upper atmosphere. 'Plasma drive overload,' Jurgen said, his expression bleak.

'Could have been one of theirs,' Halvdan said, peering into the darkness. 'The *Ironwolf's* a tough one. She can handle herself against a bunch of filthy aliens.'

Bulveye wanted to agree, but as he watched, the signs of weapons fire diminished swiftly in the wake of the explosion. The battle appeared to be over. He checked his vox-bead once more, just in case, but every frequency he tried was still being jammed.

The Wolf Lord took a deep breath, then turned to face his men. 'At this point, we have to assume that the *Ironwolf* has been destroyed,' he said curtly. Glancing past the warriors, he caught sight of Andras, leaning against the wall and breathing heavily after their swift climb. Bulveye hadn't even realised the young noble had accompanied them.

'Andras!' Bulveye called, shouldering his way through the cordon of Wolves to stand at the young man's side. 'Who are these Harrowers? What do they want?'

The Antimonan's expression was bleak. 'We don't know who they are. Every seven years their ships fill the skies and they...' He took a deep, wracking breath. 'They used to hunt us like animals. Men, women, children – the children especially. They... they seem to like the sound of children's screams the best. They would take people by the hundreds and... and torture them. I've heard stories from my father, about the times before the quota, when the Harrowers would descend on the cities and take whomever they could find.'

'When we arrived, the senators were arguing about the quota,' Bulveye said, 'and something about a lottery.'

Andras nodded, unable to meet the Wolf Lord's eyes. 'During my great-grandfather's time, the Senate thought that an offering might appease the Harrowers and spare the bulk of our population. We gave them our criminals and outcasts, penned up like sheep for the slaughter, while the rest of our people took refuge in fortified shelters built into the hills.' He shrugged. 'It worked well enough. The Harrowers never stayed for more than a year, and by the time they'd exhausted their appetites on the people we gave them, they hadn't the time or energy to root out many others.'

It was all Bulveye could do not to recoil in disgust from the young man. The idea of sacrificing human beings to such monsters disgusted and appalled him. 'Why in the Allfather's name didn't you fight back?' he said through clenched teeth.

'We *did* fight them!' Andras cried. 'At first, the armigers fought back with every weapon they had. There was a great battle at one point – the armigers ambushed a large force of raiders and killed a score of them, including their leader,' the young man said. 'And in return the Harrowers returned to their starships and rained death on Antimon for seven days and seven nights. Most of the world was laid waste, and hundreds of millions died. After that, the Senate disbanded the armigers and forbade anyone to raise a hand against the raiders.'

Bulveye clenched his fists. 'Then the Senate betrayed you one and all,' he snarled. 'A life not worth fighting for is no life at all.' With an effort, he fought down the urge to berate Andras. He couldn't be held to account for the decisions of his ancestors. 'How long have the Harrowers plagued your world?'

Andras raised a hand and wiped angry tears from his eyes. 'Two hundred years, or so the histories say. No one knows where they came from, or why they leave. No one taken by the Harrowers is ever seen alive again.'

Bulveye nodded thoughtfully. Pieces of the puzzle were falling into place. The Harrowers had found Antimon shortly after the galaxy-wide warp storms began to subside. Evidently, this part of space remained somewhat turbulent – the Imperium had encountered a number of regions across the galaxy that still experienced cycles of warp storm activity, followed by brief periods of calm. The aliens plagued the world as long as they could and then left before the storms could rise up and trap them in the system, likely moving on to terrorise yet another planet.

'The devils built the black spires after the bombardment, I suppose,' Bulveye said, thinking aloud.

Andras nodded. 'Their technology borders on sorcery,' he said with a trace of awe in his voice. 'They land their sky-ships on terraces built into the sides of the great spires, and venture out to hunt across the zone when the mood takes them.'

Bulveye nodded thoughtfully. He was starting to build a profile of the aliens in his head, analysing their actions and inferring what he could from them. High overhead, longer and brighter streaks of fire began to arc across the night sky, falling towards Antimon's surface like a sheaf of burning darts. 'What happens next?' the Wolf Lord asked.

Andras took a deep breath. 'The Harrowers will descend upon the spires and take up residence,' he said. 'They'll wait for perhaps a day, then send out their tribute parties the following night to take our offering.' The young nobleman shook his head bitterly. 'But we're not ready. They've arrived early this time. We haven't finished stocking our shelters, and we don't have enough people to fill out the quota.'

Bulveye remembered something he'd heard earlier. 'Does that have anything to do with the lottery that the senators were debating earlier?'

Andras stared guiltily up at the Wolf Lord and nodded. 'Every seven years, the incidence of crime drops sharply,' he said with bleak humour. 'Our prisons don't have nearly enough criminals to satisfy the aliens, so there will have to be a lottery to decide who else must become part of the tribute.' His gaze fell to the stone surface of the ramp. 'It's happened before, or so my father tells me. Prominent families are already trying to offer rich bribes to buy an exemption for their children.' He shook his head. 'I don't know what's going to happen now. The Senate will empty the prisons, of course, but that may be all they can manage at this point. I doubt any of the families have more than a few months' food stocked away. When they come out of their shelters to search for more, the Harrowers will be waiting for them.'

The Wolf Lord looked skywards and watched the descent of the raiders. 'I reckon they arrived when they did on purpose,' he said. 'They've become tired of your offerings, Andras, so they've arranged things to provide them some more sport.' It wasn't so difficult to imagine; he had heard of bloodthirsty reavers who'd done much the same thing during his own raiding days on Fenris.

Bulveye tried to imagine offering up Fenrisian villagers to the vile appetites of a band of ruthless xenos marauders, and his stomach roiled at the thought. He looked down at Andras and fought back a surge of deadly rage. It wasn't the boy's fault, he told himself. If anyone was to blame it was his elders. The Wolf Lord now regretted not grabbing Javren by the throat when he'd had the chance.

'Is there a particular place where you bring your tribute to the aliens?' Bulveye asked the young man.

Andras wiped more tears from his cheeks and nodded. 'There is a pavilion,' he replied, 'about ten kilometres east of Oneiros.' He glanced up at the Astartes, and was shaken by the look on Bulveye's face. 'What are you going to do?'

The Wolf Lord met the young man's gaze. 'These xenos think they can prey upon mankind like sheep,' he said calmly. 'I intend on showing them the error of their ways.'

IT WAS EARLY afternoon on the following day when the procession of bulbous Antimonan cargo haulers appeared on the road heading west from Oneiros and made their way down the length of the broad meadow towards the tribute site. The pavilion itself was square and largely featureless, little more than a chessboard of stone paving tiles more than fifty yards on each side and situated at the feet of a semicircle of large, wooded hills. Only the heavy iron rings fixed at intervals along the paving stones hinted at the site's awful purpose. Further to the west, the tall, knife-like xenos spire rose ominously into the clouds, its base wreathed in tatters of curling mist.

Bulveye and his lieutenants watched from the shadows of a hillside thicket as the cargo haulers left the white-paved utility road and rumbled across the pavilion. The Antimonans wasted little time, orientating themselves across the stone expanse according to a well-drilled plan. When the last vehicle was in place, the passenger doors on the haulers popped open and large men in padded coveralls hopped out. Each one carried a kind of power stave or shock maul, which they swung about with authority once the back gates of the haulers banged open and the shackled prisoners began stumbling out. The men and women wore shapeless, faded brown tunics and breeches, and dark inmate tattoos had been branded along the sides of their necks. Each file of stunned, shambling convicts was herded to a line of iron rings and shackled there as a group. Once they were locked in, the prisoners sank down onto the stones and waited. Some stared up at the blue sky overhead, while others seemed to fold in on themselves and look at nothing at all.

Halvdan shook his head despairingly. 'How can they just sit there, like sheep for the slaughter?' he whispered, despite the fact that the pavilion was nearly a kilometre distant. 'If I were down there, they'd have to beat me senseless before they hooked me to one of those rings.'

Jurgen pointed towards the far end of the pavilion. 'Looks like those lambs agree with you, brother,' he said grimly.

The men in the last set of haulers were struggling with a smaller group of manacled victims, who thrashed and kicked and bit at their handlers. These men and women wore a variety of clothing styles, and were obviously taken from streets and homes all over Oneiros. They struggled against their fate with an energy born of stark terror, but the lash of the handlers' shock-sticks kept matters from spiralling out of control. Twenty minutes later the last of the weeping, pleading victims were chained to the pavilion stones, and the handlers returned to their vehicles without so much as a backwards glance.

Bulveye raised his eye from the scope of a boltgun and handed the weapon back to Jurgen. There were eight of his warriors surrounding him in the thicket, including his two lieutenants. Gone were the battle-trophies and tokens of honour they'd worn the day before; they'd stripped their armour bare and smudged the gleaming surfaces with dirt and soot to minimise any telltale glint that could give their position away. Over the course of the previous night they had put aside any pretence of civility and made themselves ready for war.

As the Harrowers had begun to descend on Antimon in their multitudes, Bulveye had left Andras and the city behind, loping through the darkness to the landing field where their Stormbird waited. The pilot of the drop-ship was ready, the craft's thrusters charged and idling as the Space Wolves clambered aboard and began arming themselves from the Stormbird's large weapons lockers. The Wolf Lord had ordered the drop-ship to head west, flying at treetop level to mask its movement from alien auspex arrays, and find a place to settle down within ten or twelve kilometres of the tribute site. The pilot had found a lightly wooded hollow just big enough to put the assault ship down in, and the warriors had spent the rest of the night camouflaging it with netting and scraps of broken branches shorn off by the landing. By dawn, the Wolf Lord had led his small warband to the hills around the pavilion and begun planning his ambush. With so few men and so little in the way of equipment, his options were somewhat limited.

The Wolf Lord pointed to the western end of the field beyond the pavilion. Between the paving stones of the tithe site and the woods at the base of the surrounding hills, there was plenty of room to land an entire squadron of Stormbirds. 'They'll likely bring their ships in over there,' he said. 'That's our kill box.'

Jurgen folded his arms and nodded grudgingly. The warrior cast a sidelong glance at Halvdan, then addressed Bulveye. 'What's our objective here, my lord?'

Bulveye frowned thoughtfully. 'I'd think it was obvious,' he replied. 'We inflict as many casualties among the enemy as possible and put them on the back foot. We want them to start worrying about the possibility of an ambush every time they leave the spire.'

'That's not what I mean, my lord,' Jurgen said. 'You saw all those ships landing last night; there must be more than a hundred at this spire alone. This isn't a little raiding party: it's some kind of nomadic clan or tribe.'

The Wolf Lord gave Jurgen a hard look. 'Are you saying we're not equal to the task?'

'I'm saying it's not our fight,' the lieutenant replied. 'These people aren't Imperial citizens; in fact, their leader called you a liar and said that he wanted nothing to do with us. If the xenos hadn't shown up yesterday you'd be on the *Ironwolf* right now, planning a campaign to conquer the planet and force it into compliance.'

Bulveye's gaze narrowed angrily at the lieutenant's bald declaration, but finally he nodded. 'What you say is true, brother,' he admitted. 'But it changes nothing. We're warriors of the Emperor and protectors of mankind. *All* mankind. If we don't live up to that ideal, then all the blood we've shed during the Crusade has been for naught, and I'll be damned before I let that happen.' Before Jurgen could respond, he turned away from his lieutenant and waved at the assembled men. 'We've only got a few hours left before nightfall. Let's begin preparing our positions.'

The Astartes made their way down out of the hollow and moved quickly through the dense forests around the base of the hills. They took their time sizing up the killing field, drawing not only on the years of intensive training and hypno-instruction provided by the Allfather, but also from years of ambushing foes in the wild terrain of their homeworld. When they were content with their positions, the four remaining warriors were summoned from their temporary camp up in the hills to bring down the heavy weapons they'd secured from the Stormbird. While the last elements of the ambush were set in place, the Stormbird's pilot was situated in a camouflaged position high on one of the nearby hills to warn of the aliens' approach.

They didn't have long to wait. An hour after sunset, with a glinting field of stars overhead and deep shadows filling the meadow about the pavilion, Bulveye's vox-unit came to life. 'Fenris, this is Aesir,' the lookout called. 'Multiple contacts approaching from the west at low altitude. Many heat traces: nearly a dozen large craft and a score of smaller ones.'

At the edge of the woods, Bulveye cocked an ear westwards. Sure enough, he could hear what sounded like gravitic engines, faint but growing stronger. They had an unearthly pitch, like a chorus of wailing souls. But the sound held no dread for him; instead, it set his blood boiling at the prospect of battle. He keyed his vox-bead. 'Fenris copies. Relocate to point Alpha and prepare for extraction.'

'Copy,' the lookout answered. His job done, the pilot would retreat down the hill and head for the

Stormbird, prepping the engines and making ready for a quick escape.

Bulveye checked his weapons one last time and turned to his lieutenants. Despite the near-total darkness beneath the canopy, the Wolves' enhanced senses allowed him to see his battle-brothers clearly. 'For Russ and the Allfather, Wolf Brothers,' he said quietly, then led them out into the meadow.

Halvdan and Jurgen followed Bulveye across the wide field west of the tribute site. Wild grass and meadow flowers swished against their armoured legs. The two lieutenants held their boltguns in one hand and their bared blades in the other. Bulveye's weapons were still sheathed at the moment, and he continued to stare expectantly towards the western horizon.

They crossed the kill box and approached the tribute site, making no effort to conceal their movements. It wasn't long before the shackled victims spotted the striding giants and began to moan in fear, thinking their doom had come at last. The Space Wolves ignored the rising panic of the prisoners, however. When they were ten yards from the western edge of the pavilion they stopped and turned about, placing the tribute site at their backs.

Halvdan tested his grip on his weapons. His bale-eye glowed like an ember in the darkness. 'I don't see why we have to be the bait,' he grumbled.

Jurgen grinned cruelly. 'Obviously, Bulveye wanted the most impressive warriors he had available, to strike fear into the hearts of the enemy. Or, in your case, the ugliest.'

Before the exchange could escalate, a cluster of pale green lights appeared along the hilltops to the west, approaching swiftly. A faint chorus of cries grew louder with each passing moment, riding on the faint breeze. The Harrowers had arrived.

The Space Wolves watched as a dozen glowing lights descended upon them like a salvo of terrain-hugging missiles. Their keen night vision picked out details of the oncoming craft while they were still some distance away: they were small, sleek and rakish, with curved, blade-like stabilisers and rows of wicked barbs protruding from their undersides. Each craft carried a single rider, who appeared lithe and human-like despite the strange, articulated armour they wore. The alien jetbikes howled past the Wolves like a flock of hissing, wailing birds, sweeping by to either side of the three warriors and bearing down on the pavilion behind them. As the bikes went past, Bulveye caught a glimpse of a pale, sharply angular face etched with strange tattoos and glinting with metal implants. The rider's eyes were black and depthless as the void itself.

Behind the swarm of jetbikes came eleven larger craft, gliding with lethal grace over the hills and sinking towards the edge of the western field. These ships were the big cousins of the strange jetbikes, with sharply raked prows, spiked hulls and razor-edged stabiliser fins. Crews of pale-skinned, armoured figures swarmed around the decks of eight of the transports; they crowded at the bow, having apparently been told of the three warriors awaiting them on the plain.

Fearless and haughty in their numbers, the large craft settled easily onto the grassy field, and their crews disembarked with contemptuous grace. From a hundred yards away, Bulveye watched the aliens congregate in loose-knit mobs; most of the raiders' faces were concealed by tall, conical black helmets, and they held long-barrelled rifles in their gloved hands. Their leaders sported tall horsetail-like plumes of hair from their helmets, and their harnesses were decorated with glittering, web-like meshes that held trophies of bleached bone.

They advanced towards the waiting Space Wolves in a rough crescent, their rifles held across their chests, whispering to one another in a sibilant tongue that sounded like the rustle of dry snakeskin. The raiders were wary, studying the huge Astartes with disquieting intensity, but it was clear from their unhurried advance that they didn't consider the three Wolves a serious threat.

At the centre of the advancing mob came a hunched, pale-skinned figure cased in bizarre, ornate armour, surrounded by a cadre of stitched-together creatures that paced about the leader's heels like a pack of hounds. The hunched figure – evidently the leader of the raiding band, as near as Bulveye could tell – had half of his long, white hair shaved away, exposing a fragile scalp etched with complex scar-tattoos. The exposed ear, long and pointed like a dog's, had been expertly flensed and perforated, until it lay against the side of the alien's head like a kind of grisly lace. More scars lined the figure's angular cheeks and throat; bits of metal glittered from the thin bands of scar tissue, creating a web-work that seemed to form a kind of complex symbol or pictograph that ran from temple to collarbone. The alien's eyes were large and deep-set, and his frayed lips twitched over white teeth that had been filed to jagged points. The fingers of his left gauntlet were little more than a set of cruel blades that hung almost to his knees; they clattered and scraped against one another as the monster approached. Even from thirty yards away, Bulveye could smell the alien's acrid scent, tainted by strange elixirs and bio-modifications. The scent prickled his skin and brought the taste of bile to his mouth.

He looked upon these monsters and felt no fear; instead, there was only a terrible eagerness – a hunger to bare his blade and dive in amongst his foes, hacking and slashing with wild abandon. It was the wolf inside him – the wild gift of Leman Russ himself, and it stirred in his breast like a living thing.

Not yet, he told the beast. *Not yet.*

The aliens drew closer, still whispering in their serpentine tongue. Still more strange scents washed over Bulveye and his men, making his veins shiver plucked chords. The raiders were surrounded by a miasma of pheromones, adrenal vapours and narcotic musk; it was all his enhanced physiology could do to filter the poisons before they rendered him insensate. As it was, his head swam and his knees felt weak. He heard Halvdan curse under his breath, and knew his men were struggling as well.

Bulveye turned his head away from the aliens and looked back at the huddled victims chained to the stones of the pavilion. Many were weeping; others had their heads bent in prayer. A handful were looking at him, their eyes wide and pleading.

The Wolf Lord turned back to the advancing raiders, his hands falling to his sides. He eyed the twisted creature at the centre of the mob. 'Hear me, alien,' he called out in a clear voice. 'You've preyed on these people for centuries, so I suspect by now your people understand our tongue. I am Bulveye, axe man of the Rus and sworn brother to Leman, Primarch of the Sixth Legion. The people of this world are under my protection, monster. You tread here at your peril.'

Bulveye watched the alien leader's dark eyes widen in amusement. His lithe form trembled with deranged mirth until his lips peeled back from his jagged teeth and he cackled with feverish glee. His grotesque bodyguards gibbered and howled along with their master, raking their talons along their scarred cheekbones and tearing at their scabrous lips.

The alien grinned at Bulveye like a sea-pike, showing his needle-pointed teeth, and spoke in a gurgling voice that bubbled up from pheromone-soaked lungs. 'You will make a fine gift for my master,' the xenos said in passable Low Gothic. He flexed his clashing finger-blades. 'How he will laugh to hear your bold words as he unspools the flesh from your bones.' A shudder of pleasure gripped the alien's tortured frame. 'Your suffering shall be exquisite.'

Bulveye's icy gaze narrowed on the monster. 'So you are not the master of this vile horde?'

The xenos gave a bark of phlegmatic laughter. '*I am but a lowly servant of Darragh Shakkar, Archon of the Kabal of the Shrieking Heart. It is he who holds this world of beasts in his taloned hands.*'

The Wolf Lord nodded slowly. When he spoke again, his voice was cold as polished iron. 'Then you and I have nothing more to discuss.' Bulveye's right hand was a blur of motion as he drew the plasma pistol from his hip and shot the alien between the eyes.

The alien leader's headless body had not yet hit the ground before the rest of the Space Wolves opened fire, unleashing a stream of bolter rounds from the surrounding woods into the mass of the assembled raiders. The xenos mob was so tightly packed that every round found a target; the mass-reactive slugs punched through the aliens' light body armour and exploded within, ripping their limbs and bodies apart. With a crackling hiss, a pair of krak missiles streaked from the tree line and struck the sides of two of the larger transports, blowing them apart in a deadly shower of fire and red-hot shrapnel. The aliens spun about, shrieking with rage, and fired their rifles blindly into the darkness. Their weapons made a high-pitched buzzing as they fired, spitting streams of hypervelocity splinters into the trees.

Behind Bulveye, Jurgen and Halvdan raised their boltguns and added to the carnage, pumping streams of shells into the surprised raiders. The alien warriors twitched and fell in sprays of bitter blood.

Through the hail of fire came the bodyguards of the fallen alien leader, their hideous faces twisted into masks of drug-fuelled hatred as they hurled themselves at the Wolf Lord. Dozens of the xenos warriors took inspiration from the bodyguards' wild charge, and they joined in as well.

Streams of splinter fire hissed past Bulveye or spattered against his Mechanicum-blessed armour as the aliens bore down upon him. Overhead, a flight of xenos jetbikes hissed past, raking the northern tree-line with splinter fire. In response, a frag missile streaked skywards on a plume of flame and detonated in their midst, riddling three of the bikes with shrapnel and sending them plunging to the ground.

The Wolf Lord held his ground and pulled his power axe from his belt. Triggering its energy field, he leaped forwards to meet the xenos charge with an ancient war-song on his lips. The bodyguards surrounded him on all sides, raking at him with their claws or lunging forwards to snap at him with their fangs, but each time Bulveye answered them with a fearsome sweep of his axe. He severed arms and split trunks, spilled entrails and severed heads, until the bodies began to pile up about him. The wolf surged within his breast, demanding release, but Bulveye focused on his axe-work and held the beast at bay.

Within moments Jurgen and Halvdan joined the melee, carving into the enemy mob with sweeps of their crackling power swords. Behind the aliens, more of their transport craft exploded under the missiles and concentrated bolter fire of the remaining Wolf Guard. The surviving jetbikes continued to strafe the woods, seeking revenge against the ambushers, but the darkness and the close-set trees shielded the Astartes from much of the enemy fire.

A saw-edged bayonet glanced off Bulveye's breast-plate; another jabbed at his right leg and scored a bright line across his greave. A third weapon jabbed in from the left and a little behind the Wolf Lord, stabbing into the hollow under his arm and tangling in the cables that ran there. He swung his axe in a backhanded stroke that struck the head off one raider and buried itself in the torso of the attacker who'd stabbed him from behind. To his right, he levelled his plasma pistol and fired twice, point-blank, into the press. Aliens burst apart, vaporised by intense blasts of ionised gases or set alight by secondary thermal effects.

Then, suddenly, the xenos raiders retreated from the Wolf Lord like an outgoing tide, flowing away swiftly on all sides. More splinters crashed against his chest and arms, but they were wild bursts fired by the retreating aliens. The surviving warriors were in full flight, racing back to their remaining transports under the covering fire of the remaining jetbikes.

Bulveye and his lieutenants rushed forwards with bloodied weapons held high, singing songs of vengeance and death. A splinter struck the Wolf Lord just above the knee, causing him to stumble with a spasm of sudden pain, but his advance scarcely faltered. Two of the transports rose into the air with a whine of gravitic impellers; immediately they were targeted by a pair of krak missiles. One transport was struck on the flank, showering the troop deck with flame. The vehicle rocked beneath the blow, spilling burning bodies over the starboard rail, but it managed to lurch ahead with a shriek of thrusters and come about in a long turn to the west. The second craft blew apart in a spectacular explosion, showering the field with blazing debris. Some of the burning pieces fell among the rest of the rising transports, sowing more death and destruction across their troop compartments, but the damage wasn't enough to incapacitate them. The rakish craft swung around and disappeared swiftly into the distance, fleeing for the safety of the distant spire. Moments later, Bulveye and his men were alone, surrounded by flaming wreckage and the bodies of the dead.

The Wolf Lord summoned his men from their ambush positions. 'Jurgen, check on the men and give me a report,' he told his lieutenant, then turned and headed for the pavilion.

They cowered at his approach – a massive, armoured giant, silhouetted in flame and bearing a glowing, crackling power axe in one gauntleted hand. The Antimonans, prisoners and innocent victims alike, looked upon Bulveye with an equal mix of awe and pure, atavistic terror. He looked over the huddled mass of men and women and spoke in a clear, commanding voice.

'Hear me, people of Antimon,' the Wolf Lord said. 'From this night forwards, you will live in fear no longer. Return to your city and tell everyone you meet of what happened tonight. Tell them that the

Allfather has sent his warriors to fight on your behalf, and that we will not rest until the aliens are driven from your world forever.'

He swept his axe down in a hissing arc and sliced through the chains of the first set of prisoners. They leaped back with a shout, then held up the severed links with looks of shock and uncomprehending wonder. By the time the Wolf Lord had reached the second set of prisoners, the first men were already running eastwards as fast as their feet would take them.

Halvdan joined Bulveye in freeing the Antimonans. His power sword crackled as it split the iron rings asunder. When the last of the people had been freed and sent fleeing back to Oneiros, the lieutenant gave Bulveye a sidelong glance, his augmetic eye flat and unreadable. 'Not a bad beginning,' he said. 'But we were lucky. The damned aliens have had the run of this planet for so long that they'd become complacent. And I reckon they'll be back here in no time, looking to even the score. What do we do now?'

The Wolf Lord straightened and looked to the west. 'We call in the Stormbird and head south, drawing any pursuit after us so the Oneirans have a good chance of getting back to their home city,' he said. 'Then we find a good spot in the wastelands to set up a base and wait to see just how badly these people want their planet back.'

THERE WAS A storm building out among the ruins. Bulveye could feel the static charge building in the air like a faint caress against the exposed skin of his face and hands. A breath of hot, dry wind hissed over the broken stones of the fallen city, followed by a brassy roll of thunder far off to the east that stirred the Wolf Lord from the depths of his restorative trance. Reflexively he began the series of auto-hypnotic rotes that would bring him, layer by mental layer, back to full consciousness. Within a few moments he opened his eyes and took a deep breath to fully activate his pulmonary systems. His armour's bio-support systems finished their purification routines, leeching away the toxins excreted via the modified sweat glands along his skin and injecting metabolic stabilisers into his bloodstream. By his own estimation he'd been resting for less than an hour. It wasn't enough, based on the amount of radiation he had been exposed to, but it would have to do. He would need to inspect the warband's makeshift camp and ensure that everything was under cover and secured before the storm and its howling winds roared over them.

Their latest encampment was a hundred kilometres south of Oneiros's habitable zone, in the wreckage of a small city that still bore a high level of background radiation from the xenos holocaust of two centuries before. Over the last three months they had shifted position dozens of times, never staying in one place for more than a week and keeping to radioactive regions in the hope of confounding enemy hunter-killer patrols. It was only Bulveye's long experience as a raider himself plus the mobility afforded by their Stormbird drop-ship that allowed the Wolves to continue their hit-and-run raids against the Harrowers and evade the furious pursuits that followed.

They struck everywhere and anywhere, operating as three-man teams in nearly every one of the planet's habitable zones. With hundreds of years of combat experience and a lifetime stalking through the woods of their native Fenris, the Astartes sprang lightning-quick ambushes against isolated xenos raiding parties, or used missile launchers to attack low-flying transports moving between the alien spires and the Antimonan cities. They would strike fast, inflict as many casualties as possible, then fade just as quickly into the countryside, avoiding detection until the opportunity arose to strike again. Bulveye meant to draw off as many of the Harrowers as he could and disrupt their raids against the Antimonans, and judging by the intensity of the xenos response, the strategy appeared to be succeeding. The aliens now kept constant patrols searching the wastelands, some venturing as far north and south as the planetary poles, and in the last few weeks had even resorted to unleashing random orbital bombardments against some of the larger ruins in the hope of flushing out their prey.

The Astartes succeeded for no other reason than they were willing – and able – to suffer far more privation and hardship than their foes. The small store of emergency rations aboard the Stormbird had been exhausted within a month of careful rationing, but the warriors' enhanced metabolic functions allowed them to draw nutrients from plants, animals and even inorganic materials that would kill a normal human. They camped in wild, desolate places that left them at the mercy of the worst weather that the planet could produce, and exposed themselves to levels of background radiation that would have killed a normal human within hours. More than once, an enemy hunter-killer team had caught the Wolves' trail, but were ultimately forced to abandon their pursuit when the land became too deadly for them to travel through.

For all that, the Wolves paid a steep price for their success. The constant exposure to radiation had suppressed their natural healing abilities, and coupled with the aliens' predilection to poison their weapons, it meant that many of the warriors were wounded to a greater or lesser degree. Of the twelve Astartes under the Wolf Lord's command, three had succumbed to their wounds and lapsed into the Red Dream, a deep coma that freed the warrior's body to try and cope with the gravest of injuries. Currently, Bulveye had two teams of three on extended deployments around the planet at all times, with a third team providing security for their fallen brothers while they regained their strength for another patrol.

The going had been difficult, but there were encouraging signs that they were having an impact on the balance of power across Antimon. The Harrowers still attacked the local cities, sometimes with a savagery that bordered on the bestial, but the fierce, uncoordinated attacks rarely produced significant results. More importantly, there were signs that Bulveye's message had somehow managed to circulate among the Antimonans across the entire world. The tribute fields had fallen into disuse after the events of that first, fateful night – or at least, they were no longer used for the purpose they'd been intended. Instead, the Wolves would sometimes pass near the pavilions and find offerings of food or medicines wrapped in parcels of waterproof cloth, or simply wreaths of local flowers or bottles of wine. Sometimes the parcels would contain notes written in the local dialect, and the warriors would puzzle for hours over the strange script, trying to divine their contents. To Bulveye, the message was clear enough: the people of the battered world knew what his warband was doing on their behalf, and they were grateful.

The Wolf Lord caught sight of movement at the bottom of the low hill where he sat. Moments later, Halvdan emerged from the ruins of a small dwelling and began limping haltingly up the slope towards him. The burly warrior had been hit in the thigh by an envenomed dagger wielded by a white-haired xenos female, and the wound so far showed no signs of healing. How he continued to walk, let alone fight, in the face of such terrible pain was a wonder to Bulveye.

'Stormbird's on the way back,' the lieutenant said hoarsely as he reached the top of the hill. Bulveye beckoned for the warrior to sit, and Halvdan sank to the ground with a grateful nod. The skin around his eyes was pale and lined with strain as he pulled a water flask from his belt and took a deep draught of the contents.

Bulveye nodded. 'Both teams recovered?'

'Aye, thank the Allfather,' Halvdan replied. 'Jurgen said he had casualties, though.' The bearded warrior looked off to the east, towards the distant brown smudge of the approaching storm. He took another swallow from the flask. 'I've finished taking stock of our supplies, as you requested.'

The Wolf Lord arched an eyebrow. 'That was fast.'

Halvdan let out a grunt. 'There wasn't much to count,' he said. 'We're down to forty rounds of bolt-gun ammo per man, eight grenades, twelve melta charges and two krak missiles, plus whatever else the two patrols manage to bring back with them. We don't have a single complete medicae kit left, and armour damage varies anywhere from ten per cent to eighteen per cent per warrior. In short, we're close to the end of our rope. We can manage another set of patrols, or perhaps one major engagement, and that will be that.' He sighed, fixing the Wolf Lord with his baleful red eye. 'We're four weeks overdue at Kernunnos at this point. They're bound to send someone to look for us. A battle group could arrive at any time.'

The Wolf Lord regarded his sword-brother. 'What are you getting at?' he said.

Halvdan took another drink. From the smell, it was clearly filled with Antimonan wine. The warrior shrugged his massive shoulders. 'I don't like these damned aliens any more than you do, lord, but I think we've done all we can at this point. Leman himself couldn't have asked our brothers to fight any harder. You know that. When the Stormbird gets back, why don't we go to ground somewhere a little more liveable and lay low until relief arrives?'

The suggestion took Bulveye aback. 'We can't stop now. *Especially* now. The tide is turning in our favour. If we don't keep up the pressure we'll be relinquishing the initiative to the enemy, and I guarantee they will do all they can to capitalise on it.'

'Yes, but…' Halvdan paused, searching for a tactful way to say what was on his mind. After a moment, he gave up and simply ploughed ahead. 'My lord, we owe these people *nothing*. They rejected you out of hand. You know what that means.'

The Wolf Lord's eyes narrowed angrily. 'I know full well,' he growled. 'And if it comes down to that, I'll do my duty, like any other servant of the Allfather. You can't look at the wreck I've made of this subsector and imagine otherwise.'

Halvdan raised a placating hand. 'Look, I'm not saying you've gone soft-hearted–'

'I know exactly what you're saying, brother,' Bulveye said. 'You wonder why I'm going to such effort to fight for people we will just have to turn around and conquer later.'

The Wolf Lord rose to his feet. Dust spilled from the joints of his armour and billowed away in the rising breeze. 'We are crusaders, Halvdan. The Allfather sent us forth to save the lost worlds of humanity and bring them back into the fold. If there is a chance, however slim, that we can convince these people of our intentions and avoid repeating what we did to Kernunnos, then I'll do whatever I must. I'll fight to my last breath if that is what it takes.'

Halvdan stared up at Bulveye, his expression hard, but after a moment he simply shook his head and sighed. With an effort, he forced himself back onto his feet and clapped his hand on the Wolf Lord's shoulder.

'The drop-ship should be back at any moment,' he said. 'We'd best go meet it and see if Jurgen's brought us back any presents.'

Together, the two Astartes made their way down the hill and out into the dusty plain west of the ruined town. No sooner had they arrived than a black shape appeared on the horizon, streaking in low to mask its flight path from orbital surveyors. At once, the two Wolves could see that the drop-ship was in trouble: smoke was streaming from one of its engines, and its flight path was erratic. It was clear that the pilot was struggling desperately to keep the Stormbird straight and level at such a dangerous altitude.

Within minutes the assault craft was flaring its jets over the landing field and settling down hard on the dusty ground. Moments later the ramp opened and four Wolves – including the pilot – exited quickly with portable fire suppressors in their hands. They raced aft and doused the smoking engine. Jurgen, meanwhile, appeared at the top of the ramp and approached Bulveye and Halvdan, who were still standing a few yards distant.

'You missed quite a trip,' Jurgen said as he stepped up to his lord. 'A brace of alien fighters picked us up as we were transiting the Oneiran habitable zone. They gave us quite a run before we managed to knock them down.'

'How bad is it?' Bulveye asked.

Jurgen's expression turned grim. 'You'll have to ask the pilot about the drop-ship. Two more of our brothers have gone into the Red Dream. One of them is likely going to lose both his legs, if he survives at all.'

The Wolf Lord accepted the news with a curt nod. 'Were the patrols successful?'

'Yes,' Jurgen said without hesitation. 'Perhaps more so than we might have expected.'

'Oh? How's that?'

The lieutenant folded his arms. 'Well, as we were flying back, the pilot picked up a lot of aerial activity around Oneiros. It appeared that the Harrowers were conducting a major series of raids on the city, so I decided to try and get a closer look. We infiltrated the zone and set down near the tribute field. That's where our patrol found something interesting.'

Bulveye frowned at the news. 'Another package?'

'No,' Jurgen said. 'A message.' He reached into a pouch at his belt and drew out a scrap of paper. 'It was wrapped around the hilt of a dagger that was driven into a gap between the paving stones of the pavilion.'

The Wolf Lord examined the paper. To his surprise, it was written in archaic Low Gothic – less like the local dialect and more like the parent tongue that nearly every human world understood. The note contained a vox frequency, a time and a name. *Andras*.

Jurgen studied Bulveye's reaction to the message. 'What do you think it means?' he asked.

Bulveye queried his armour's chrono. The time mentioned on the note was just a few hours away. 'It means that the Antimonans are ready to take the next step.'

THEY ARRIVED FOUR hours before the scheduled rendezvous time, after moving overland through the wastes and then slipping through the wooded hills until they were in position to observe the tribute field. Bulveye had no doubt that it was Andras whom he spoke to over the vox, but that didn't mean an ambush was out of the question.

Xenos aircraft flew overhead at constant intervals while the Wolves sat and waited: transports and fighters, most bound in the direction of Oneiros. As Jurgen had reported, it appeared that the Harrowers had committed a great deal of their local strength to pillaging the city, no matter the cost. Bulveye watched the flights pass overhead and added the data to his evolving plan.

At precisely the appointed time, a trio of cloaked figures slipped from the woods bordering the road to the east of the pavilion and headed for the tribute site. The Wolves were impressed; no one had caught wind of the Antimonans until they'd broken cover. Bulveye watched them approach and crouch down at the rendezvous point, and made his decision.

'I'm going down,' he told his lieutenants. 'Hold position here until I say otherwise.' Then he rose from the shadows and made his way out onto the plain where they'd first ambushed the Harrowers some twelve weeks before.

The Antimonans saw him coming from a long way off. They watched him intently from the depths of their hoods, but made no move until he was just a few yards away. One of the figures rose smoothly and moved to join Bulveye. He could tell from the way the man moved that it was Andras.

'Well met,' Bulveye said quietly, extending his hand. Andras took it, clasping the Wolf Lord's wrist in a warrior's grip.

'We've been waiting for two weeks, hoping you'd find the message,' the young nobleman replied. 'We're glad you came. How are you faring?'

'Well enough,' Bulveye said carefully. 'We're grateful for the gifts your people have left for us. Has the Senate had a change of heart?'

'The Senate is no more,' Andras replied. 'The raiders killed them last month.'

The news surprised Bulveye. 'What happened?'

'Our food stores are swiftly running out,' Andras explained. 'It's the same all over Antimon. My father and the other senators decided to open negotiations with the leader of the Harrowers and try to organise some kind of settlement before our situation became untenable.' The nobleman's body stiffened. 'The alien leader agreed on a meeting at the Senate building, but he did not come to talk. Instead, he and his warriors seized the senators and spent an entire week torturing them to death. Since then, the raiders have gone wild in Oneiros, filling the streets and tearing into the hill shelters with every tool and weapon at their disposal.'

'What became of the alien leader?' Bulveye inquired.

'He personally took part in torturing the senators, but returned to the spire afterwards.'

The Wolf Lord nodded thoughtfully. 'And what do you wish of us, Andras, son of Javren?'

Andras reached up and drew back his hood. A fresh scar marked the left side of his face, and livid bruises coloured his brow. 'We want to join you,' he replied. 'There were always those of us in the aristocracy who secretly kept the ways of the armigers alive. When you fought the raiders here on that first night, it inspired us to take action ourselves. Lately we've been making attacks against the raiders inside the city and enjoyed some success, but we would be a hundred times more effective if we could fight with you and your warriors beside us!'

To Andras's evident surprise, Bulveye shook his head. 'Fighting aliens inside Oneiros will accomplish very little at this point.'

'What are you talking about?' Andras hissed. 'How is that any different from what you have been doing these last three months?'

'Because everything I've done so far has been with one objective in mind,' Bulveye said. 'And that is to divide the raiders and ultimately turn them against one another.'

Andras scowled at the Wolf Lord and shook his head in frustration. 'I don't understand,' he said.

'That's because you were never a raider yourself,' Bulveye replied. 'I was, a very long time ago, and everything I've seen about the Harrowers so far tells me they aren't much different from the reavers I dealt with back on Fenris.'

'What does that mean?' Andras replied.

'It means that they're a greedy lot, and greed makes a person treacherous,' Bulveye explained. 'A raiding band is only as strong as its leader, who holds the group together by dint of being harder, meaner and cleverer than the rest. He takes the best of the plunder for himself, but so long as everyone manages to get a cut, the gang stays more or less content. When the loot dries up, though, watch out. That's when things get dangerous.'

Andras thought about that for a moment. 'And you've been making it hard for the Harrowers to take many slaves.'

'And killing as many of them as I can in the bargain,' Bulveye said. 'Every time a raiding party is ambushed, or a transport is shot down, the Harrowers' leader is made to appear weak. And I guarantee that some of his lieutenants are feeling tempted to try and take control of the band themselves.'

'So if the current leader dies, the rest will turn on each other to see who gets to be next in charge.' Andras said.

'Exactly,' Bulveye agreed. 'And now, while the majority of the Harrowers are in Oneiros, we've got our best chance of killing him and setting the bloody contest in motion.'

'How do you plan on doing that?' the nobleman asked. 'I told you, he's back at the spire now.'

'All I need is a Harrower transport,' Bulveye said. 'The aliens think they're safe in their floating citadels. I'm going to show them otherwise.'

Andras stared up at the Wolf Lord. 'I can get you a transport,' he told Bulveye. 'But only if you let us help you attack the spire.'

Bulveye held up a hand. 'I appreciate your courage, but we don't need the help.'

'Really? Do you know how to fly one of those transports?'

'Not at the moment,' the Wolf Lord replied. 'Do you?'

'Not… at the moment,' Andras grudgingly admitted, 'but over the last couple of centuries my people have gleaned quite a bit about the aliens' tongue.' The young nobleman drew himself up to his full height, which still left him at roughly chest-height next to the huge Astartes. 'We can deliver a transport into your hands and tell you how to read its controls. All we ask is that you allow us to accompany you when you attack the spire.'

Bulveye could not help but admire the young man's courage. 'How fast could you accomplish this?'

'We can strike tonight if you wish,' Andras said confidently.

'Is that so? All right. Tell me of your plan.'

ONCE ANDRAS AND Bulveye had agreed upon the plan, the Wolf Lord gathered his battle-brothers and the Antimonans led them back to Oneiros on foot. At the outskirts of the city the Wolf Lord saw first-hand the devastation wrought by the xenos occupiers. The sky above the city was orange with flames from burning buildings at the city centre, and

Bulveye could see signs of activity on the hills surrounding Oneiros as the aliens besieged a great many of the white stone hill-shelters. Fliers buzzed back and forth through the night air, but Andras and his companions led the Astartes on a circuitous route down the winding streets towards a large square just a few kilometres from the Senate building. In the square sat four of the alien transports and close to forty of the raiders in an improvised field base.

Andras led the Wolves into the burnt-out shell of a municipal building and left them there while he and his compatriots went to set his plan in motion. Andras returned with eight others a short while later, this time wearing the curious scaled armour and weapons of Antimon's warrior caste. The hexagonal links of the armour were polished to a mirror-bright sheen, and carried a faint scent of ozone that wrinkled Bulveye's nose.

'It's done,' the young nobleman said. 'We'd been planning this for some time, but for a different purpose. The diversion had been intended to draw the Harrowers away so that other groups could leave their shelters and forage for food.' Andras's expression turned grim. 'Hopefully, if our plan works, there won't be a need for such desperate measures.'

Bulveye nodded. 'How long?'

Andras glanced at his chrono. 'Another twenty minutes, give or take.'

The warriors settled down to wait, checking their weapons and observing the activity in the plaza. Bulveye settled down beside Andras. 'You asked me a number of questions before,' he said. 'Now I'd like to ask one of you.'

Andras looked up from the partially disassembled pistol in his lap. 'All right,' he said evenly. 'What do you want to know?'

'When we first arrived over Antimon, no one answered our hails – except for you,' the Wolf Lord said. 'Why did you disobey the Senate and answer our call?'

Andras didn't reply at first. His lips compressed into a tight line and his eyes grew haunted. 'The Harrowers took my mother and my sister when I was only four,' he said. 'They broke into our shelter. My father had barely enough time to hide me, but the raiders found everyone else. They spared him because he was a member of the Senate, but they... they took the others away, and he didn't even try to stop them. My sister was only two at the time.' The young man reached up and pinched the corners of his eyes. 'When I was ten I crept into the attic and started practising with my great-grandfather's blades. I swore to myself that if I ever had the chance, I was going to make the Harrowers pay for what they'd done. When your ship arrived in orbit, I thought that chance had finally come.'

Bulveye laid a hand on Andras's shoulder. 'It has, Andras. You have my oath on it.'

Off in the distance came the faint but unmistakeable sound of an explosion, followed by the rattle and pop of gunfire. The sounds of fighting intensified within moments, until it sounded like a full-fledged battle was underway.

Andras straightened. 'That would be the diversion,' he said. 'Now we wait and see what the Harrowers will do.'

Out in the plaza, the aliens had sprung into action. Within minutes, three of the transports were lifting off and rushing over the hilltops in the direction of the fighting.

Andras smiled as the transports faded from sight. 'They always leave one back in reserve,' he said, nodding towards the grounded craft. 'Now all we need to do is take care of the ten warriors that are left.'

Bulveye nodded. 'Leave that to us.'

The building they were concealed in was down a side street just off the square, about a hundred yards from the transport and its complement of raiders. Bulveye summoned his eight warriors with a curt command, and the Astartes readied their weapons. 'Be swift, brothers,' he told the Astartes. 'This is not the time for stealth. Kill the bastards as quick as you can, and let's be away.'

Without waiting for a reply, the Wolf Lord led the way into the street and set off towards the Harrowers at a dead run.

He'd barely covered fifty metres when the aliens spotted him. His enhanced hearing picked up a stream of hissed orders from the enemy officer, and the warriors quickly took cover and opened fire. Splinters hissed through the air all around Bulveye or rang off the plates of his armour. In reply, he raised his plasma pistol and let off two shots: the first struck the xenos officer as he ran from one position of concealment to another, cutting the alien nearly in two. The second blast struck a raider just as he rose from cover to take shot with his rifle, vaporising the alien's head and shoulders.

Bolter fire rang out all around the Wolf Lord, and howls of battle-fury split the night. Once again, Bulveye felt the beast inside him stir at the sound, but still he held it back. *Not yet*, he thought to himself. *Not yet, but soon.*

Firing on the move, the Space Wolves felled one alien after another, until the last three lost their nerve and fled down a side street on the opposite side of the plaza. Wasting no time, Bulveye reached the transport and leaped aboard, his axe held ready. He landed just in time to see the transport's pilot dive over the opposite side of the craft and flee as well.

Within a few moments the rest of Bulveye's warband and Andras's warriors had climbed aboard the alien craft. Right away, the Wolves' pilot, an Astartes named Ranulf, and two Antimonans whom Andras claimed were conversant with the alien's strange language, clustered by the transport's controls and began to puzzle them out. A minute later Ranulf keyed a number of controls, and the craft's powerplant activated with a rising whine. Then the pilot took hold of what looked like a control yoke and slowly, carefully, the transport rose into the air. It swung its nose ponderously to the west and began gliding gracelessly forwards.

'Faster!' Bulveye urged. 'The aliens will be on us at any moment! If we don't get to the spire before they raise the alarm we're all done for!'

'Aye, lord,' Ranulf answered. 'Everyone hang on to something!' he said, and pulled a lever. At once, the craft surged forwards, gathering speed until the city and the twilit countryside blurred away beneath them.

As the transport sped like an arrow towards the xenos spire, Andras worked his way forwards to stand beside Bulveye. 'Are you sure this is going to work?' he asked.

Bulveye considered his answer. 'If we can reach the reactor chamber, then I'm sure we can bring down the spire,' he said. 'As to the rest…' He shrugged. 'It's in the hands of the Fates now.'

'But how can you be certain we'll find their leader?' the nobleman asked.

The Wolf Lord answered with a savage smile. 'Once he realises what we intend to do, don't worry. He'll come to us.'

Ten minutes later they saw the alien spire. The massive structure was silhouetted against the night sky, limned in a faint blue glow cast by the citadel's gravitic suspensors. Pale green lights flashed at intervals along the surface of the spire, and here and there a craft rose from a landing spot on the side of the structure and sped away into the night.

Suddenly, Ranulf called out from the control room. 'My lord! The vox in here's started hissing! I think we're being challenged!'

Bulveye bent at the knees, placing as much of his body behind the armoured railing of the transport as he could. The rest of the Wolves followed suit. The Wolf Lord looked over at Andras. 'I'd get down were I you,' he said. 'Here's where things get interesting.'

All at once the night sky lit up with beams of energy and stitching streams of fire as the spire's defensive batteries went into action. Energy blasts struck the prow of the transport, blasting holes through the armour plate and showering the passengers with molten shrapnel. Bulveye turned back to the control room. 'Aim for the centre of the spire!' he told Ranulf. 'There have to be landing pads there for maintenance and supply!'

The transport plunged onwards through the hail of fire. Its high speed and the surprise of the spire's gunners made it a difficult target, and it crossed the distance to the citadel in a matter of seconds. Ranulf caught sight of a suitable landing pad at the spire's midpoint and raced towards it. Only at the last minute did he try to flare the engines back and come in for a landing.

They touched down with a bone-jarring crunch and a long, rending sound of tearing metal. Everyone was thrown forwards, piling up in the craft's mutilated bow as the transport skidded wildly down the landing pad in a shower of sparks. Finally, friction asserted itself and the transport slowed, skidding to a stop less than a dozen metres from the far edge of the pad.

It took several moments for the warriors to extricate themselves from the bow of the transport. Jurgen and Halvdan led the way, leaping over the rail onto the landing pad with weapons at the ready. The rest of the Wolves and Andras's warriors quickly followed, their faces concealed by armoured veils. Bulveye yelled to Ranulf as he reached the rail. 'Make sure this bucket is ready to fly by the time we get back,' he said, 'otherwise it's going to be a long walk back to Oneiros!'

The Wolf Lord leaped over the rail and landed with a clang onto the pad. Five yards away, a long, low hatchway led into the spire. Bulveye waved his battle-brothers towards the hatch. As they advanced, Andras came up beside him, closely trailed by his warriors. 'What now?' he asked.

Bulveye nodded at the hatch. 'This has to be a loading hatch for carrying parts and supplies into the citadel,' he said. 'The passageway beyond will take us to the reactor chamber sooner or later.' He nodded to Halvdan. 'Melta charge! Make us a hole!'

The lieutenant nodded and fitted one of their six anti-armour charges to the hatch. Moments later there was a *whoomp* of superheated air, and a large, molten hole had been blown through the door's thick plating. Without hesitation, Jurgen and two of the Space Wolves dived inside, and boltguns echoed in the space beyond. The staging area beyond was littered with wreckage from the blast; smashed containers spilled half-melted debris across the black floor and smouldering, armoured corpses attested to the force of the melta charge's focused blast.

The Wolf Lord and the rest of the assault team charged through the breach as Halvdan pulled a small auspex unit from his belt. The Astartes keyed in a series of commands, and the unit lit up immediately. 'I'm getting a strong energy source at about seven hundred metres,' he said, gesturing towards the centre of the spire. 'That's got to be the reactor.'

'Take point,' Bulveye said with a curt nod. 'Find us the shortest route to the core and stop for nothing.'

For the next twenty minutes the assault team drove their way deeper into the spire, navigating by the energy traces on Halvdan's auspex unit. Bulveye and his Wolves moved swiftly and lethally through the access corridors of the alien citadel, orchestrating a well-rehearsed dance of death that tore through everything the Harrowers put in their path. The huge passageways were teardrop-shaped and oddly faceted, as though the entire citadel had been carved from a strange kind of crystal, and the walls hummed with stored energies. Every surface was suffused with a purplish light, picking out strange, graceful carvings on the crystalline walls but leaving much else in shadow.

The xenos defenders sealed all the hatches leading into the spire and organised hasty defences behind each of them, but each time the Wolves would use a melta charge to create a breach and then dive through firing while the defenders were still recovering from the effects of the blast. It was a time-honoured technique that the Astartes had mastered in boarding actions over the course of decades, and so long as they kept up their momentum the warriors were difficult to stop.

Bulveye knew they were getting close when they blasted their way into a large room lined with strange, pulsing controls and filled with almost fifty xenos warriors. The Wolves made their breach and broke through into a storm of hissing splinter fire. Jurgen and the two warriors who went in first were struck dozens of times, but the armour succeeded in deflecting most of the deadly needles. Without hesitating they rushed at the mass of aliens, their power swords and chainaxes held high, and in moments were locked in a savage melee.

The Wolf Lord was next through the breach, and found himself attacked from three sides by armoured raiders brandishing rifles and jagged knives. He drove back the assailants on his left with a shot from his plasma pistol, then slashed furiously at the rest with his power axe. The keen blade split rifle barrels and armoured torsos with equal ease, and the aliens fell back in disarray. Bulveye charged after them, allowing room for Halvdan and the rest to make their way into the chamber behind him.

Splinters howled through the air, and the crackle of Antimonan pistols replied in kind. Andras came up on Bulveye's left, slashing at the aliens with his sword. Splinters raked him, but the projectiles sparked and deflected away from the noble – evidently the armiger harness incorporated a defensive force-field of some kind. The rest of the Antimonans joined in with ferocious zeal, shooting and stabbing at every Harrower they could see.

The aliens fought to the last, emptying their weapons and then using their bayonet-tipped rifles as pole-arms until they were finally cut down. One of Andras's men lay dead among them, and every one of Bulveye's warriors had sustained a number of minor wounds. 'Press on,' the Wolf Lord commanded, indicating the open archway at the far end of the chamber.

They emerged into a vast room whose ceiling rose to a peak far above their heads. Control consoles lined the walls of the octagonal chamber, and three other archways led off in different directions from the room. At the centre of the chamber, suspended in a complex network of struts and field induction matrices, rested an enormous, spindle-shaped crystal. The feeling of ambient power was thick inside the chamber; each pulse shivered along the Wolf Lord's bones. 'This is it,' he said. 'Halvdan, set the remaining charges. The rest of you cover the other entrances.'

'Two had best be enough,' the lieutenant said, limping forwards and scrutinising the crystal to determine where his charges would do the most damage.

The rest of the warriors raced forwards, fanning out around the huge reactor room to block access via the other three entrances to give time for Halvdan to do his work. Bulveye was only a few steps behind them, crossing to the opposite side of the chamber, when the Harrowers launched their counter-attack.

They struck from all three sides at once, pouring splinter fire through the openings that ricocheted dangerously around the room. The fire was so intense that the defenders had to duck away and take cover, which gave the xenos troops the opening they needed to launch their charge. Armoured warriors burst into the chamber from left and right, driving back the Antimonans and coming to grips with the warriors of Bulveye's Wolf Guard.

Across the chamber, Bulveye saw one of Andras's
warriors lean into the third archway and open fire
with both pistols. Splinter fire sparkled across his
shields – then a pair of indigo energy beams struck
the warrior full in the chest, collapsing the energy
field and blasting the man apart. Right on the heels
of the energy bolts charged a force of black-
armoured warriors wielding long, powerful glaives
that crackled with blue arcs of electricity. Within
moments another of the armigers was dead, cut in
two by the blow of one of those deadly weapons,
and the two Wolves guarding the entrance had been
driven back, hard-pressed by the fearsome attackers.

Into the space created by the sudden charge came
a tall, lithe figure, clad in intricate, arcane armour
and wreathed in a corona of swirling, indigo-hued
energy. A long, curved black blade hung loosely in
his right hand, and a long-barrelled pistol was ready
in his left. His hair was long and black, hanging
unbound past his shoulders, and his face… The
sight of his face caused Bulveye's blood to run cold.

The xenos chieftain had no face – or rather, he had
a multitude of them. Ghostly, agonised human faces
flickered and wailed in the place where the alien's
face ought to be. Men, women, children – each face
twisted in a mask of unutterable terror and pain.
From across the room, Bulveye could feel the horror
radiating from the terrible holo-mask, as palpable as
a knife drawn against his cheek.

The wolf inside him rose up, baring its fangs. Its
rage and bloodlust filled him. *Now?* It seemed to
ask.

Now, Bulveye answered, and he let the rage of the Wulfen fill him. The Wolf Lord raised his glowing axe and howled, a primal sound born in the primeval forests of ancient Terra itself, and then charged at his foe.

Two of the chieftain's bodyguards leaped into the Wolf Lord's path, their glaives held ready. He shot them both with blasts of his plasma pistol, dropping them with glowing craters blasted in their chests. A third bodyguard leaped forwards, stabbing with his glaive. The motion was almost too swift for the eye to follow, but the battle-madness had taken hold of Bulveye, and his body moved almost without conscious thought. He swept the blade aside with the flat of his axe, then brought the weapon around in a back-handed blow that sheared through the warrior's neck. Bulveye shouldered the headless corpse aside and charged on, howling as he went.

The xenos chieftain was waiting for him, his blade still held almost casually to one side. Heedless, berserk, the Wolf Lord swung a blow that would have split a normal man in two, but the power weapon struck the dark field surrounding the alien and slowed as though cutting through wet sand. When the edge struck the chieftain it scarcely marked his intricate armour.

Bulveye might have died then if it had not been for one of his warriors. One of the Wolf Guard covering the portal, a fearsome warrior named Lars, had despatched his foe and now hurled himself at the alien chieftain as well. His axe struck the alien's force-field and glanced harmlessly off the chieftain's helm. In return the xenos leader lashed out with his curved blade and struck off Lars's head.

Furious, Bulveye pressed his attack, aiming a series of swift blows at the chieftain's arms and torso, but the chieftain became a whirling blur of deadly motion, dodging the Wolf Lord's every stroke or parrying effortlessly with his flickering blade. The alien's black blade struck again, and Bulveye dimly felt the point sink deep into his side. The chieftain drew his sword free and leaped lightly backwards, hissing with pleasure. The Wolf Lord let out a roar of thwarted rage and shot the nimble figure with his plasma pistol, but the bolt dissipated harmlessly against the alien's force-field.

Before he could pursue further, a black-armoured figure crashed against Bulveye from the right. The bodyguard knocked the Wolf Lord off his feet, and the two went down in a tangle of limbs and weapons. Both struggled to pull their blades free quick enough to deal the killing blow. Out of the corner of his vision, Bulveye saw the xenos chieftain drawing nearer, his sword ready. Then suddenly he heard the sound of an Antimonan pistol at close range and a bullet punched through the bodyguard's helm.

Bulveye hurled the alien's body away as Andras raced past with two of his armigers to challenge the alien leader. Their pistols blazed in their hands, but the bullets seemed to vanish in the swirling void surrounding the Harrower. The chieftain's blade flashed, but the armigers' force-fields succeeded in deflecting the alien's attacks. Antimonan swords sliced and thrust at the alien, but the chieftain avoided the attacks with contemptuous ease. Still, the momentary distraction was enough to allow Bulveye to recover.

The Wolf Lord leaped to his feet amid the raging melee, and found himself in a slowly tightening circle as the alien attackers drove his warriors back towards the centre of the room. Many of the Wolf Guard had surrendered themselves to the Wulfen as well, and they wrought a hellish slaughter among the enemy, but for every warrior they slew it seemed that two more took his place. In another few minutes it seemed that they would be overwhelmed.

A shout carried across the chamber from behind Bulveye. He turned to see Halvdan standing by the towering crystal, and the sliver of reason that remained to him told the Wolf Lord that the charges for the reactor had been set.

Bulveye turned back to the xenos chieftain and realised what he had to do. He lunged forwards, gathering speed as he charged towards the alien.

By this time, both of Andras's warriors were dead, and the young nobleman was fighting the chieftain on his own. He wielded his blade with superlative skill, but the alien was far swifter and more experienced; only the Antimonan's energy shield had saved him from certain death. Each blow against Andras's shield sent arcs of energy crackling along the surface of his scale armour, and it was clear that it was close to failing.

The chieftain was so intent on killing Andras that he didn't notice Bulveye's charge until it was nearly too late. He shifted position in a blur of motion, swinging his weapon in a decapitating stroke, but the Wolf Lord surprised him by dropping his plasma pistol and seizing the alien's sword arm at the wrist. The field's energy sank through Bulveye's armour like ice water, a cold so sharp it sank like a knife into his bones, but he gritted his teeth and held on nonetheless.

Surprised, the alien spat a stream of curses and tried to pull away, but Bulveye let go of his axe and clamped his right hand around the chieftain's neck. With a roar of pure, animal fury, he picked the lithe alien off the deck, turned and hurled his body at the power crystal a few metres away. When the chieftain's energy field struck the crystal there was an actinic flash and a concussion that knocked nearly everyone from their feet. The chieftain's body was vaporised instantly by the blast; pieces of his shattered, smouldering armour ricocheted around the room like shrapnel from a grenade.

The next thing Bulveye heard was a strident, atonal sound that seemed to reverberate through the structure of the spire itself. Shocked from his battle-madness by the blast, he saw the last of the Harrowers fleeing from the chamber as fast as they could.

Andras stood close to the Wolf Lord, still reeling from the shock of the battle. 'What's happening?' he yelled.

Bulveye grabbed his weapons off the deck. 'That sounds like an alarm of some kind,' he shouted. 'The reactor must have been damaged by that energy field. We need to get back to the transport right now!'

Five of Andras's men and two of Bulveye's Wolf Guard lay dead, surrounded by heaps of alien bodies. Jurgen and Halvdan were already helping the survivors to grab the bodies of the fallen and carry them out as well. Together they raced back the way they'd come, ready to kill anyone who got in their way, but the alarm had sent every Harrower on the spire scrambling for their own means of escape. By the time they staggered out onto the landing pad, the skies were starting to fill with Harrower transports hastily lifting off from the doomed citadel. Alien bodies – some armoured, some not – were piled in heaps before the damaged transport, their bodies torn apart by boltgun shells or ravaged by the whirring teeth of Ranulf's chainsword. The pilot stood with his feet planted on the landing pad before the transport's gangway, his armour spattered with alien gore. Bulveye raised his axe in salute to Ranulf's dogged defence, and ordered everyone onto the xenos craft.

'How long until your charges blow?' Bulveye asked Halvdan as they clambered aboard.

'Another fifteen seconds, give or take,' the lieutenant replied.

'Morkai's teeth!' Bulveye cursed. 'Ranulf, get us the hell out of here!'

With a whine of tortured impellers and a ragged scraping of metal, the crippled transport shuddered into the air and yawed dangerously to port. The craft didn't so much take off as fall off the side of the landing pad, taking its passengers on a stomach-churning drop as the vehicle's motors struggled to repel the force of gravity.

Ten seconds later the spire was lit from within by a series of explosions that rippled outwards from the centre of the structure. Arcs of lightning a thousand yards long whipsawed across the spire's surface, cutting away landing pads and carving furrows in the crystal surface. Then, slowly, like a toppling tree, the massive spire began to settle towards the planet's surface. Its tip hit the rocky ground and shattered, scattering debris in a billowing cloud of dirt that stretched for kilometres in every direction, then the spire fell onto its side and vanished in massive detonations.

The shockwave of the blast spun the transport around like a top and sent it corkscrewing through the air. For several vertiginous moments, Bulveye was certain they were going to crash, but Ranulf managed to ride out the wave and get the craft stabilised a scant hundred metres off the ground. Behind them, a rising pillar of dirt and smoke was highlighted by the first, pink rays of dawn.

'What now?' Andras said, leaning ashen-faced against the craft's dented rail.

Bulveye scanned the skies, watching as dozens of Harrower ships boosted their thrusters and climbed into the sky, heading for orbit. 'We return to Oneiros,' he said, 'and wait to see what the survivors do. Either they'll start fighting amongst themselves to see who will be their next leader–'

'Or?'

The Wolf Lord shrugged. 'Or we'll be having visitors in a very short amount of time.'

THROUGHOUT THE MORNING the sky was full of vapour trails from Harrower ships boosting into the upper stratosphere. As the first of Oneiros's citizens crept tentatively out from their shelters and gaped at the towering column of dirt and smoke staining the sky to the west, Bulveye and Andras led their warriors to the Senate building and awaited Antimon's fate.

For the first few hours they dressed their wounds, shared out ammunition and fortified the structure as best they could. Then, as the day wore on and sounds of jubilation rose from the surrounding hills, Andras sent an armiger into the city in search of food and wine. By late afternoon a procession of joyous Oneirans began arriving with the last scrapings from their larder: preserved meats, shrivelled vegetables and sweet, cloying wine. To Bulveye's warriors, it was a feast worthy of a primarch.

As the sun set, the warriors drank and ate and enjoyed the fellowship of battle-brothers who had faced death side by side. Bulveye observed the gathering with no small amount of pride. The Antimonans had acquitted themselves well. In centuries to come, he was sure the planet would provide the Imperium with fine soldiers for the Army, or perhaps even young aspirants to the Allfather's Legions.

Night fell, and sharp-eyed lookouts manned the terraces outside the Senate building and searched the sky for signs of attack. Not a single flash of light was spotted, nor could the Astartes detect the faint specks of ships orbiting the planet. Bulveye took this to be a bad sign, and he and Andras spent a sleepless night preparing to make a final stand inside the Senate building.

It was just before dawn when an Astartes lookout saw the first tell-tale streaks of light in the sky. Bulveye and Andras were sitting together at the foot of the steps that led to the Speaker's chair when the Wolf Lord's vox bead activated.

'Fenris, this is *Stormblade*. Fenris, this is *Stormblade*. Are you receiving, over?'

The voice sent a jolt through Bulveye. He clambered to his feet, looking skywards as though he might suddenly glimpse the Space Wolf cruiser hovering up near the ceiling. '*Stormblade*, this is Fenris! I hear you! What's your status?'

'Our battle group arrived in-system twenty hours ago and made a stealthy approach to the planet,' the officer on the *Stormblade* answered. When we were still about eight hours away, we were engaged by a large fleet of xenos vessels, but we inflicted heavy losses and forced them to disengage an hour later. The survivors have fled towards jump points near the edge of the system.'

By this point, the rest of the Wolf Lord's warband were on their feet, as well as Andras and his warriors. Every one had a questioning look on his face. Bulveye regarded them all with a triumphant look and cried, 'A battle group has arrived from Kernunnos and defeated the Harrowers! Antimon is free!'

Armiger and Astartes alike broke out into cheers at the news. Andras stepped forwards and clapped Bulveye on the shoulder. 'We owe you more than we will ever be able to repay, my friend,' he said to the towering warrior. 'From this day forwards we will remember today as the day of Antimon's deliverance.'

The Wolf Lord only shook his head. 'There is no debt between us, brother,' he replied. 'Just serve the Allfather faithfully in the years to come and give your due to the Imperium, and that will be thanks enough.'

The young nobleman's smile faltered. 'I don't understand,' he said.

Bulveye laughed and waved his hand dismissively. 'That's nothing to worry about at the moment,' he said. 'It will be months before the Imperium can send representatives to begin integrating your world with the rest of the worlds in this subsector. For now, I expect you'll be want to restore the Senate, which is a good first step. The Imperial governor, when he arrives, will need their support to ensure full certification of the planet. And then the real work will begin!'

Andras's hand fell away from the Wolf Lord. He took a step back. 'There's been a misunderstanding,' he said. 'We have no desire to be part of your Imperium – especially now, when we've only just regained our freedom!'

Bulveye felt his heart turn to lead. Jurgen and Halvdan sensed the change in their lord's demeanour and stepped close. Andras's trio of armigers did the same, their expressions tense.

The Wolf Lord paused, desperate for the right words to change what he feared was about to happen. 'Andras,' he began. 'Listen to me. I came here because the Imperium needs this world. It needs *every* human world to come together and rebuild what was lost before. Believe me, the galaxy is a dangerous place. There are alien races out there that would like nothing more to see our extinction – or worse. You and your people know this better than anyone.'

He took a step closer to the young nobleman. His armigers laid their hands on the hilts of their swords. 'We must be united in a common cause, Andras. We *must*. The Allfather has commanded it, and I'm honour-bound to obey. Antimon is going to be part of the Imperium, brother. One way or another.' He held out his left hand. 'An age of glory awaits you. All you have to do is take my hand.'

A look of anguish crossed Andras's face. 'How can you say this to me, after all we've been through? Weren't you the one who said that a life not worth fighting for is no life at all?' The young man's voice trembled with anger. 'Antimon is free, and will stay that way. Her armigers will protect her!'

Bulveye shook his head sadly. 'The Imperium will not be denied, Andras. So I ask you one last time: will you join us?'

The young warrior's expression turned hard and cold. Slowly, he shook his head. 'I will fight you if I must.'

Bulveye's empty hand sank to his side. His heart felt cold as lead. 'Very well, brother,' he said heavily. 'So be it.'

The axe was an icy blur between the two warriors. Andras never saw the blow that ended his life. A half-second later boltguns roared, and the two shocked armigers fell dead as well.

Bulveye stared at the bodies of the young men for a long time, watching their blood spread in a widening stain upon the floor. Abruptly, his vox-bead crackled. 'Fenris, this is *Stormblade*. The battle group is in orbit and awaiting your instructions. We have assault troops mustered and ready, and surveyors have identified targets for preliminary bombardment. What are your orders?'

The Wolf Lord tore his gaze away from the dead men at his feet. When he spoke again, his voice was like iron. '*Stormblade*, this is Fenris,' he said. 'This world has refused compliance. Execute crusade plan epsilon and commence combat operations at once.'

With a heavy tread, the Wolf Lord stepped over the bodies of Andras and his men, leaving bloody footprints on the steps as he climbed his way to the Speaker's chair. The wood creaked under his weight as he sat himself upon it and rested his bloody axe across his knees. Outside, the people of Antimon were still cheering their deliverance when the first bombs began to fall.

SCIONS OF
THE STORM

Anthony Reynolds

ISOLATED FOR COUNTLESS millennia in the stygian darkness of Old Night, the inhabitants of the world designated Forty-seven Sixteen had at first rejoiced to be reunited with their long-lost brothers. For over four thousand years they had thought themselves alone in the universe, and had come to regard ancient Terra as little more than a vague, half-forgotten race-memory; an allegorical myth, a fabled genesis world invented by their ancestors. They had greeted the Word Bearers envoys with open arms, gazing upon the immense, grey-armoured Astartes warriors with awe and reverence.

'Irrevocably corrupt worshippers of a heathen deity,' First Captain Kor Phaeron stated damningly upon his return from the meeting.

'Is it not the duty of the crusade to embrace all the distinct strands of humanity, even its most wayward sons?' said Sor Talgron, Captain of Thirty-fourth Company. 'Would not the God-Emperor wish His most devoted Legion to lead these blind children to enlightenment?'

Officially, the expanding Imperium of Man was a secular one, promoting and expounding the 'truths' of science and reason over the 'falsehoods' of religion and spiritualism. The XVII Legion, however, understood the truth, though it was, at times, a heavy burden to bear. Sor Talgron knew that the time was drawing near when the acknowledgement of the Emperor's divinity would be universally embraced. Faith would become the greatest strength of the Imperium, greater than the untold billions of soldiers that constituted the Imperial Army; greater even than the might of the Legions of Astartes. Faith would be the mortar that held all the disparate elements of mankind together.

Even the most blinded of Legions, those who most vocally denied Lorgar's holy scripture, would in time come to understand the inherent truth in the primarch's words. And they would be forced to beg his forgiveness for having ever cast doubt upon his words. That the Emperor denied His divine nature did little to smother the fires of devotion within the XVII Legion; *only the truly divine deny their divinity,* Lorgar himself had written.

'You know the Emperor's mind now, Talgron?' Kor Phaeron growled. 'If you have such insight, please enlighten us lesser mortals.'

'I claim no such thing, First Captain,' Sor Talgron snapped.

Sor Talgron and Kor Phaeron glared at each other with undisguised venom through the cloying incense smoke rising from dozens of hanging censers. The circular, tiered room where the war council was taking place was deep in the heart of the *Fidelitas Lex*, Lorgar's flagship, and the captains of the other Grand Companies stood silently around its circumference, watching with interest from the shadows to see how this confrontation would develop. However, Erebus, the softly spoken First Chaplain of the Legion, interposed himself between Kor Phaeron and Sor Talgron, ever the mediator, moving into the centre of the sunken command pulpit and breaking their venomous glares.

'The First Captain and I shall consult with the Urizen,' Erebus said smoothly, ending the discussion. 'Lorgar's wisdom shall guide us.'

Still glowering, Sor Talgron had bowed to the First Chaplain before spinning on his heel and striding from the room along with the other dismissed captains. He waved skulking robed servants out of his path, intending to travel by Stormbird back to his own cruiser, the *Dominatus Sanctus*, and rejoin Thirty-fourth Company.

It had been more than a month since Sor Talgron had seen the blessed primarch of the XVII Legion, and the Urizen's absence at the war council had been keenly felt. Tempers were fraying, and dissent was beginning to spread through the ranks; the Legion needed Lorgar to return to them.

The holy primarch had been locked within his personal shrine-chamber in self-exile for a full Terran month – ever since his audience with the Emperor of Mankind. In that time he had allowed none bar Kor Phaeron and Erebus, his closest advisors and comrades, into his presence. The entire Forty-seventh Expeditionary Fleet had sat dormant while it waited for its primarch's orders.

Sor Talgron had snatched a momentary glimpse of his primarch as the Urizen was ushered into his private quarters upon his return from his meeting with the Emperor, and had been shocked to the core of his being by what he had seen.

Always, Lorgar had radiated a palpable aura of passion and belief, an unassailable shield of faith that was at once awesome and terrifying. Whereas it was said that the Wolf's strength was his irrepressible ferocity, the Lion's his relentless tenacity, and Guilliman's his strategic and logistical brilliance, Lorgar's strength was his unshakeable faith, his profound self-belief, his ruthless and unwavering devotion.

Though Erebus had sought to hide the Urizen from the gaze of the Legion, Sor Talgron's eyes had locked with those of his primarch for the briefest of moments before a hatch had slammed down, blocking his vision. The depth of despair he had seen in Lorgar's eyes had forced him to his knees. His eyes had filled with tears and his stomach had knotted painfully, his mind reeling. What could possibly have transpired upon the Emperor's battle-barge to have so shaken the unshakeable?

He had not even reached the embarkation deck of the *Fidelitas Lex* when he was contacted by Erebus, requesting his return to the war chamber: the Urizen had made his decision.

As he marched back through the labyrinthine corridors of the *Fidelitas Lex*, Captain Sor Talgron prayed that Lorgar himself would be present, though in this he was to be disappointed.

Still, at least a decision had been made – after a month of idleness, the XVII Legion at last had purpose.

'In his great mercy,' Erebus said, addressing the reassembled gathering of Word Bearers captains, 'the Urizen wishes that this long-lost strand of humanity be brought to compliance; that they be embraced into the fold of the Imperial Truth.'

Murmurs spread around the gathered captains, and Sor Talgron nodded his head in approval. Such was the way that the XVII Legion had operated since the start of the crusade. They had brought the glory of the Imperial Truth to every world that they had encountered thus far, and though their progress might not have been as swift as that of some of the other Legions, those worlds left behind by the XVII Legion were the most devout and loyal of all. Those who refused the word and those deemed unworthy were, of course, zealously crushed, ground to dust beneath the armoured heel of Lorgar's Astartes, but those who accepted their teachings were embraced into the Imperial truth, their loyalty assured.

Sor Talgron cast a triumphant glance towards Kor Phaeron, but the First Captain did not look displeased by the proclamation, for all that he had been braying for war earlier.

'However,' Erebus continued, 'it is with sadness and remorse that the Urizen has come to his decision. The Emperor is displeased with our Legion, brothers.'

Absolute silence descended over the chamber, every set of eyes focusing on the First Chaplain. Sor Talgron felt his blood run cold.

'The Emperor, it seems, is not satisfied with the rate of our progress. The Emperor is not content with the worlds, compliant and faithful, that we have delivered to Him. In His *wisdom*,' Erebus continued, his voice soft and yet with a growing edge of bitterness, 'the Emperor has rebuked our blessed primarch, His most faithful and devoted of sons, and ordered him to hasten our crusade.'

Dark mutterings passed between the gathered captains, but Sor Talgron blocked them out, focused on the words of the First Chaplain.

'Our blessed primarch feels that, given time, the inhabitants of Forty-seven Sixteen could be taught the error of their ignorant, heathen ways; that they would make model Imperial citizens once guided towards the light of truth by our Chaplains and warrior-brothers. However, the Emperor's orders are clear, and the Urizen is a faithful son; he cannot refuse his father's order, though it causes him much lamentation.'

'And what are those orders, First Chaplain?' said Captain Argel Tal of the Seventh Company.

'That we do not have the time necessary to convert these ignorant heathens to the Imperial Truth,' Erebus said, with some reluctance. 'Their profane beliefs are deemed incompatible with the Imperium. As a result... Forty-seven Sixteen must burn.'

Sor Talgron reeled at the proclamation, shocked and horrified that an entire world that might have been brought into the Imperial Truth was condemned to death merely because of... what? The Emperor's impatience? He immediately felt ashamed, guilt swelling up within him for even thinking such blasphemy. Once this war was done, he swore that he would attempt to atone for his errant thought through hours of penance and self-flagellation.

Nevertheless, after they had recovered from the initial shock of Lorgar's orders, every captain of the XVII Legion, Sor Talgron included, threw themselves fully into preparations for the forthcoming war with a focus bordering on fanaticism. He was a warrior of Lorgar, Sor Talgron reminded himself; it was not for him to attempt to interpret the orders of his betters. He was a warrior first and foremost, and he fought where – and against whom – he was commanded.

Less than twenty-four hours later more than a hundred and ninety million people were dead – over ninety-eight per cent of the doomed world's population.

The cruisers and battleships assigned to the Forty-seventh Expeditionary Fleet anchored at high orbit, and for twelve hours unleashed their payload upon the condemned, storm-wracked planet. Cyclonic torpedoes and concentrated hellfire broadsides pierced the storm clouds spanning the planet. Entire continents had disappeared in flames.

One city survived the carnage. This was the seat of
the planet's governance and the centre of its blas-
phemous worship. Protected within a bubble of
coruscating energy was the profane palace-temple of
the enemy, a structure as large as a city in itself.
Unwilling to allow even a single heathen blasphe-
mer to remain alive, for that would have been
against their lord's orders, five full companies of the
XVII Legion were mobilised, striking down towards
the planet's surface to finish the job.

Sor Talgron led Thirty-fourth Company down
towards Forty-seven Sixteen, the Stormbirds carrying
his loyal Astartes warrior-brothers descending into
the storm-wracked atmosphere. Despite the weight
of the preliminary bombardment that had pre-
empted the ground assault, it soon became apparent
that the enemy defences were not completely neutralised; blinding arcs of energy screamed up from
below, smashing several of the Stormbirds out of the
air even as they entered the planet's atmosphere, the
lives of almost a hundred precious warrior-brothers
lost in the blink of an eye.

Sor Talgron ordered the Stormbirds to pull off
their current trajectory, and sent swift warnings to
his brother captains of Fourth, Seventh, Ninth and
Seventeenth Companies following in his wake,
advising them to come at the dome from a different
angle. Even as the vox transmissions were sent, Talgron's Stormbird was hit, sheering away one of its
wings and shorting out its controls, sending it into a
fatal, spiralling dive towards the ground. Assault
hatches were blown, and at nineteen and a half

thousand metres Sor Talgron leapt from his granite-grey Stormbird, leading his Space Marines screaming down towards the ruined city below as their jump packs roared into life.

The ruined enemy city was spread out below as Sor Talgron's Assault squads broke through the storm clouds, the speed of their descent enhanced by the powerful engines of their jump packs. From their altitude the curvature of the world could be seen clearly, and the shattered remains of a city pummelled into the ground by ordnance was spread out as far as the eye could see in every direction. At the centre of the shattered city was the flickering dome, a blister of energy in the fire-blackened flesh of the enemy land.

That dome was easily twenty kilometres in diameter, and rose almost a quarter of that distance above the ground. As he descended towards the city, arcs of lightning stabbing down from the clouds around him and up from the ground below, the captain of Thirty-fourth Company calmly identified a landing zone and transmitted the coordinates to his men.

They landed five kilometres from the flickering dome. The enemy city was a single grand super-structure hundreds of levels high, its grand valley-like boulevards criss-crossed with thousands of arched walkways and lined with balconies and terraces. Much of it had been blasted into oblivion, but more had survived than Sor Talgron had expected – the glassy material that everything on this world was constructed from was apparently more resilient than it appeared. Before the bombardment had begun, the city must have looked stunning, though Sor Talgron found such opulence deeply suspicious. Beauty, he felt, was to be mistrusted.

Nothing living had survived the brutal bombardment outside the shimmering dome. Those inhabitants of Forty-seven Sixteen that had been exposed to the full brunt of the barrage had been obliterated, flesh, muscle and bone instantly consumed in roaring flames, leaving only circles of ash where they had stood as evidence to their ever having existed at all. Charred bodies in their millions, those who were inside when the bombardment commenced, were strewn throughout the glass buildings of Forty-seven Sixteen. Tens of thousands of them were discovered in the profane temple-shrines dotted all over the city, their flesh melted together into obscene, congealed, fleshy lumps that were almost unrecognisable as having ever been human.

The scale of the slaughter was nothing if not impressive.

Drop-pods streamed like a deadly shower of meteors down from the battle-barges in the upper atmosphere. Scores were destroyed as they dropped through the storm, their occupants instantly slain.

At first it appeared that they faced no ground resistance. Then the first of the robotic, three-legged war constructs marched unscathed through the flickering shield-dome to meet them, lightning spitting from their blade-arms, and battle was met.

THE STORM-WRACKED WORLD was in its final death throes. Lightning ripped across the bruised skyline.

The flashing of electricity was constant, a blinding strobe that threw the battle-scarred ruins of the alien superstructure into stark relief. Sor Talgron's primary heart was pounding, pumping over-oxygenated blood through his veins. Hyper-stimulated adrenal glands fired, fuelling his aggression and sending fresh energy shooting through his nervous system. The stink of ozone and discharging electricity was strong in his nostrils.

He pressed himself hard up against a shattered, glass-smooth spire, taking cover as another of the enemy war constructs fired a blast of harnessed lightning towards him. The crackling arc of energy slammed against the spire half a metre away, sending flickering sparks of energy dancing across its smooth surface. Mouthing a curse, Sor Talgron slammed a fresh sickle clip into his bolt pistol. Thunder rumbled deafeningly overhead, an unrelenting churning roar that made the Space Marine captain's insides reverberate.

Another blast struck, this time catching one of his warriors, Brother Khadmon, full in the chest as he broke from cover. The Astartes warrior was hurled backwards by the force of the blast, smashing him into another spire with bone-crushing force. He slid to the ground, his armour blackened and bubbling, and Sor Talgron knew that he was dead. Khadmon continued to twitch for several minutes, as flickers of electricity danced across his corpse. His flesh had been cooked within his power armour, his innards and blood boiling; the heat generated by the lightning-weapons of the enemy was easily a match for the lascannons borne by the Devastator-Havoc squads.

Sor Talgron swore. Too many of his company brothers had already died this day, and he felt his anger and resentment building.

Apothecary Uhrlon was already moving towards the fallen warrior, risking himself as he leapt towards the dead Astartes to drag the corpse into cover.

'Be quick, Apothecary,' Sor Talgron shouted. 'We can't stay here. We have to take down those spires!'

Not for the first time, Sor Talgron prayed that this plan of Kol Badar's was going to work. If the spires were brought down, would that cause a rent in the seemingly impenetrable shield-dome as the favoured sergeant predicted? He believed that it would, but if Kol Badar was wrong, then even more of his brothers would die before the day was out.

For a moment he watched as the Apothecary carried out the grisly duty of extracting Brother Khadmon's precious gene-seed. The drill screeched as it penetrated Khadmon's ceramite armour and flesh, splattering his armour with blood.

More forks of lightning struck around him. No more of his warriors were caught in the killing blasts, but it was only a matter of time before the enemy flanked their position, repositioning themselves to draw a direct bead on them. The robotic war constructs of the enemy were formidable foes. Far from unthinking, predictable automatons, they had proven to be wily and dangerous enemies, constantly adapting and refining their tactics and strategies to best defeat the invaders.

Artificial intelligence.

Such a thing was an abomination.

The Emperor Himself had decreed such research forbidden, part of the compact agreed between Terra and Mars, and to go against the word of the Emperor was heresy of the highest order. That the inhabitants of Forty-seven Sixteen could not possibly know this was of little consequence.

'Squadron Tertius, do you read?' said Sor Talgron, broadcasting across the vox-net.

'Yes, captain,' came the prompt reply, the voice muffled and devoid of emotion. 'Orders?'

'I need you here. We're pinned down. The enemy are positioned upon fortified balcony positions. Distance is…' He turned towards the Astartes sergeant nearby, Brother Arshaq.

'One hundred and forty-two metres, elevation eighty-two degrees,' said Sergeant Arshaq, risking a glance around the spire to get a lock on the enemy. He ducked back as several blasts of lighting stabbed towards him, striking the glassy spire with shocking force.

'You get that, Tertius?' said Sor Talgron across the vox.

'Affirmative,' confirmed Squadron Tertius. 'On our way.'

They were positioned on one of the high flyover walkways that criss-crossed the immense, man-made valleys separating the different sections of the city's superstructure, pinned in place by the weight of incoming fire.

Glancing down, Sor Talgron could make out thousands of granite-grey armoured battle-brothers, accompanied by scores of the Legion's tanks, fighting hard for every inch of ground as they closed in on the shimmering shield-dome from all directions. The flash of muzzle flare from thousands of bolters was like so many flickering candles at this distance, and the roar of the weapons was drowned out by the relentless booming thunder overhead. Missiles left lingering coils of smoke in their wake as they spiralled towards the enemy, a deadly robotic army that knew nothing of fear or mercy, and gouts of retina-searing, white-hot plasma spat from overheating weapons.

The deceptively delicate-looking war constructs of the enemy stalked through the mayhem all but unscathed. Slender insectoid legs carrying them inexorably forwards, they stepped steadily through the hail of bolter fire, each of them protected by a sphere of lightning that flashed and sparked as they absorbed the incoming fire. Their return fire exacted a horrifying toll, lightning weapons slaughtering Astartes and sending Predator and Land Raider tanks flipping end over end.

Concentrated lascannon fire struck again and again at the constructs' shields, finally overloading several of them and blasting the robotic machines apart, but the sheer weight of fire required to neutralise even a single machine was staggering.

With the practicalities of war and the difficulties of his mission occupying his mind, Sor Talgron had pushed aside any moral qualms he had regarding the validity of the war. That the humans of Forty-seven Sixteen were divergent was undeniable. Their unrepentant and wilful manufacture of thinking machines alone was enough to condemn them.

Yet for all this, the captain of Thirty-fourth Company could not help but feel pity for those whom his Legion had been sent to slaughter. A stab of resentment lanced through him, shocking him with the strength of the emotion.

Why had the Emperor not allowed the XVII Legion to even *attempt* to bring Forty-seven Sixteen to enlightenment?

Since landing, Sor Talgron had not seen a single living human – all they had faced so far had been their war constructs, though the gory, dismembered and obliterated remains of people were everywhere.

'Here they come,' said Sergeant Arshaq, drawing Sor Talgron out of his reverie.

Squadron Tertius came streaking up from below, three boxy grey shapes moving at great speed. These were new innovations from the forges of Mars, and the land speeder pilots threw their anti-grav attack vehicles from side to side, jinking to avoid incoming fire that speared towards them. They screamed underneath the flyover on which Sor Talgron and his veteran squad were taking cover, engines roaring as they zeroed in on the location that Sergeant Arshaq had provided, and as they rose in altitude and began their attack run, their weapons began to belch.

Heavy bolters spat hundreds of high-velocity explosive rounds towards the enemy constructs above, and multi-meltas screamed as they fired, sending superheated blasts into the foe, overriding their shields and rendering the robotic war machines molten.

'Targets neutralised,' came the word from the land speeder squadron, barrelling underneath a bridge spanning the man-made valley of glass buildings, before performing a tight loop around it and screaming overhead.

'Good work, Tertius,' said Sor Talgron, stepping out into the open once more.

Glowing green targeting matrices flashed before his eyes. Information feeds streamed across his irises as he focused on the target location for his next jump. Two hundred and seventy-four metres, his head-up display informed him.

In a clipped voice, he conveyed the coordinates of the leap to his warrior-brothers. Confirmations of his orders flooded in, and without ceremony, Sor Talgron broke into a run towards the low balustrade of the flyover. Placing one foot upon the railing, he launched himself out into open space.

Before the force of gravity began to drag him to the ground, his jump pack roared into life. Powerful vectored engines screamed, and he accelerated sharply into the air, flames and dirty black smoke spewing out behind him.

Warrior-brothers of Thirty-fourth Company leapt into the air behind their captain, flames roaring in their wake. Sor Talgron could see more of his Assault squads in the distance, streaking towards their targets like fireflies, trailing fire as they ascended vertical precipices and criss-crossed gaping expanses between glass structures in bounding leaps, attempting to avoid the heavy weight of incoming fire.

Targeting crosshairs appeared in the corners of his vision, drawing his attention, and he turned his head to see another group of enemy war constructs a hundred metres to his side, stepping smoothly out onto a terrace built into the side of a cliff-like section of the city's superstructure. They lifted their lightning-rod arms in the direction of Sor Talgron and his veteran squad, and he saw the sparking build-up of power along those silver lengths.

Barking a warning, Sor Talgron threw himself into a barrelling spin, taking him off his current trajectory. A fraction of a second later, a trio of blinding streaks of lightning speared by him. Deafening, supersonic cracks of thunder accompanied these blasts, though the damping systems of his helmet made the sound bearable.

Two warriors of Talgron's veteran Assault squad were hit, struck out of the air by forks of energy. Electricity leapt from their bodies to those nearby, shorting out life-systems and sending targeting arrays haywire.

'Take them,' Sor Talgron said, turning in the air towards the enemy even as those warrior-brothers that had been hit fell, smoking, down into the maelstrom of battle far below. Gunning the engines of his jump pack, anger filling him at the thought of his fallen brethren, the captain of Thirty-fourth Company angled his flight to take him down amongst the enemy machines.

There were three of the constructs, and he lifted his bolt pistol and began firing as he descended towards them, each pull of the trigger sending a mass-reactive bolt screaming towards its target. Lightning-shields flashed into existence around the enemy robots, his rounds merely stitching flashing impacts across their surface.

Blasts of lightning tore up towards the descending Word Bearers, making the air crackle and reverberate with power, and Sor Talgron saw the information feed from another of his warriors go dead.

Angry, and eager to unleash this anger on these unliving foes, Sor Talgron came in to land fast, his rapid descent bringing the glass terrace racing up towards him. The vectored engines of his jump pack swivelled towards the ground as he swung his legs out in front of him, and a fiery blast slowed his descent.

His boots skidded on the surface of the smooth terrace as he touched down, and his heavy power mace was in his hand instantly, coruscating energy wreathing its flanged head with a press of its activation stud. While the lightning fields that protected the constructs could effortlessly shrug off a direct hit from a bolt gun, Sor Talgron had learnt that they afforded less protection against blows landed in hand-to-hand combat, or shots fired at point-blank range. Closing the distance quickly was imperative.

The sight of the enemy constructs up close filled him with loathing. *Abominations.*

They were synthetic mockeries of humans, their very existence an offence. Perhaps he had been wrong in thinking this war unjustified, Sor Talgron pondered as gazed upon their blasphemous forms.

They stood almost as tall as a Dreadnought, though they were far less bulky than the deadly war machines of the Astartes Legions. Each of them had a human-like torso made of the same semi-transparent glassy material that formed the entire city – manufactured perhaps for its non-conductive properties – and featureless heads filled with circuitry sat upon their shoulders. In place of humanoid legs, each of the constructs was borne upon three slender multi-jointed insectoid limbs – each perhaps three metres long if extended straight. These legs gave the machines a disturbing, arachnid feel, like some twisted amalgamation of man and spider, though there was nothing organic about them.

The arms of the constructs were like those of men, except that their forearms ended in long, tapering spikes of silver instead of hands. Electricity sparked between these arms as they were brought close together.

Veins of silver ran through the bodies of the abominations, all leading to their 'hearts', the battery-centres of harnessed storm energy in the centre of their torsos. Electrical pulses flickered along these metallic threads, seemingly powering all of its functions: movement, thought, weapons and the lightning-fields that made them all but invulnerable to ranged fire.

The constructs moved with the jerky precision of long-legged hunting birds as they reacted to the Word Bearers' attack. Dirty flames belched from Astartes jump packs as more of Sor Talgron's brethren touched down around them. Bolt pistols roared, and flamers belched, bathing the robotic machines in gouts of super-heated promethium, though the worst of these attacks were, of course, deflected by the protective domes of lightning that flared around each of the constructs.

Sor Talgron leapt towards the nearest of the abominations with a roar.

The sentient stepped away from him and brought its silver lightning-rod arms together with a clap of thunder. A jagged spear of light flashed towards the captain of Thirty-fourth Company, but he had pre-empted the strike, and threw himself to the side. The crackling arc scythed by him, making the oath-papers affixed to the rim of his shoulder pad burst into flame.

He closed the distance quickly, recognising that the abomination needed time for its lightning weapon to recharge. With a sweep of his crackling mace he struck the construct's shield, the stink of ozone rising as the two power sources came together with a deafening crack. The sphere of energy was torn apart by the blow, sparks and energy wreathing Sor Talgron's weapon as the shield dissipated.

Stepping in close and grunting with the effort, Sor Talgron smashed his power maul into one of the construct's insectoid legs. Though fragile looking, the slender limb was as hard as tempered plasteel, and while thousands of tiny cracks spread up and down the glassy limb, it did not shatter.

A pained, whistling sound, something akin to the musical trill of a song-bird, erupted from the war machine. It tried to back away from him, but its damaged limb buckled as soon as it placed weight upon it, and it crumpled to the floor.

Sor Talgron closed in on the fallen construct, even as it struggled frantically to right itself. Its two intact legs skittered off the smooth, glassy terrace floor, and again it emitted its pained bird-song like whistle. It flailed with its pair of lightning-rod arms, discharging electricity wildly, narrowly missing him. Sor Talgron pressed his heavy boot down upon the chest of the construct and smashed his power maul into its domed head, shattering it. Sparks spat from its ruptured cranium, and the power core located in its chest faded, the silver veins running through its transparent body turning dark and lifeless.

The shield of another of the constructs was brought down, and a melta-blast turned the torso of the machine molten, super-heated glass running like lava, dripping down its legs and onto the floor with a hiss. Spinning, Sor Talgron fired his bolt pistol at the last of the war machines, but the lightning-field sprang up before him, absorbing the power of the bolts.

Its arms came together with a deafening crack and another of Sor Talgron's veterans was killed, lifted from his feet and hurled out into open space, his body swathed in electricity.

Brother Sergeant Arshaq launched himself at the construct from its side. He punched with his immense power fist, the blow dispelling the construct's shield with a powerful explosion of energy.

Bolt pistols bucking in their hands, Sor Talgron and his veterans stepped towards the now unshielded construct. It reeled beneath the blows, emitting pained bird-cries, and spider-web cracks appeared upon its torso and head. Sergeant Arshaq planted another bolt into its artificial cranium as it staggered. The high explosive round found a crack and detonated within the constructs head, spraying shards of glass in all directions.

However, even in death it was a deadly foe. It floundered, staggering drunkenly, electricity leaping from the stump of its neck. Its arms flailed, and as it turned towards Sor Talgron those silver limbs came together, and a lethal fork of energy shot towards him, accompanied by a deafening crack.

He saw it coming, and managed to twist his body so that it did not strike him with the full brunt of its power, yet it still lifted him off his feet and sent him flying through the air. His vision instantly turned black as the photochromatic lenses of his helmet were melted by the intense heat. The acrid stink of liquefying wires and cables filled his helmet. He was slammed hard into a wall, cracking its glass surface with the force the impact. Spinning off the angled surface of the wall, Sor Talgron was thrown over the edge of the terrace.

He was freefalling then, arms and legs flailing wildly. Still blind, he spun in the air, groping for a handhold. His ceramite encased fingers merely scratched against glass, screeching loudly.

Abruptly his fall came to an end as he landed on a lower terrace with bone-jarring force, cracking its surface. The thirty-metre fall would likely have killed a lesser man, but Sor Talgron pushed himself unsteadily to his knees, his bones bruised but unbroken. Smoke rose from his blistering power armour and lingering sparks of electricity flickered across his body. Sor Talgron tore his damaged helmet from his head. Seeing that it had been rendered useless by the electrical blast, he hurled it away from him, his face flushed and angry.

The stink of burning flesh – his own – was strong in his nostrils, and he blinked as he was momentarily blinded by the lightning tearing apart the heavens.

While many warrior-brothers of the XVII Legion had the noble countenance of their primarch, Sor Talgron had the face of one born to fight, with broad, thick features and a nose that had been broken so many times it was nothing more than a fleshy lump smeared across his face. He scowled darkly and swore as he pushed himself unsteadily to his feet, his muscles protesting.

Sergeant Arshaq, flames spewing from his jump pack, landed alongside him, followed closely by the other members of Veteran Squad Helikon.

'Are you all right, captain?' asked the sergeant.

Sor Talgron nodded his head.

'The construct?' he said.

'Destroyed,' confirmed Arshaq, reaching a hand out to his captain. 'The path to the shield-dome is clear.'

Sor Talgron accepted Arshaq's outstretched hand, allowing the veteran sergeant to help him back to his feet. The last vestiges of the electricity that had engulfed him flickered over his gauntlets and up

Arshaq's arm. Nodding his thanks, Sor Talgron turned towards the flickering shield-dome, shielding his eyes against its glare.

They were only five hundred metres from the lightning-shield now, and the air crackled with intensity, making his short-cropped black hair stand on end.

The weight of fire being directed against the immense lightning-dome from the ground was awesome. Hundreds of tanks were bombarding the flickering, curved sides of the shield at a scale that would have long ago felled city blocks. A demi-legion of Titans, immense machines of destruction crafted by the adepts of Mars that stood as tall as buildings, unleashed the full power of their weapons against the shield, yet even these, amongst the most potent weapons the Imperium of Man was able to construct, appeared to have little effect.

From within the shield-dome, more of the blas-phemous enemy war constructs were marching, passing through the shield unscathed, protected within their bubbles of energy. They stalked out to meet the Word Bearers in the streets below, moving forwards in staggered lines, lightning forking from their silver arms as they brought them together. How many more of them did the enemy have, Sor Talgron wondered?

Sor Talgron was almost blinded as another sear-ing orbital strike split the sky, lancing down through the upper atmosphere to smash against the top of the shield. Still it held, an impenetrable barrier that it seemed would not be breached, no matter the amount of ordnance thrown against it.

'I really hope this plan of Kol Badar's is going to work,' said Sergeant Arshaq.

'You and me both, my friend,' said Sor Talgron.

His eyes settled on the immense tower-spires encased in silver that ringed the shield-dome. Each was struck time and again by lightning spearing down from the tumultuous storm clouds, and an intense humming of power reverberated from these giant rods as the power built within them. Several times a minute this harnessed energy was expelled from one of the spires in great lightning arcs that stabbed down into the streets below, striking at tanks and squads of Astartes with deafening thunderclaps, killing dozens with every strike.

Even as Sor Talgron and Squad Helikon looked on, electricity leapt from one of the silver spires in a jagged line, striking at one of the giant Warlord-class Titans blasting at the shield-dome from afar. The cataclysmic sound of the discharge hit them a fraction of a second later, the sound threatening to rupture Sor Talgron's unprotected eardrums. The Titan's void shields were stripped away by the force of the strike and it rocked backwards as if in pain. Another immense blast of energy forked from the silver spires, striking the Titan in its head even as it attempted to step back away from the danger, and the forty-metre-high colossus toppled, smashing down on top of a pair of Land Raider battle tanks, crushing them like paper.

Interspersed between these towering spires were smaller ones, and while those too were frequently struck by the fury of the storm, when they discharged their power, it was not towards the Astartes but rather towards the shield-dome itself. Sor Talgron had studied these spires from afar, and he believed that Kol Badar was correct in suggesting that these were what was keeping the shield intact. The lightning they absorbed forked from their silver lengths into the shield, strengthening it and keeping it solid. These were Sor Talgron's targets, for he believed that if they were destroyed, then the shield would fall.

Located high up on the superstructure, they were hard to target from the ground, and the defensive spires surrounding them would strike down any aircraft approaching to drop its payload upon the shield-spires. It fell to his Assault squad to launch the strike.

However, less than a quarter of his jump pack-equipped warriors had made it this far – the strength of the enemy's resistance had not been foreseen. He had only enough Assault squads remaining to take down three of the spires, and he had no idea if that would be enough to have any real effect on the shield.

Still, he was not going to back off now.

He could see grey armoured figures in the distance, fire and smoke trailing behind them, leaping towards the spires he had allocated as targets. The time to test Kol Badar's theory had come, and again he prayed that this was going to work.

'It has to work,' Sor Talgron said grimly to himself. He took a deep breath, then opened up a vox-channel to his Assault squads.

'Report,' he said.

'First wave, target secured,' growled the voice of Kol Badar, his most trusted veteran sergeant, and the one who had suggested this course of action. Tactically astute and fearless in battle, Sor Talgron knew he would go far.

'Awaiting your mark,' said the sergeant.

'Second target secured, captain,' said Sergeant Bachari, in command of the second wave. 'Melta charges locked in position.'

From his position, Sor Talgron could see the warriors of Bachari's second wave in the distance surrounding the slender silver spire that had been designated as their target, less than fifty metres from the flickering veil. Kol Badar's first wave would be surrounding a similar spire, fifty metres higher up the structure.

'Sergeant Paeblen? Does Squad Lementas control the third target?' said Sor Talgron.

'Engaging the enemy, captain,' came Paeblen's voice. The sound of roaring chainswords, Astartes shouting and weapons discharging echoed in the background. There was a loud explosion, and the line abruptly descended into static white noise. A moment later, a new voice crackled across the vox.

'Brother Aecton here, captain,' said the voice.

'Go ahead, brother,' said Sor Talgron.

'Sergeant Paeblen is down, captain,' said Brother Aecton. 'I am taking temporary command of the third wave.'

Aecton was an experienced member of Squad Lementas, a battle-scarred veteran that Sor Talgron knew could be relied upon to keep his wits in the most nightmarish situations. As the longest-serving member of Lementas, it fell to him to take command if anything happened to his sergeant. A moment later the vox crackled, and Aecton's voice came through once more.

'Target secured, captain. Melta charges are in place.'

'Good work, Brother Aecton,' said Sor Talgron.

'All squads: blow your charges on my mark,' said Sor Talgron. Turning to Sergeant Arshaq, he nodded solemnly.

'Moment of truth,' remarked the sergeant.

Sor Talgron smiled grimly.

'Do it,' he said.

THE MELTA BOMB clusters placed around the base of the three silver spires detonated simultaneously. For a moment, Sor Talgron saw no real effect, and he felt certain that the ploy had failed. Then he saw one of the three targeted spires begin to shudder. As the melta charges turned its base to a superheated morass of bubbling liquid and hissing gas, the spire began to sag. With a metallic groan, accompanied by wildly discharging electricity, the kilometre-high spire collapsed and fell inwards, straight towards the shield-dome.

Even as that one spire began to fall slowly towards the lightning-dome, so too did the other two shudder and collapse, falling slowly at first and then with increasing velocity.

If the fall of the spires had any effect at all, created any breach in the shield whatsoever, then Sor Talgron felt certain that it would only be a momentary gap.

'Now!' roared Sor Talgron, leaping into the air, the flames of his jump pack carrying him straight towards the dome. He accelerated fast, the engines of his jump pack straining against the forces of gravity.

He could feel the power of the shield-dome intensify as he drew nearer, making his skin tingle and his eardrums reverberate painfully.

He was no more than fifty metres from the veil when the first spire struck. An explosion of light and electricity erupted, far more intense than any he had yet seen.

A moment later, the other two spires hit, creating a blinding discharge of electricity. Bolts of power leapt madly between the three silver spires, and a rent was momentarily ripped open between them, a hole sheared in the fabric of the dome.

Without pause, Sor Talgron angled towards the temporary gap, pushing the engines of his jump pack to their limits, burning rapidly through the last reserves of fuel.

Jagged arcs of lightning criss-crossed back and forth across the tear in the shield-dome as the veil began to reform its impenetrable mesh. With a shout, Sor Talgron pushed on, knowing that he was committed now; there was no turning back.

He roared through the ever-diminishing hole, and his entire body was jolted as a barbed fork of lightning passed through him, using his flesh as a conduit.

His jump pack shorted out completely, sparking and smoking, though the force of his momentum carried him through the rapidly diminishing rent in the veil. His vision was fading in and out, and he dropped like a stone, a smoking, charred body, landing heavily on a palatial balcony within the flickering dome.

Sor Talgron twitched involuntarily for a moment as the last vestiges of electricity left him, dissipating across the smooth glassy floor. Pushing himself up to one knee, smoke rising from the burnt, stinking flesh of his face, he unclipped the release clamps upon his breastplate, and his now useless, smoking jump pack dropped to the ground with heavy clunk.

'That was... unpleasant,' said Arshaq, pushing himself to his feet nearby. The veteran sergeant's cream-coloured tabard was hanging off him in fire-blackened strips. Some parts of the robe were still on fire, and Arshaq casually ripped the remnants of the fabric away from him.

Only the warriors of Squad Helikon had made it through the gap. The other three of the surviving Assault squads were stuck outside the shield-dome. Sor Talgron swore.

It had taken all of the squads' melta bombs to create even that momentary crack in the enemy's defence – it would not be a move that his Assault squads would be able to replicate, nor was he able to contact his brother Space Marines beyond to advise them of a new course of action – evidently, the shield-dome blocked vox traffic as easily as incoming lance strikes. The all-encompassing lightning-dome they were now ensconced within obscured everything beyond.

Sor Talgron's scorched face was stinging, but he ignored the pain, his eyes fixed in the distance.

The city within the dome had been untouched by war, and it was an awe-inspiring sight. Pristine crystal domes, glass spires and interconnected walkways that gleamed like spider-webs dipped in quicksilver sprawled before them.

But Sor Talgron paid none of these structures any mind; he was completely focused upon the looming glass structure in the distance – and upon the giant statue that towered above it.

His eyes narrowed as he glared up at the titanic statue. It stood more than a kilometre tall, a titanic silver and glass colossus in the form of a man, standing with arms raised. Lightning from the shield-dome struck the statue's outstretched hands every few seconds, bathing it in flashes of flickering energy that coiled around its arms and torso.

Sor Talgron felt loathing rise up within him.

This was no was statue of a heroic founder or local legend; this was an effigy of the god of the people of Forty-seven Sixteen.

'So it is true, then,' said Arshaq, disgust in his voice. 'These people are heathen idolators.'

'Lorgar, give me strength,' Sor Talgron murmured.

'Captain,' said Sergeant Arshaq, consulting his auspex. 'We have multiple contacts, moving on our position. What are your orders?'

'We go there,' said Sor Talgron, pointing towards the statue. 'And we kill everything we find. Those are our orders.'

STRANGELY, THEY HAD encountered little resistance since passing through the dome.

After the brutal battle towards the centre of the enemy superstructure, the utter absence of the enemy here was eerie.

They traversed over expansive arched walkways of delicate glass, moving warily towards the immense central spire, covering all the angles and scanning for movement.

The battle outside the sphere of lightning had been bloody in the extreme – the artificial war constructs were deadly foes, utilising weaponry unlike anything that any of the crusade fleets had encountered, as far as he understood. Yet here, within the sheltered, impenetrable dome of energy, it was peaceful – almost serene.

Through vaulted hallways and soaring cathedral-like passages they moved, footsteps echoing loudly upon the smooth glass.

'It's like a tomb,' remarked Arshaq.

Sor Talgron was forced to agree. He almost wished for an enemy to appear, just to break the tension. Almost.

The Word Bearers moved warily along a wide bridge spanning two glittering crystal spires, closing steadily on the central temple structure that rose up before them like an exotic crystal flower, atop which stood the colossal statue of the enemy's false god. Sor

Talgron could not look upon the vile storm-god statue without feeling his gorge rise.

On more than one occasion they glimpsed enemy constructs stalking along bridges and walkways far below, moving towards the shield-dome and the battle raging outside, but they appeared unaware –or unconcerned– with the Astartes already within the shield.

It seemed that the entire superstructure of the enemy continent-city revolved around this strangely alien building, and all the walkways, ramparts and flyways within the veil led towards it. Undoubtedly, it was a structure of great importance, and Sor Talgron felt strongly that the last vestiges of humanity on this doomed world were hidden within.

They covered the ten kilometres to the heart of the city swiftly, moving at a fast pace that they could have maintained for days on end.

At last they drew near the central temple-building. The storm-god statue loomed above them, its arms bathed in lightning. They were just stepping out from beneath a towering archway of crystal splinters, stalking warily towards this central structure, when Sergeant Arshaq spoke.

'Life readings,' he warned, consulting the squad's auspex. They were the first life signs that the device had registered since their arrival on Forty-seven Sixteen.

Sor Talgron barked an order and Squad Helikon formed a defensive perimeter around their captain. They continued to advance, drawing ever closer to the huge, cylindrical temple that rose up before them.

Gaping, triangular portals were cut into the sides of the temple. The interior was filled with blinding light – nothing within its brilliance could be discerned.

Warily, the Word Bearers advanced towards the nearest portal. Sor Talgron shielded his eyes against the bright light. There was a delicate shimmering sound emanating from within, and with a nod he ordered Squad Helikon in.

Stepping inside was like being transported to a completely different location. Sor Talgron felt the change in the air against his burnt skin. The air here was cool and vaguely fragrant, where outside it was hot and filled with the acrid stink of electricity. His gaze was immediately drawn upwards. The immense structure was formed around a vast cylindrical shaft, which disappeared into the distance overhead. This lofty expanse was filled with shimmering light that descended from above like an ethereal waterfall falling in slow motion. A strange, lilting sound accompanied this fey light, something akin to the sound of glass chimes, overlaid with the hum of energy. Hundreds of arcing balconies and gantries ringed this central shaft, and walkways criss-crossed the expanse. So focused on these disturbing wonders was Sor Talgron that he barely registered the panes of glass silently sealing the portal behind them.

Standing atop a fluted pillar of glass was an exact replica of the colossus half a kilometre overhead, though this statue was a 'mere' fifty metres tall. Its head was thrown back rapturously, its arms held skywards in what might have been praise or glory.

Shimmering light bathed this statue in radiant brilliance.

The floor sunk away below them in a steep series of tiers – hundreds of them. And upon each tier crowded the kneeling figures of men, women and children. These were the first people that the Word Bearers had encountered since their arrival on Forty-seven Sixteen – the last of the world's population.

All had their heads bowed to the floor in prayer, facing towards the glass idol of their profane stormlord. Sor Talgron guessed there must have been some forty thousand people packed into the stadium-like temple, all of them murmuring in low voices and rocking from side to side, as if lost in a trance. None seemed to have noticed the appearance of Sor Talgron and Squad Helikon.

Upon a dais at the bottom of the circular tiers, a diminutive old man stood leaning upon a staff of glass and silver. He raised his head, staring up at Sor Talgron and his brethren. He did not appear surprised or shocked at their appearance; rather, he wore a mournful expression on his cracked parchment face.

'Stay with me,' said Sor Talgron. 'Hold your fire, and follow my lead.'

His eyes were locked on the one who could only be the religious leader of the enemy civilisation. This was the one that Kor Phaeron had met with less than two days earlier. Flanked by the warrior-brothers of Squad Helikon, he began marching down the steep stairs towards the enemy leader.

At some unspoken command, the entire congregation of men, women and children stood, turning to
face the intruders into their realm. The Word Bearers
tensed, levelling weapons towards the crowd. Sor Talgron expected to see the flush of anger and
resentment in their faces, but they stared at the towering Astartes forlornly and, perhaps, with a little
disappointment.

'Nobody engage,' warned Sor Talgron.

For all that the enemy appeared to pose little threat,
he knew from experience that it took but a single
individual to turn the mood of a mob murderous –
indeed, the Chaplains of the Legion were skilful at
inciting just such emotion. Were the crowd to turn on
them, the resulting massacre would be terrible. He
and his brothers would reap a bloody toll, taking
down hundreds, perhaps thousands, of these people,
but there were only half a dozen, facing more than
forty thousand. Even Astartes would eventually be
dragged down by such numbers.

The warriors of XVII Legion descended the steep
tiers, eyeing the crowd that parted before them warily.
The people regarding them stood in absolute silence,
which was, Sor Talgron thought, perhaps more dis-
concerting than had they been braying for blood; at
least *that* he would have understood.

The old man regarded their approach solemnly.

'What are we doing?' hissed Sergeant Arshaq, using
a closed vox channel so none of his squad could hear.

'I want to see how divergent these people really are,'
said Sor Talgron, replying on the same closed channel.

He had known Arshaq for decades, both having been raised in the same temple on their grim home world of Colchis, and the captain overlooked such breaches in protocol from the sergeant, valuing his opinion. The sergeant's silence to his answer was enough to tell him that Arshaq did not approve, but he knew him well enough to know that the sergeant would back him up, no matter what.

They descended to the bottom of the tiers, and started up the steps of the dais towards the old priest. Sor Talgron levelled his bolt pistol at the elderly man's head.

'Squad Helikon,' said Sor Talgron in a low voice. 'Establish a perimeter.'

'Yes, captain,' said the sergeant of Squad Helikon, nodding. With clipped commands, Arshaq directed his squad members into position. They spread apart, facing outwards, scanning the crowd for potential threats.

Talgron stepped onto the final level of the dais and came to a halt before the old priest. The elderly man came up barely to his mid-section, and though he was clearly ancient, his eyes were bright and alert. Something in his gaze made Sor Talgron vaguely uneasy. Was he a sorcerer? He dismissed the notion immediately. The old man was unnerving, but he felt no threat from him. He lowered his pistol.

'I am Sor Talgron, Captain of Thirty-fourth Company, XVII Legion,' he said, his voice ringing out loudly, breaking the silence.

'Why do you bring death to my world, warmonger?' said the old man, speaking a corrupted, archaic form of Low Gothic.

'You will order the complete surrender of your armed forces, effective immediately, and relinquish control of the world designated Forty-seven Sixteen,' said Sor Talgron, ignoring the old priest's words. 'Understand?'

'Why do you bring death to my world?' said the priest again, but again Sor Talgron refused to acknowledge his words.

'You will lower the lightning-shield protecting this structure,' he said firmly. 'You will order your people and your infernal thinking machines to cease all hostilities. Do I make myself clear?'

The old priest sighed, and nodded his head vaguely. With a gesture, he drew Sor Talgron's attention towards a dark glass cube that was rising smoothly from the floor. Was it some form of weapon? His pistol was in his hand instantly.

There was something forming within the solid mass of the prism, and sensing no immediate danger, Sor Talgron stepped cautiously towards it. The perfect glass cube would have come up to the chest of a regular human, but Sor Talgron was forced to bend forwards to peer at the image taking shape within.

At first the object forming within was hazy and transparent, like a ghost-image, but within several heartbeats it solidified. It was somewhat like the three-dimensional representations that he had seen produced by advanced pict-devices, but those images were always poor representations of reality. This image looked real, a solid artefact, encased in the glass cube.

It was an open book, he saw, painstakingly illuminated with ink and gold leaf. The borders were replete with impossibly intricate, coiling designs and interweaving patterns. Sor Talgron saw that stylised figures and creatures were worked into these borders, hidden amidst the twisting patterns and coiling spirals. Each of the pages was covered in dense lines of script written in a firm, austere and vaguely familiar hand.

Every warrior-brother of the XVII Legion spent several hours every day engaged in solitary illumination, but never had he seen a work such as this. The penmanship and artistry was phenomenal, far beyond anything that Sor Talgron or any warrior-brother could ever hope to achieve. It was a work of undeniable genius – something that surely no mortal hand could ever hope to match. Indeed, the only illuminated works that he had ever seen that were even vaguely comparable was those penned by the Urizen himself, and he had only been allowed fragmentary glimpses of those great works…

He leaned in closer, eyes widening. The text was written in the variation of High Gothic utilised only by the religious elite of his homeworld, Colchis.

'What is this?' said Sor Talgron in shock, his mind whirling.

He threw a glance towards the priest, standing nearby, but it was impossible to read the expression in the old man's eyes. He turned back towards the book seemingly trapped within the black cube.

'…and in faith shall the universe be united…' he said, reading aloud a line that leapt out from the dense script. His voice faltered. He knew these words. Indeed, he had memorised this work in its entirety. He swallowed heavily.

'...*united behind the... the God-Emperor of all mankind,*' he said in a hoarse whisper, completing the hallowed line.

He looked back at the old priest in confusion and shock.

'I don't understand,' he said.

'We are the Scions of the Storm,' said the old man, gesturing with both arms to encapsulate all the people standing around the temple dais.

'What in Lorgar's name is that supposed to mean?' growled Sor Talgron.

The old priest snorted, and shuffled past Sor Talgron. He leant forwards and brushed his fingertips across the smooth surface of the cube. The pages of the book within the glass prism turned in response, flicking rapidly. Each was intricately illuminated and covered in dense script. Sliding his fingertips more slowly across the surface of the cube, the old priest made the pages turn slower, flicking slowly until he came to the densely illuminated frontispiece of the holy text.

He flashed Sor Talgron a sad smile, pointing at the page.

The captain of Thirty-fourth Company stared wide-eyed at the full-page illumination. It showed a radiant figure bedecked in wondrously detailed armour, detailed in gold leaf. The divine figure's head was thrown back, and surrounded by a golden halo.

The God-Emperor of Mankind.

Sor Talgron's eye was drawn to the golden armour worn by the God-Emperor, to His ornate and ancient breastplate, the breastplate He was said to have worn while leading the ancient armies of unification across the ravaged surface of old Terra… the breastplate that bore the ancient symbols of His rulership, symbols that were recognised and rightfully feared before even the commencement of Old Night, the symbols mirrored on the golden armour of the Legio Custodes, the Emperor's personal guard.

These symbols rose in bas-relief from the Emperor's armour; they represented the Emperor's wrath – *thunder bolts*.

Understanding dawned.

The inhabitants of Forty-seven Sixteen were worshipping the Emperor.

SOR TALGRON SWALLOWED thickly, still staring at the image of the Emperor.

Scions of the Storm, the old man had called his people; sons of the storm. They were worshipping the Emperor as a god, the personification of the storms that wracked their world.

'Now you understand,' said the priest. He tapped a finger onto the smooth surface of the cube, and the three-dimensional image of the holy work disappeared.

'This war should never have been sanctioned,' said Sor Talgron. 'Your people are not heretics.'

'No,' said the old priest. 'We wished to join your Imperium – long had we thought ourselves alone in the darkness.'

'We can stop this,' said Sor Talgron. 'You must lower your shield – I cannot contact my commander while it is intact.'

How many people had already died here? And for what? Sor Talgron felt hollow inside. They had committed genocide because of a misunderstanding.

The Scion smiled sadly, and stepped towards Sor Talgron. He placed a wrinkled hand upon the captain's chest plate, over his heart.

'Give me your word that the last of my people will live, and the shield shall be lowered,' the old man said.

'I swear it,' said Sor Talgron.

The shield-dome encasing the temple-palace of the Scions flickered and disappeared, and Sor Talgron hastily patched in to the *Fidelitas Lex*, speaking of what he had learnt.

'Understood, Talgron,' came Kor Phaeron's muffled reply. 'The Urizen has been informed. Hold position.'

The long-range vox-channel was cut off, and for long minutes Sor Talgron and Squad Helikon stood by uneasily, waiting for fresh orders. The squad still kept their weapons upon the crowd, and Sor Talgron stared up at the statue of the Emperor above.

Long minutes passed. Now that the shield-dome was down, vox-reports began to flood in – it appeared that all fighting across Forty-seven Sixteen had ceased.

'Teleport signature,' reported Arshaq finally.

'This will all be over soon, old one,' Sor Talgron said in a respectful tone. 'The Urizen will be pleased to have learnt that you are believers.'

A moment later, scores of coalescing shapes began to appear around the circumference of the tiered prayer-levels above, teleporting in from the *Fidelitas Lex* in low orbit overhead. They appeared at first as little more than vague shimmers of light, then as more solid forms as realisation was completed.

One after another, a hundred Terminator-armoured Astartes materialised, weapons trained on the human worshippers of Forty-seven Sixteen. Sor Talgron raised an eyebrow.

'A little dramatic, brother,' he commented, under his breath. He raised a hand in greeting to his brother-captain. The distant figure of Kor Phaeron nodded curtly in response, though he made no move to descend the tiers.

Two more shapes began to coalesce, this time on the dais alongside Sor Talgron. His eyes widened as he saw who it was that was teleporting in, and he dropped to one knee, his head bowed and his heart hammering in his chest as the teleportation was completed.

A warm hand was placed upon the crown of his head, its pressure firm, yet nurturing.

'Rise, my son,' said a voice spoken with quiet, understated authority that nevertheless made a shudder of unaccountable panic ripple through Sor Talgron. It was not an experience common for an Astartes.

Pushing himself to his feet, Sor Talgron lifted his gaze and looked upon the shadowed face of a demigod.

* * *

LORGAR WAS AS magnificent and terrible to behold as ever. His scalp was completely hairless, and every inch of exposed flesh was caked in gold leaf, so that he gleamed like a statue of living metal. The sockets of his soulful, impossibly intense eyes were blackened with kohl, and Sor Talgron was, as ever, unable to hold the Urizen's gaze for more than a fraction of second.

There was such vitality, such depth of pain, such intensity and yes, such suppressed violence in Lorgar's eyes that surely only another primarch could hope to stare into them without breaking down weeping before this living god.

He stood a head taller than Sor Talgron, and his slender physique was encased within a magnificent suit of armour. Each overlapping plate was the colour of granite and inscribed with the intricate cuneiform of Colchis. Over this he wore an opulent robe the exact shade of congealed blood, the fabric heavy with gold stitching.

The Urizen, the Golden One, the Anointed; the primarch of the XVII Legion had many names. To those whom he deemed heretic, he was death incarnate; to his faithful, he was everything.

'We are pleased with your success, brother-captain,' said a smooth voice. Almost gratefully, Sor Talgron turned his gaze towards the figure that accompanied the primarch. Erebus. Who else would dare answer for the primarch?

'Thank you, First Chaplain,' said Sor Talgron, bowing his head respectfully.

'This is the one?' said Lorgar, his intense gaze fixing upon the figure of the old priest, who stood transfixed at Sor Talgron's side. The captain of Thirty-fourth Company had all but forgotten about him. The elderly hierarch leant heavily on his staff, his eyes wide with horror. He was shaking his head slightly from side to side, moaning wordlessly.

'This is he, my lord,' replied Sor Talgron. 'This is the one I believe to be the leader of this world's cult of Emperor-worship.'

Erebus smiled, though the smile did not reach his eyes. Sor Talgron knew that look well, and his blood turned to ice.

'I gave my word that no further harm would befall his people,' insisted Sor Talgron. 'Don't make a liar of me, Erebus.'

'You're going soft, brother,' said Erebus.

'It is my belief,' Sor Talgron said, looking towards Lorgar, 'that a race memory of the God-Emperor lingers in the subconscious of the inhabitants of Forty-seven Sixteen. They are devout, and worship Him faithfully, albeit as a crude, elemental force. It would be an easy thing to direct them towards the Imperial Truth, my lord. I feel that had such knowledge been known beforehand, the war on Forty-seven Sixteen would have been deemed unnecessary and inappropriate.'

Erebus craned his neck to look up at the statue of the storm-god above them. He raised an eyebrow and exchanged an amused glance with his primarch before looking Sor Talgron in the eye once more.

'You've done your duty, captain,' said Erebus, stalking around behind the old priest like a wolf circling its prey. 'And you've saved the lives of many of our brothers. For that, you are to be commended.'

'There is more,' insisted Sor Talgron. 'I believe that they have been… picking up our signals, my lord. I saw a copy of…'

His voice faltered as the Urizen turned his gaze towards him once more, and he felt a shudder of unease beneath the power of the primarch's gaze.

'A copy of what, captain?'

'The *Lectitio Divinitatus*, lord,' said Sor Talgron.

'Really?' said Lorgar, clearly surprised.

'Yes, my lord,' said Sor Talgron.

'Walk with me,' said Lorgar. Sor Talgron found himself responding instantly. Such was the power and control in the primarch's voice that he would not have been able to resist had he any wish to.

'Bring him,' the Urizen said over his shoulder, and Erebus guided the old priest, gently but firmly, in their wake. Squad Helikon fell in behind them at a nod from the First Chaplain, leaving the dais empty.

The primarch stepped off the dais and strode towards the steep, tiered stairway that would take them up to the ring of Kor Phaeron's First Company, standing motionless around the circumference of the arena above. Sor Talgron had to hurry to keep pace. Abruptly, the primarch came to a halt at the bottom of the stairs, turning to face the captain of Thirty-fourth Company, a rare, sardonic smile curling the corners of his lips.

'It was a lifetime ago when I wrote the *Lectitio Divinitatus*,' said Lorgar.

'It is the greatest literary work ever to have been conceived,' said Sor Talgron. 'It is your masterpiece.'

Erebus laughed lightly at that, and Sor Talgron felt his choler rise. Lorgar broke into motion once more, taking the stairs four at a time, and he struggled to keep up. Of the thousands of people who stared open-mouthed at this golden, living god walking among them, the Urizen paid no notice.

'Much has happened these past months,' the primarch said. 'My eyes have been opened.'

'My lord?' said Sor Talgron.

'The *Lectitio Divinitatus* is nothing,' said the primarch. There was a quiet but forceful vehemence to his voice. '*Nothing.*'

Sor Talgron could not comprehend what he was hearing, and he furrowed his brow. Was this some test of his faith and devotion?

'I am composing a new work,' declared Lorgar, favouring Sor Talgron with a conspiratorial glance. They were almost at the top of the tiered steps. 'It is almost complete. It is to be my opus, Talgron, something with *true* meaning. It will make you forget the *Lectitio Divinitatus.*'

'What is it, lord?' said Sor Talgron, though he immediately feared he had overstepped his mark.

'Something special,' said the Urizen, tantalisingly.

They reached the top of the tiered amphitheatre, where they were greeted by Kor Phaeron, who dropped to one knee before his lord primarch. When he stood, his eyes were burning hot with the flames of fanaticism. He licked his lips as he stared

at the old priest, who was being helped up the final
stairs by an attentive and gentle Erebus.

'My lord,' said Sor Talgron, his mouth dry. He felt
the gaze of the priest upon him, but avoided it. 'Are
we to condemn these people for… for merely being
cut off from Terra?'

Stony silence greeted Sor Talgron's words, broken
finally by Kor Phaeron.

'Ignorance is no excuse for blasphemy, *brother*,' he
said.

Lorgar glared at his First Captain, who backed
away, dropping his gaze and visibly paling.

Then the primarch put his arm around Sor Talgron's shoulder, and drew him away from the others.
At such close proximity, he smelt of rich oils and
incense. The scent was intoxicating.

'Sometimes,' said Lorgar, his tone one of regret,
'sacrifices must be made.'

He turned Sor Talgron around. The priest was still
looking at him, eyes filled with dread. Out of the
corner of his vision, Sor Talgron saw the primarch's
almost imperceptible nod.

A knife, its blade curved like the body of a serpent,
was suddenly in Erebus's hand. Sor Talgron cried
out, but Lorgar's grip around his shoulders was
crushing, and he could do nothing as the blade was
plunged into the old priest's neck.

Holding the old man upright with one hand, Erebus ripped his knife free and a fountain of blood
spurted from the fatal wound. Hot arterial blood
splashed across the plates of Erebus's blessed
armour, staining it dark red.

Dipping a finger into the geyser of blood, Erebus swiftly drew an eight-pointed star upon the dying man's forehead, though the meaning of the symbol was lost on Sor Talgron. Then, the First Chaplain hurled the old man away from him, sending him crashing down the stairs that he had just helped the old man climb. The priest's body tumbled and flopped end over end. It came to rest halfway at the foot of the stairs, a broken, lifeless marionette, blood pooling beneath it, arms and legs bent unnaturally.

Before the shocked worshippers of Forty-seven Sixteen could react, the entirety of the First Company began firing. The sound was deafening, blotting out the screams. Bolters and autocannons were swung methodically from left and right, mowing down unarmoured men, women and children indiscriminately. Heavy flamers spewed their volatile liquid fire down into the packed masses.

Ammunition was expended, and the First Company Terminators calmly reloaded, slamming fresh magazines into place, replacing drums of high-calibre rounds, threading fresh belts through arming chambers and replacing empty canisters of promethium with fresh ones. Then they simply continued firing.

'Do you trust me, Sor Talgron?' said Lorgar, his breath hot against the captain's face. Shocked and horrified by the scale of the brutal massacre, Sor Talgron was unable to answer.

'Do you trust me?' the Urizen said, more fiercely, his voice quivering with such intensity of feeling that

Sol Talgron felt that his legs would surely have given way beneath him had he not been supported.

The captain of Thirty-fourth Company turned his face towards the impassioned, golden face of his primarch, lord and mentor. He nodded his head slightly.

'Then believe me when I say that this is necessary,' said Lorgar, his voice full of righteous fury.

'The Emperor, in His *wisdom*, has driven us to this point,' said Lorgar. 'This is *His* will. This is *His* mercy. The blood of these innocents is on *His* hands.'

The deafening roar of the slaughter slowly died. At a barked order from Kor Phaeron, the Terminators of First Company began descending the tiers, inspecting the kills and executing those who had, miraculously, survived their concentrated fire.

'I need to know who I can trust,' said Lorgar, his voice filled with such intensity that Sor Talgron knew fear – *real* fear – such that an Astartes should never know. 'I need to know that my sons would follow me where I must go. Can I trust you, Word Bearer?'

'Yes,' said Sor Talgron, his throat cracked and dry.

'Would you walk into hell itself alongside me if I asked it?' asked Lorgar.

Sor Talgron made no immediate response. Slowly, he nodded his head.

Lorgar stared at him intently, and he felt his soul shrivel beneath the penetrating gaze. In that moment Sor Talgron felt certain that Lorgar was going to kill him then and there.

'Please, my lord,' gasped Sor Talgron. 'I would follow you. I swear it. No matter what.'

The intensity suddenly left Lorgar's face, washed away as if it had never been. How could he ever have thought the Urizen meant him harm, he thought? He almost laughed out loud, the notion was so ludicrous.

'You asked me before what the great work I am scribing was,' said Lorgar, his tone casual and light. 'For now, I am calling it the *Book of Lorgar*.'

The primarch of the Word Bearers released his grip on Sor Talgron. Lorgar's golden lips turned into a smile, and despite everything, Sor Talgron could not help but feel his heart lift.

Lorgar laughed softly to himself.

'Such hubris, I know,' he said. 'I'd like you to read it.'

Lorgar looked him directly, his eyes flashing.

'What do you remember of the old beliefs of Colchis, Sor Talgron?'

THE VOICE

James Swallow

IN SILENCE, ONLY truth remains.

But to find it; ah, there is the task. For, one must ask herself, what place is truly silent? Where can the absolute stillness of tranquillity be found?

The question was a common one placed to novices at the very start of their induction, and it was a rare aspirant who showed the wisdom to come even close to the correct answer.

Many would look to the stars, through the portals of the great ebon-hulled craft they found themselves aboard, and they would point to the void. Out there, they would say. In the airless dark, there is silence. No atmosphere to carry the vibrations of sound, no passage there for voice nor song nor shout nor scream. The void is silence, they would say.

And they would be corrected. For even where there is no air to breathe, there is still clamour, the...

chaos, as it were. Even there, broadcast across wavelengths that unaugmented humans could not
perceive, there was the riot of cosmic radiation and
the constant rumble of the universe's great stellar
engines as it turned and aged. Even darkness itself
had a sound, if one had the ears with which to hear
it.

So then. The question again. Where is silence?

Here. Leilani Mollitas mouthed the words, her
voice stilled. *It is here, within me.* She touched her
chest with both hands, palms flat and blades of fingers extended, thumbs crossed in the shape of the
great Aquila. Inside her thoughts, behind her closed
eyes, beyond the rush of blood in her veins, the
novice strained to listen and find the tranquillity of
self; for it was only within the human heart that the
absolute purity of silence could be found, the peace
that only the mute could know.

A frown grew upon her pale, pleasant face. She
could not reach it. Even as that thought formed in
Leilani's mind, she knew she was lost to the
moment. The perfect embrace of serenity faded
from her and she allowed a breath to escape her
lips.

In the flat hush of the sanctum the noise of her
exhalation was like the rush of a wave breaking
against a shore, and she felt her cheeks colour
slightly. Her eyes snapped open and she blinked,
displeased with herself.

Her mentor stood a few feet away, observing her
with the same perpetually watchful air that was the
very meter of her character. The other woman

moved her head slightly, the top-knot of purple-
black hair about her otherwise shorn scalp shifting
to pool on the shoulders of her golden battle-
bodice. Below the flexible duty armour, reinforced
red thigh-boots and studded gloves covered her
limbs, with more plate metal for her sleeves and a
snake-skin of dense mail as leggings. Tabards hung
free from her waist and she was without weapons,
her helmet or the finery of her furred combat cloak.

Amendera Kendel of the Storm Dagger cadre,
Oblivion Knight and Sister of Silence, stood before
her without a sound. Her amber eyes betrayed a
teacher's concern for a promising student.

Leilani smothered her startled reaction quickly.
She had thought herself alone in the Black Ship's
meditation chamber, utterly unaware of the other
woman's arrival. The girl could not help but wonder
how long Kendel had been there, how long she had
been studying her as she tried and failed to find her
inner focus. By contrast, the novice was dressed
only in her mail undersuit and the lightweight
hooded robe of an unvowed aspirant. Leilani raised
her bare hands and began to sign, but her mistress
halted her with a short shake of the head. Instead
the woman held the tips of two fingers to her chin.
Give voice, commanded the gesture.

The novice's lips thinned. She longed for the day
when words would no longer pass from her mouth,
but as she had just demonstrated, it would not be
today. At this moment, Novice-Sister Leilani Mollitas felt further away from taking the Oath of
Tranquillity than she ever had before.

'Sister Amendera,' she began, and even her whispers rose to fill every corner of the cavernous Sanctum Aphonorium, 'How may I be of service to you?'

Kendel's hand fell to the crimson leather of her belt and her fingers toyed with it a moment; Leilani knew the subtle cue from her many months of service as the Oblivion Knight's adjutant. Her mistress was framing her thoughts, marshalling them into ready formations in much the same way she commanded her Witchseeker squads. The novice wondered if Kendel had ever made an ill-considered statement in her entire life.

~You continue to be troubled.~ The Knight spoke in ThoughtMark, one of the symbolic sign languages employed by the Silent Sisterhood. Small in scale, full of delicate gestures of finger and thumb, it served to convey concepts of great subtlety or intricate nature. It was far more graceful than the large, sharp motions of BattleMark, the command language used by the Sisters to communicate on the field of conflict, far more complex and nuanced. Many of the fine inferences of Kendel's intent could not have been translated directly into spoken Imperial Gothic. There were shades of degree in her statement that no human voice could ever have delivered, and thus Leilani felt hobbled as she replied with crude words.

'It is so,' she agreed. 'The news from the outer rim is difficult for me to assimilate.' The words tumbled out of her in a rush, echoing slightly off the curved steel walls of the meditation chamber. The novice was feeling increasingly uncomfortable speaking out loud in this hallowed place. The *Aeria Gloris*, as with every starship in service with the Divisio Astra Telepathica, was equipped with aphonoria, great spaces within their hulls where sound-deadening technologies rendered the closest equivalent to absolute quiet. To break that silence seemed an obscenity, a defacement; yet Sister Amendera made no move to step aside and usher Leilani into the nearby antechamber, concealed from them by ornate curtains of black and gold.

Perhaps it was some sort of test, like the question? Yes, that had to be it. Kendel had made it clear during Leilani's duty under her command that she expected much from the young aspirant, and not for the first time the novice-sister wondered if she would be found wanting. 'What we witnessed in the Somnus Citadel,' she continued, 'the... creature brought back from Isstvan aboard the starship *Eisenstein*.' The girl shook her head, recalling a mutated Astartes warrior that had run riot across the Sisterhood's lunar stronghold, the freakish aberration that had once been a loyal warrior of the Emperor. 'These things pull at my reason, mistress, and I find it difficult to hold my mind upon the tasks at hand.' She looked away, to the steel decking beneath her boots. 'All this talk of traitors and heresy. Horus...'

The Warmaster's name left her lips and it seemed louder than a gunshot. She stumbled over her thoughts and looked up once more.

Kendel nodded once. ~These reports of his rebellion are hard news. It would be a lie to say that no sister remains unaffected by the terrible duplicity that is said to be unfolding.~

'It has robbed me of my focus,' Leilani admitted. 'I think of good men, of the noble Astartes we have often fought alongside, and then to conscience such monstrous deceit among their ranks...' She shivered. 'The Astartes and the primarchs are line kindred of the Emperor of Mankind himself, and if they are wracked by such division then...' The novice's throat went dry as she tried to utter the words. 'What if such horror reaches our ranks, mistress?'

The other woman looked away. ~You would not be aware,~ she signed, ~but I met him once. The Warmaster. He was everything they say of him. And if he truly has turned his face from the rule of Terra, then it will be the war to end all wars to give him his censure.~

Leilani felt sobered by the Oblivion Knight's direct statement. In her service to the Sisters of Silence, the novice had been exposed to many sights – psykers driven insane by their ability to touch the churning madness of the warp, human beings whose flesh and minds had been twisted beyond all recognition, things less than alive that boiled with infernal psychic power – but all these were enemies she could understand, they were foes that, although reviled, Leilani could grasp in her reason. But the traitors? What possible motive could they have? This was the greatest era of humankind, with the galaxy turning at their feet and the Great Crusade at its height; why would one so highly placed as the Warmaster Horus wish to put a match to the Emperor's utopia, when its completion was so close at hand?

~Who can know?~ replied Sister Amendera.

The novice blushed, suddenly aware of the echo around her, realising that she had voiced those last few thoughts aloud.

The swish of the fine silk curtains hanging across the chamber entrance drew the attention of both women, as the Null Maiden Sister Thessaly Nortor entered. Her taut, scar-sharpened face was drawn in a scowl and she gave a blunt BattleMark reply, clearly having heard the novice's last words. ~Target Warmaster. Traitor. Uprising status Flawed/In Error Condition. Insurrection will be Terminated in short order before Rebellion can Expand/Cause Collateral Damage.~

Nortor shot Leilani a hard look, a clear scolding in her eyes. The second-in-command of the Storm Dagger cadre had made no secret of her disdainful opinions of the Warmaster's mutiny. The other woman's breath rasped quietly through the mechanical apparatus at her neck; where Mollitas and Kendel showed bare flesh, almost three-quarters of Nortor's throat had been replaced with a mechanical augment. Made of a polished silver-steel, her artificial implant served the function of flesh destroyed during an engagement against the Jorgalli, inside one of the xenos's bottle-worlds. As well as her neck, much of the Null Maiden's lungs were also synthetic proxies assembled by the Sisterhood's biologians. On one level, Leilani was privately envious of the dour Sister Thessaly; Nortor's larynx had been lost to the acidic bite of the bottle-world's alien atmosphere, and she had refused to allow her augmentation to be fitted with an artificial replacement. The woman was as silent a Sister as was humanly possible.

'We can only hope that the Warmaster sees the error of his ways,' offered Leilani, but even as she said the words they seemed little more than weak and foolish optimism.

~He must recant.~ Nortor's obvious annoyance calmed slightly and she switched to the more reasoned language of ThoughtMark. ~To oppose the Emperor is the height of madness. The only explanation is that the Warmaster has grown envious of his father's greatness.~ She shook her head. ~That, or he has lost his mind.~

In the other Sister's retort, the novice heard the echo of similar words that had chimed from elsewhere in the Sisterhood. Even as news of the rebellion spread, so too there was the talk of a different movement in motion: a growing sect of veneration for the leader of humankind. Such reverence seemed ill-fitting; Leilani balked at the use of the term 'worship' in connection with a being so avowed to a secular path for his people, and yet this so-called Lectitio Divinitatus was raising its head in the strangest of places. If anything, the novice found the question of this school of thought almost as hard to swallow as the concept of Horus's perfidy; and yet, while the Emperor was no deity, it could not be denied that his magnificence was so great that granting him such exalted status was at least an understandable mistake. But it was something to be expected of common, unsophisticated tribals from the feral worlds, not the educated men and women of the Imperium.

Sister Amendera became aware of a pict-slate in her subordinate's white-knuckled grip, and she gave her a quizzical look. In turn, Sister Thessaly bowed slightly and offered the device to her commander. Leilani could guess what the slate contained – an updated skein of mission orders from the command stratum of the Sisterhood on Luna, sent directly from the high offices of the Departmento Investigates.

THE FULL SCOPE and range of the Black Ships and their duties were known only to a select few among the upper tiers of the Silent Sisterhood, the lords of the great Council of Terra and the Emperor himself, but the basic tenet of their works were well recognised. The exact number and disposition of Black Ships that prowled the galaxy purposely remained an unknown; all that could be certain was that the worlds of the Imperium would witness one of them appear in their skies at a preordained time of tithing, ready to accept their cargo. The vessels did not take tribute in the form of riches or chattel – as much as they were warships, the *Aeria Gloris* and her sister-craft were also great asylum-barges where those revealed to show the taint of the pskyer were interred. Every world beneath the Emperor's light was duty-bound to give up those of its populace marked with the potential – latent or not – for psychic talent; and those that were not given freely, those that escaped the net, these too were the quarry of the Black Ships and the Sisterhood.

In the dark holds of their dungeon decks, psykers of every stripe and power were corralled and tested. Many did not endure the process well, and perished under the harsh glare of the Vigilators and Prosecutors. Others, those too damaged by their own warped psyches or too dangerous to be allowed to live, would quietly be put down and the ashes of their corpses cast into suns.

The ones who were strong enough to survive and pliant enough to accede to the will of the Imperium were the lucky few. For them, further, harder testing lay ahead in the ironclad mind-halls of the City of Sight on Terra itself, the headquarters of the Divisio Astra Telepathica. There, they would take the first steps upon the road to the ritual of soul-binding and recruitment into the ranks of the astropathic choirs.

The duty of the hunt and the stewardship was a harsh one that no ordinary human could hope to accomplish; indeed, to even conceive of crewing a Black Ship with mere troopers from the Imperial Army, or even the great Astartes, would be a path to ruin. Such were the powers of some psykers that the perceptions of a mind could be twisted and re-ordered to their will. It was not uncommon for the worst of the psi-witches to cloud thoughts, to coerce and control through pure exercise of will. A normal man could be made to unlock cages and think no ill deed done, never knowing that he had freed a monster. Mindless servitors alone could not be trusted to deal with so complex an obligation. Only the Sisterhood, who brought with them the gift of Silence, had the strength to hold the witches in check. This they did through fealty to the Emperor, this they did through the very action of their beating hearts and the blood in their veins. This duty they marked with their vow never to speak.

For the Sisters of Silence were poison to witchkind. Chance mutation within the human genome, once in every million, might create a psyker; but in once in several *billion* would yield the precious jewel of the Pariah gene, the Untouchable. It was the cold logic of evolution that brought them forth. If the unfettered mental power of a psyker existed, then in balance there had to be those at the opposite end of the genetic spectrum – those whose minds were the absolute antithesis of the warp-touched, whose presence alone was enough to nullify the raging psi-fire. Each Sister was an Untouchable, a psychic 'blank' forever protected from the sorcery of the witches they hunted. Immune to psychic attack, their very aura enough to disrupt and distress their prey, there were no better warriors to fulfil this great duty.

But still, at day's end, they were not superhuman. Trained hard to fight alongside the elite of the Emperor's military, certainly, respected and venerated by all, undoubtedly, but still human. Still weighed down with human doubts and human fears.

AMENDERA KENDEL CONSIDERED this as she weighed the pict-slate in her hand, watching Novice-Sister Leilani and the churn of thoughts writ large across her face. She did not need the preternatural power of a telepath to read the girl's mind. The great dread over the rebellion of Horus hung across everything like a dark cloak, blotting out the light with a haze of confusion. Every Sister aboard the ship, if she admitted it or not, found her thoughts turning to the matter of this unprecedented event in moments of introspection. In the hush of the *Aeria Gloris*, it was easy to find oneself drifting into reverie, for the mind to fill in the stillness with thoughts and wondering that, if left unchecked, could spiral out of control. Typically, the iron discipline of the Sisterhood and the call of their duties tempered such things; but the sheer scope of the Warmaster's rebellion... of his *heresy*... It tore at reason and composure like a wild, clawed thing.

Kendel forced the thoughts away and glanced down at the pict-slate, drawing her focus back to the mission at hand. Upon it she glimpsed the seal of Celia Harroda, the Witchseeker Pursuivant, and above it a notation from the high office of Sister-Commander Jenetia Krole. She licked dry lips. Krole, mistress of the Raptor Guard and one of the Emperor's personal battle confidantes, was the highest-ranking Sister alive. The mark of her notice upon this operation made the gravity of the situation clear, in no uncertain terms.

She removed a glove and placed her bare skin on the sensing pad, letting the slate prick her finger. A moment later the blood-lock released the cipher that untwisted the text from encoded gibberish back into readable Gothic.

The first few pages reiterated what Kendel had already been told in her earlier briefing at

Evangelion Station. The *Aeria Gloris* had been called from its normal circuit pattern and placed under an emergency re-tasking diktat, dropping from the warp to hastily resupply at the orbital platform before making space for the Opalun Sector. The Black Ship had only just begun its tithe cruise, and as such the dungeon decks were practically empty; Kendel suspected this was an important factor in the choice of the *Aeria Gloris* for this task, but she had not made mention of it.

The orders were deceptively direct. One of their sister-craft, an older, larger vessel called the *Validus*, had failed to make three scheduled astropathic check-ins and was now officially logged as missing, status unknown. The *Validus*, in contrast to Kendel's ship, was at the end of her cruise, her decks groaning with a bounty of telepaths, pyrokenes, kineticates, dreamers and mind-witches of every stripe. She should have hove to in Luna's orbit one month ago. Sister-Senior Harroda had commanded Kendel in brisk, severe BattleMark. ~Mission/Task: seek-locate-evaluate. Determine cause of anomaly. Recover if possible.~

Those words encompassed a multitude of possibilities. Black Ships had gone missing in the past, on more than one occasion. For all their combat capability and advanced stealth technologies, the craft in service to the Astra Telepathica were not invulnerable. They largely travelled alone for good reason, but this also meant that they could fall prey to enemy craft in greater numbers or become mired if caught by stellar phenomena. She remembered the *Honour*

Haltis, ambushed and obliterated in battle with eldar reavers; the *White Sun*, taken by warp storms, and all the others.

But a missing Black Ship also conjured up the very worst of possibilities: a breakout. On a vessel laden with witches, such a thing was a true horror to consider. As such, Harroda's orders had concealed the implication that, if needed, Sister Kendel's remit would stretch to the application of a most final end to the voyages of the *Validus*.

The *Aeria Gloris* was now only hours from the area confirmed as the last known location of the errant vessel, and with each passing moment Amendera Kendel felt her unease grow. She chided herself that the source of her concern was not simply the obvious matter of what caused the craft to go dark, but also a trivial personal disquiet. She felt slightly guilty at her outward treatment of her adjutant. Novice-Sister Leilani had allowed her anxiety over the Warmaster's rebellion to occupy too much of her thoughts and it was affecting her meditation; but by the same token, Kendel dwelled on something that was, in all honesty, far more inconsequential.

The *Validus* carried the flag of the Oblivion Knight Sister Emrilia Herkaaze, and the woman was not unknown to Amendera Kendel. Far from it; they had first met in the dark iron halls of a Black Ship just like this one, both of them drawn to the notice of the Sisters of Silence as children. Each of them recruited from worlds in the Belladone Reach, Kendel and Herkaaze had shared a vague kinship throughout their aspirant trials, but as they had

grown into full Sisterhood, the women's early
friendship soured. Now, years later, they were bitter
rivals, each nursing antipathy for the other. She
refused to draw up the reasons from her memory,
instead letting them bubble and churn just below
the surface of her thoughts. To dwell on such things
would only dilute her focus still further.

Sister Amendera wondered if the Witchseeker
Harroda was aware of their ill-feeling towards one
another; she thought it likely, as little seemed to
pass beneath the notice of Sister-Senior Celia's
diamond-sharp gaze unnoticed. Perhaps, in its way,
this was a test for her. Ever since the incident at the
Somnus Citadel and her involvement with the
renegade Death Guard Garro, Kendel had become
aware that she was being scrutinised by her peers.
To what end, she could not be certain.

The Knight became aware of her adjutant and her
second watching her intently, waiting for her to
proceed. She nodded and scrolled further on
through the data encoded on the pict-slate. ~This is
confirmation of what we have already been told,~
she signed with her free hand. ~Records of the
ship's tithe and previous ports. Estimation of current weapons load-out and systems capacities–~

She halted abruptly. The dense data transmission sent out to them via machine-call vox had
some additional matter appended, key among
them a single digitised datum captured from a
partial astropathic communication. The protocols
associated with Black Ship signals were completely absent; normally, any communication sent

from vessel to vessel would be prefixed with a number of codicils and ciphers. There were none. The message had been sent uncoded, in the clear.

Out loud.

Kendel pushed the 'execute' key and the slate replayed the datum. In the quiet of the Aphonorium it seemed like shouting.

A woman's words, rough and strangely toned, as if it had been a very long time since she had used them and could not quite remember how to speak. Two words. Just two words, but they brimmed with a terror so powerful that Sister Amendera felt her hands contract into fists, and she saw Nortor and Mollitas fall breathless.

'The voice...' said the woman. 'The voice...' And then once more, as a ragged scream. *'The voice!'*

'What does it mean?' The novice blinked and frowned, staring at the pict-slate. 'It must have been a sister, but she spoke the words... She spoke them aloud.'

At her side, the Null Maiden nodded slowly. Typically, Sisterhood transmissions sent to locales beyond line-of-sight were despatched not with words but in an ancient machine-readable variant of ThoughtMark known as Orsköde, a mechanical rattle of clicking that to untrained ears would resemble the sounds of turning cogwheels. For this woman, undoubtedly one of Herkaaze's cadre, to not only eschew that but to willingly break her Oath of Tranquillity... The implications were ominous.

~The ship never exited the empyrean,~ noted Thessaly. ~We can only guess at what they might have encountered in warp space.~

Amendera felt a cold chill across her, as one might feel on a summer's day if a shadow passed before the face of the sun. She remembered the stink of death and decay in the corridors of the Somnus Citadel, a fly-swarmed man-shape of something insectile and foul, killing and corrupting with every clawed footstep.

She did not need to guess at what horrors the warp could hold. She had already seen them, spilled out into the real world.

A MADDENED SEA of blood-churned surf, curtains of nameless and impossible colour, great howling halls of flayed emotion; the hellish nightmare of the immaterium raged around the *Aeria Gloris* as the Black Ship closed the distance towards its drifting sister-vessel. The incalculable monstrosity of warp space thundered and screamed, beating at the energy bubble of the Geller field, clawing at the craft that dared to penetrate this realm of pure psychic force; even the massed numbers of Untouchables aboard were not enough to hold such energies at bay. Without the protective barrier, the *Aeria Gloris* would be engulfed.

The *Validus* floated there, the only sign of any life the dull emerald glow from the emitter coils visible about her warp motors. Power still flowed through the derelict, but the craft made no moves to turn to meet them, nor to offer communication through vox or tight-beam laser. Alive and yet dead, the *Validus* floated, serene against the madness.

If the two vessels had met in normal space, it would have been policy to send across a scout party on a boarding craft, allowing the *Aeria Gloris* to stand off and bring her cannons and torpedo launchers to bear, lest the *Validus* suddenly become a threat worth terminating. But here inside the screaming caverns of the empyrean such protocols could not be followed. Instead, an altogether more delicate approach was required.

With care, the shipmaster's bridge crew brought the *Aeria Gloris* closer and closer until the glimmering non-matter of her Geller field brushed that of the *Validus*. Cogitators programmed for just such tasks passed orders, via festoons of golden commwire and mechadendrites, to servitors using scrying scopes to measure the energy spectra being broadcast from the other Black Ship. By agonising moments, they brought the vessel's protective envelope into synchrony with its neighbour. Like two bubbles meeting on the surface of a pond, they touched one another, shifted and finally merged. Such an operation was a difficult one, but then the Black Ships were crewed by some of the finest crop of thinking serfs available to the Imperium. It would take their constant stewardship to maintain the merging of fields; a single miscalculation would collapse both, and open the starships to the ocean of insanity lapping at their keels.

And yet the *Validus* drifted as if upon a calm sea. Seasoned veterans among the crew serfs talked among themselves and spoke ill of such unusual circumstance. Some, those who thought themselves safe to do so beyond the sight of the Sisters, even bent at the knee and offered a prayer to Terra and the Emperor.

The warp was rage, and constant with it. But here, in this place, there was a cavity within the churn and thunder, an expanse where all seemed becalmed. If it had been the surface of a planetary ocean, then there would have been no breath of air, only glassy water from horizon to horizon. Such things were unknown by the shipmaster, and with the tradition of all sailors dating back to the times of mankind's first voyages in craft of wood and sail, he and his men feared and cursed it.

Elsewhere, on the lower decks of the *Aeria Gloris*, power moved to mechanisms capable of tunnelling through the layers of space-time, and a great flare of boiling light enveloped the ship's teleportarium stage. The women stood upon it shimmered like mirages and were gone.

THE TRANSITION FLASH faded into the darkness and Sister Amendera gestured with her drawn sword. To her right, Leilani held a bolt pistol in one hand and an auspex in the other, her attention on the chiming reports of the sensor device.

To her left, Thessaly was already cutting order-gestures in the air, flinging the shapes towards the three Sister-Vigilators that had accompanied them.

Kendel ran a finger over her forehead without conscious thought, absently tracing the red lines of the Aquila tattoo there. She took a careful breath, glancing around the low, wide corridor they had appeared in. The Knight had expected to find the chamber cold, perhaps the air inside thin from slowed life support functions and proximity to the outer hull; she had ordered the teleport servitor not to target them too deeply into the *Validus*'s mass, for fear that the risk of a mis-integration would grow with the distance of projection. But the air here was warm and dry, like a desert just after sunset. And more than that, there was peculiar stillness to it, as if the motes of dust around them were suspended in some sluggish fluid.

Kendel stepped forwards, letting her blade lead her, making small, experimental cuts in the air. Despite her faint discomfort, she couldn't find anything immediately wrong. The gravity seemed normal, and she could smell... nothing.

'Thermal blooms in that direction,' offered Sister Leilani, her voice strangely flat. She pointed ahead, towards the end of the corridor. Ahead there were shapes piled untidily beyond the low greenish glow of the lumes in the walls, sharp-edged metal frames of tubes and wire.

~Cages,~ signed Nortor.

The Knight nodded and advanced. She had ventured no more than a few steps when a gasp of alarm made her turn about. One of the Vigilators had approached a support pillar made of iron, which extended from the deck to the ceiling above. Her

hand was in a fist and she opened it to her commander. Amendera watched a rain of metal sand fall
lazily from her fingers, glittering in the lume-light.
The Vigilator gestured to the pillar and showed
where she had touched it. The Sister's gloves had left
dents in the iron. It crumbled beneath even the
lightest of touches, becoming more powder.

Kendel snapped her fingers and Sister Leilani duti-
fully moved to the stanchion, tracing the scanning
device over its length. She frowned and repeated the
action, clearly unhappy with the initial reading.
'Odd,' she admitted, her words dulled and distant-
sounding. 'The auspex suggests that this piece of the
ship's structure is far older than the rest of the metal
in this corridor…' Her frown deepened. 'By the
order of several million years.'

The Knight allowed herself the rarity of a faint
grunt of dismissal and beckoned her troop onwards.
Strange as that was, it would not do to become
bogged down in such minutiae so quickly. The
group moved on, towards the discarded cages, and at
once Kendel understood exactly where the teleport
flash had deposited them. They were at the perimeter of the *Validus*'s husbandry yards, where the
hunting animals deployed by the ship's prosecutor
squads would be corralled.

The thought had only just occurred to her as she
crossed some invisible membrane and a barrage of
sensation suddenly assaulted her. There was no
force-field barrier, no detectable wall to divide one
section of the corridor from another; it was simply
that one moment the air about her was dead and

quiescent and the next it was dense with smells and
sounds. Perhaps, like the warping of time around
the metal stanchion, the two ends of the passageway
existed in differing states.

Nortor came to her side and she saw the other Sister's face wrinkle in faint disgust. Here, the air was
thick with the coppery stink of old, spilled blood, a
heavy perfume of rust that almost concealed other,
earthier stenches of rotten meat and faeces. The
tainted air here also carried sound differently; it was
clearer, harsher on the ears. Kendel heard a scraping, a dripping, from one of the shadowed corners.
She stepped over a flattened enclosure, seeing a
mush of small bones, flesh and white feathers
inside. Among the pieces of the dead raptor were
shiny golden psiber circuits that flashed as they
caught the light.

One of the Sister-Vigilators aimed her bolter in
the direction of the sound and thumbed a switch on
the weapon's flank; an illuminator rod fixed to the
barrel snapped on, casing a cold oval of white light
before it. The scraping paused, and there at the edge
of the torchlight a pair of eyes glowed. More beams
stabbed out to reveal a large, pale-furred mastiff as
it sniffed in the direction of the women. The snout
of the enhanced canine was brown and wet, and as
it panted, the glassy vials of accelerant fluids
implanted in its back clinked together. To one side,
Nortor snapped her fingers in a command string,
but the animal ignored her. After a moment, the
hound looked away and bowed its head, returning
to its task. Kendel took a careful step closer and the

animal was fully revealed, lapping at a wide comma of blood pooled about the head and neck of a crew serf. The top of the man's skull was open, and in one hand he held a Sisterhood-issue stake-thrower. She studied him for a moment; he appeared to have used the weapon first to nail his legs to the deck by firing a long quarrel through each ankle, then one more through his other hand.

'He tried to crucify himself,' said Leilani.

The en-dog was looking up at them again, and slowly its lips drew back to show metal teeth, a low growl building in its throat. Kendel heard the fluid in the tubes bubble and hiss. She had seen the damage these animals could do firsthand when she herself had given orders to release them. The Knight threw a glance at Sister Thessaly and made an open-handed gesture.

~Flamer.~

There was a snap-hiss as the pilot lamp lit, and Nortor brought her weapon off the strap and around in one smooth action. Before the en-dog had the chance to rock forwards off its steel-clawed feet, the Sister squeezed the trigger bar and bathed the animal in a cloud of burning promethium. It died with a squeal and they left it where it fell, moving on towards a bank of access shafts.

Kendel saw her novice dally a moment around the animal's corpse and snapped her fingers. Leilani's head bobbed in acknowledgement, and she followed.

The light from the gun torches swept left and right around them as Kendel gave the other woman a sideways look. ~That will not be the only death we see this day,~ she signed. ~Look.~

The Vigilators moved on, and in heaps here and there, piled up against the walls or amid the smashed cages, there were dead after dead. Raptors, hounds and servitors.

But not a single Sister.

THE DECK PLANS of the *Validus* had been encoded into the memory tubes of Leilani's auspex, and once the boarding party had found their bearings, it was a simple matter to orientate themselves in order to scale the Black Ship's inner tiers towards the commandery and bridge. Sister Thessaly took a moment to send a vox message back to the *Aeria Gloris*, a staccato chatter of clicks that signified all was well, that the mission was proceeding as planned; but the novice could not help but wonder how anything they encountered here could be 'as planned'.

The *Validus* was a death ship, a floating tomb, and if it had not been silent before, then it truly was so now. Leilani knew the emergency protocols as well as any Sister. The standing orders aboard Black Ships were rigid and unchangeable: in the event of any shipboard catastrophe of such magnitude that the command crew could not overcome it, failsafe switches would flood the dungeon decks with Life-Eater, a bio-weapon of terrible swiftness and horrific virulence. If the Sisters aboard this ship were as dead as the serfs they had found, then so were the witches. It had to be so; if it were not, then why were the boarding party still alive, why had they not been attacked the moment they teleported aboard? More-over, she knew that whatever had killed the unfortunates they had found had been no gas or bio-weapon.

They moved deeper into the Black Ship's interior, past long corridors of testing cells walled in with spherical shields made of psi-toxic phase-iron, across the gantries between the utility decks. Overhead, stalled carriages on angular rail channels that in other times would shuttle crew and material from tier to tier and down the city's-length of the vessel were frozen in mid-journey, faint lights burning inside. Along the way they found more signs of curious phe-nomena: other places where hull metal had been turned into dust or wet slurry by means unknown, one section where the air was hazed by a smoke that hung like a frozen image until they passed through it, and chambers where the walls, floor and ceiling were painted over with a molecule-thin layer of human blood. It seemed without rhyme or reason to Leilani; perhaps it was the touch of the warp at the hand of these things.

At last, they reached the command deck, another broad corridor that branched off into smaller ancil-lary chambers, with the open amphitheatre of the *Validus*'s bridge at the far end. Lit in the yellow smoul-der of the lumes were masses of bodies, piled atop one another in a disordered fashion, as if a thronging crowd had perished instantly on its feet and been left where they had fallen. Ahead of her, Sister Thessaly hesitated and held up a hand to halt the rest of the group. There was a strange murmur in the air, an ebb and flow like the sound of surf on a shore. It took a moment for the novice to realise that it was breathing.

She peered at a group of the bodies closest to her – they were crew serfs, their duty uniforms simple tan affairs with a minimum of braid and sigils – and was startled. They were not dead; none of them were. Instead, the whole mass of the crewmen lay, blank eyes seeing but not seeing as if in some form of catatonia.

Nortor prodded one of them with the tip of her boot. When there was no reaction, she reached down and took the hand of a serf. Without pause, the Silent Sister broke the man's finger. The wet snap of bone sounded, but little else.

Sister Amendera picked her way through the bodies to peer into an open iris hatch on the far wall; Leilani followed her, recognising the doorway as the entrance to a saviour pod. There were more bodies inside, some of them strapped into the seats of the escape capsule, others lying on the floor where they had dropped. Like the serfs in the corridor, all of them were alive but insensate. The novice studied the face of one man, a bridge officer by the rank tabs on his shoulder boards. His eyes were those of a doll, glassy and infinitely empty.

'Whatever did this destroyed their minds.' She glanced around the corridor again. 'All of them. All at once.' Leilani's throat became arid as she imagined this scene replicated all through the *Validus*, with every crewmember reduced to a fleshy husk, minds ruined by some catastrophic, instantaneous flash of psychic force. 'In Terra's name,' she whispered, 'what happened here?'

Further down the corridor, one of the Vigilators rapped on the steel wall to attract their attention. ~No Sisters,~ she signed.

~Onwards,~ ordered the Oblivion Knight.

THE VIGILATORS SHOULDERED away the bodies of fallen crew choking the entrance to the bridge proper, and the Silent Sisters entered with weapons at the ready, casting their sight into every shadowed corner on the ready for attack. A long platform that extended out over the main oval of the control pit several metres below, the bridge was designed in such a way that the Black Ship's commanding officer could stand at the rail as if at the prow of an ocean-going vessel, and see his staff ranged out beneath him. Only the most senior crew had stations on this level, and the wide banners of flickering hololithic screens formed an arc of glassy lenses in the air above their consoles. Most of the monitors were little more than rains of static, but some still functioned, showing the process of autonomic systems inside the Black Ship's drive core, the steady tick of life support. Leilani noticed one screen displaying a feed from an exterior camera; the blunt bow of the *Aeria Gloris* was visible, rendered in shadow against the churning red-purple hell of warp space. Other active screens were lined in dark crimson, trailing pennants of emergency warning glyphs. One of the Vigilators scrutinised an engineer's panel, her long leather-clad fingers moving over the keys.

~The kill-switch was not activated,~ she signed.
~There was no release of the termination option
here.~

Nortor looked up from a console by the command throne. ~Shipmaster's log is intact.~

Kendel sheathed her sword with a grimace and
gestured for Sister Thessaly to continue. The other
woman tapped a string of keys on the console and
a crackling hum issued out from vox grilles hidden
in the steelwork.

Leilani caught sight of a man in a commander's
dark kepi, sprawled out on the deck in lee of a Y-
shaped stanchion; it was this man's voice that filled
the dank air of the bridge as the data-spool
rewound. Each entry was short and precise, punc-
tuated by a clicking code indicating numerical data.
The shipmaster spoke of an urgent signal that had
reached them outside the normal strictures of contact protocol, a faint entreaty that the astropaths
aboard the *Validus* had considered strangely
phrased and slightly disturbing. The bonded psykers complained of their disquiet at the
communiqué, and they were sickened by a peculiar
resonance that clung to the signal, an echo of pha-
sure displacement that troubled them greatly. And
yet, the message was in order, bearing the ciphers
that guaranteed the authority of the highest levels
of the Silent Sisterhood. The novice saw her mistress scowl at this, her eyes narrowing. The briefing
imparted by Sister Harroda had mentioned nothing of any message sent to the craft before its
disappearance.

The shipmaster spoke of a single, simple order contained in the transmission. The *Validus*'s captain was commanded to bring the vessel to a halt in this region of the ever-turbulent warp and await further contact. This they had done, only to encounter the first incidents of the atemporal phenomena that the Sisters had witnessed on their passage through the lower decks. The entry ended, and after a pause Nortor triggered the next in the sequence.

~This is the last,~ she noted.

Again the voice of the shipmaster; but this time he seemed like a different man, the matter-of-fact clarity with which he had recorded his earlier logs gone. Leilani listened carefully and heard spikes of raw panic in the captain's words fighting to overwhelm his self-control. She heard him pause and mutter, his voice rising and falling as he fretted over the fate of his ship.

There, amid the sudden and alien calm, something had begun down on the dungeon decks. Moving like a tide, radiating like a nova, inside the iron holding cells the massed psyker cargo awoke as one, burning out the neuroshackles that held them in check, the potent dampening filters pumped into their blood-streams becoming weak and ineffective. The *Validus*'s astropathic choir began to scream. There was weeping and bellowing and–

Silence.

~The final entry ends here,~ signed Sister Thessaly. ~There is nothing else.~

Leilani felt sickened, as if an invisible patina of dirt was suddenly coating her flesh. The idea of rampant, uncontrolled psykers in such number was utterly abhorrent to her. It was everything the Sisterhood stood against, and it made her feel soiled to think she was in close proximity to such a thing.

Fighting down a shudder, the novice-sister found her gaze drifting up to the gantry above the bridge platform. There was a single hatch up there, a thick disc of metal set in a heavy ring of black iron; beyond it would be a narrow tunnel leading to the astropath habitat, where the ship's tame psykers would parse messages for transmission across the interstellar deeps. Such sections of a starship were always heavily shielded, for even the smallest amount of telepathic interference could upset their delicate sensory paths; aboard a Black Ship, the matter was magnified a thousandfold.

Only the most highly trained, the most tightly controlled of the astropath kindred could ever serve aboard a vessel that was such a riot of psi-noise, and even then the life expectancy for them was a fraction of that of their fellows aboard normal ships of the line. Even their sanctorum, isolated from the rest of the craft through advanced technologies, energy fields and thick walls of psi-resistant metals, was pale shelter for them. Leilani could not help but wonder what had transpired in there after this... awakening.

She looked back to find the Oblivion Knight watching her. Sister Amendera gestured in Battle-Mark, having clearly come to the same conclusion. ~Investigate and evaluate.~

Grimly, the novice accepted her orders with a nod and shucked off her cloak, so that she could more easily enter the narrow conduit overhead. Removing her bolt pistol, Leilani checked the weapon and reached for the access ladder, willing her hands not to tremble.

The hatch yawned open to present her with a shallow, gloomy tunnel lit from the far end by pale blue illuminators. Without looking back, she ascended, leading with her pistol. She smelled decay in the stalled, stagnant air.

The chamber was spherical and smooth-walled, the faint light spilling from oval lumes arranged in a ring around the interior equator. The inner surface of the murky chamber glittered gently where intricate lines of microscopic text ranged around from pole to pole. Leilani felt a moment of confusion, of wrongness, and in the next second she had the reason why.

'Gravity,' she said aloud. 'There's gravity in here.'

Usually, the astropaths aboard a craft of this class would live in a null-gee bubble, cut off from the graviton generators of the rest of the ship so that they could float freely without concern for the vagaries of something so base, so mundane as walking upon their feet. But here, the nullifying field was inactive, and she sought and found a sparking control panel some distance up the curved walls where the command switches has been forcefully disabled.

It was then that she saw them, and understood. There were three astropaths in the choir of the *Validus*, and it appeared that, while afloat overhead, with great care they had removed their outer robes and fashioned them into nooses, fixing one end to

the upper ranges of the hollow chamber and the
others about their necks. Then, one of them must
have destroyed the controls and allowed the pull of
gravity to reclaim their bodies, and snap their necks.

The corpses of the dead psykers swayed slightly in
the flow of new air that had followed Leilani up the
access tunnel. In the low light, she could not make
out any features upon the three; their faces were
puffy, blood-streaked orbs, turned to ribbons of wet
meat where they had clawed at themselves in some
sort of frenzy.

WHEN SISTER LEILANI returned to the bridge platform,
Kendel read what the young woman had seen in the
astropath chamber from the paleness of her face.

~All targets self-terminated.~ The novice-sister gave
her report in BattleMark without thinking, but
Kendel chose not to correct her. The sight had shaken
the girl. Mollitas was far stronger than she gave herself credit for – if she had not been, the Oblivion
Knight would never have chosen her as her adjutant
– but she was reluctant to test her own limits and,
until she did, the Oath of Tranquillity, the mark of
the Aquila and true Sisterhood would be beyond her
reach.

~Orders?~ Sister Thessaly stood before her commander, toying with her weapon.

The Oblivion Knight hesitated for a moment, then
nodded to the senior of the Sister-Vigilators. ~Split
squads,~ she signed. ~Vigilators, aft approach.~
Kendel touched her chest. ~This unit, forwards.
Descend and converge.~ She brought her hands

together and clasped them. In one context the symbol could mean *alliance*, in another *collision*, or even *amalgam*. In this, it indicated a target to be located and isolated. It was not necessary for her to outline their objective; the last words of the shipmaster had made that certain.

She switched speech. ~We will find our sisters,~ she told them. ~This is our order and our obligation.~

Nortor made the sign of the Aquila.

'In the Emperor's name,' whispered Mollitas.

THEY EMERGED INTO an icy cavern, boots crunching on rimes of hoarfrost and snow, the access channel to the dungeon decks carpeted with a blanket of oily grey slush. It was a peculiar sight to see inside the metal halls of a starship, more suited to a winter's day upon some distant colony world. Kendel's breath emerged from her mouth in trails of white and she threw a questioning look to the novice. They were deep inside the *Validus* now, nowhere near the exterior hull where the leeching cold of space could reach them. The Knight raised a hand to her armoured collar to toggle a vox control, intending to signal the Vigilators. Were they seeing the same thing? Was this yet another of the strange spot-effects that were scattered throughout the interior of the derelict Black Ship?

But a motion from Nortor made her hesitate. The other Sister nodded towards tall columns of dirty ice clustering in one corner. There was movement behind them and breath, white in the air.

'Who is there?' The novice-sister gave voice to the question. 'Show yourself.'

Kendel felt a weak, familiar pressure at the back of her skull. It was like the sense of heaviness in the sky before a storm, or the very faintest of echoes. She was drawing her eagle-head sword when a figure suddenly bolted from between the ice pillars, half-running, half-skidding towards them.

A man in a frost-caked overall came at her, an iron manacle and length of broken chain clattering about one ankle. She saw a leering grin and eyes wide, showing too much white. Haloes of vapour formed around his hands and she felt the already-low temperature drop still further. He was conjuring snow out of the air, grabbing it and moulding it into blades of ice.

Kendel knew the kind well: a cryokene. She held up a hand to halt Nortor from placing a bolt shell through his breastbone as a matter of course, and let the psyker come on towards her, his bare feet slapping at the frozen deck plates.

In the man's eyes she saw the moment, as she had so many times before with her other quarries, when understanding hit him. In mid-run, the psyker pushed into the edge, the faint, ghostly periphery where Kendel's Pariah gene began to exert its influence upon him. He entered the invisible zone about her where the Sister's Untouchable nature created a pool of nothingness in the shadow-space of the warp. Some of Amendera's kindred were stronger in this than others, and in some the great gift of Silence manifested itself in different ways; for the Oblivion Knight it was an unseen sphere that extended beyond her flesh, dampening the power of any psyker with increasing severity the closer they came.

The cryokene stumbled, the ice storm he had been creating from thin air suddenly evaporating in his clawed hands, the ice shattering. Kendel met his gaze with a warning glare and shook her head in mute censure.

The psyker bounced on the balls of his feet; even an animal would have had the sense to react to such a barrier, to be cowed and back off. But if reason had ever been in this man, it was long gone now. Undeterred, he screamed and threw himself at her, scratching at her eyes.

The Pariah effect, as potent as it was, could only protect against the sorcery of telepathic contact and other witch ploys. Against physical attack, against shot or blade or claw, it was no shield; but for those, the Sisters of Silence had their years of training in the schola bellus of Luna. Almost as an off-hand motion, Kendel creased the cryokene's scalp with the heavy brass crown on the pommel of her weapon. It connected with a dull crack and he went back to the deck on his haunches, sliding on the thin ice.

'Can you not see what we are?' called Sister Leilani. 'In our silence, you cannot harm us.'

'You cannot hear!' he shouted, his voice a sudden, atonal bark of sound. 'If I cannot hear, you must not!' He scrambled back to his feet, and again he threw himself towards Kendel. 'You must not hear!'

He was insane, that was not in doubt. Perhaps, whatever release of energy had killed the minds of the crew serfs and servitors had only scrambled the wits of this one, and in the disorder that followed he had found his escape from the Black Ship's cells. Not that it mattered. There would be nothing to glean from this witch.

The Oblivion Knight stepped into his attack, with her hand-and-a-half sword still held in a reversed grip. Turning, she brought the blade up to meet the cryokene's throat and took him there, decapitating his body with a lean stroke that let the victim's momentum do the work for her. Crimson fluid gouted briefly into the air, spattering across the grubby snow. Specks of blood dotted Kendel's golden cuirass, but the arterial spray was sporadic and quickly stilled.

She stepped over the corpse and walked on through the ice and snow as the last gushes of red pooled on the cold deck, a thin wisp of steam rising from the length of her sword blade.

~What did he mean?~ Sister Thessaly matched her pace, signing carefully. ~He spoke of hearing something. Perhaps there is a connection with the last words of communication from this ship?~

Kendel held the tips of two fingers to her chin, and Nortor nodded in slow agreement.

'Give voice,' murmured Sister Leilani. 'But to what?'

THE FURTHER THEY progressed, the stronger the sense became of a new, strange denseness in the atmosphere, a thickening of the air that brought with it a greasy, metallic tang that Leilani could not clear from her throat, no matter how many times she sipped water from the dispenser nozzle in her portcullis-shaped gorget. She knew that the

Oblivion Knight and the Null Maiden sensed it as well; their moods became wary and sullen as they passed through the outer sections of the holding areas, the cells where the less dangerous denizens of the dungeon decks were typically held. The novice chanced a look in through the locked doors of cells she chose at random; inside each there were odd, wet pastes of matter that might have been bodies, if flesh were wax and pressed to a flame. The air was unnaturally still, cloying to the point that it took on the properties of a membrane. Leilani felt the ghost-touch of it on her bare face, like the gossamer caress of spider webs.

Ahead, ever at the lead, Thessaly Nortor's boot scraped to a halt and the novice froze, ready for the next maddened psyker or freakish phenomenon to rear its ugly head. Instead, the Null Maiden turned towards the other two women and made the sign for *Sister*.

They came across her in the middle of the chamber; she sat cross-legged on the dark iron deck plates, her head bowed in concentration and her sword drawn, both hands clasped around the slim hilt. Leilani was aware of a peculiar calm that seemed to radiate from the woman's body, an absence of emotion or energy. A silence, for want of a better word.

Her mouth was moving but no sound emerged; still, the novice had only to read a word or two and she knew what litany was being unspoken. Without realising it, Leilani said the words aloud. 'We are Seekers and we shall find our Prey. We are Warriors

and woe to those we Oppose...' She trailed off, her
cheeks colouring.

A frown formed on Sister Amendera's face and
Leilani looked again at the distaff Sister. The other
woman had a top-knot of rust-red hair that hung
loosely, lank and sweat-soaked, over her bald skull.
There was a line of livid pink puckering down the
left side of the Sister's face and neck from her cheek-
bone, pointing like an arrow towards the
lightning-bolt symbols etched on her shoulder
plates. She bore the same rank as Kendel, and it was
with that realisation that Leilani recognised the
woman.

With a dry gasp, Sister Emrilia Herkaaze of the
White Talons cadre opened her eyes, her battle meditation broken, and looked up at her. The woman's
left eye, framed by the scarring, was an intricate augmentation of blue glass and golden clockwork. She
gave Leilani a cold, evaluating once-over.

Herkaaze ignored the offer of Nortor's open hand
and got to her feet, shrugging off stiffness. The
Oblivion Knight turned her glare towards Kendel;
the lower half of the woman's face was concealed
behind a half-mask resembling barred gates, but the
novice could tell her mouth was twisting in a sneer.

~I knew that someone would come,~ signed the
other Knight, ~but I never would have expected it to
be you.~

Kendel's expression cooled. ~The mission fell to
us. The Storm Daggers go where they are sent.~

The tension between the two Knights was strong,
and Leilani could not help but think back to the

rumours she had heard about Kendel and Herkaaze's thorny rivalry. One story, told to her by another of the novices, said that the women had once fought with a fire-witch on Sheol Trinus; Herkaaze, unwilling to fall back before a powerful enemy and regroup, had been struck by burning debris and later turned the blame to Kendel for refusing to support her. Leilani had not believed the tale at the time, but now looking at Sister Emrilia's old wounds, she wondered if there might have been some truth in it.

Herkaaze caught her staring and pushed closer to the novice. ~Seen enough, speaker?~ She asked, her augmetic eye glittering. Leilani looked at the deck, cowed.

~I sense witchkind,~ noted Sister Thessaly. ~Close at hand.~

The scarred Knight nodded but did not address the other woman, instead focusing her intent back on her former comrade. ~Are you all there is? You three?~

Sister Amendera shook her head. ~A lance of Sister-Vigilators attend us. I sent them by a secondary path, via the aft decks–~

Herkaaze made a derisive noise in the back of her throat. ~You sent them to their deaths, then.~

At this, Nortor clasped her fist into her palm, tapping out an interrogative tone-message through the signal-generating touchpads on the knuckles of her glove. Leilani heard the short-range signal echo through the vox in her wargear. They waited for a moment for the standard 'all-clear' reply from the other team, but there was only the hiss of static. Nortor paled slightly and shook her head.

~Horrors are loose aboard this ship. I lost many Sisters of my own to the witches who ran free in the madness.~ Herkaaze nodded to herself. ~We killed as many as we could.~

Anger flared on Kendel's face and she grabbed the other Knight's arm. She did not sign, but her question was clear.

With exaggerated care, Sister Emrilia peeled the other woman's hand from her grip. ~There was no time to send a full warning. We had to come here, to build the wall. Else all would have been lost.~

'The wall?' Herkaaze winced at the sound of her voice, but Leilani ignored it. 'I do not understand.'

Nortor folded her arms across her armoured breasts, fists to elbows. The sign meant *wall* but also *bastion* and *enclosure*.

'What happened here?' asked the novice.

~Answer her,~ demanded Kendel.

Herkaaze shot the young woman an acid look, and finally nodded. She began to sign in ThoughtMark, quickly and sharply; the motions were so swift, so animated that to an unschooled observer they would have resembled the training kata of some dance-like martial art.

Sister Emrilia gathered up the threads of events left unwoven by the curious warning detected by Evangelion Station and the logs of the *Validus's* shipmaster.

After the Black Ship had hove to and in turn been becalmed in this odd void-within-a-void, from all

about the craft probing psychic impulses forced their
way into the vessel. At first, some of the crew-serfs
claimed to see ghosts stalking the corridors; such
sightings were not uncommon on ships where the
raw agony of caged telepaths left psychic stains upon
the bulkheads, but these were no ordinary wraiths.

These ghosts moved in concert, intent on tasks
that seemed more military than otherworldly. And
soon, the rioting erupted across the dungeon decks.
Many of the psykers killed themselves or died when
the pulses of psi-force lashed their cells. Too late,
Herkaaze admitted, she and her Sisters had realised
that the probing attacks were not random, but targeted at the most powerful psykers aboard the
Validus. Each impulse blew open cells and holding
cordons – but when granted their sudden freedom
the captured witches did not flee. Stranger still, they
moved deeper into the dark prison spaces, seeking
each other. A troop of Sister-Prosecutors dared to
venture in and witness what sorcery the mutants
were creating; those women died, but not before
passing on reports of what they saw.

In her studies, Leilani had read many of the great
texts in the towering stacks of the libraria in the
Somnus Citadel, from the earliest volumes of the
Psykana Occultis to the *Voiceless Judgements of Melaena
Verdthand*. In these tomes of psychic research and
lore, the young sister-in-waiting had learned much
of the witch. She believed that faith in sword and
bolter and silence were but one half of a sister's
armoury, that knowledge of their quarry carried
equal weight. In this, she had read much of the

strangest extremes of psyker-kind; and so even as Kendel and Nortor watched Herkaaze's terse report with growing disbelief, the novice found herself nodding, knowing that such freakish things were indeed possible.

The grim-faced woman continued. ~The very worst and the very strongest of the *Validus*'s tithe of witchkind shambled together and became an amalgam.~ Sister Emrilia was very careful to use the sign-gesture for that word, bringing her hands together and clasping them. An amalgam, in the manner of *fusion* or *joining*.

Leilani felt her blood run cold. 'This I have read of,' she broke in. 'A group-mind, the spontaneous formation of a shared telepathic consciousness. On Ancient Terra, in the Age of Strife, the nation-state of the Jermani had a word for it. *Gestalt*.'

Sister Amendera took a warning step towards the other Knight. ~The Life-Eater,~ Kendel snapped her hands back and forth. ~Why was it not used?~

Herkaaze eyed her. ~Malfunction,~ she replied, ~Sabotage/Outside influence. Cause unknown.~

The four of them stood for a long moment, weighing the import of what had been described. Whatever the instigating force, whatever the impetus was that had created this freakish confluence of minds, the question now at hand was how to deal with it; how to kill it, Leilani corrected herself, for such a radical mutation would not be allowed to live in the Emperor's secular, ordered galaxy.

The scarred woman returned to her explanation, and this time she seemed less angry, more morose at the thought of what orders she had been forced to give. Knowing full well that the squads of Witchseekers, Vigilators and Prosecutors aboard the *Validus* could not hope to defeat a monster fuelled by the power of witches raised to such geometric heights, Sister Emrilia did the only thing that she could.

Her last order to her Sisters was to deploy about the dungeon decks, each of the warriors to find and take a space where they could kneel and recite the creed, a place where they could draw within and bring forth the gift of silence from themselves. There were some among the common citizenry who called the Sisterhood the 'Daughters of the Gates', partially in respect to the half, three-quarter or full helmets they wore, fashioned in designs after the portcullises of archaic castles, but the name also came in respect to their mission – to stand as the barrier between the rampant insanity of unchained witches and the safety of the Imperium. In echo of this, Herkaaze gave the command to encircle the group-mind aboard the *Validus* and hold it in place. Each Sister of Silence, her Pariah's mark burning cold in the minds of the psyker freaks, was one bulwark in a ring the witches could not cross. However, by the same token, no Sister could step away. It was an impasse.

~But now you are here,~ Sister Emrilia signed, switching back to ThoughtMark once again, ~and you can take my place while I move in and kill it.~

KENDEL'S LIPS THINNED. Her former comrade had not changed at all since Sheol; if anything, the beating she took on that desolate sphere had not humbled her, but instead hardened her intractable manner. Here they stood, Knight and Knight, their ranking equal and unquestioned, yet still Herkaaze spoke to her as if she were addressing an inferior.

~We are not here as your reinforcements,~ Kendel gestured. ~We are here to rescue you.~

The other woman glared at her, the old scar tissue on her cheek darkening. Like the eye she had replaced, it would have been a simple matter for the Sisterhood's chirurgeons to have patched and regrown the damaged flesh on Emrilia's face, to have made her seamless and whole again; but instead she wore the disfigurement visible to the world, as if it were some sort of badge of honour. Amendera's lip twisted; such a gesture was something she might have expected of an Astartes, but not a Sister.

~We cannot break the line.~ Herkaaze's body language was severe and accusatory. ~One severed link and that horror will be freed to prey upon the galaxy. This is the only option. I go in and I kill it.~

~We,~ corrected Kendel, drawing in all of them in one flick of her hand. ~We will kill it.~

Nortor was nodding. ~Mollitas can take the Knight's place here, in the ring. We three will venture deeper.~

Kendel glanced at the novice-sister and shook her head. For all her book-learning and potential, Sister Leilani was not ready for this challenge. She had too many doubts, too much churning inside her thoughts to find the serenity needed to truly bring forth the silence. The Oblivion Knight indicated that

the Null Maiden would take Herkaaze's place there
and kneel on the deck.

For a moment, an instant so slight that one who
did not know Thessaly Nortor would not have seen
it, Kendel's second wavered; then she bowed and
drew her sword, falling into the meditative stance.
Before she bowed her head she drew her flamer and
handed it to Mollitas without statement or ceremony.

Leilani took it with a nod, drawing herself up, digging deep for her courage. Sister Thessaly closed her
eyes and began to mouth the words of the creed.

In the next second Herkaaze was stepping to stand
in front of the other Knight. ~No support required.~
Her BattleMark was sharp and angry. ~Stand down.~

~In the past you censured me for failing to aid
you. Now you will do the same when I make that
offer freely?~ Kendel signed the words and watched
the other Knight's scarring turn crimson, the old
wound showing Herkaaze's anger like a beacon.

There was a moment when Sister Emrilia seemed
on the edge of actually uttering her rebuke out loud;
but then she turned away. ~Come, then. But this is
my vessel and command here is mine.~ Herkaaze
did not wait for Kendel to acknowledge her, and
walked on, towards the far hatch.

~Confirmed.~ Sister Amendera made the cross-
fingered gesture at her chest and looked up to find
her adjutant watching her intently.

INSIDE HERKAAZE'S WALL there was madness; madness and phantoms.

The ghosts attacked them in a horde, coming out of the decking and the ceiling, falling out of shadows and from behind support pillars. They were shimmering and wailing, the noise of them at the furthest end of the spectrum from the Sisters.

Bolt shells and pulses of fire from the flamer moved through them, and swords were of little use. The wraiths closed and faded even as they screamed, evaporating like morning dew as their energies collided with the limits of the Pariah effect; but there were some that were flesh and blood, hidden in the morass like a dagger wrapped in a cloak. They were crewmen of the *Validus*, drained of mind like those on the upper decks, but unlike those poor fools, these were rendered into the bloody realms of psychosis. Concealed in the crush of their spectral doubles, they laid into Kendel, Herkaaze and Mollitas with clubs fashioned from broken pieces of metal or severed limbs.

Corralled inside the invisible barrier, the forces that had twisted the psyches of these serfs had turned upon themselves. Their minds like rabid animals trapped in a snare, they were gnawing upon their own reason, all trace of what made them men gone now. Inside those thought-hollowed skulls, there could be nothing but darkness and void. By chance Kendel matched gazes with a man in a ship-fitter's tunic and she knew without doubt that he, like all of them, was ruined inside. It made her angry: these poor fools were not even the enemy, just the overspill of the witchery left to fester here in the bowels of the *Validus*.

Still, she did not allow this emotion to prevent her from giving the mindless ones their due despatch. Her sword moved in flashing arcs, opening bodies to the air and sending aerosols of crimson to spatter across the walls.

The two Oblivion Knights fought as mirrors of one another, the ingrained training of the Sisterhood's blade schola rising to the fore without the need to frame it in conscious thought. Behind them, Sister Leilani spent fire upon the foe in grunting chugs of exhaust from the flamer's bell-shaped mouth. They died as they were cut down or turned to shrieking torches. The bodies of the unreal became motes of dust in the still, stale air of the corridor, while the bodies of the real carpeted the decking.

Then there came the moment's pause, the three of them panting hard. Kendel watched Herkaaze clean her blade on the jacket of a dead serf and she wondered if the White Talon warrior had thought of these poor creatures in the same manner as she had. Amendera doubted it; Sister Emrilia had always been one for a singular worldview of black and white, good and bad. She did not have any room for shades of grey; that, if Kendel was honest with herself, was at the heart of the disputes they had shared more than any other matter.

Nearby, Sister Leilani returned Thessaly's flamer to its strap across her shoulder and blew out a shuddering breath. 'Throne's sake,' she husked. 'They swarmed upon us as soldier ants would those invading their mounds. I dread to think what force compelled them.'

Herkaaze gave the novice another disapproving look, as if she were trying to glare the younger woman into silence. Mollitas did not seem to notice, too caught up in the train of her own thoughts. The Knight saw her face grow pale as some terrible notion came upon her.

'Mistress,' she began, with a wary tone. 'What if this...' Leilani indicated the walls of the Black Ship. 'If all this is the framework of some gambit by the rebel Astartes?' Suddenly, words began to fall from her lips in a cascade. 'It is known that some of their Legions have been said to engage with witchery, and–'

The hard report of brass upon steel sounded, silencing the novice, and Kendel turned to see where Herkaaze had rapped the pommel of her sword against the deck. ~Must she speak so often?~ demanded the other Knight.

~Do you fear she may be right?~ Kendel signed the question back in reply.

Herkaaze did not even bother to grace her with an answer, and moved on. She pointed with her drawn blade, the tip aiming at a great oval hatch up ahead. The metallic stink of psyker spoor was strongest there, the echo of it throbbing at the base of Amendera's temples. Emrilia walked on towards the massive door, never looking back.

BEYOND THE HATCH was a chamber that ended in a smouldering molecular furnace. It was this sight that would be the last for the most powerful and unruly of the psyker-kind processed aboard the ship.

Executed here, on the iron deck, then cast into the open maw of the machine, their bodies would be reduced to ash; it was believed that no psychic could reconstitute themselves after such a killing.

Perhaps, then, it was fitting that they found the group mind here, the men and women that were its component parts huddled together in a crowd, some standing, others on the floor or lying against the walls in an unearthly accumulation. Unlike the mind-dead on the other tiers, these ones seemed on the surface to be animate and alive; in some ways that made the sight of them all the more horrible.

'They have no faces,' said Leilani. In fact, she was only half-correct. The hundredfold members of this unnatural psychic amalgam each had the suggestion of eyes, nose, a mouth, but they were in a constant flux, never settling to become anything like a human aspect. Instead, they were sketches, half-finished approximations of what a person might look like, all of them the same. One moment, long of nose and narrow of eye, then fatter about the cheeks and with a tiny moue of a mouth. Bone beneath their skins made ticking, popping sounds as the structure of their skulls was warped and altered, second by second, over and over again.

All of them turned to stare at the Sisters and cocked their heads in quizzical fashion. The novice grabbed for the flamer at her shoulder and flicked her gaze down at the volume meter: half-full. Her fingers found the trigger bar and the weapon's emitter bell hissed in readiness.

~This is it,~ signed Herkaaze. ~This is the Voice.~

They advanced across the chamber and the pieces of the gestalt closest to them retreated, propelled back by the proximity of the Untouchables' psi-toxic presence. The three women moved in a tight triangle, each watching an angle of attack.

But unlike the cryokene, unlike the en-dog, these shifting faces betrayed no clear intention, no emotion that could be read and predicted. They simply observed, with expressionless stares, the glimmer of intellect and intent broken into shards that barely registered in a hundred pairs of eyes.

Leilani began to wonder how such a thing could be killed; the weapons the Sisters carried with them were not enough to terminate so many at once. And if they began a cull piecemeal, how would the group-mind react?

The swaying, blank figures all took an abrupt breath, their faces shifting into a hatchet-browed aspect and solidifying.

'Far enough.' The rasping and atonal words were spoken by groups of them in a dislocated chorus that made her skin crawl; each syllable was uttered by a different cluster of voices in unearthly harmony. 'Stay your weapons–'

Leilani saw the expression on Herkaaze's face twist into one of fury, incensed at the temerity of the demand. The Oblivion Knight surged forwards with a snarl, and the cluster of psykers nearest to her recoiled as she came at them. Sister Amendera reached out to hold her back, but she was not quick enough. Her sword still warm from earlier kills, Herkaaze struck out and carved into a woman in a prisoner's shipsuit, the brand of a telekinetic on her forehead. The cut that ended her was a downwards slash that opened the woman's torso, and without pause the scarred Knight extended and severed the hand of another psyker, this one a male. He fell to the floor, one arm ending in a red stump jetting fluid.

The other psykers moved with sudden speed, and Leilani recalled the flocking motion of arboreal birds on her home world. The disparate pieces of the group-mind moved like water, flowing away from the attacker, leaving the dead and injured among their number where they fell. Leilani realised she was already seeing them as a single entity, no longer thinking of the psykers as discrete people within a larger whole.

Cut off from the horde, the man with the missing hand suddenly screamed and there was cracking anew from the bones of his face as his flesh attempted to reset itself. Abandoned by his kind, he began to resemble the crazed remnant they had encountered outside. Herkaaze silenced him by opening his throat with her blade-tip.

'Stay your weapons!' This time it was a shout, every member of the gestalt bellowing as loudly as their lungs would allow. The sound was so strong in the low-ceilinged furnace chamber that it gave the Sisters pause.

Leilani experienced a moment of confusion. Any handful of the psykers present in the chamber would have been more than a match for two Oblivion Knights and a novice-sister, and as one in this strange meta-concert, they doubtless wielded enough power to kill them all in an instant, crushing them by bringing down the deck above, by burning off all air in the chamber by pyrokene firestorm or any one of a dozen methods.

Why then were they still alive?

'What do you want?' she asked.

The answer from a myriad of throats made her blood chill. 'Leilani Mollitas. Emrilia Herkaaze. Amendera Kendel. I have been waiting for you.'

'They know our names...' The novice's words seemed tiny in comparison to the voice of the crowd.

~Witchery!~ Herkaaze signed furiously. ~They have plundered our thoughts!~

~Impossible,~ Kendel replied silently. ~No telepath can penetrate the bastion of our minds. We are Untouchable.~

'I know who you are,' echoed the chorus, 'and I must speak with you.' The faces of the assembled mass moved and altered again, melting and flowing in meter to the mood of the words.

With each utterance, Leilani felt the ebb and drag of psychic force shifting about her like an ocean of clear oil. The presence of the group-mind rebounded around them in captured echoes. The novice gripped the flamer tightly, and struggled to keep herself from shaking. First, in the things she had read in the libraria, then in the living, breathing madness she had witnessed in the transformed Astartes on Luna, and now here, before her in this ship... Every half-truth and myth Leilani had heard about the powers that lurked within the empyrean were made true.

~Whatever dark corner of the warp spawned you, creature, you will not manifest here.~ Kendel sheathed her blade and in its stead drew her bolter to the ready.

Laughter pealed around the crowd. 'This is not the face of Chaos. What you see here is only a message and the messenger.'

~What message?~ Kendel demanded her answer with savage jabs of motion.

'A message,' repeated the voices. 'Once before a message came and it was too late to change the pattern of things. You were there, Amendera Kendel. You saw this.'

Leilani saw the Knight nod slowly, making the sign for an Astartes. 'Garro...' whispered the novice.

'A new message. A warning.' The breathy choir paused. 'For the ears of the Emperor of Mankind. Darkness comes, Sisters. The great eye opens and Horus rises. The history of tomorrow is known to me.'

Kendel exchanged glances with her subordinate. Precognition was a known and documented psionic effect, although extremely rare and difficult to interpret. Leilani could imagine her mistress turning the words over in her mind; if this confluence of psychic had power enough to pierce the veil, perhaps... perhaps they might have some insight into the skeins of events yet to occur.

Herkaaze spat noisily on the deck and brandished her sword. ~Destroy this monstrosity!~ she signed. ~It is some ploy, either of the witches' origin or even the turncoat Warmaster himself! We cannot ferry this abhorrence into the Emperor's divine presence. It must be killed!~ She advanced with her blade raised high, head sweeping back and forth like a hunting hawk looking for her next prey.

Members of the group-mind broke apart from the main pack as she came at them, forming into smaller flocks that retreated from her along the ashen-stained walls. 'I am not your enemy!' came the multiple cry. 'The storm is about to break, but the course of things can be changed!'

Herkaaze's only answer was to lunge and strike down another psyker.

'Millennia of endless warfare can be prevented!' Panic and desperation entered the voice of the chorus. 'Believe me!'

From out of nowhere, a cluster of figures rushed towards Leilani and she raised the flamer, ready to immolate them in a heartbeat; but their flowing, waxen faces turned to her, imploring as they altered, begging her to hear them out. 'What do you want?' she screamed out the question again.

In turn, they howled back at her. 'I am only the portal, the messenger and the message. Across the madness of the warp, where time and space become unravelled and the tapestry of events falls apart. I call to you from then.' Hands grabbed at her robes. 'I warn you from your tomorrows. Your now is my past. I am living in the hell I wish you to uncreate, centuries gone and the fires still raging.'

* * *

AMENDERA KENDEL HAD once believed that the universe could do nothing to shock her; the horrors that she had witnessed in service to the Silent Sisterhood, the years that matured her from a callow novice to an Oblivion Knight of rank and stature, these things had shown her much, from the glories of the human heart to the very depths of monstrosity that nature could create. But she had lost that arrogance, truly lost it when word had come of the Heresy, when she had looked into the eyes of a creature cut from the raw matter of corruption. She had known then that there was more that moved upon the face of the universe than could be encompassed in her judgement.

And here, now, she found herself challenged again. It would be easy for her to take the path Emrilia followed, to decry and shout for death. To question and wonder, even for a moment, that was beyond Herkaaze's insight. There had been moments when Kendel had thought she too had become reactionary and hidebound – and this was one more reason why she selected the girl Leilani as her adjutant. At times, she saw the mirror of herself in the novice-sister, keeping her close so that she might reinforce that dormant sense of wonder.

But to comprehend this… A voice, speaking not from the here and now but a time yet to happen. A future? Try as she might, Sister Amendera could not find it in herself to deny that such a thing, as incredible as it seemed, was not possible. It was the warp, after all; and in the warp, all things were malleable. Emotion, distance, thought, reality. If dimensions such as these were distorted here, then why not time itself?

'This place and this instant,' cried the psykers. 'I am here as you are, peering in from my unfuture to the shifting sands of the past.' All together, they moved their hands to their faces, the tips of two fingers to their chins. 'To give voice.'

Herkaaze was frozen, kneading the hilt of her sword, turning in place, daring the witchkin to come within reach of a cut. She did not see the cluster grouping around Sister Leilani, entreating the girl with open hands and upturned faces. Kendel moved towards the girl, unsure of how to proceed.

'You know me,' they told the novice, flesh shifting again, bones crackling. 'Look. See.'

There was something new in the chanted words, a cadence and pitch that seemed at once eerily familiar to Kendel, but unknown as well. Older, somehow. Her breath was struck from her lips as the group-mind's aspect altered once again, the sketch of a face thickening, becoming firm and definite. A cold sensation crawled along the base of the Knight's spine.

'You know me,' they said, and each one of them was the mirror of Leilani Mollitas.

THE NOVICE SCREAMED in fright at the faces surrounding her. They were some strange mimicking of her own plain features, but lined and aged by years and hardship. She looked and saw dozens of elder sketches of herself, renderings of what she might be should she live a hundred years. The timbre of the voices echoed in her memories, and she was suddenly thinking of her mother. The similarity was uncanny and it terrified her. She could not deny it: the voices were hers. The flamer dropped from her nerveless fingers to the deck, and she stumbled back a few steps.

'How… can this be?'

The chorus inhaled together and replied. 'I have done terrible things to get to this place,' said the voice. 'Pacts and accords that have scarred my soul.'

'We are Untouchable,' Leilani husked. 'They say we have no souls.'

'We have,' came the reply. 'Else I would have had nothing to burn, no coin to pay my way here.' She became aware of the Oblivion Knights either side of her, each watching with expressions of horror and wonderment. The voice pealed like a bell. 'That price I… *you* paid willingly. Now trust me. Take me to him, and we will be able to reorder a galaxy yet unsullied by–'

There came a sound; not quite a howl, not a gasp or a cry but some strangled merging of all three. It burst from Herkaaze's mouth in a flash of spittle and rage. Her revulsion was so towering that she could not hold in the exhalation. Her free hand flew about her face in a wild dance.

~Traitor bitch!~ she signed, almost too fast for the eye to follow. ~If this insanity is to be believed, then you have consorted with mind-witches! You have betrayed your oath to the Throne of Terra and the Lord Emperor!~

Leilani tried to find the words to explain, but her thoughts were confused. It was not her, but some other possible incarnation of the woman she would become who had done this deed; and yet the novice shuddered as she looked wildly around at the psykers who wore her face. If such a thing had been done, what was the magnitude of these sinister pacts her elder self mentioned? Treating with witchkind was the least among them; in order to make this bridge across the warp, sorcery of the darkest stripe would be needed. Her Pariah gene, burned from her DNA. Her literal self, subsumed into a mass-mind for the sole purpose of punching a hole into the past. What magnitude of event could have been so great to have made that choice seem a reasonable one?

The novice felt conflicted. Sickened by the scope of such mad sacrifice, it was all she could do not to retch, but even as she was revolted, Leilani found a kernel of understanding. 'Yes,' she whispered, 'I would do such a thing. If that was required of me, if the cost was so high, yes. I would do this deed.'

She turned her gaze inwards, and touched the tranquillity inside herself, newly revealed beneath a light of new self-knowledge. In Leilani's silence, only the truth of who she was remained.

It was this thought that followed her into darkness, as the tip of Herkaaze's sword carved through her spine and erupted from the chest plate of her battle-bodice.

KENDEL BARELY HELD in the scream, her mouth gaping open but the utterance smothered by the force of her sacred oath.

Sister Leilani's eyes rolled back and she coughed out a great tide of blood, her body collapsing as Herkaaze drew back her blade from where she had stabbed the girl in the back. The novice-sister fell in a clatter of armour and flesh against the corroded decking. Crimson spread around her in a rippling halo.

The Knight brought up her bolter and aimed it at the other woman, the weapon trembling in her grip. She felt wetness on her cheeks. *Why?* Kendel mouthed the words, her other hand tight in a mailed fist. She wanted to shout the question, but her voice would not come.

~How can you ask that?~ Herkaaze gave her a defiant glare, daring her to shoot. ~I have stopped this monstrosity before it started. Strangled the horror in its crib.~

Around them the psykers were whispering, then mumbling, then speaking and finally screaming. They clawed and howled at each other, tearing the flesh of their faces into rags. Their cries were just one word, repeated until the chamber resonated with the sound.

'No. No no no no no no no no no–'

The air trembled and the deck groaned with it. Kendel ducked as one of the psykers, a pyrokene, suddenly erupted into flames and caught a cluster of his fellow prisoners alight. Elsewhere, a tornado of force flashed where a psychokinetic lost control of herself. As if they were untrained hounds whose leashes were suddenly cut, the witches were running wild. Mollitas's death tore them down, and the

Oblivion Knight saw the group-mind fracturing, self-destructing.

Clipped by the psi-fires, pieces of the metal ceiling broke away and crashed to the ground. Plumes of gas and drifts of meat-smoke stinging her nostrils, Kendel saw Herkaaze disappear behind a cascade of tumbling pipes and spun away to avoid a gout of flame. The *Validus* trembled and moaned again; she thought of the calmed void outside in warp space. How long would it last now, with the witches in disarray?

She took two steps and hesitated, half-turning, remembering Leilani's corpse there on the deck, but all around her steel and iron was turning into rains of gritty powder. Kendel thought she heard the echoing report of a bolter firing from deeper into the chamber; the Knight ignored it and fled, cutting down a pair of ferals who tried to block her path. Into the corridor beyond, she felt her boots slip and become mired as the deck softened beneath her steps. All over the walls, tendrils of decay snaked out, aging everything they touched. Time itself was digging its fangs into the hull of the *Validus*, the freakish effects no longer confined to locations here and there throughout the vessel.

Kendel's tapped out the emergency all-channel recall on her glove, searching the smoky gloom for any sign of Sister Thessaly or the White Talons who were still on the ship. Her vox crackled but no reply codes came. She reached beneath her combat cloak and her fingers touched her teleport recall beacon. The Oblivion Knight gripped the slim golden rod in her hand, her thumb hesitating over the activation stud. Why did Nortor fail to answer her? Where were the others? What mad hell had this death ship come from?

Kendel spat and glared at the rod's winking indicator; then the deck beneath her gave way, and she knew nothing else.

LIGHT CUT INTO her eyes and she coughed.

Blinking owlishly, Amendera Kendel became aware of a restraint harness around her and the thin whisper of liquids enveloping her body. She tried to focus, staring at a shimmering shape on a dark wall. After a while it resolved into a reflection, and she orientated her perceptions. She lay suspended in a bath of pale pink fluids, her body for the most part naked except for places where metal devices were joined with puckered, inflamed skin. A narthecia tank, a great cocktail of medicines and liquids that mended burned flesh or torn skin. The Knight had often seen the like in the medicae decks of the *Aeria Gloris*, but in all her service she had never found herself in one of them. The fluids resisted her attempts to move, pulling on her. She could shift a little, and then only her head and neck, raised above the enamelled steel walls of the tank.

The chamber was dim, lit only by the glow of a single lume set low and the red laser-optics of a hunchbacked servitor. It moved slowly just to her right, orbiting between two sculpted consoles that chimed in time with her heartbeat and breathing.

Kendel glanced down at her hand and saw a line of burn scarring across the palm that had held the teleport beacon. Not dead, then. The sight seemed to be the final confirmation for her. She drew in a breath and found it hard to hold it; her lungs ached.

'Awake.'

The word fell from the shadows beyond the far end of the tank. Kendel blinked and threw a look at the servitor, but the machine-helot did not appear to notice. The Knight pushed again at the restraints holding her in place, but they were of dense plastiform and immovable.

'Don't.' The voice was harsh and broken. 'You will reopen the wounds you have spent so long healing.' Parts of the shadows detached from the dark and moved.

Kendel saw a figure, a woman, a Sister. The shapeless coils of a robe, the lume-light touching a shorn scalp and the cascade of a top-knot beyond it. At once she was shocked; even in shadows, Kendel could see this was no unavowed novice but a ranked Sister of Silence. For a Sister to speak aloud was anathema.

The woman seemed to sense her amazement. When she spoke again, there was a cruelty in her words. 'We are alone here, you and I. The servitor cannot report. None will know that I have given voice.' In the dimness, the Sister touched two fingers to her chin. 'You are aboard the *Aeria Gloris*,' she continued. 'That errant harpy Nortor came to your rescue as you lay insensate. The teleport recovered you.' The figure shook its head once. 'The Null Maiden did not survive the translation.'

A sharp tension twisted in Kendel's chest. She had known Thessaly Nortor for many years, and her loss cut deeply.

'Some of the White Talons escaped in saviour pods.' Kendel heard a low, wry chuckle. 'We were the lucky ones. Treated to such a show.' The Sister spread her hands. 'The *Validus*, consumed by a wash of psychic fury, eaten alive by rabid time. The vessel torn to shreds, the warp about it churned into a maelstrom. Ah.' She shivered. 'It is such a delicacy to say these things without gesture.'

In defiance, Kendel moved her right hand just enough that the other woman could read the signs. ~You sully your oath. You break the silence.~

'He will forgive me.' The woman stepped closer, and Emrilia Herkaaze's face revealed itself. 'It was He who guided me to the pods when you left me to die. He who guided my blade when I executed your errant novice. He, who saved me when you abandoned me on Sheol Trinus.'

The Knight snarled with fury and pulled at her restraints, the pink fluid splashing around her. Thin whorls of new blood issued out through the liquid from ruptured sutures. Disgust filled her at the towering injustice of it, that this callous and narrow-hearted woman should live and poor Leilani perish.

Herkaaze came close and halted, bowing her head. 'Whatever it was that we witnessed in there, I killed it as I said I would. Your novice, she had some connection to the monstrosity, that is not disputed.' She sighed. 'Perhaps there was some truth to the ravings of the voice. If it was indeed a messenger from our unbound future, then her death here annulled that skein of time. Those events will not unfold.' The other Knight nodded to herself. 'In a way, I saved her from herself. She died unsullied, with the seed of corruption still dormant inside. And so the order of the universe is preserved.'

~The message,~ signed Kendel, wincing in pain. ~You killed the messenger. Whatever truth there was for us to learn goes unheard! She spoke of wars we could prevent, a great burning!~

Sister Emrilia shook her head. 'No one will believe you if you make mention of that. Give voice to it and you will destroy your reputation, for I will decry you. At best, you will ruin yourself. At worst, you will split the Sisterhood.' She glared at the other woman, clearly relishing the feel of words on her tongue. 'Do you wish that, Amendera?'

~You are a blind fool. Arrogant and superior.~ Kendel turned her head away. ~You and every one of your stripe are a cancer on the Imperium.~

'I see better than you,' she replied, walking back towards the shadows. 'My eyes are open to the truth. Only one so divine as the God-Emperor has the right to tamper with the weave of history.'

At the utterance of the word 'god', Kendel turned back, a questioning look on her face; but the other woman was still walking, speaking almost to herself.

'If there is to be war, it is because He wishes it. I am the vessel for His voice, sister, and all who are mute before His glory will not rise with me.'

Herkaaze vanished into the darkness and Kendel closed her eyes. Inside she sought out silence, but it remained lost to her.

CALL OF
THE LION

Gav Thorpe

IN A STORM of kaleidoscopic violence, reality was torn apart. From the seething warp-point burst forth a starship, slab-sided and bristling with weapon systems. Within moments of the warp rift opening, the *Spear of Truth* had smashed into realspace, and almost immediately its launch bays were opening, shafts of red light spilling from the yawning maws of its hangars.

The battle-barge spewed forth a swarm of unmanned probes that darted out from the warship's armoured hull in all directions, turning and weaving a complex pattern like bees around their hive, their scanners seeking any sign of immediate threat. A few minutes later, patrol craft erupted from their mechanical wombs on white-hot plasma jets. They formed up into three squadrons, one fore, one aft and the other circling the battle-barge amidships.

Thus protected, the *Spear of Truth* began the long process of slowing its immense speed.

On the bridge of the *Spear of Truth*, Chapter Commander Astelan was geared and armed ready for battle, as were the rest of his crew, heedful of the standing orders for vessels to be ready to fight immediately. Such orders were not merely dogma. Despite her guns and patrol craft, the *Spear of Truth*, like all starships, was most vulnerable dropping out of warp space. Just as a man requires time to orientate himself upon recovering consciousness, so too did the battle-barge and its inhabitants need to adjust to realspace.

Astelan was clad in his power armour, as were his three companions, Galedan, Astoric and Melian, each a captain of the companies carried aboard the battle-barge. Their armour was shadow-black, broken only by the red winged-sword insignia of the Legion upon their left shoulder pad and their company markings on the right. The dull grey of exposed piping and cables broke through from under the overlapping ceramite chestplates, coiling under the arms to the backpacks that supplied power to the suits.

Though painstakingly maintained, each showed small but tell-tale signs of wear and tear – spots of corrosion, repaired battle damage and makeshift replacement parts. Astelan had heard that newer versions of armour had been developed, with reinforced joints and fewer weak spots, but it had been more than four years since his Chapter had been in contact for a substantial resupply.

Around the massive figures of the four Astartes were several dozen functionaries clad in simple robes or white coats. Most stood at workstations, while some were on hand with dataslabs to record any orders given by their commanders. The only sounds were the thrumming of logic machines, the chitter of readouts, the tread of boots on mesh decking and the murmurs of the technicians. All were well practised; there was no need for idle chatter, only clipped reports from the bridge crew.

'Local scan negative for planetary bodies.'

At Astelan's waist hung a power sword and his holstered bolt pistol. They had been in his possession since he was promoted to sergeant, only fourteen years ago, and they were as much a badge of office for him as the insignia inscribed upon his chest plastron. He tapped his fingers against the hilt of the sword as he waited for the sensor screen to re-establish itself.

'Local scan negative for artificial bodies.'

'Wide sensor array operational.'

The seconds ticked by slowly, as the *Spear of Truth* metaphorically shook away its dizziness and regained its sight and hearing.

'Tactical display coming online.'

The mood of concentration did not lighten at the news, for although the *Spear of Truth* was now no longer swathed in a sensorial limbo, it would take a while before the data being relayed back to the ship was collated and analysed.

'Local comm-web established.'

A few more minutes passed until a technician spoke again.

'Localised scanning complete,' he said. 'Zero threats detected.'

Though there were no obvious sighs of relief or relaxation, the tension aboard the bridge dissipated somewhat. Alertness turned to focused activity; caution to curiosity.

Astelan looked up at the huge digital display that rendered all of the incoming data into an understandable image. It was crude at the moment, little more than a wire-frame schematic of the system and its major planetary bodies, and would take several days for the picture to be completed as the surveyor probes raced through the system sending back their findings.

Over the coming hours, eighteen more vessels broke from warp at various points around the star system's outer reaches, each spawning its own small brood of escorts and augury devices. Seven more battle-barges, three fleet carriers and eight light cruiser-class warships descended upon the silent worlds orbiting the deep-red orb at the system's centre. Invisible, tight-beam laser communications criss-crossed the void seeking the whereabouts and conditions of the other fleet members.

After several hours, contact was fully re-established. The fleet correlated their courses and calculated velocity descents for rendezvous, inbound towards the core worlds.

The Dark Angels began their exploration of system DX-619 in earnest.

Astelan was patient. It would be at least seven more days before the fleet had decelerated to something approaching orbit-navigable speed, and he was determined to use that time to gather as much information as possible about this uncharted stretch of the galaxy.

A radio signature, faint or perhaps even non-existent, had brought the Dark Angels here; the merest chattering murmur against the background radiation of the universe. It would most likely be nothing, a cosmic anomaly caused by an irregularity in the star's emissions or a millennia-old echo of a civilisation long since turned to dust by the passing of an age. Such had been the case for ninety-five per cent of the systems the task force had investigated over the last five years. Almost all were deserted, for even at the height of mankind's spread across the stars they were scattered thinly, pockets of humanity amongst the impossible vastness of interstellar space.

In the early years the forces of the Great Crusade had met with huge success, bringing the Imperial Truth to hundreds of worlds in the relatively densely populated systems around Terra. Here, in the yawning chasm between spiral arms, such colonies had always been sparse, and through the isolation of the Age of Strife it was possible that none at all had survived.

With every warp jump, Astelan always readied himself for action, for unexpected discovery, but with every jump he also hardened his expectations with the overwhelming probabilities involved in finding these far-flung outposts of humanity.

It was thus understandable that Astelan watched the data monitors in a less-than-expectant mood. As the fleet gradually converged, he subconsciously processed the scan results scrolling across dozens of screens that filled the walls of the bridge. Technicians fussed over control dials and comm-units, cursing as connections were lost, grinning to their colleagues when unexpected feedback results were received.

Astelan ignored them all, focusing entirely on one part of the main screen – the radio signature inter-cept relay. It was on that small wavering graph line that Astelan heaped his thoughts. It was a dull white line against the black of the screen, barely moving, showing nothing more than the static background hum of the universe's birth.

Four days, he told himself. Four days for a positive contact. Four days before he ordered the fleet to turn around and head outsystem for another jump. It would be a waste of time to decelerate for longer, with the attendant need to accelerate again ready for warp jump, and so he gave his hopes four days to manifest.

Already resigned to disappointment by recent experience, Astelan tore his eyes away from the radio relay and gave a nod to his second-in-command, Galedan. The captain accepted control of the bridge with a nod of his own and took the Chapter com-mander's place as Astelan turned and left.

'COMMANDER REQUESTED ON the bridge.'

Galedan's voice sounded metallic through the comm-grille of Astelan's quarters, and its flat, precise tone gave no sense of the captain's mood. Astelan was sat at his small desk, garbed in an open-fronted robe, poring over weapons manifests. There was no need to respond. Galedan would have been more specific if the Chapter commander's presence was urgently needed, and the lack of a general alarm reassured Astelan that this was probably nothing more than some routine logging or scan result requiring his authorisation.

He placed the manifests neatly into the desk's drawer and stood. A glance out of the small port showed the DX-619 star, much closer now. The dark shape of a planet could be clearly seen intruding upon the edge of the orb. That was nothing new, either. They had been closing on the world for three days now and they would reach it in two more. It was just a small shadow at the moment, like any other ball of rock they had encountered.

With a resigned weariness, Astelan made his way along the metal and plascrete innards of the ship to the bridge.

As the heavy double doors hissed open, Astelan was confronted by a scene of intense activity. The technicians were gathered in small clusters of fours and fives around certain instruments, and seemed to be checking each other's calculations and findings.

Galedan turned, and Astelan saw a glimmer in his companion's eyes and an expectant look. Unlike the Chapter commander, Galedan was in his armour, as befitted the bridge commander. Servos creaked as the captain gestured towards the main panel.

Astelan's eyes immediately fixed on the radio relay as he strode into the room. He stopped in his tracks

only three paces in. There was a spike on the small
line. It was not particularly tall, but it was a definite
abnormality. Regaining his composure, Astelan
stepped up beside Galedan. The captain turned an
inquiring look at one of the chief technicians and
received a wordless nod in reply.

'Report,' said Astelan.

'Confirmed artificial radio signature, commander,'
Galedan replied, unable to keep the hint of a smile
from his lips.

Astelan turned his attention to the chief technician,
a lanky man with thinning hair and grey stubble.

'Automated? Location?' said Astelan. A couple of
times before they had come across old beacons or
communications satellites miraculously still functioning centuries after those that had launched them
had perished.

'Fourth planet, definitely fluctuating, very likely to
be non-automated,' the technician reassured him.

'Sound general alarm,' ordered Astelan. It was a
wise precaution, but Astelan did it as much to alert
the crew that something was happening as he did out
of military prudence. 'Signal the rest of the fleet with
our findings. Rendezvous adjustment to point sigma-
absolute. Please convey an invitation to Chapter
Commander Belath to join me as soon as possible.'

FURTHER SCANNING REVEALED that the planet's inhabitants had the capability to communicate by radio,
and technicians soon confirmed that the inhabitants
were human and spoke a dialect of the Terran language. The news that the fleet had indeed discovered

an isolated human world brought Belath to the *Spear of Truth* for a meeting between the two Chapter commanders.

With the fleet at general quarters once more, Astelan stood in one of the *Spear of Truth*'s docking bays clad in his armour, awaiting the arrival of Belath. Accompanying Astelan were his three on-board company commanders and an honour guard from the First Company.

Around them the hangar was full of drop-pods, the immense shapes of Castellan-class bombers and Harbinger assault craft, as well as the hawk-like forms of five Deathbird interceptors. Racks of bombs and missiles, crates of ammunition and stacks of power packs filled much of the remaining space.

A dull clang above the Chapter commander signalled the arrival of Belath's transport. In the ceiling, gears ground into action and a breeze wafted upwards as the inner lock doors opened and the air inside the hangar was drawn up into the void above. Hydraulics wheezing, the heavy lift brought down the sleek, eagle-prowed craft, lights strobing an orange warning to those below and throwing dancing shadows around the assembled Space Marines.

As the lift descended, Astelan considered how little he knew of his visitor. This was the first opportunity that he had been granted to meet his fellow Chapter commander face-to-face. He had exchanged comm contacts with Belath but only on a very formal basis. Belath's fleet and Chapter had joined Astelan's only two weeks earlier in the Calcabrina system. Astelan had been informed by Belath that the Dark Angels' primarch, the Lion, had sent Belath to add his forces to the expedition.

Astelan knew nothing of Belath, but these days that was not surprising. The massive influx of warriors into the Legion following the rediscovery of Caliban meant that there were many commanders who had never met each other, tossed together on task forces and in warzones all across the galaxy.

That one such Chapter commander had been despatched to assist Astelan was curious for the simple fact that there had been little enough for Astelan's Chapter to do and additional forces were unlikely to change that.

'The Lion probably wants Belath to gain some experience alongside the veterans before sending him off on his own,' said Galedan, guessing his commander's thoughts by way of their long history together.

Astelan merely grunted a non-committal reply and kept his gaze upon the shuttle as the lift thudded to the hangar floor. With a hiss, the beak-like prow of the ship opened up to form a boarding ramp, and a lone power-armoured figure strode down.

To Astelan, Belath looked incredibly young, perhaps only thirty or thirty-five years old. Given that the Legion's strength had increased by almost twenty thousand in the last few years, it was no shock to see that relatively junior Astartes were occupying command positions. After contact with Caliban many company officers had been promoted to Chapter commanders over the new recruits, and it was this that had seen Astelan's own rapid rise to prominence. It had since been decided not to split the existing Terran veterans too much across the new Calibanite Chapters and so it was inevitable that some of the more recent additions would be commanded by all but untested warriors.

Belath had the pale skin and dark hair that was common to many Calibanites, though his eyes were a deep blue rather than the usual brown or grey. His hair was cropped exceptionally short, in stark contrast to Astelan's long braids, and Belath's expression was of tight-lipped solemnity.

The arrival stopped in front of Astelan and held a fist to his chest in salute. As Astelan nodded in greeting, he noticed something that caught his eye.

'What's that?' Astelan asked, pointing to a heraldic symbol on Belath's right shoulder plate, where normally a Space Marine's organisational and rank markings would be painted. It was decorated with a quartered shield, white and blue, emblazoned with a sword held in the grip of a taloned foot.

'That is the symbol of my order,' replied Belath, somewhat taken aback. 'The Order of the Raven's Wing.'

Astelan turned an inquiring look to Galedan.

'One of the knightly orders,' the captain said. 'A Calibanite rank badge.'

'And that?' said Astelan, redirecting his accusing finger to Belath's other shoulder pad, which was painted a dark green beneath the Dark Angels symbol.

'The glorious Lion El'Jonson has decreed that Calibanite warriors are to wear the green of our home world's forests,' said Belath with no small hint of defiance. 'It is to act as a remembrance of the battles fought to tame Caliban under the leadership of the Lion.'

Astelan merely nodded without comment. The two Chapter commanders stood gauging each other in silence for several heartbeats before Astelan spoke again.

'Welcome aboard the *Spear of Truth*,' he said, extending a hand. 'I am pleased to make your acquaintance.'

Belath hesitated, and then broke into a disarming smile and shook Astelan's hand.

'It is my honour and privilege,' the young Chapter commander said.

Followed by his entourage, Astelan led Belath from the docking bay into the dorsal concourse that ran the length of the *Spear of Truth*. As they headed towards a nearby conveyor, they passed open archways through which Astelan's Space Marines could be seen readying for battle. Squad upon squad of power-armoured warriors ran through weapons or maintenance drills under the stern eyes of their sergeants. Banners were carefully taken down from their honoured positions on the walls of the chambers, paint carefully applied to dents and scratches on armour and solemn oaths renewed before the symbols of the Legion.

'My Chapter is also ready to fight,' assured Belath as the group stopped before the mesh door of the conveyor.

One of the honour guards stepped forwards and pushed a broad plate on the wall. The conveyor door slid aside for the pair to enter. Astelan dismissed the escort as he stepped inside. The conveyor was a cube some ten feet by every dimension, lined with thick plascrete walls. Astelan turned two dials as Galedan, Astoric and Melian followed the two Chapter commanders.

'Are they ready *not* to fight?' asked Astelan as the door slammed shut.

The conveyor jolted into action, rapidly rising up through the decks of the battle-barge.

'I do not understand,' said Belath, raising his voice so that it could be heard over the clatter of chains and gears.

With a shudder the conveyor halted for a moment and then continued, now heading horizontally towards the prow of the battle-barge. Astelan considered his reply for a moment before speaking.

'We exist to bring the Emperor's peace to the galaxy,' said Astelan finally. 'While we may bring war to millions, we should not crave it.'

'We were created to fight,' countered Belath.

'Yes, and we are also charged with the responsibility of choosing who we fight against,' said Astelan. 'When we go to war, we must do so in the sure and utter knowledge that it is right. From this comes our wholehearted dedication to victory. We must be a terrible foe, and must do terrible things, in order that others will learn from our enemies' follies. Once unleashed, out anger cannot, and should not, be stayed. Relentless on the attack, intractable in defence, these are the hallmarks of the Astartes. Yet, it is perhaps all too easy to stir ourselves to angry war for small reason. You must remember that a world crushed beneath our heel may be resentful, and requires garrisons and resources to guard it. A world that comes freely to accept the wisdom of the Emperor must be embraced as a brother for they will add strength and not detract it.'

'We are perfected in body and mind to be the sword of the Lion,' said Belath. 'Where he directs, our blade falls. It is not our part to judge the punished, merely to administer the punishment. Let diplomats and bureaucrats argue the reasons and let us be dedicated to the annihilation of our enemies.'

As if to punctuate the young Chapter commander's remarks, the conveyor suddenly halted and a bell rang somewhere above it. Galedan opened the door and the three captains stepped out into the corridor beyond. Belath made to take a pace but Astelan laid a hand upon his arm and held him back, turning Belath to face him.

'You command more than a thousand of the finest warriors in the galaxy, as do I,' said Astelan. 'The Emperor has placed in me that power, but with it must come the judgement to wield it wisely. I do not know what you learnt about war in the Order of the Raven's Wing, but it is bloody and costly and only a fool desires it.'

'The Lion has chosen me to lead this Chapter,' said Belath, gently but insistently prising his arm from Astelan's grip. 'I have my orders from the primarch and I will not hesitate to carry them out.'

Without offering a reply Astelan strode from the conveyor and turned left along the corridor. A great double door of carved wood stood out incongruously from the plascrete walls and metal decking. The carvings were of an angular, abstract design. Astelan ran his gauntleted fingers over the lines and curves, tracing them.

'I fashioned these doors myself,' the Chapter commander said, looking at Belath. 'For many hours I laboured, copying designs from memory seen on the long halls I grew up in upon the Sibran Steppes of Terra. There is a tale in these patterns, for those who know how to read it.'

'What tale?' said Belath, his anger replaced by intrigue.

'Later,' replied Astelan reluctantly as he opened the doors. 'We have a campaign to plan.'

'Later then,' said Belath, stepping past Astelan into the room beyond.

Inside was the operations room of the *Spear of Truth*. The walls were filled with banks of blank screens and comm-units, faced by long benches as yet vacant. The thrum of latent power filled the air, waiting to turn the quiet chamber into the epicentre of a military action that could conquer worlds.

Belath gave the equipment no second glance, having similar facilities upon his own vessel, and instead strode to a huge glass-topped oval tablet at the centre of the chamber. Astelan followed him with the others and directed Astoric to activate the hololith.

The glass flickered into life, a dull grey at first but warming up to a bright green. As the captain deftly manipulated the controls, a glowing three-dimensional sphere rose up from the table, slowly rotating. The press of more buttons illuminated small patches on the surface of the globe, and flickering lights sprang up in a haphazard maze around them.

'This is the system's fourth world,' announced Astelan. 'We are currently standing out some seven hundred thousand kilometres from low orbit on the standard ecliptic plane. No visual data is yet available, but I have highlighted sources of energy spikes and radio interference. Most likely they are urbanised areas.'

'Populated?' asked Belath with considerable excitement.

'Yes, populated,' said Astelan with a smile. 'You seem to have joined us just in time. Five years we have been out in this wilderness with barely a glimmer of life to be seen. I hope you realise how fortunate you are.'

'Certainly,' said Belath. He took a deep breath and then turned to face Astelan, his fist held formally against his chest. 'With your permission I would like to lead the assault.'

Astoric and Galedan both laughed, but were quickly silenced by a look from Astelan.

'While your enthusiasm is commendable, it is a bit early to be talking of assaults,' the Chapter commander told his young peer.

'Do you plan to make contact?' asked Belath, his eyes fixed on the hololithic representation of the world.

'I have not yet decided,' said Astelan. 'It is a delicate situation.'

'As far as we can determine, the inhabitants are as yet unaware of our presence,' said Galedan, staring at the flickering three-dimensional image as if it was the world itself. 'Contact would reveal us and we would lose the element of surprise.'

Astelan nodded in agreement.

'It's a mess of communications,' he admitted. 'I do not know how we would make contact, or with whom. There appear to be no planet-wide official frequencies. It seems that we have several states and governments to deal with.'

Belath looked up at this, his face thoughtful.

'That could prove to be an advantage,' he said. 'We could introduce ourselves to one nation and deal directly with them – use them as a partner to reveal ourselves to the remaining populace.'

'But with whom would we initially ally ourselves?' said Astelan with a shake of his head. 'We have no means of determining which power bloc is dominant, if any. Such an intercession could provoke conflict between the states, even civil war.'

'We need more information before we can proceed,' said Astoric. He glanced at the others before continuing. 'Local knowledge.'

'Communications techs are analysing everything that's incoming,' said Astelan. 'We can unravel more through studying the comms-feed.'

'Why not just go and take a look?' said Belath. 'Better still, we should capture some of the inhabitants for questioning.'

'We'll need somewhere isolated,' said Galedan, peering at the hololith. He nodded in satisfaction and indicated an area on the southern continent. 'This area seems sparsely populated. There's scattered urban centres, but plenty of open space for us to land undetected.'

Astoric turned his attention to data streaming past the image of the planet.

'It will be nightfall over that part of the planet in just under three ship hours,' the captain said. 'One moon will be in recession, the other dark.'

'I will lead a short sortie to the surface to establish a ground base and gather more information,' announced Astelan. 'We'll drop tonight with a reconnaissance force and see what we can find.'

'Is that wise, commander?' asked Galedan. 'It would be more prudent if I or one of the other captains led the mission, you are too valuable to risk until we know more.'

Astelan fixed them all in turn with a fierce stare.

'It's been three years since I last set foot planetside,' he growled. 'I'm bloody well going to step onto this one first!'

As ASTELAN HAD wished it, so he was the first to step from the assault ramp of the huge Harbinger drop-transport. The drop-ship could be more likened to a small fortress than a transport, silhouetted against the cloudy sky. The outline of the drop-ship was broken by eight armoured turrets armed with lascannons. Smaller automated defences swivelled back and forth; rocket multi-launchers and anti-personnel heavy bolters peered towards the horizon with unliving eyes.

The whine of anti-grav engines caused Astelan to step aside from the ramp. Ten jetbikes swept past in pairs, their riders clad in stripped-down armour. A few metres from the drop-ship their engines erupted into piercing howls and the reconnaissance squadron fanned out swiftly. Soon the flicker of their jets disappeared into the darkness. Following closely behind, heralded by the deeper thrum of their engines, two land speeders shot from the bowels of the Harbinger, their heavy weapons ready to provide support to the bikers.

Squads of Astartes pounded down the ramps, the drop-ship trembling with the weight of dozens of booted feet upon plasteel. Squad by squad the company assembled under their captain before being dispersed to positions around the site.

Astelan cast his gaze left and right, taking in his surrounds, the landscape digitally projected onto his eyes by his helmet's auto-senses so that the dark was almost as bright as day. According to Astoric there was a medium-sized conurbation three kilometres away. The dropsite was located in a patchwork of fields separated by chest-high walls and ditches. Here and there were dotted clusters of plain buildings. To the west was a thick forest, beyond which lay the town. The fields rose up onto steep-sided hills to the north, but the rest of the terrain was open and flat. It was these long fields of fire that had contributed towards Astelan's decision to land at this point.

It was here that Astelan hoped to make contact with the planet's inhabitants.

Having been present at three other first-contact situations, he knew that the next minutes and hours

294   GAV THORPE

would be vital. Scans had shown no orbital craft,
even basic communication satellites, so the shock of
visitors arriving from space might well be considerable. Astelan had chosen this relatively small
backwater to acclimatise to the world and to act as a
gentle introduction to the natives – it was unwise to
drop armoured warriors into the heart of a planet's
major cities unless widespread panic was the desired
result.

That the world did not have space-capable craft was
surprising but not unknown. So much knowledge
had been lost during the long centuries of darkness,
many worlds had even returned to cruel barbarism
and superstition. At the moment, the world was neither friendly nor enemy, simply an intriguing enigma
that Astelan wished to swiftly unravel.

Astelan set up his command post some five hundred metres from the Harbinger inside an
abandoned farmstead. It was a set of simple cubic
constructions of plascrete, of a pattern laid down by
the standard template data seen all across the galaxy
during mankind's expansion to the stars. As other
units moved to similar positions in buildings and
along walls surrounding the dropsite, Astelan idly
mused whether other standard template construct
materiel would be found. It was not a particular concern of his, but the Mechanicum of Mars would be
interested.

The sound of a distant detonation tore Astelan from
his thoughts and he dashed outside, ducking his considerable frame beneath the low lintel of the doorway.
Amongst the trees a pall of smoke rose into the air. He

saw flashes of flame and a few moments later came the crash of more explosions.

His comm-piece crackled inside his helmet and Astelan gave the sub-vocal command that activated the pickup. It was Sergeant Argeon, the leader of the recon sweep.

'It looks like our small town is, in fact, a military installation, commander,' the sergeant reported blithely. 'I don't think they were expecting visitors.'

Astelan swore loudly. The jetbikes were almost three kilometres distant, several minutes from supporting units. Before he could make any further analysis, the keen auto-senses of his armour attracted his attention.

It was the unmistakeable whine of approaching jets.

The defence arrays on the Harbinger also detected the incoming craft and a hail of missiles streaked skywards upon trails of fire, screaming to the west. Explosions blistered in the low clouds that hung over the whole sky, but there was no way of telling if any had hit their targets.

No more than a minute later the answer came. Small black shapes appeared, a long chain of them drifting downwards towards the Harbinger. They erupted in blossoms of incendiary destruction around the drop ship and upon its hull, splashing some form of burning fuel in their wake. Evidently at least one aircraft had survived.

As the Chapter commander processed this new development, Argeon's voice was in Astelan's ear again.

'They are readying for an attack on our position,' the sergeant said. 'What are your orders?'

'Pull back a kilometre and establish a new cordon,' Astelan replied. Jetbikes were for scouting, not for mounting a resistant defence.

'Acknowledged, commander,' said Argeon.

The tactical display showed that Sergeant Cayvan was moving his three squads forwards on his own initiative, securing the boundary of the woods. Astelan left the experienced sergeant to his own devices, confident that he knew what he was doing.

'Withdrawal pattern, commander?' asked Sergeant Jak in the comm-piece.

'Not until we know what their aerial capability is,' said Astelan. There was little sense in piling the troops back onto the burning Harbinger until Astelan knew whether the enemy had the means to shoot down the transport.

A different tone signalled a message incoming from orbit.

'I have coordinates for orbital barrage confirmed.' It was Belath, his tone quiet and assured.

'Negative,' responded Astelan. 'They might not have orbital craft but we have no idea if they have ground-based defences capable of striking back. Do not give away your position.'

'I understand,' said Belath. 'I am dispensing craft for atmospheric dominance.'

'Yes, cover the landing zone and put your companies on their ships in preparation for landing,' Astelan said.

'They already are, Astelan,' replied Belath with a note of umbrage.

'Stand ready for my word then,' said Astelan.

By now the Harbinger was ablaze along half its length. Its surviving turrets were firing a near-continuous stream of anti-air rockets into the clouds. Their approach all but masked by the din, more unseen jets screeched overhead and a short while later the ground was rocked by massive explosions.

The heavy bombs tore huge craters in the grassy mud and sent plumes of stones and dirt high into the air. Several scored direct hits on the landing craft, tearing out great chunks of plasteel armour and rock-crete superstructure.

More thunderous detonations swiftly followed, the explosions much smaller than those of the bombs though more accurate and numerous. It appeared that artillery was also being brought to bear on the drop zone.

The rattle of small-arms fire drifted from the woods, interspersed with the heavier cracks of bolter rounds. Cayvan's squads were being engaged by their new enemy. Astelan swore again. He had so little information with which to construct a suitable strategy. The enemy had unknown numbers, unknown positions and unknown capabilities.

In the face of his own ignorance, the Chapter commander fell back on the principal strategy of the Astartes – attack and dominate.

'Cayvan, hold position,' Astelan barked quickly over the comm-net. 'Sergeant Argeon, I want the locations of those artillery pieces relayed to Chapter

Commander Belath. Jak, deploy your Devastators onto the hills and provide cover fire. Move the rest of your squads north and support Cayvan. Melian, stand ready to reinforce either flank.'

His warriors thus set into motion, Astelan ducked back inside the farmhouse. It was empty inside but for a few broken pieces of furniture and discarded rags. Sergeant Gemenoth had erected a tactical display unit in the centre of the main room. It was a simple vertical glass plate and projector, linked into the comm-net of the Dark Angels' battle-barge in geostationary orbit thousands of kilometres above them.

The screen showed the rough topography of the surrounding area, and the locations of Astelan's squads were marked out by symbols that juddered across the artificial battlefield. Astelan tried to match the fragmented display and the gunfire and explosions outside with the reports buzzing over his helmet's comm-link. It was no good; he still felt he had no clear picture of what was happening.

'Squads two and three, form up on my position,' he told his guards as he moved back outside.

The Dark Angels closed in on Astelan as another salvo of shells tore at the ground around the farmstead, showering them with clods of earth, shrapnel and pieces of stone clattering upon their armour. As Astelan vaulted over the low wall encompassing the group of buildings, he cast his gaze to the woods.

There was still a considerable amount of firing and detonations tore at the treetops. There seemed little threat from other directions so it was towards the forest that he led his men.

Another barrage landed around the Dark Angels as they jogged towards the treeline. Astelan felt the shockwave buffet him, while battle-brothers Rathis and Kherios were thrown from their feet by the impacts. Astelan stopped and turned with concern but the two Astartes pushed back to their feet and retrieved their bolters, their armour pitted and scored but not breached. Assured that neither was injured, Astelan continued towards the trees at a brisk pace, slipping his power sword from its sheath and unholstering his bolt pistol.

The trees were closely packed, the thick canopy of foliage swathing the woods in darkness. A few ferns broke through the leaf mould but the woods were otherwise free of undergrowth. The ground was soft underfoot and the heavy Astartes sank into the mulch, their boots leaving deep prints in the rotting leaves.

Muzzle flashes and the roar of bolters drew them to the left, and barely a hundred metres under the trees, Astelan saw the first of Cayvan's squads. The Astartes were standing just beneath the lip of a long, low ridge, trading fire with an enemy as yet out of Astelan's view. Bullets kicked up sprays of mud and pattered from the Dark Angels' armoured suits.

Astelan reached the squad, and their sergeant turned to address him.

'Sergeant Riyan is flanking to the north, Chapter commander,' the Astartes said. 'He believes several hundred attackers, maybe up to a thousand, are trying to push through to the landing site.'

'Then we must push back,' said Astelan.

He waved for the squad to follow him and stepped over the ridge. Astelan saw immediately that the enemy were using the trees and undulating ground for cover, darting into view, firing their crude automatic rifles and then ducking back out of sight.

As soon as he strode over the ridge, the intensity of fire rose sharply. The flare of gunfire seemed concentrated to his right as the fusillade tore bark from trees and slashed through low-hanging branches. He felt impacts across his chest and right shoulder but paid them no heed.

Behind him the squad advanced in two sections, one laying down a storm of bolter fire while the other advanced. The foremost Astartes then took up position and unleashed their own weapons while the rest of the squad moved up past them. The explosive-tipped bolts tore chunks out of the trees and ripped apart any enemy soldier unfortunate enough to be hit.

As they closed in, Astelan could make out his foes more clearly. They were dark-skinned and dressed in drab blue overalls. They looked more like farmhands or factory workers than soldiers, but they held their ground as the Astartes approached and their fire was both accurate and determined.

Glancing around, Astelan saw the bulky shapes of other Astartes moving in from the left and the right, pressing forwards alongside their Chapter commander.

A bullet struck Astelan's helmet, its impact knocking his head back. Dizzied by the hit he fell to one knee. Static blurred the vision in his right eye as his helmet's auto-senses attempted to recalibrate themselves.

Astelan could see indistinct shapes along a low ridge just to his right. Though half-blinded, he raised his pistol by instinct and fired off eight shots, the whole magazine, in the direction of the enemy. Two soldiers were torn apart by the bolts and the rest ducked for cover. Several seconds passed and still the vision in his right eye was fuzzy.

With a grunt, the Chapter commander stepped sideways and stood with his back to a tree. Shells were now erupting around him, blasting apart foliage and bark, and bullets whined and splintered close by. Unperturbed, Astelan stowed his weapons and then twisted the helmet free, which came away from the neck guard with a hiss of escaping gases. He hooked the helmet to the belt band of his armour.

Tasting blood, he reached up to his right cheek. There was blood on the fingertips of his gauntlet. Astelan had no idea how deep the wound was, but registered no discomfort, so he assumed it was superficial. His enhanced blood would have clotted the wound already. He calmly reloaded his bolt pistol and drew his sword again.

Astelan resumed his advance, cracking off single shots as heads and limbs moved into sight from behind the trees. At close quarters the fighting was becoming chaotic. Rounds zipped and screamed past every few seconds, though none struck him. The artillery fire was slackening, perhaps for fear of hitting their own soldiers or perhaps from some action by the Astartes. Still, a few shells were detonating close at hand, spraying Astelan with charred leaves and baked mud.

A new sound entered his consciousness: the throbbing bass note of an autocannon. The sound was reassuring, and Astelan looked to his right and saw an Astartes laying down a curtain of fire with the heavy weapon, his legs braced wide apart, a torrent of shell casings clattering off his backpack.

This proved too much for the enemy and their fire quickly diminished as fighters were driven into cover by the autocannon's fearsome torrent of fire. In the lull, the Astartes charged forwards, bolters coughing, battle cries ringing from the trees.

It seemed that Riyan's flanking manoeuvre had been successful, for the enemy were streaming away from their positions, heading back westwards, while more Astartes moved in from the north. Tongues of fire licked out through the trees from flamers, while bright lances of multilaser fire strobed with deadly effect along the foxholes and shell scrapes the enemy had dug into the ground.

The retreat turned into a rout before the fury of the Dark Angels. Some of the soldiers threw down their weapons in their flight, their panicked shouts drowned out intermittently by the crack of exploding bolter rounds, the hiss and boom of frag missiles and the distinctive snap of lascannons.

'Hold pursuit,' Astelan ordered. 'Find me a dozen wounded for prisoners.'

'Armour! Armour! Armour!' Riyan suddenly shouted over the comm. 'Tracked fighting vehicles approaching our position from the north and west.'

There was the sound of an explosion close at hand and the line buzzed with static. Another voice cut in.

'This is Brother Nikolan,' the Astartes said. 'Armour has large-calibre weapons. Sergeant Riyan is seriously wounded.'

'Jak, move up to Riyan's position and take command,' snapped Astelan.

The sergeant gave an affirmative and headed off northwards at a run. Astelan waved for the remaining Astartes to follow him to the north-west.

Within a few minutes, the growl of combustion engines drifted through the trees. Denied his autosenses, Astelan relied on the reports of his battle-brothers to identify the tanks' positions in the darkness. Exhaust plumes lit up like fireworks on their helmet displays and a steady stream of coordinates was passed across the comm-net.

The stench of oil-based fuel wafted from the west, and Astelan peered into the gloom. A moment later he saw the glaring blossom of a muzzle flash highlighting a tank less than two hundred metres away, its bulk concealed behind an outcrop of rock. The shell exploded just behind the Chapter commander and he heard cries from wounded Astartes as grit and dirt showered down onto him.

Now that he knew where it was, Astelan could make out the tank's shape a little better. It was compact, its turret seemingly oversized for its hull, with a short-barrelled cannon. Secondary weapons opened fire with flashes, and more bullets screamed past. The turret adjusted slightly and the main gun angled down towards the Dark Angels' position.

'Disperse!' bellowed Astelan, sprinting to his right. His power armour took him across the ground in huge leaps, covering half a dozen metres with every pace.

The explosion smashed apart a tree trunk just metres from where the squad had been stood. Brother Andubis was flung sideways by the detonation, smashed head-first against another tree. He sat up and raised his arm to show that he was not badly injured.

As the squad regrouped, Brother Alexian took up a firing position with his lascannon. He shouldered the anti-tank weapon like an immense sniper rifle, peering along its sight towards the hull-down tank. A beam of blinding energy spat forwards as he pressed the firing stud, smashing into the tank just above the turret ring. Flames sprang up immediately, and in their light Astelan saw helmeted figures popping the hatches and scrambling free. Two cleared the wreck before the ammunition inside ignited, blowing apart the vehicle in a spectacular detonation that sent fire and shrapnel high into the air. The light of the explosion revealed scores of soldiers were now moving back into position to attack, bolstered by their armoured support. The Astartes levelled their weapons and began to fire once more.

Over the din of bolter rounds and the burning tank, Astelan recognised a loud roar overhead: the tell-tale engines of a Castellan bomber. Explosions rippled through the blasted trees barely a hundred metres from the Astartes' positions, tearing apart scores of enemy. The rapid barking of heavy bolter fire heralded a strafing run that cut down dozens more. Satisfied with his work, the pilot banked his craft back towards the landing zone.

Astelan sent the order for the rest of the force to fall back by squads and secure the perimeter of the landing zone once more. Though the enemy attempted a counter-attack, the swift intervention of Castellans and Deathbirds pouring missiles and fire into the woods soon convinced the opposing soldiers to allow the Astartes to pull back in peace.

Back at the landing site, Astelan saw that though the enemy had suffered horrendously, the Dark Angels were not without their losses too, mostly from bombs, artillery strikes and tank guns.

Clusters of wounded Astartes sat or lay around the force's three Apothecaries, who stapled wounds, cauterised gashes and did what else they could to patch up the injured warriors until they could receive proper treatment back aboard ship. Most were back on their feet and ready to fight within minutes. Three would never fight again.

Astelan watched with grim resignation as Vandrillis, his Chief Apothecary, moved from one dead Astartes to the next. He disengaged the cables of the Astartes's backpack and pulled it aside. Vandrillis then used his reductor, a complex array of blades mounted on his forearm, to cut through the back armour plate to expose the flesh below.

The shiny, hard shell of the battle-brother's black carapace was slick with blood. Vandrillis drilled down into the flesh of the dead Astartes and then punched the reductor deep into the exposed spine. With a twist and a yank, he tore free the lower progenoid, an egg-shaped gland that stored the Astartes's gene-seed so that it could be recovered and implanted into a new recruit. Vandrillis placed the precious organ into a vacu-flask and continued his bloody work on the Astartes's neck.

Though it was a reminder of the fate of every Astartes, to die in battle, it was also reassuring. Every warrior carried within him the primarch's gene-seed and with it the means to create more Astartes. To know that even in death the Legion would be strengthened was a thought that allowed the Astartes to fight without fear, to make the noblest sacrifice without hesitation.

Astelan knew that his fate would not be on the end of a reductor, for his progenoids had matured over two decades ago and had been removed in the relative safety of a shipboard medical bay. He had made his contribution to future generations of Dark Angels and could fight now safe in the knowledge that others would be able to follow.

Turning away from the grisly scene, Astelan signalled for Gemenoth to bring him the long-range comm-array; with his helmet damaged it was the only way for Astelan to contact the fleet. He punched the frequency of Belath's battle-barge into the readout.

'Signal received, this is Belath,' the Chapter commander answered. 'What is your situation?'

'Get us off this rock,' Astelan replied.

* * *

THE WITHDRAWAL OF Astelan's landing force was to last for the rest of the night, during which the local forces tried three more times to attack the drop-zone. Under heavy air cover, three more Harbingers were brought down from Belath's fleet and the Dark Angels were able to collapse back to their transports under the covering fire of the heavy weapons and armoured support that the reconnaissance force had lacked.

Astelan was the last to leave, staring balefully at the ravaged drop-zone as the ramp closed in front of him. All he had wanted was to secure some locals for intelligence, and now he had overseen a significant battle. In the dim light of dawn he looked at the ravaged forests and crater-pocked field that had been the battleground. This did not bode well for a peaceful introduction to the Enlightenment of the Emperor.

HE WAS NOT surprised to find Belath aboard the *Spear of Truth's* operations room, awaiting his arrival.

'We must move fast and regain the initiative,' said Belath. 'We have lost the element of surprise and even now the armed forces of the world will be at full readiness. The more time we give them, the harder the battles ahead.'

'What are you proposing?' asked Astelan, his gaze directed towards the glowing orb above the hololith.

'While you were sparring with the locals, I conducted more analysis of the transmissions data,' said Belath, leaning with his fists on the edge of the glass tablet, his eyes fixed on Astelan. 'The locals refer to the world as Byzanthis. There are six continents, each in essence a separate nation-state. We strike at each state simultaneously, dropping from orbit into their capitals. We disable their governments and military command within hours, and isolate power and transport networks in a matter of days.'

'Divide and conquer?' said Astelan, finally meeting the stare of Belath.

Before Belath could answer, the door hissed open and Galedan strode in.

'You should listen to this,' he said, crossing to the comms centre. As he dialled in a frequency a tinny voice crackled from the speakers.

'–ed. Unwarranted attack on the sovereign territory of Confederate Vanz will not be tolerated,' the voice was saying. 'Byzanthis Committee of Nations has convened to decide a response. Confederate Vanz will not stand alone. Aggressor strangers will be resisted. Unwarran–'

'It's a looped message on a broad range of frequencies,' said Galedan, switching off the unit.

'We can reply?' asked Astelan.

'Of course,' said Galedan.

'This is a distraction,' said Belath. 'We need to strike now!'

'We have a means to make peaceful contact,' said Astelan. 'Why choose to ignore it?'

'There is little sense of a planetary nationhood,' Belath argued. 'Two states are currently at war, the others have all fought against one another on and off over the past centuries. Crush each state individually and the world falls.'

'There is a global council, this Committee of Nations,' said Astelan. 'The situation is easily retrieved through them.'

'Diplomats and ambassadors for the most part,' countered Belath. 'You have not heard what I have heard. The Committee of Nations is considered weak and ineffective. They have no real power or control.'

'Then we will give them that power,' said Astelan. 'We shall make amends for the inadvertent conflict and communicate with the council. The state governments will be forced to treat with us through the Committee of Nations, and from that we will forge a common fate for the whole planet.'

'And if they refuse?' said Belath, straightening. 'We simply give them more time to swell their armies. Not only will more delays give these forces time to build their strength, they will spread propaganda about their supposed victory over us.'

'It does not strike me as right that we give these people no chance for a peaceful solution,' argued Astelan. 'What would history think of us? What would Caliban be now if the Emperor had come with a closed fist rather than an open hand?'

'Caliban is different,' said Belath.

'Because it is your world?' said Astelan, pacing towards Belath.

'Because we have the Lion,' said Belath confidently. 'The Emperor had no choice but to treat with us. Any invasion would have been costly and counter-productive.'

'And so because no primarch dwells here, we should offer them no choice?' snarled Astelan, stepping right in front of Belath, who stood his ground. 'Their blood, their lives, are worth less because of a chance of fate?'

'It was not chance that brought the Lion to Caliban,' said Belath with quiet assurance. 'Destiny brought our leader to us.'

Astelan did not speak for a moment and stepped back, rubbing the sweat from his forehead with the back of his hand.

'I will contact the Committee of Nations and explain our peaceful intentions,' Astelan said finally. 'Galedan, make preparations.'

The captain left the room, casting a wary glance at Belath as he walked past.

'I cannot consent to this course of action,' said Belath as soon as the door had hissed shut. He raised a placating hand before Astelan could respond. 'It is clear we cannot agree on this. We must send word to the primarch for guidance, so that his orders might be understood by us.'

Astelan laughed but there was no mirth in tone.

'We are Chapter commanders of the Dark Angels,' he said scornfully. 'We cannot run to the Lion or the Emperor every occasion that we face difficulty. We are leaders of an Astartes Legion. We must act, not vacillate. If you wish to cry off to Caliban, then you are free to leave. I am staying here and contacting the council.'

'This is a war of reconquest,' spat Belath. 'What we are building is more important than the lives of a few men, larger than the sacrifice of thousands, even millions. You are soft, and I wonder what the Lion will make of your lack of courage.'

With a wordless shout Astelan seized Belath by the edges of his breastplate and charged him into the wall, plascrete cracking under the impact.

'Your lack of respect will not be tolerated,' snarled Astelan.

'Nor yours,' replied Belath calmly, his blue eyes piercing in their intensity.

'I fought for the Emperor and he chose me to be the tip of his spear,' said Astelan, his tone low and measured. 'My Chapter has fought on a dozen worlds against foes the like of which you have no comprehension. We have earnt battle honours given to us by the Emperor of Mankind, and I have earnt his respect and praise.'

'I too have my honours,' replied Belath with no sign of trepidation. 'I was the first of my order to be chosen by the Astartes, I am the first to be made Chapter commander. I have been raised on traditions far older than your Legion, Terran. Many generations of my forefathers fought for the Order of the Raven's Wing and their blood flows in my veins. You may look down in dismay at the heritage of Caliban, but it is your home now. Its people will be your people. It is the world of the Lion, and his traditions shall be the traditions of the Dark Angels. It is by his judgement that I mark my worth, not by yours.'

Astelan released his grip and sighed.

'I say not these things to insult your heritage, nor as a threat, but as a warning,' the Chapter commander said quietly. 'Be ready for battle at all times, but do not rush heedlessly towards it. It is not just the lives of those below that you condemn, but some of your own. Your battle-brothers will shed their blood in this cause, and some will lay their lives upon its altar for you. Do you not owe it to them to make sure that what you do is righteous and unavoidable?'

Belath turned away and walked towards the door. He stooped just short of it and turned.

'It was your mistake that has precipitated this situation,' he declared. 'I cannot forgive that but I shall allow you the chance to redeem yourself. You have seniority and I would not have it known that I abandoned a battle-brother.'

With that he opened the door and strode out, leaving Astelan with his dark thoughts.

ASTELAN CAST HIS gaze upwards in frustration, his fists clenched. He was sat at the main comms panel of the operations room, with Galedan, Belath and a horde of technicians on hand. He had spent the greater part of the last two days dealing with various Byzanthisian functionaries in his attempts to organise a delegation; two days spent talking to bureaucrats and politicians had left his patience very thin. Now he was finally talking to somebody who had the power to convene the Committee of Nations.

'There was no premeditated attack,' he repeated, forcing himself to remain calm. 'I only acted to defend my men.'

There was a pause while his message was transmitted. A few seconds passed before the response came from the planet below.

'What assurances do you give that you do not "defend" yourselves again?' the voice of Secretary

Maoilon hissed from the speakers. 'You expect to land troops at a military base and not consider it provocation?'

'Our choice of landing site was an error that I deeply regret,' said Astelan, and never had he felt the truth of his own words so strongly. 'I will attend a meeting of your committee and explain everything. All of your questions are best answered face-to-face.'

Again there was a pause filled with static.

'You alone will come?' asked Maoilon. 'Unarmed?'

'I and my fellow commander,' said Astelan. 'Two of us. Unarmed. Transmit the location of the chambers and a time suitable for the meeting.'

'Treachery will be dealt with harshly,' said Maoilon.

'There will be no treachery,' said Astelan and then he signalled for the radio link to be cut. He swivelled in his chair to face Galedan. 'Organise whatever needs to be organised. Belath and I will teleport in.'

'We should have squads ready to follow us,' said Belath. 'They will be able to deploy within moments onto our location should the locals attack us.'

Astelan considered arguing, but from the expression on Belath's face he had already made his decision.

'Do what you will as precaution, but you will accompany me unarmed,' said Astelan.

'Agreed,' said Belath.

CRACKLING ENERGY SWATHED Astelan, bathing the Chapter commander and his squad in an actinic glare as the teleporter activated. Astelan felt the usual jarring dislocation and a burning sensation throughout his whole body. In milliseconds the transition was over, but just like the *Spear of Truth* emerging from the warp, Astelan needed a moment to gather his wits.

He blinked rapidly to clear his fogged vision and found himself in a wide circular hall built from white marble, or some similar local stone. It was a circular amphitheatre in layout, with rows of seats ranged around the low central platform on which he was stood. Five sets of steps led up to tall, narrow double doors spaced evenly around the hall's circumference. Halfway between each set of doors were windows of the same proportion through which Astelan glimpsed a deep-blue sky.

The hall was filled with people, some dressed in strangely cut suits, others in bright robes or simple smocks. There were all manner of different skin colours and features, jewellery and headdresses, but the hundreds packed into the auditorium had one thing in common: the absolute terror written upon their faces.

Most were wide-eyed and open-mouthed, some were visibly shaking and sweating and others were on their feet or cramming themselves into the backs of their chairs in an effort to put as much distance between themselves and their new arrivals.

A few moments later more teleporter energy crackled across the floor to Astelan's left, and where there had been empty air now stood Belath. He was dressed, as was Astelan, in simple robes of black. At his right ear Belath wore a comm-piece and Astelan could see that it was on open transmission; the Chapter commander's troops in orbit would hear everything said.

Astelan raised his arms out and held his palms up to show that he held no weapon.

'I am Chapter Commander Astelan of the Dark Angels Legion.' Astelan's voice boomed out and rebounded from the walls and ceiling, carrying easily to every part of the broad chamber. 'I am here as the representative of the Emperor of Mankind. Who here has authority to speak with me?'

The assembled delegates glanced nervously at each other until an elderly man limped forwards, a walking cane in his right hand. He was bald but for a few wisps of hair and a thin beard that hung to his chest. His skin was like dried leather and a cataract scarred his left eye. The remaining good eye regarded Astelan with a mixture of apprehension and awe.

The elderly man hobbled forwards to stand in front of the giant Astartes. Astelan was almost two feet taller than the man who stood before him, and his broad body could have contained his frail frame ten times over. The man stood regarding the newcomer with his good eye, and Astelan returned his stare with a steady gaze.

'I am Chairman Paldrath Grane,' said the man. His voice was strong and unwavering, utterly at odds with his physical condition. 'I speak for the Committee of Nations, but others will speak for their own.'

'Your world is but one of many thousands spread across the stars,' Astelan said, speaking slowly and clearly. 'The ancient empire of man was shattered, but a new power has arisen. From ancient Terra the Emperor of Mankind now builds a new galaxy upon the remnants of the old. Humanity unites under his leadership and benefits from his protection.'

'Of ancient Terra, we know not,' said Grane. 'Old worlds, old star empires, this we recall in our most prized histories. You come with war and offer peace. What right has your Emperor to rule Byzanthis?'

'By his own power and destiny has he been chosen to lead us,' said Astelan. 'Prosperity, technology and peace will be yours if you embrace the Emperor's Enlightenment.'

'And if we refuse?' This was from an equally ancient man sat in the front row of seats just to Astelan's left. The Chairman turned with a scowl, which was returned in kind.

'Identify yourself,' said Belath, stepping forwards.

'President Kinloth of Confederate Vanz,' the man replied. Though old, he was more sturdily built than Grane, with a full head of short grey hair and a close-cropped beard. His eyes were sunken and ringed with dark lines and his teeth much stained. 'It was my army you attacked four days ago.'

'A misunderstanding, it was not our intent to fight but to make peaceful contact,' said Astelan.

'And what peace you bring to families of two thousand, seven hundred and eighty men killed?' demanded Kinloth. 'What peace you bring to one thousand, six hundred and fifteen more that lie in hospitals?'

'The peace of the knowledge that no more need die here,' said Belath.

'They will be remembered for their sacrifices and gloried by the Emperor's servants,' said Astelan quickly, hiding his annoyance. 'None fall in the Emperor's service and go neither unheeded nor unremarked, nor their families unrewarded.'

'If what you say is true, Confederate Vanz will welcome your Emperor when he arrives,' Kinloth said. His eyes had lit up at the mention of reward and it was clear he saw some personal gain in the unfolding events.

'Lashkar Kerupt will not welcome your Emperor,' said another dignitary, a short middle-aged woman in a flowing silken red dress embroidered with butterfly designs. Her dark hair was bound into a tight knot, and her face was painted with yellow and her lips with black. She stood and turned to address those behind her.

'Listen to me!' she cried out. 'Strangers come with hand offering peace while holding gun behind backs. Our astro-stations detect strangers' ships above our cities. Warships intent on destroying. Strangers come to kill or enslave our world. We must take hostages to guarantee freedom.'

Astelan darted a glance towards Belath at the mention of ships in orbit above the world's cities, but the Chapter commander gave no acknowledgement.

'Seize them!' cried the woman and the doors were flung open. From entrances all around the hall black-unformed soldiers burst into the room, stubby carbines in their hands.

'Wait!' Astelan shouted, both a warning to the soldiers and a command to Belath.

'Protect your commanders!' snapped Belath, his eyes regarding Astelan with cold hostility.

No more than two seconds after his command, the air around the pair snapped with energy. Bulky figures shimmered into view encircling the pair; ten massively armoured Terminators raised their combi-bolters and opened fire. The initial salvo was devastating, tearing holes in chests, ripping off limbs and decapitating by the score. Such desultory return fire as existed pinged harmlessly from the inches-thick ceramite-and-adamantium bonded shells of the warriors' armour.

'Withdraw,' said Astelan as bullets skipped from the tiled floor and plucked at his robe.

Facing foes coming at them from every direction, the Terminators formed a defensive ring and began to walk towards one of the doorways. Hysterical shouting and panicked shrieks mixed with the deafening crash of combi-bolters. The delegates clawed and kicked at each other as they streamed away from the Astartes. Some snatched up weapons from fallen soldiers but were blasted apart in turn. Stepping over blasted and blistered bodies, the Astartes retreated up the steps, through the doorway and into the room beyond.

They were in some form of small antechamber, filled with soldiers. As the Astartes entered, the soldiers turned and fled without firing a shot. Two Terminators moved forwards to secure the other doorway, and for the moment Astelan found himself in a centre of calm.

'They detected your ships!' he bellowed at Belath. 'I told you not to move without my command!'

'I have made no move as yet,' Belath replied calmly. 'Drop forces stand by to respond to my command. I await your consent.'

Astelan opened his mouth but said nothing, unable to give voice to the mixture of rage and incredulity that was boiling up inside.

'Should I strike now or shall we withdraw again?' Belath asked, his voice barely heard by Astelan through the thundering of his heartbeat in his ears.

'What?' Astelan said.

'Shall I order the attack or shall we teleport back to orbit?' Belath said. 'All of their leaders are here. Those who wish to surrender can do so now. Those that wish to fight will face the consequences of their decisions.'

'This is how you wanted it to happen, isn't it?' said Astelan.

'I had no idea the natives were capable of detecting a vessel in low orbit,' said Belath. 'However, we cannot rectify that and should act as necessary to preserve our troops and foster victory. To delay further would be a grave error.'

Astelan took a few paces back and forth, his brow creased in a frown as he considered what to do. Eyes narrowed with anger, he turned his glare upon Belath.

'Do it!' Astelan snapped. 'Order the assault!'

Belath nodded, showing no signs of emotion. He turned away and whispered something into his comm-piece.

'It is done,' Belath said, turning his attention back to Astelan. 'What of the council?'

'I fear there is little to be salvaged here,' said Astelan.

The two of them pushed past the Terminators guarding the door back to the main chamber, whose weapons had been silent for more a minute. The council hall was a scene of utter ruin. The marble was slicked with blood, chairs smashed and bodies, of soldier and delegate, were piled up around the doors. Some still moved, groaning from their wounds. Slumped at the bottom of a flight of steps was Grane, a fist-sized hole in his lower back. Astelan crossed the chamber to gaze down at the decrepit Chairman. There was no sign of life.

A thunderous rumble shook the floor and Astelan looked up sharply. Another followed swiftly after, shaking the entire hall and sending dust and shards of stone showering down from the ceiling above.

'It has begun,' said Belath, gesturing towards a high window. Astelan followed his pointing finger and gazed outside.

As he walked towards the window Astelan could see fire raining down from the heavens as the ship lying in space above unleashed its bombardment. The city stretched for kilometres in every direction around the hill upon which the council chambers sat. Avenues of high buildings radiated outwards and long terraces of houses clung upon steep hills in the distance. Plasma warheads detonated upon the boulevards and bombardment cannon shells obliterated parks and tenements.

After several minutes the devastating torrent of fury abated. Astelan looked upwards and saw the dark shadows of drop-ships growing in size. On fiery tails drop-pods screamed downwards, slamming into the roofs of buildings and smashing into cracked and burning streets. Their doors opened like armoured petals and the Astartes within disembarked with bolter and flamer. Astelan could hear nothing from here but could imagine the crack of bolter and the screams of the dying.

The wrath of the Dark Angels had been set free.

Belath stepped up to the window and gazed out, the fires reflected in his eyes. He turned his head and looked at Astelan.

'The cities will be under our control within hours,' he said. 'The world, in a few days.'

'The blood of all who die is on your hands,' said Astelan. 'I will not let this go unpunished.'

Belath smiled at that moment, and it was a hard, emotionless expression that chilled Astelan to see it.

'You do not decide guilt or punishment,' said the young Chapter commander. 'My astropaths already send word to Caliban of what occurs here. You will soon learn the consequences of disobedience, Terran.'

THE LAST CHURCH

Graham McNeill

MIDNIGHT SERVICES HAD once been crowded at the Church of the Lightning Stone. Fear of the darkness had drawn people in search of sanctuary in a way the daylight could not. For as long as anyone could remember, the dark had been a time of blood, a time when raiders attacked, monstrous engines descended on wings of fire and the violence of the warlike thunder giants was fiercest.

Uriah Olathaire remembered seeing an army of those giants as it marched to battle, when he had been little more than a child. Though seven decades had passed since then, Uriah could picture them as though it were yesterday: towering brutes who carried swords of caged lightning and were clad in plumed helmets and burnished plate the colour of a winter sunset.

But most of all, he remembered the terrible magnificence of their awesome, unstoppable power.

Nations and rulers had been swept away in the dreadful wars these giants made, entire armies drowned in blood as they clashed in battles the likes of which had not been seen since the earliest ages of the world.

Now the fighting was over, the grand architect of this last world war emerging from the host of toppled despots, ethnarchs and tyrants to stand triumphant on a world made barren by conflict.

An end to war should have been a wondrous thing, but the thought gave Uriah no comfort as he shuffled along the nave of his empty church. He carried a flickering taper, the small flame wavering in the cold wind sighing through the cracks in the stonework and the ancient timbers of the great doors to the narthex.

Yes, the midnight service had once been popular, but few now dared come to his church, such was the ridicule and scorn heaped upon them. Changed days from the beginning of the war, when fearful people had sought comfort in his promises of a benign divinity watching over them.

He held his gnarled claw of a hand around the fragile flame as he made his way towards the altar, fearful that this last illumination would be snuffed out if his concentration slipped even a little bit. Lightning flashed outside, imparting a momentary electric glow to the stained-glass windows of the church. Uriah wondered if any of his last remaining parishioners would brave the storm to pray and sing with him.

The cold slipped invisibly into his bones like an unwelcome guest and he felt something singular about this night, as though something of great import were happening, but he couldn't grasp it. He shook off the sensation as he reached the altar and ascended the five steps.

At the centre of the altar sat a broken timepiece of tarnished bronze with a cracked glass face, and a thick, leather-bound book surrounded by six unlit candles. Uriah carefully applied the taper to each candle, gradually bringing forth a welcome light to the church.

Aside from the magnificence of the ceiling, the interior of his church was relatively plain and in no way exceptional: a long nave flanked by simple timber pews and which was crossed by a transept that led to a curtained-off chancel. Upper cloisters could be reached via stairs in the north and south transepts, and a wide narthex provided a gallery prior to a visitor entering the church itself.

As the light grew, Uriah smiled with grim humour as the light shone upon the ebony face of the bronze timepiece. Though the glass face was cracked, the delicate hands were unscathed, fashioned from gold with inlaid mother-of-pearl. The clock's internal mechanisms were visible through a glass window near its base, toothed cogs that never turned and copper pendulums that never swung.

Uriah had travelled the globe extensively as a feckless youth, and had stolen the clock from an eccentric craftsman who lived in a silver palace in the mountains of Europa. The palace had been filled with thousands of bizarre timepieces, but it was gone now, destroyed in one of the many battles that

swept across the continent as grand armies fought
without care for the wondrous things lost in their
violent spasms of war.

Uriah suspected the clock was perhaps the last of
its kind, much like his church.

As he had fled the palace of time, the craftsman
had cursed Uriah from a high window, screaming
that the clock was counting down to doomsday and
would chime when the last days of mankind's existence were at hand. Uriah had laughed off the
man's ravings and presented the clock to his
bemused father as a gift. But after the blood and
fire of Gaduaré, Uriah had retrieved the clock from
the ruins of his family home and brought it to the
church.

The clock had made no sound since that day, yet
Uriah still dreaded hearing its chimes.

He blew out the taper and placed it in a shallow
bowl at the front of the altar and sighed, resting his
hand on the soft leather of the book's cover. As
always, the presence of the book was a comfort and
Uriah wondered what was keeping the few faithful
that remained in the town below from his doors
this night. True, his church stood at the summit of
a high, flat-topped mountain that was difficult to
climb, but that never usually stopped his dwindling
congregation from coming.

In ages past, the mountain had been the tallest
peak upon a storm-lashed island shrouded in mists
and linked to the mainland by a sleek bridge of silver, but ancient, apocalyptic wars had boiled away
many of the oceans, and the island was now simply

a rocky promontory jutting from a land that was said to have once ruled the world.

In truth, the church's very isolation was likely all that had allowed it to weather the storm of so-called *reason* sweeping the globe at the behest of its new master.

Uriah ran a hand over his hairless scalp, feeling the dry, mottled texture of his skin and the long scar that ran from behind his ear to the nape of his neck. He turned towards the doors of his church as he heard noises from outside, the tramp of feet and the sound of voices.

'About time,' he said, looking back at the clock and its immobile hands.

It was two minutes to midnight.

THE GRAND DOORS of the narthex opened wide and a cold wind eagerly slipped inside, whipping over the neat rows of pews and disturbing the dusty silk and velvet banners that hung from the upper cloisters. The ever-present rain fell in soaking sheets beyond the doors and a crack of lightning blistered the night sky alongside a peal of thunder.

Uriah squinted and pulled his silk chasuble around him to keep the cold from his arthritic bones. A hooded figure was silhouetted in the doorway to the narthex, tall and swathed in a long cloak of scarlet. Uriah could see the orange glow of burning brands carried by a host of shadowy figures who stood behind him in the rain. He squinted at these figures, but his aged eyes could make out no detail beyond firelight glittering on metal.

Displaced mercenaries looking for plunder?

Or something else entirely…

The hooded figure stepped into the church and turned to shut the doors behind him. His movements were unhurried and respectful, the doors closed softly and with care.

'Welcome to the Church of the Lightning Stone,' said Uriah, as the stranger turned towards him. 'I was about to begin the midnight service. Would you and your friends wish to join me?'

'No,' said the man, pulling back his hood to reveal a stern, but not unkind face – a remarkably unremarkable face that seemed at odds with his martial bearing. 'They would not.'

The man's skin was leathery and tanned from a life spent outdoors, his hair dark and pulled back into a short scalp-lock.

'That is a shame,' said Uriah. 'My midnight service is considered quite popular in these parts. Are you sure they won't come in?'

'I'm sure,' repeated the man. 'They are quite content without.'

'Without what?' quipped Uriah, and the man smiled.

'It is rare to find a man like you with a sense of humour. I have found that most of your kind are dour and leaden-hearted men.'

'My kind?'

'Priests,' said the man, almost spitting the word as though its very syllables were a poison to him.

'Then I fear you have met only the wrong kind,' said Uriah.

'Is there a right kind?'

'Of course,' said Uriah. 'Though given the times we live in, it would be hard for any servant of the divine to be of good cheer.'

'Very true,' said the man as he moved slowly down the aisle, running his hands over the timber of each pew as he passed. Uriah walked stiffly from the altar to approach the man, feeling his pulse quicken as he sensed a tangible threat lurking just beneath the newcomer's placid exterior, like a rabid dog on a slowly fraying rope.

This was a man of violence, and though Uriah felt no threat from him, he knew there was something dangerous about him. Uriah fixed a smile and extended his hand, saying, 'I am Uriah Olathaire, last priest of the Church of the Lightning Stone. Might I have your name?'

The man smiled and shook his hand. A moment of sublime recognition threatened to surface within Uriah's mind, but it was gone before he could grasp it.

'My name is not important,' said the man. 'But if you wish to call me something, you may call me Revelation.'

'An unusual name for one who professes a dislike of priests.'

'Perhaps, but one that suits my purposes for the time being.'

'And what purpose might that be?' asked Uriah.

'I wish to talk to you,' said Revelation. 'I wish to learn what keeps you here when the world is abandoning beliefs in gods and divinity in the face of the advances of science and reason.'

The man looked up, past the banners to the incredible ceiling of the church, and Uriah felt the unease that crawled over his flesh recede as the man's features softened at the sight of the images painted there.

'The great fresco of Isandula.' said Uriah. 'A divine work, wouldn't you agree?'

'It is quite magnificent,' agreed the man, 'but divine? I don't think so.'

'Then you have not looked closely enough,' answered Uriah, looking up and feeling his heart-beat quicken as it always did when he saw the wondrous fresco completed over a thousand years ago, by the legendary Isandula Verona. 'Open your heart to its beauty and you will feel the spirit of god move within you.'

The ceiling was entirely covered in a series of wide panels, each one depicting a different scene; nude figures disporting in a magical garden; an explosion of stars; a battle between a golden knight and a silver dragon; and myriad other scenes of a similarly fantastical nature.

Despite the passage of centuries and the fitful lighting, the vibrancy of hues, the fictive architecture, the muscular anatomy of the figures, the dynamic motion, the luminous colouration and the haunting expressions of the subjects were as awe-inspiring as they had been on the day Isandula had set down her brush and allowed herself to die.

'And the whole world came running when the fresco was revealed,' quoted Revelation, his gaze lingering on the panel depicting the knight and the dragon. 'And the sight of it was enough to reduce all who saw it to stunned silence.'

'You have read your Vastari,' said Uriah.

'I have,' agreed Revelation, only reluctantly tearing his gaze from the ceiling. 'His works are often given to hyperbole, but in this case he was, if anything, understating the impact.'

'You are a student of art?' asked Uriah.

'I have studied a great many things in my life,' said Revelation. 'Art is but one of them.'

Uriah pointed to the central image of the fresco, that of a wondrous being of light surrounded by a halo of golden machinery.

'Then you cannot argue that this is not a work truly inspired by a higher power.'

'Of course I can,' said Revelation. 'This is a sublime work whether any higher power exists or not. It does not *prove* the existence of anything. No gods ever created art.'

'In an earlier age, some might have considered such a sentiment blasphemy.'

'Blasphemy,' said Revelation with a wry smile, 'is a victimless crime.'

Despite himself, Uriah laughed. 'Touché, but surely only an artist moved by the divine could create such beauty?'

'I disagree,' said Revelation. 'Tell me, Uriah, have you seen the great cliff sculptures of the Mariana Canyon?'

'No,' said Uriah, 'though I have heard they are incredibly beautiful.'

'They are indeed. Thousand-metre-high representations of their kings, carved in stone that no weapon can mark or drill can cut. They are at least as incredible as this fresco, somehow worked into a cliff that had not seen sunlight in ten thousand years, yet a godless people carved them in a forgotten age. True art needs no divine explanation, it is just art.'

'You have your opinion,' said Uriah politely. 'I have mine.'

'Isandula was a genius and a magnificent artist, that much is beyond question,' continued Revelation, 'but she also had to make a living, and even magnificent artists must take commissions where they are to be found. I have no doubt this undertaking paid very well, for the churches of her time were obscenely wealthy organisations, but had she been asked to paint a ceiling for a palace of secular governance, might she not have painted something just as wondrous?'

'It's possible, but we shall never know.'

'No, we won't,' agreed Revelation, moving past Uriah towards the altar. 'And I am tempted to believe there is an element of jealousy whenever people invoke the divine to explain away such wonderful creations.'

'Jealousy?'

'Absolutely,' said Revelation. 'They cannot believe another human being can produce such sublime works of art when they cannot. Therefore some deity reached into the artist's brain and inspired it.'

'That is a very cynical view of humanity,' said Uriah.

'Elements of it, yes,' said Revelation.

Uriah shrugged and said, 'This has been an interesting discussion, but you must excuse me, friend Revelation. I have to prepare for my congregation.'

'No one is coming,' said Revelation. 'It is just you and I.'

Uriah sighed. 'Why are you really here?'

'This is the last church on Terra,' said Revelation. 'History will soon be done with places like this and I want a memory of it before it's gone.'

'I *knew* this was going to be an unusual evening,' said Uriah.

URIAH AND REVELATION repaired to the vestry and sat opposite one another at a grand mahogany desk carved with intertwining serpents. The chair creaked under the weight of his guest as Uriah reached into the desk and removed a tall bottle of dusty blue glass and a pair of pewter tumblers.

He poured dark red wine for the pair of them and sat back in his chair.

'Your good health,' said Uriah, raising his tumbler.

'And yours,' replied Revelation.

Uriah's guest took a sip of the wine and nodded his head appreciatively.

'This is very good wine. It's old.'

'You have a fine appreciation of wine, Revelation,' said Uriah. 'My father gave it to me on my fifteenth birthday and said I should drink it on my wedding night.'

'And you never married?'

'Never found anyone willing to put up with me. I was a devilish rogue back then.'

'A devilish rogue who became a priest,' said Revelation. 'That sounds like a tale.'

'It is,' said Uriah, 'But some wounds run deep and it does no good to reopen them.'

'Fair enough,' said Revelation, taking another drink of wine.

Uriah regarded his visitor over the top of his tumbler. Now that Revelation had sat down, he had removed his scarlet cloak and draped it over the back of his chair. His guest wore utilitarian clothes, identical to those worn by virtually every inhabitant of Terra, save that his were immaculately clean. He wore a silver ring on his right index finger, which bore a seal of some kind, but Uriah couldn't make out what device was worked upon it.

'Tell me, Revelation, what did you mean when you said this place would soon be gone?'

'Exactly what I said,' replied Revelation. 'Even perched all the way up here, you must surely have heard of the Emperor and his crusade to stamp out all forms of religion and belief in the supernatural. Soon his forces will come here and tear this place down.'

'I know,' said Uriah sadly. 'But it makes no difference to me. I believe what I believe and no amount of hectoring from some warmongering despot will alter my beliefs.'

'That is an obstinate point of view,' said Revelation.

'It is faith,' pointed out Uriah.

'Faith,' snorted Revelation. 'A willing belief in the unbelievable without proof...'

'What makes faith so powerful is that it requires no proof. Belief is enough.'

Revelation laughed. 'I see now why the Emperor wants rid of it then. You call faith powerful, I call it dangerous. Think of what people in the grip of faith have done in the past, all the atrocities committed down the centuries by people of faith. Politics has slain its thousands, yes, but religion has slain its millions.'

Uriah finished his wine and said, 'Have you come here just to provoke me? I am no longer a violent man, but I do take kindly to being insulted in my own home. If this is all you are here for, then I wish you to go now.'

Revelation placed his tumbler back down on the desk and held up his hands.

'You are right, of course,' he said. 'I am being discourteous, and I apologise. I came here to learn of this place, not to antagonise its guardian.'

Uriah nodded graciously. 'I accept your apology, Revelation. You wish to see the church?'

'I do.'

'Then come with me,' said Uriah, rising painfully from behind his desk, 'and I will show you the Lightning Stone.'

URIAH LED REVELATION from the vestry back into the nave of the church, once again looking up at the beautiful fresco on the ceiling. Shards of firelight danced beyond the stained glass of the windows, and Uriah knew that a sizeable group of men waited beyond the walls of his church.

Who was this Revelation and why was he so interested in his church?

Was he one of the Emperor's warlords, here to earn
his master's favour by demolishing the last church on
Terra? Perhaps he was a mercenary chief who sought
to earn the new master of Terra's gratitude by destroying icons of a faith that had endured since the earliest
days of mankind's struggle towards civilisation?

Either way, Uriah needed to know more of this Revelation, to keep him talking and learn what he could
of his motives.

'This way,' said Uriah, shuffling towards the chancel, an area behind the altar that was curtained off
from the rest of the church by a rich emerald drape
the size of a theatre curtain. He pulled a silken cord
and the drape slid aside to reveal a high, vaulted
chamber of pale stone in which stood a tall megalith
that rose from the centre of a circular pit in the
ground.

The stone was napped like flint and had a distinct,
glassy and metallic texture to its surface. The mighty
stone was around six metres tall and tapered towards
the top, such that it resembled an enormous speartip.
The stone reared up from the ground, the tiled floor
of the pit laid around it. Patches of wiry, rust-
coloured bracken clustered at its base.

'The Lightning Stone,' said Uriah proudly, descending a set of stairs built into the ceramic-tiled walls of
the pit to place a hand on the stone. He smiled, feeling the moist warmth of it.

Revelation followed Uriah into the pit, his gaze
travelling the length of the stone as he circled it

appreciatively. He too reached out to touch it and said, 'So this is a holy stone?'

'It is, yes,' said Uriah.

'Why?'

'What do you mean? Why what?'

'I mean why is it holy? Was it deposited on the ground by your god? Was a holy man martyred here, or did a young girl receive some revelation while praying at its base?'

'Nothing like that,' said Uriah, trying to keep the irritation from his voice. 'Thousands of years ago, a local holy man who was deaf and blind was walking in the hills hereabouts when a sudden storm came in over the western ocean. He hurried back down to the village below, but it was a long way and the storm broke before he could reach safety. The holy man took shelter from the storm in the lee of the stone and at the height of the storm it was struck by a bolt of lightning from the heavens. He was lifted up and saw the stone wreathed in a blue fire in which he saw the face of the Creator and heard His voice.'

'Didn't you say this holy man was deaf and blind?' said Revelation.

'He was, but the power of god cured him of his afflictions,' said Uriah. 'He immediately ran back to the village and told the people there of the miracle.'

'And then what happened?'

'The holy man returned to the Lightning Stone and instructed the townspeople to build a church around it. The story of his healing soon spread and within a few years, thousands were crossing the silver bridge to visit the shrine, for a spring had begun to flow from the base of the stone and its waters were said to be imbued with healing properties.'

'Healing properties?' asked Revelation. 'It could cure diseases? Mend broken limbs?'

'So the church records say,' said Uriah. 'This bathing chamber was built around the stone and people came from across the lands to bathe in the sacred waters while they still flowed.'

'I knew of a similar place far to the east of this land,' said Revelation. 'A young girl claimed to have seen a holy vision of a woman, a holy woman that bore a conspicuous similarity to a religious order of which her aunt was a member. Bathing houses were set up there too, but the men that ran the site were afraid the output of their holy spring would be insufficient, so they only changed the water in the pools twice a day. Hundreds of dying and diseased pilgrims passed through the same water every day, so you can imagine what a horrible slop it was at the end: threads of blood, sloughed-off skin, scabs, bits of cloth and bandage, an abominable soup of ills. The miracle was that anyone emerged alive from this human slime at all, let alone was cured of anything.'

Revelation reached out to touch the stone once more, and Uriah saw him close his eyes as he laid his palm flat on the glistening stone.

'Haematite from a banded ironstone formation,' said Revelation. 'Exposed by a landslip most likely. That would explain the lightning strike. And I have heard of lightning curing people of blindness and deafness, but mostly in those whose suffering was a result of hysterical complaints brought on by earlier traumas rather than any physiological effect.'

'Are you trying to debunk the miracle this church was founded upon?' snapped Uriah. 'There is a malicious streak to you, if you would seek to destroy another's faith.'

Revelation came around the Lightning Stone and shook his head. 'I am not being malicious; I am explaining to you how such a thing could have happened without the intervention of any godly power.'

Revelation tapped a finger to the side of his head and said, 'You think that the way you perceive the world is the way it actually is, but you cannot perceive the external world directly, none of us can. Instead, we know only our ideas or interpretations of objects in the world. The human brain is a marvellously evolved organ, my friend, and it is especially good at constructing images of faces and voices from limited information.'

'What has that to do with anything?' asked Uriah.

'Imagine your holy man sheltering from the storm in the cover of this great stone when the lightning bolt hit, the fire and the noise, the pounding surge of elemental energy pouring through him. Isn't it possible that an already-religious man might, in such desperate circumstances, perceive sights and sounds of a divine nature? After all, humans do it all the time. When you wake with dread in the dead of night, is that darkness in the corner not an intruder instead of just a simple shadow, the creak of a floorboard the tread of a murderer instead of the house settling in the cold night?'

'So you're saying that he imagined it all?'

'Something like that,' agreed Revelation. 'I don't mean to suggest he did so consciously or deliberately, but given the origins and evolution of religions in the human species, it seems a far more likely and convincing explanation. Don't you agree?'

'No,' said Uriah. 'I don't.'

'You don't?' said Revelation. 'You strike me as a not unintelligent man, Uriah Olathaire. Why can you not concede at least the possibility of such an explanation?'

'Because I too have seen a vision of my god and heard His voice. Nothing can compare with knowing personally and completely that the divine exists.'

'Ah, personal experience,' said Revelation. 'An experience utterly convincing to you and which cannot be proved or disproved. Tell me, where did you receive this vision?'

'On a battlefield in the lands of the Franc,' said Uriah. 'Many years ago.'

'The Franc were long ago brought to Unity,' said Revelation. 'The last battle was fought nearly half a century ago. You must have been a young man back then.'

'I was,' agreed Uriah. 'Young and foolish.'

'Hardly a prime candidate for divine attention,' said Revelation. 'But then I've found that many of the men who appear in the pages of your holy books are far from ideal role models, so perhaps it's not surprising at all.'

Uriah fought down his anger at Revelation's mocking tone, turning away from the Lightning Stone and climbing from the pit. He made his way back towards the candlelit altar, taking a few seconds to calm his breathing and slow his racing heartbeat. He lifted the leather-bound book from beside the candle and took a seat on one of the pews facing the altar.

He heard Revelation's footsteps and said, 'You come in an adversarial mood, Revelation. You say you wish to learn of me and this church? Well come, let us joust with words, thrust and parry one another's certainties with argument and counter-argument. Say what you will and we will spar all night if you desire. But come sunrise, you will leave and never return.'

Revelation descended the steps of the altar, pausing to admire the doomsday clock. He saw the book in Uriah's hands and folded his arms.

'That is my intention. I have other matters to attend to, but I have this night to talk with you,' said Revelation, pointing to the book Uriah clutched to his thin chest. 'And if I am adversarial, it is because it infuriates me to see the blinkered wilfulness of those who live their lives enslaved to such fantastical notions as are contained in that book and others like it – that damnable piece of thunder in your hands.'

'So now you mock my holy book too?'

'Why not?' said Revelation. 'That book is nine centuries worth of agglomerated texts assembled, rewritten, translated and twisted to fit the needs of hundreds of mostly anonymous and unknown authors. What basis is that to take guidance for your life?'

'It is the holy word of my god,' said Uriah. 'It speaks to everyone who reads it.'

Revelation laughed and tapped his forehead. 'If a man claimed his dead grandfather was speaking to him he'd be locked up in an asylum, but if he were to claim the voice of god was speaking to him, his fellow clerics might well make him into a saint. Clearly there is safety in numbers when it comes to hearing voices, eh?'

'This is my *faith* you are talking about,' said Uriah. 'Show some damned respect!'

'Why should I?' said Revelation. 'Why does your faith require special treatment? Is it not robust enough to stand some questioning? No one else on this world enjoys such protection from scrutiny, so why should you and your faith be singled out for special treatment?'

'I have *seen* god,' hissed Uriah. 'I saw His face and heard His words in my soul...'

'If you have had such an experience, you may believe it was real, but do not expect me or anyone else to give it credence, Uriah,' said Revelation. 'Just because you believe a thing to be true does not *make* it so.'

'I saw what I saw and I heard what I heard that day,' said Uriah, his fingers clenching tightly on the book as long-buried memories swam to the surface. 'I know it was real.'

'And where in Franc did this miraculous vision take place?'

Uriah hesitated, reluctant to give voice to the name that would unlock the box in which he had shut the memories of his past life. He took a breath. 'On the killing field of Gaduaré.'

'You were at Gaduaré,' said Revelation, and Uriah couldn't tell if Revelation's words were a question or simply an acknowledgement. For the briefest second, it sounded as though Revelation already knew.

'Aye,' said Uriah. 'I was.'

'Will you tell me what happened?'

'I'll tell you of it,' whispered Uriah. 'But first I'll need another drink.'

ONCE AGAIN, URIAH and Revelation returned to the vestry. Uriah reached into a different drawer and removed a bottle, identical to the first, except that this bottle was half-empty. Revelation sat, and Uriah noticed the chair protested once more at his weight, though the man was not especially bulky.

Uriah shook his head as Revelation held out the pewter tumbler and said, 'No, this is the good stuff. You don't drink it from a tumbler, you drink it from a glass.'

He opened a walnut cabinet behind his desk and lifted out two cut crystal copitas and deposited them on the desktop amid the clutter of papers and scrolls. He uncorked the bottle and a wonderful peaty aroma filled the room, redolent with the memories of high pastures, fresh, tumbling brooks and dark, shadow-filled woods.

'The water of life,' said Uriah, pouring two generous measures and sitting opposite Revelation. The liquid was heavy and amber, the crystal of the glass refracting slivers of gold and yellow through it.

'Finally,' said Revelation, lifting his glass to take a drink. 'A spirit I can believe in.'

Uriah said, 'No, not yet, let the vapours build. It intensifies the flavour. Swirl it a little. See the little slicks on the side of the glass? They're called tears, and since they're long and descending slowly we know the drink is strong and full-bodied.'

'Can I drink it now?'

'Patience,' said Uriah. 'Carefully nose the drink, yes? Feel how the aromas leap out at you and stimulate your senses. Allow yourself to react to the moment, let the scents awaken the memories of their origin.'

Uriah closed his eyes as he swirled the golden liquid around the glass below his nose, letting the fragrances of a lost time wash over him. He could smell the mellow richness of the alcohol, his memory alight with sensations he had never experienced: running through a wild wood of thorns and heather at sunset, the smoke from a fire in a wooden hall with a woven roof of reeds and which was hung with shields. And above all, he sensed a legacy of pride and tradition encapsulated in each element of the drink.

He smiled as he was taken back to his youth. 'Now drink,' he said. 'A generous sip. Swirl the drink over your tongue, cheeks and palate for a few seconds before you let it slide down as you swallow.'

Uriah sipped his drink and revelled in the silky smoothness of its warmth. The drink was powerful and tasted of toasted oak and sweet honey.

'Ah, that's a flavour I've not had in a long time,' said Revelation, and Uriah opened his eyes to see a contented smile on his visitor's face. 'I didn't think any remained.'

Revelation's features had relaxed and Uriah saw his cheeks glow with a rosy health. For no reason he could identify, Uriah felt less hostile to Revelation now, as if they had shared a moment of sensation that only two connoisseurs could appreciate.

'It's an old bottle,' explained Uriah. 'One I was able to rescue from the ruin of my parents' home.'

'You make a habit of keeping old alcohol around,' said Revelation.

'A throwback to my wild youth,' said Uriah. 'I was fond of drink a little too much, if you take my meaning.'

'I do. I have seen many great individuals brought low by such an addiction.'

Uriah took another sip, a smaller one this time, and savoured the heady flavours before continuing. 'You said you wanted to know of Gaduaré?'

'If you are ready and willing to tell me of it, yes.'

Uriah sighed. 'Willing, yes. Ready… Well, I suppose we will find out, eh?'

'Gaduaré was a bloody day,' said Revelation. 'It was hard on all who were there.'

Uriah shook his head. 'My eyes are not what they once were, but I can still tell that you are too young to know of Gaduaré. You would not even have been born when that battle was fought.'

'Trust me,' said Revelation. 'I know of Gaduaré.'

The tone of Revelation's words sent a shiver down Uriah's spine and, as their eyes met, he saw such a weight of knowledge and history that he felt suddenly humbled and ashamed for arguing with Revelation.

The man put down his glass and the moment passed.

'I should tell you a little of myself first,' said Uriah. 'Who I was back then and how I came to find god on the battlefield of Gaduaré. If you've a mind to hear it, that is…'

'Of course. Tell what you feel you need to tell.'

Uriah sipped his drink and said, 'I was born in the town below this church, nearly eighty years ago, the youngest son of the local lord. My clan had come through the final years of Old Night with much of their wealth intact and they owned all the land around these parts, from this mountain down to the mainland bridge. I wish I could say I was treated badly as a child, you know, to give some reason for why I turned out the way I did, but I can't. I was indulged, and became something of a spoiled brat, given to drinking, carousing and bouts of petulance.'

Uriah sighed. 'Looking back, I realise what a shit I was, but of course it's the lot of old men to look at themselves as youngsters and realise too late all the mistakes they made and regrets they carry. Anyway, I decided in my adolescent fires of rebellion that I was going to travel the world and see whatever free corners of it remained in the wake of the Emperor's conquests. So much of the world had been brought under his sway, but I was determined to find one last patch of land that wasn't yet under the heel of his thunderbolt and lightning armies.'

'You make it sound like the Emperor was a tyrant,' said Revelation. 'He ended the wars that were destroying the planet and defeated dozens of tyrants and despots. Without his armies, mankind would have descended into anarchy and destroyed itself within a generation.'

'Aye, and maybe we'd have been better off that way,' said Uriah, taking another sip of his drink. 'Maybe the universe decided we'd had our chance and our time was up.'

'Nonsense. The universe cares not a whit for our actions or us. Our fate is wrought by our own hands.'

'A philosophical point we'll no doubt return to, but I was telling you of my youth…'

'Yes, of course,' said Revelation. 'Continue.'

'Thank you. Well, after I announced my intention to travel the world, my father was good enough to grant me a generous stipend and a retinue of soldiers to protect me on my journeys. I left that very day and crossed the silver bridge four days later, travelling across a land recovering from war and which was growing fat on labours decreed by the Emperor. Hammers beat out plates of armour, blackened factories churned out weapons and entire towns of seamstresses created new uniforms for his armies.

'I crossed to Europa and caroused my way across the continent, seeing the eagle-stamped banner everywhere I went. In every town and city, I saw people giving thanks to the Emperor and his mighty thunder giants, though it all seemed hollow, like

they were going through the motions because they
were too afraid not to. I'd seen an army of the
Emperor's giants once when I was a child, but this
was the first time I had seen them in the wake of
conquest.'

Uriah's breath caught in his throat as he remembered the warrior's face, leaning down to regard him
as though he had been less than an insect. 'I was
drunk and whoring my way down the Tali peninsula
when I came upon a garrison of the Emperor's
super-soldiers at a ruined clifftop fortress and my
romantic, rebellious soul couldn't help but try and
bait them. Having seen them in battle, I shudder
now to think of the hideous danger I was in. I
shouted at them, calling them freaks and servants of
a bloodthirsty, tyrannical monster whose only
thought was the enslavement of mankind to his own
towering ego. I paraphrased the works of Seytwn and
Galliemus, though how I remembered the old masters when I was so drunk, I'll never know. I thought
I was being so clever, and then one of the giants
broke ranks and approached me. Like I said, I was
monumentally drunk and filled with that sense of
invincibility that only drunks and fools know. The
warrior was a hulking figure, more massive than any
human being should ever be. His brutish frame was
encased in heavy powered armour that enclosed his
chest and arms, and which I thought was ridicu-
lously exaggerated.'

'In previous wars, most warriors preferred to grapple with one another in close combat rather than use
long-range weapons,' said Revelation. 'The power of

a warrior's chest and arms were of paramount importance in such feats of arms.'

'Ah, I see,' said Uriah. 'Well, anyway, he came over and lifted me out of my chair, spilling my drink and upsetting me greatly. I kicked at his armour and beat my fists bloody against his chest, but he just laughed at me. I screamed at him to let me go and he did just that, telling me to shut my mouth before tossing me off the cliff and into the sea. By the time I'd climbed back to the village, they were gone and I was left with a hatred as strong as any I'd known. Stupid really, I was asking for it and it was only a matter of time until someone put me in my place.'

'So where did you go after Tali?' asked Revelation.

'Here and there,' said Uriah. 'I've forgotten a lot of those years, I was drunk a lot of the time. I know I took a sand-skimmer across the Mediterranean dust bowl and traversed the wastelands of the Nordafrik Conclaves that Shang Khal reduced to ashen desert. All I found were settlements that paid homage to the Emperor, so I carried onwards far into the east to see the ruins of Ursh and the fallen bastions of Narthan Durme. But even there, in places so far away as to be the most desolate and remote corners of the world, I still found those who gave thanks to the Emperor and his gene-engineered warriors. I couldn't under-stand it. Didn't these people see that they'd just exchanged one tyrant for another?'

'Humanity was heading for species doom,' said Revelation, sitting forwards in his chair. 'I keep telling you that without Unity and the Emperor there would be no human race. I can't believe you don't see that.'

'Oh, I see it all right, but back then I was young and full of the fires of youth that see any form of control as oppression. Though they don't appreciate it, it's the function of youth to push at the boundaries of the previous generation, to poke and prod and establish their own rules. I was no different from any other youth. Well, perhaps a little.'

'So you'd travelled the world and hadn't found any corner of it that hadn't sworn allegiance to the Emperor... Where did you go next?'

Uriah refilled their glasses before continuing. 'I returned home for a spell, bearing gifts I'd mostly stolen along the way, then set off again, but this time I went as a soldier of fortune instead of a tourist. I'd heard there were rumours of unrest in the land of the Franc, and fancied I could earn myself renown. The Franc were a fractious people before Unity and did not take kindly to invaders, even ones posing as benign. When I reached the continent, I heard of Havuleq D'agross and the Battle of Avelroi and rode straight for the town.'

'Avelroi,' said Revelation, shaking his head. 'A town poisoned by the bitterness of a madman whose meagre talents fell far short of his ambition.'

'I know that now, but the way I heard it at the time, Havuleq found himself wrongly accused of the brutal murder of the woman the Emperor had appointed as his governor. He was set to be shot by a firing squad when his brothers and friends attacked the Army units tasked with his execution. The soldiers were torn to pieces, but some of the townsfolk got themselves killed in the fighting, including the local arbiter's son, and the mood of the people turned ugly. For all his other faults, and there were many, Havuleq was a speaker of rare skill and he fanned the flames of the townsfolk's ire at the Emperor's rule. Within the hour, a hastily formed militia had stormed the Army barracks and slain all the soldiers within.'

'You know, of course, that Havuleq *did* assault and murder that woman?'

Uriah nodded sadly. 'I learned that later, yes, when it was too late to do anything about it.'

'And then what happened?'

'By the time I reached Avelroi, full of piss and vinegar for the coming fight, Havuleq had rallied a number of the local townships to his cause and had amassed quite an army.'

Uriah smiled as the details of his early time in Avelroi returned, clearer than they had been for decades. 'It was a magnificent sight, Revelation, the icons of the Emperor had been torn down and the city was like something from a dream. Colourful bunting hung from every window and marching bands played in the streets every day as Havuleq marched his soldiers up and down. Of course, we should have been training, but we were buoyed up with courage and our own sense of righteous purpose. More and more of the surrounding towns were rising up against their Army garrisons, and within the space of a few months around forty thousand men were ready to fight.

'It was everything I'd dreamed of,' said Uriah. 'It was a glorious rebellion, courageous and heroic in the grand tradition of the freedom fighters of old. We were to be the spark that would light the fuse of history that would see this planetary autocrat tumbled from his self-appointed rulership of the world. Then we heard that the thunderbolt and lightning army was marching from the east and we set off in grand procession to meet it in battle. It was a joyous day as Havuleq led us from Avelroi, I'll never forget it: the laughter, the kisses from the girls and the spirit of shared brotherhood that filled us as we marched out to battle.

'It took us a week to reach Gaduaré, a line of high hills directly in the path of our enemies. I had read my share of the ancient stories of battle and knew this was a good place to make our stand. We occupied the high ground and both our flanks were anchored on strong positions. On the left were the ruins of the Gaduaré Bastion, on the right a desolate marsh through which nothing could pass.'

'It was madness to oppose the Emperor's armies,' said Revelation. 'You must have known you could not defeat them. These were warriors bred for battle, whose every waking moment was spent in combat training.'

Uriah nodded. 'I think we knew that as soon as our enemy came into sight,' he said, his features darkening at the memory, 'but we were so caught up in the mood of optimism. By now our army was fifty thousand strong, and we faced less than a tenth of that number. It was hard not to feel like we could win the day, especially with Havuleq riding up and down and firing our blood. His brother tried to calm him, but it was already too late and we charged from the hillside like mad, glorious fools, screaming war cries and waving swords, pistols and rifles above our heads. I was in the sixth rank and we'd covered nearly a kilometre by the time we got anywhere near the ranks of the giants. They hadn't moved since we'd set off, but as we got close, they shouldered their guns and opened fire.'

Uriah paused and took a long gulp of his drink. His hand was shaking and he carefully and deliberately set his glass down on the desk as he continued.

'I'll never forget the noise,' he said. 'It was like a thunderstorm had suddenly sprung into existence, and our first five ranks were completely cut down, dead to a man without even the time to scream. The enemy's bolts tore limbs from bodies or simply burst men apart like wet sacks. I turned to shout something, I forget what exactly, when I felt a searing pain in the back of my head and I fell over the remains of a man who'd had his entire left side blown off. It looked like he'd exploded from the inside out.

'I rolled onto my knees and felt the back of my head. It was sticky and matted with blood and I realised I'd been hit. A ricochet or a fragment. Anything larger and I'd have lost my head. I could feel the blood running from me and looked up in time to see our enemies fire again. That's when I started to hear screams. Our charge had ground to a halt, men and women milling around in confusion and fear as they suddenly understood the reality of what Havuleq had begun.

'The thunder warriors put up their guns and marched towards us, unsheathing swords with serrated edges and motorised blades. The noise, oh god, I'll never forget the noise they made. A roar like something out of a nightmare. We were already beaten, their first volley had broken us, and I saw Havuleq lying dead in the middle of the field. The lower half of his body had been blown clean off and I saw the same terror I was feeling on every face around me. People were begging for mercy, throwing down their weapons and trying to surrender, but the armoured warriors didn't stop. They marched right up to us and hacked into us without mercy. We were cut apart and brutalised with such economy of force that I couldn't believe so many people could die in so short a time. This wasn't war, at least not as I'd read about it, where men of honour fought in glorious duels, this was mechanised butchery.

'I'm not ashamed to say I ran. I ran, soiled and bleeding, for safety. I ran like all the daemons of legend were after me and all the time I was hearing the awful sound of people dying, the wet sound of flesh splitting open and the stench of voided bowels and opened bellies. I can't remember anything much of my flight, just random flashes of dead bodies and screams of pain. I ran until I couldn't run any more, and then I crawled through the mud until I lost consciousness. When I woke, which I was surprised I did at all, I saw it was dark. Pyres had been lit and the victory chants of the thunder warriors drifted over the killing field.

'Havuleq's army had been destroyed. Not routed or put to flight. Destroyed. In less than an hour, fifty thousand men and women had been killed. I think I knew even then that I was the only survivor. I wept beneath the moonlight and as I lay there bleeding to death in agony, I thought of how pointless my life had been. The heartbreak and ruin I'd visited upon others in my reckless pursuit of hedonism and self-interest. I wept for my family and myself and that was when I realised I wasn't alone.'

'Who was with you?' asked Revelation.

'The power of the divine,' said Uriah. 'I looked up and saw a golden face above me, a face of such radiance and perfection that my tears were no longer shed for pain, but for beauty. Light surrounded this figure and I averted my eyes for fear I'd be blinded. I'd been in pain, but now that pain was gone and I knew I was seeing the face of the divine. I couldn't describe that face to you, not with all the poetic images in the world at my disposal, but it was the most exquisite thing I had ever seen.

'I felt myself lifted up and I thought that this was the end for me. And then the face spoke to me, and I knew I was destined to live.'

'What did this face say to you?' asked Revelation.

Uriah smiled. 'He said, "Why do you deny me? Accept me and you will know that I am the only truth and the only way."'

'Did you reply?'

'I couldn't,' said Uriah. 'To utter any words would have been base. In any case, my tongue was quite stilled by the awesome vision of god.'

'What made you think it was god? Did you not hear what I said earlier about the brain's ability to perceive what it wants to? You were a dying man on a battlefield, surrounded by your dead comrades and you were having an epiphany of the futility of the life you had led. Surely you can think of another explanation for this vision, Uriah, a more likely explanation that does not require the supernatural?'

'I need no other explanation,' said Uriah, firmly. 'You may be wise in many things, Revelation, but you cannot know what goes on in my own mind. I heard the voice of god and saw His face. He bore me up and set me into a deep slumber, and when I awoke, my wounds were healed.'

Uriah turned his head so that Revelation could see the long scar on the back of his neck. 'A piece of bone shrapnel had been embedded in my skull, barely a centimetre from severing my spinal cord. I was alone on the battlefield and I decided to return to the land of my birth, but when I returned I found my family home in ruins. The townsfolk told me that Scandian raiders from the north had heard of my family's wealth and come south in search of plunder. They killed my brother then violated my mother and sister in front of my father to force him to tell them where he hid his treasures. They couldn't know my father had a weak heart and he died before they could learn his secrets. I found my home in ruins and my family little more than bleached cadavers.'

'I am sorry to hear of your loss,' said Revelation. 'If it is any consolation, the Scandians would not accept Unity and were wiped out three decades ago.'

'I know, but I do not revel in death any more,' said Uriah. 'The men who killed my family will have been judged by god and that is justice enough for me.'

'That is noble of you,' said Revelation, real admiration in his voice.

'I took a few keepsakes from the ruins and made my way to the nearest settlement, thinking I'd get blind drunk and then try to figure out what to do with my life. I was halfway there when I saw the Church of the Lightning Stone and knew I had found my purpose in life. I had spent my life until that point living only for myself, but when I saw the spire of the church I knew that god had a purpose for me. I should have died at Gaduaré, but I was saved for a reason.'

'And what reason was that?'

'To serve god,' said Uriah. 'To bring His word to the people.'

'And that's what you've been doing here?'

Uriah nodded. 'It's what I've been trying to do, but the Emperor's promulgators traverse the globe with his message of reason and the refutation of gods and the supernatural. I assume that is why you are here and why none of my congregation has come to the church tonight.'

'You are correct,' said Revelation. 'In a manner of speaking. I *have* come to try and convince you of the error of your ways, to learn of you and to show you that there is no need for any divine powers to guide humanity. This is the last church on Terra and it falls to me to offer you this chance to embrace the new way willingly.'

'Or?'

Revelation shook his head. 'There is no "or", Uriah. Come, let us go back out into the church as we talk, I want to instruct you of all that belief in gods has done for humanity down the ages, the bloodshed, the horror and the persecution. I will tell you of this and you will see how damaging such belief is.'

'And then what? You'll be on your way?'

'We both know that's not what's going to happen, don't we?'

'Yes,' said Uriah, draining the last of his drink. 'We do.'

'LET ME TELL you a story that happened many thousands of years ago,' said Revelation.

They walked along the north transept of the church, coming to a set of spiral stairs that led to the upper cloisters. Revelation followed after Uriah, talking as he climbed. 'It is a story of how a herd of gene-bred livestock caused the death of over nine hundred people.'

'Did they stampede?' asked Uriah.

'No, it was a handful of half-starved creatures that escaped from their paddocks outside Xozer, a once-great city of the Nordafrik Conclaves.'

They reached the top of the stairs and began walking along the cloister, its confined walls dark and cold. Dust lay thick on the stone-flagged floor and a handful of thick candles that Uriah could not remember lighting guttered in iron sconces.

'Xozer? I've been there,' said Uriah. 'At least I saw what my guide told me were its ruins.'

'Quite possibly. Anyway, these hungry animals walked through a building holy to one of the many cults that called Xozer home. This cult, which was known as the Xozerites, believed that gene-bred meat was an affront to their god and they blamed a rival sect known as the Upashtar for the defilement. The Xozerites went on a rampage, stabbing and clubbing any Upashtar they could find. Of course, the Upashtar retaliated and rioting spread throughout the city and left close to a thousand people dead.'

'Is there a point to that story?' said Uriah, when Revelation did not continue.

'Absolutely, it tells a universal tale and typifies religious behaviour that has been recurring since the beginning of human history.'

'A slightly far-fetched example, Revelation. One freakish story cannot serve as a proof that belief in the divine is a bad thing. Such belief is the bedrock of moral order. It gives people the character they need to get through life. Without guidance from above, the world would descend into anarchy.'

'Sadly, millions once held that view, Uriah, but that old truism just isn't true. The record of human experience shows that where religion is strong, it causes cruelty. Intense beliefs produce intense hostility. Only when faith loses its force can a society hope to become humane.'

'I don't believe that,' said Uriah, stopping by one of the arches in the cloister and looking down onto the nave. Dust swirled across the floor, blown by the storm winds chasing around the lonely church. 'My holy book gives instruction on how to live a good life. It has lessons humanity needs.'

'Are you sure?' asked Revelation. 'I have read your holy book and much of it is bloody and vengeful. Would you live your life literally by its commandments, or do you view the people who populate its pages as exemplars of proper behaviour? Either way, I suspect the morals espoused would be horrifying to most people.'

Uriah shook his head. 'You're missing the point, Revelation. Much of the text is not meant to be taken literally, it is symbolic or allegorical.'

Revelation snapped his fingers. 'That's *exactly* my point. You pick and choose which bits of your book to take literally and which to read as symbolic, and that choosing is a matter of personal decision, not divinity. Trust me, in ages past, a frightening number of people took their holy books *absolutely literally*, causing untold misery and death because they truly believed the words they read. The history of religion is a horror story, Uriah, and if you doubt it, just look at what humanity has done in the name of their gods over the millennia.

'Thousands of years ago, a bloody theocracy that venerated a feathered-serpent god rose in the Mayan jungles. To appease this vile god, its priests drowned maidens in sacred wells and cut out the hearts of children. They believed this serpent god had an earthly counterpart and the temple builders drove the first pile through a maiden's body to pacify this non-existent creature.'

Uriah turned to Revelation in horror and said, 'You can't seriously compare my religion to such heathen barbarism?'

'Can't I?' countered Revelation. 'In the name of your religion, a holy man launched a war with the battle cry of "Deus Vult", which means "god wills it" in one of the ancient tongues of Old Earth. His warriors were charged with destroying enemies in a far-off kingdom, but first they fell upon those in their own lands who opposed the war. Thousands were dragged from their homes and hacked to death or burned alive. Then, satisfied their homeland was secure, the zealous legions plundered their way thousands of miles to the holy city they were to liberate. Upon reaching it, they killed every inhabitant to "purify" the symbolic city of taint. I remember one of their leaders saying that he rode in blood up to the knees and even to his horse's bridle, by the just and marvellous judgement of god.'

'That is ancient history,' said Uriah. 'You cannot vouchsafe the truth of events so lost in the mists of time.'

'If it were one event, I might agree with you,' replied Revelation, 'but just a hundred or so years later, another holy man declared war on a sect of his own church. His warriors laid siege to the sect's stronghold in ancient Franc, and when the city fell his generals asked their leader how they might tell the faithful from the traitor among the captives. This man, who followed *your* god, ordered the warriors to "Kill them all. God will know His own". Nearly twenty thousand men, women and children were slaughtered.

'Worst of all, the hunt for any that had escaped the siege led to the establishment of an organisation known as the Inquisition, a dreadful, monstrous plague of hysteria that gave its agents free rein to stretch, burn, pierce and break their victims on fiendish pain machines to force them to confess to disbelief and identify fellow transgressors. Later, with most of their enemies hunted down and killed, the Inquisition shifted its focus to wychcraft, and priests tortured untold thousands of women into confessing that they engaged in unnatural acts with daemons. They were then burned or hanged for their confessions and this hysteria raged for three centuries in a dozen nations, a madness that saw whole towns exterminated and over a hundred thousand dead.'

'You pick the most extreme examples from the past, Revelation,' said Uriah, struggling to maintain his composure in the face of such tales of murder and bloodshed. 'Times have moved on and humanity no longer behaves in such ways to one another.'

'If you believe that then you have been shut away in this draughty church for far too long, Uriah,' said Revelation. 'You must have heard of Cardinal Tang, a mass-murdering ethnarch who practised a crude form of eugenics. His bloody pogroms and death camps saw millions dead in the Yndonesic Bloc. He died less than thirty years ago after seeking to return the world to a pre-technological age, emulating the Inquisition's burning of scientists, mathematicians and philosophers who contradicted the church's view on cosmology.'

Uriah could stand no more and walked towards the stairs at the far end of the cloister that led down into the narthex. 'You fixate on the blood and death, Revelation. You forget all the good that can be achieved through faith.'

'If you think religion is a force for good, Uriah, then you're not seeing the superstitious savagery that pervades the history of our world,' said Revelation. 'It's true that just before the descent of Old Night, religion gradually lost its power over life, but like the worst kind of poison, it lingered and fostered division amongst the people of the world that endured. Without belief in gods, divisions blur with passing ages; new generations adapt to new times, mingle, intermarry and forget ancient wounds. It is only belief in gods and divine entities that keep them alien to one another, and anything that divides people breeds inhumanity. Religion is the canker in mankind's heart that serves such an ugly purpose.'

'Enough!' snapped Uriah. 'I have heard enough. Yes, people have done terrible things to one another in the name of their gods, but they have done terrible things to one another without the recourse to their beliefs. An acceptance of gods and an afterlife is a vital part of what makes us who we are. If you take that away from humanity, what do you suggest takes its place? In my many years as a priest I have ministered to many dying people, and the emotional benefits of religion's power to console them and those left behind cannot be underestimated.'

'There is a flaw in your logic, Uriah,' said Revelation. 'Religion's power to console gives it absolutely no more credence or validity. It might very well be a comfort to a dying man to believe that he will go to some bountiful paradise of endless joy, but even if he dies with a wonderful smile on his face, it means nothing in the grand scheme of things as far as the truth of the matter is concerned.'

'Maybe not, but when my time comes, I will die with my god's name on my lips.'

'Are you afraid to die, Uriah?' asked Revelation.

'No.'

'Truly?'

'Truly,' said Uriah. 'I have my share of sins, but I have spent my life in the service of my god and I believe that I have served Him faithfully and well.'

'So why is it then, when you go to these people who are dying and clinging to their beliefs that they don't welcome the end of their life? Surely the gathered family and friends should be of good cheer and should celebrate their relative's passing? After all, if eternal paradise awaits on the other side, why are they not filled with gleeful anticipation? Could it be that, in their heart of hearts, they don't really believe it?'

Uriah turned away and made his way down the narthex stairs, his anger and frustration giving him force of pace that quite outweighed the stiffness in his limbs. A cold wind blew in from the outer doors and he could hear the mutter of voices and the scrape of metal on metal from outside. The narthex of the Church of the Lightning Stone was an austere place, stone walls with niches in which sat statues of various saints that had passed this way in the thousands of years the church had stood. A swaying candelabra, empty of candles, hung from the roof, but it had been many years since Uriah had been able to climb the stepladder in the store room to replace them.

He pushed open the door to the church and walked stiffly down the nave towards the altar. Four of the six candles he had lit there had gone out and the fifth guttered and died in the wind that entered with him.

The lone candle burned beside the clock and Uriah made his way towards it as he heard Revelation enter the church behind him. Uriah reached the altar and lowered himself to a kneeling position with some difficulty.

He bowed his head before the altar and clasped his hands together.

'The Lord of Mankind is the Light and the Way, and all His actions are for the benefit of mankind, which is His people. So it is taught in the holy words of our order, and above all things, god will protect…'

'There's no one there to hear you,' said Revelation from behind him.

'I don't care what you say any more. You have come here to do what you feel you need to do and I'll not buttress your ego and self-righteousness by playing along any longer. So just end this charade.'

'As you wish,' said Revelation. 'No more games.'

A golden light built behind Uriah and he saw his shadow thrown out onto the graven surface of the altar. The pearlescent hands of the clock shimmered in the reflected light and the ebony face gleamed.

Where once the church had been gloomy and filled with shadows, it was now a place of light.

Uriah pulled himself to his feet and turned to see a wondrous figure standing before him, towering and magnificent, clad in golden armour fashioned with love and the greatest skill, every plate embossed with thunderbolts and eagles.

Gone was Revelation, and in his place was a towering warrior of exquisite splendour, an exemplar of all that was regal and inspirational in humanity. The armour bulked his form out beyond measure and Uriah felt tears spilling from his eyes as he realised he had seen this breathtakingly, achingly perfect face once before.

On the killing fields of Gaduaré.

'You...' breathed Uriah, stumbling back and collapsing onto his haunches. Pain shot through his hip and pelvis, but he barely felt it.

'Now do you understand the futility of what you do here?' said the golden giant.

Long dark hair spilled around the warrior's face, a face that Uriah could only see through the hazy lens of memory. He could see the unremarkable features of Revelation subsumed into the warrior's countenance, itself so worthy of devotion that it took all Uriah's self-control not to drop to his knees and offer what remained of his life to its glorification.

'You...' repeated Uriah, the pain in his bones no match for the pain in his heart. 'You are the... the... Emperor...'

'I am, and it is time to go, Uriah,' said the Emperor.

Uriah looked around at his now gleaming and brightly lit church. 'Go? Go where? There is nowhere else for me in this godless world of yours.'

'Of course there is,' replied the Emperor. 'Embrace the new way and be part of something incredible. A world and a time where we stand on the brink of achieving everything we ever dreamed.'

Uriah nodded dumbly and felt a firm hand gently take his arm and lift him to his feet once more. Strength flowed from the Emperor's grip and Uriah felt the aches and ailments that had plagued him for decades fade until they were little more than evil memories.

He looked up at Isandula Verona's magnificent fresco, and the breath caught in his throat. Colours once dulled by the darkness now blazed with life and the ceiling seemed to burst with life and vitality as the Emperor's light gave it fresh animation and vibrancy. The skin of the painted figures shone with vitality, and the livid blues and lusty reds radiated potency.

'Verona's work was never meant for darkness,' said the Emperor. 'Only in the light can it achieve its full potential. Humanity is the same, and only when the suffocating shadows of a religion that teaches us not to question is gone from this world will we see its true brilliance.'

Uriah only reluctantly tore his eyes from the impossibly beautiful fresco and cast his gaze around his church. The stained-glass windows shone with new life and the intricate, subtle architecture of the interior gleamed with the skill of its builders.

'I will miss this place,' said Uriah.

'In time I will build an Imperium of such grandeur and magnificence that this will seem like a pauper's hovel,' said the Emperor. 'Now, let us be on our way.'

Uriah allowed himself to be guided down the nave, his heart heavy with the knowledge that the course of his life had been altered by, at best, a mis-understanding, at worst, a lie. As he followed the Emperor towards the narthex doors, he looked up at the ceiling once more, recalling the sermons he had delivered here, the people who had hung on his every word and the good that had flowed from this place and into the world.

He smiled suddenly as he realised that it didn't matter whether his life and faith had been based on a falsehood. He had believed what he had seen and he had come to this place with a heart open and emptied by grief. That openness had allowed the spirit of his god to enter his soul and filled the emptiness within him with love.

What makes faith so powerful is that it requires no proof. Belief is enough.

He had devoted his life to his god, and even with the understanding of how his fate had been manip-ulated by random chance, he found no resentment in his heart. He had spread a doctrine of love and forgiveness from his pulpit and no amount of clever words would make him regret that.

The door to the narthex was still open and, as they passed through its cold embrace, the Emperor pushed open the main doors of the church.

Howling wind and sheets of rain blew inwards and Uriah clasped his robes tightly to his body, feeling the night's cold stab into his body like a thousand shards of ice.

He looked over his shoulder towards the altar of his church, seeing the lone candle beside the doomsday clock snuffed out by the gale. Once again, his church was swathed in darkness and he sighed to see this last illumination extinguished. The wind blew the internal doors shut and Uriah followed the Emperor out into the darkness.

Rain soaked him instantly and a crash of lightning lit the heavens with an actinic blue glow. Hundreds of warriors stood in ordered ranks before the church, brutal giants in pugnacious armour he had last seen on the battlefield of Gaduaré.

They stood immobile beneath the downpour, the rain beating against the burnished plates of bronze in an unrelenting tattoo and causing their scarlet helmet plumes to hang limply at their shoulders. There had been some refinements, saw Uriah, the armour now all-enclosing and each warrior sealed from the elements by an interlocking series of artfully designed plates.

Huge backpacks vented excess heat in steaming plumes like breath, and each of the warriors carried a burning torch that hissed and fizzed in the downpour. Huge guns were slung over their shoulders and Uriah shivered as he remembered the murderous volley, like the thunder at the end of the world, that had felled so many of his comrades.

The Emperor put a long cloak about Uriah's shoulders as a group of armoured warriors stepped towards the church with flame lances raised. Uriah wanted to protest, to speak out against what they were about to do, but the words died in his throat as he realised they would have no effect.

Tears streamed down his face along with the rain as torrents of flame erupted from the warriors' weapons and licked over the roof and walls of the church. Other warriors fired grenades that smashed through the stained-glass windows of the church and percussive booms thudded from inside as the hungry flames took hold of the roof.

Thick smoke billowed from the windows, the rain doing nothing to dampen the destructive ambition of the flames, and Uriah wept to think of the wondrous fresco and the thousands of years of history that was being destroyed.

He turned to look up at the Emperor, the warrior's face lit by the fires of destruction.

'How can you do this?' demanded Uriah. 'You say you stand for reason and the advancement of understanding, but here you are destroying a repository of knowledge!'

The Emperor looked down at him and said, 'Some things are best left forgotten.'

'Then I hope you have foreseen the consequences of a world bereft of religion.'

'I have,' replied the Emperor. 'It is my dream. An Imperium of Man that exists without recourse to gods and the supernatural. A united galaxy with Terra at its heart.'

'A united galaxy?' said Uriah, averting his gaze from his blazing church as he finally grasped the scale of the Emperor's ambition.

'Indeed. Now that Unity has been achieved on Terra, it is time to reclaim humanity's lost empire among the stars.'

'With you at its head, I presume?' said Uriah.

'Of course. Nothing of such grand scale can be achieved without a singular vision at its heart, least of all the reconquest of the galaxy.'

'You are a madman,' said Uriah. 'And you are arrogant if you believe you can subjugate the stars with warriors such as these. They are powerful to be sure, but even they are not capable of such a thing.'

'You are right,' agreed the Emperor. 'I will not conquer the galaxy with these men, for they are but men. These are the precursors to the warriors I am forging in my gene-labs, warriors with the strength and power and vision to bestride the battlefields of the stars and bring them to compliance. These warriors shall be my generals and they will lead my great crusade to the furthest corners of the galaxy.'

'Didn't you just tell me of the bloody slaughters perpetrated by crusaders?' said Uriah. 'Doesn't that make you no better than the holy men you were telling me about?'

'The difference is I know I am right,' said the Emperor.

'Spoken like a true autocrat.'

The Emperor shook his head. 'You misunderstand, Uriah. I have seen the narrow survival path that is all that stands between humanity and extinction, and this is the way it must begin.'

Uriah looked back at the church, the gleeful flames reaching high into the darkness.

'It is a dangerous road you travel,' said Uriah. 'To deny humanity a thing will only make them crave it all the more. And if you succeed in this grand vision of yours? What then? Beware that your subjects do not begin to see you as a god.'

Uriah looked into the Emperor's face as he spoke, now seeing past the glamours and the magnificence to the heart of an individual who had lived a thousand lives and walked the Earth for longer than could be imagined. He saw the ruthless ambition and the molten core of violence at the Emperor's heart. In that instant, Uriah knew he wanted nothing to do with anything this man had to offer, no matter how noble or lofty his ambitions might be.

'I hope in the name of all that is holy you are right,' said Uriah, 'but I dread the future you are forging for humanity.'

'I wish only the best for my people,' promised the Emperor.

'I think you do, but I will not be a part of it,' said Uriah, casting off the Emperor's cloak and walking back towards his church with his head held high. The rain beat down on him, but he welcomed it as a baptismal.

He heard footsteps approaching him, but he heard the Emperor say, 'No. Leave him.'

The outer doors of the church stood open and Uriah walked into the narthex, feeling the heat of the flames as they billowed around him. The statues were on fire and the doors to the nave were gone, blown off their hinges by the blasts of grenades.

Uriah marched into the blazing heat of the church, seeing a wall of flame devouring the pews and silken hangings with insatiable hunger. Smoke filled the air and the fresco above him was almost obscured by the roiling blackness.

He looked at the clock face on the altar and smiled as the flames closed in around him.

THE WARRIORS REMAINED outside the church until it collapsed, the roof timbers crashing down into the building in a tremendous flurry of flying sparks and wreckage. They stayed until the first rays of sunlight crested the mountains and the rain finally extinguished the last of the flames.

The ruins of the last church on Terra smouldered in the chill morning air as the Emperor turned away and said, 'Come, we have a galaxy to conquer.'

As the Emperor and his warriors marched down the hillside, the only sound to be heard was the soft chiming of an old and broken clock.

AFTER DESH'EA

Matthew Farrer

'YOU DON'T HAVE to do this,' said Dreagher, breaking the long silence, and the relaxing of tension from the other War Hounds was audible even without Astartes senses. Khârn looked around the loose square of warriors and saw sneaking relief in their expressions. Someone had finally come out and said it.

'You need not do it.' Dreagher could not quite bring himself to step between Khârn and the doors, but his voice was steady. 'You should not do it.'

But other signs gave the lie to the composure in Dreagher's voice. Khârn watched his fellow captain's respiration move at just below combat-preparation speed, watched the veins in his face and shorn scalp tick at an elevated rate, took in the motions of his eyes, the subtle shifts of his shoulders as his body went through the muscle-loosening routines that had been part of their deep conditioning. Dreagher's skin carried the scent of scouring-gel but underneath it, coming off his skin, was the scent of adrenaline and the inhuman essences that the Astartes body made for itself when the danger instincts rang.

They were all keyed up; Khârn's own metabolism was escalated too. He could hardly have helped it. The air cyclers had not yet been able to carry away the tang of blood that had washed through the anteroom the last time the double doors had opened.

As Khârn worked his palate and tongue, processing and tasting the air, he realised something else: the rest of the ship had fallen as silent as the anteroom they stood in. The anteroom's semicircular outer wall opened through to the barrack-decks, and normally the broad colonnade was alive with sounds. Voices, the clank of boots and the softer tread of the menials and technomats, the distant sound of shots from the ranges, the almost subsonic buzz of the new power weapons, all gone now. The decks were as silent as the great chamber beyond the steel-grey double doors at Dreagher's back. The strangeness of that silence tautened his nerves and muscles further still.

Khârn ignored his body, letting it do what it will. He kept his eyes cold.

'Eighth Company makes me the ranking captain aboard, now,' he told them. 'My rank, my oath and my Emperor. Together they close the matter. In case anyone is insolent enough to think there's even a matter to close.'

'No,' came a voice from beside him. Jareg, the Master Shellsmith from the artillery echelon. 'The matter to close is that we must find a way to, to…' Jareg motioned wordlessly towards the doors, face twisted in distress.

'We… don't know how this will end,' said Horzt, commander of the Ninth Company's Stormbird squadron. Khârn watched the man's hands form fists, shaking to match the shake in his voice. 'And so we have to plan for the worst. One of us here, now, may need to command the Legion yet, and–'

He broke off. In the space beyond the doors a voice, deeper than a tank-rumble, mightier than a cannon-blast, was roaring in anger. If there were words to it, they were blurred and muffled by the slabs of metal in the way, but still the War Hounds fell silent. They had shouted oaths and orders and obscenities over the clamour of gun, grenade and chainaxe, over the scream of Stormbird jets, over the keen and bellow of a dozen different xenos, but Khârn was the only one who dared to speak now over that distant, muted voice.

'Enough,' he said, and his voice was flat. 'I'm not stupid enough to deny what we all think and know. You all owe Horzt a salute for being the only one to find enough Astartes guts in his belly to say it. The Emperor has brought us our lord and commander. The heartspring of our own bloodline. That is who is with us now. Our general. The one of whom we are echoes. Do you remember that? Do you?' Khârn looked from one to the next, and the War Hounds stared back at him. Good. He would have struck any of them who hadn't met his eyes. On the other side of the scarred grey plate of the doors, the distant voice roared again.

'Now, this,' he went on, 'this thing we are doing here, this is right. It is not for any Lord Commander, it is not for any high-helmed, gilt-edged custodian, it is not for anyone–' his shout stiffened their backs, widened their eyes '–to come between the War Hounds and their primarch and live. Only for the Emperor himself will we stand aside, and the Emperor has shown his wisdom. He has taken this duty and he has laid it on our shoulders.'

He looked at Dreagher again. Like Khârn, the man was dressed in white, bands of blue glittering across the high-collared tunic, boots and gauntlets a dark ceremonial blue rather than functional shipboard grey. The Emperor's lightning-bolt emblem gleamed at his collar and shoulder. His dress matched Khârn's own: the formal garments with which the War Hounds symbolised they were about their most solemn business. It was obvious why. Dreagher wanted to go in Khârn's place. Wanted to go in and die.

'We have our primarch now,' Khârn told them, and even now he felt a little shiver at the words. All these years since they had launched outwards from Terra, watching as one mighty creation after another emerged from unreclaimed space to take their places in the ranks. Khârn had heard how the Salamanders had waited in orbit around the burning moon, waited for the Emperor's word that the one he had found there was indeed their sire. He remembered the first sight of chilly-eyed Perturabo walking at the Emperor's shoulder the day they took ship for Nove Shendak, and the change in the Iron Warriors when they knew who was to command them. Every Legion still with that empty place at its head felt the same longing, sharper with every voyage, every campaign. Would this next star be the one where their blood-sire lived? Would this ship, this communiqué, bring the news that their father-commander had been found, out there in the dark? And then that electric day when the word had come to the mustering docks at Vueron, the news that their own primarch had been found, their lord, their alpha, their...

And it had come to this.

'We have our primarch now,' he repeated, 'and he will lead his Legion in whatever manner he chooses. We are his just as we are the Emperor's. What we wish or plan no longer matters. The commander of the War Hounds will meet the primarch of the War Hounds, and what happens will be as the primarch wills it. So be it. No more talk.'

Besides, he thought as Dreagher saluted and silently walked to the doors, I don't suppose it will be long before he works his way down to you. He was surprised at the thought, but surprised also at the lack of emotion that came with it. For all that the War Hounds were a hot-blooded Legion, Khârn found his thoughts flat and colourless. He took a moment to wonder if this were how others felt, the enemies who had advanced to their doom under War Hound chainaxes, or the condemned men of the auxilia in the days before the Emperor had banned the Legion from decimating allies who disgraced them on the field.

Dreagher worked the key controls and the doors swung silently outwards. Beyond them, oddly prosaic, a plain set of broad steps went down into shadows. Another roar, wordless and deep-throated, came echoing up from the gloom.

Khârn shook the thoughts away, walked forwards, and let the darkness fold over him as Dreagher swung the doors closed at his back.

KHÂRN CAME DOWN the broad, shallow steps into the great space that had been built into the ship as Angron's triumphal hall. He had been in it many times but it was a different space now, even with most of it lost in the dark. It felt different. Khârn registered that sensation, of walking into a strange space unfamiliar to him, and wondered if any room that held a primarch could feel the same again. He walked three slow, measured paces onto the smooth stone chamber floor, and pushed his enhanced vision through its darkness adjustments – the primarch had shattered most of the lights, or torn them from their mountings. Here and there the survivors cast glow-pools that did little more than texture the darkness around them. Some of the glows showed dark spatters and puddles across the floor, but Khârn did not bother to look closely. Even if the smell of it were not drowning his senses, he had seen the aftermath of death too many times not to know it.

He felt the urge to look around him for his brothers. Gheer, the Legion Master, who had come

in here first when the Emperor had told the War
Hounds they must take this duty upon themselves
and then taken ship to meet the Thirty-seventh Fleet
at Aldebaran. Kunnar, the First Company
Champion, who had donned his formal cape, taken
up his axe-staff and walked down the steps after the
noises coming through the doors had convinced
them that Gheer was long dead. Anchez, who had
captained the assault echelon, had walked down
next. He had joked with Khârn and Hyazn as the
doors had been opened for him, despite the blood
they could already smell on the air. The man had
never known what fear was. Hyazn had been next,
and two of the banner-bearers from his personal
command coterie had insisted on marching down
the steps into the dark with him. They had meant to
block the primarch's fury for long enough that
Hyazn could speak with him. It hadn't worked.
Vanche, the master-at-arms to old Gheer, had
insisted on being next, even though the next to
inherit the Legion's command, and so the duty of
taking up embassy to their lord, should have been
Shinnargen of the Second Company. The point was
moot now. Shinnargen had met his end in here an
hour after Vanche.

I am, primarch, the servant of your will, thought
Khârn, and I would never dare to pronounce you the
servant of mine. But still, my newfound lord, if you
would make your peace with your Legion while
there are still any in your Legion to draw breath…

He exhaled, and took another step into the room.
For a moment he thought he could hear movement,

the padding of feet, a rush of air that felt like breath before everything splintered and whirled and he crashed into a pillared wall to land hard on his back, gasping in pain.

By the time the gasp had entered his lungs, reflex had taken over and he was up on one knee, turning to put his broken right arm and shoulder to the wall and holding and tensing his left arm ready to ward as he scanned for motion, eyes sifting the gloom, pushing into infrared to see the hulking shape hurtling forwards to fill his vision–

Will overrode reflex, and with an iron effort Khârn forced his hand towards his side. Then he was skittering on his back across the floor, breath hammered out of his lungs and cracked clavicle flaring. Unthinkingly he drew his knees to his chest, turned the skidding tumble into a backwards roll. Training, determination and Astartes neural wiring let him shunt the pain to the back of his mind as he came up into a combat crouch.

Then will took over again, and Khârn made himself stand upright and placed his hands by his sides. He looked back and found the spot where he had rested a moment ago, but the floor was empty, no shape or heat-trace.

Was this how it was for the others? He caught himself wondering, and stopped thinking about it when the lapse in concentration started him swaying on the spot. He focused, half-heard movement closing in behind him and opened his mouth to speak, and a moment later was jerked up from the floor, the back of his head and neck in the grip of a hand that felt bigger and harder than a Dreadnaught's rubble-claw. Will, will over instinct: Khârn stopped himself from kicking backwards, trying to wrench free.

'Another one? Another one like the rest?' The voice in his ear was a rasp, a rumble, words like handfuls of hot gravel. 'Warrior made, warrior garbed, uhh...' For a moment the grip on the back of Khârn's neck juddered and his body shook like a Stormbird hitting atmosphere, then the animal growl from behind him became a roar.

'Fight!'

He was being carried forwards one-handed in long blurring strides across the width of the hall.

'Fight me!' With the words, a slam into the wall hard enough to leave Khârn's wits red-tinged and reeling.

'Fight me!' Another slam and the red was shot through with black. His limbs felt sluggish and only half there. The voice was bellowing, drowning his hearing, pouring into his head and trampling his jangled thoughts.

'Fiiight!' Another steel-hard grip closed about his broken arm and for a brief moment Khârn whirled through the air. Another impact and his back was to the wall, his feet dangling, broken shoulder incandescent with pain as one of the great hands pinned him against the dark marble.

It took a moment for things to clear. Astartes bio-chemistry stabilised his pain and his cognition, glanded stress-hormones slammed into his system and Khârn looked at his primarch's face with clear eyes.

Wiry, copper-red hair curled away from a high brow, pale eyes sat deep behind cheekbones that angled down like axe-strokes to an aquiline nose and a broad, thin-lipped mouth.

It was the face of a general to follow unto death, the face of a teacher at whose feet the wise would fight to sit, the face of a king made for the adoration of worlds: the face of a primarch.

And rage made it the face of a beast. Rage pushed and distorted the features like a tumour breaking out from the skull beneath. It made the eyes into yellow, empty pits, debased the proud lines of brow and jaw, peeled the lips back from the teeth.

And yet it was a face so maddeningly familiar, the face of the sire whose template had made the War Hounds themselves. Khârn could see his brethren in the bronze skin, the set of the eyes, the lines of jaw and skull. Pinned there and staring, the thought that flicked into his mind was of the Legion's battles against the capering xenos whose masks wove faces out of light, taunting them with distorted mockeries of themselves.

The primarch's grip tensed, and Khârn wondered if he had heard the thought – didn't they say some of their sires had that trick? Slowly Angron's other hand rose up before Khârn's face. Even in this light he could see the crackling shell of quick-clotting blood coating the fingers. The hand made a trembling fist before his face that seemed to hang there for an age before it slowly opened to make a stiff-fingered claw. Khârn could tell how the claw would strike: a finger in each eye, powerful enough to punch through the back of the socket and into his brain, the thumb under his jaw to crush his throat, the whole hand then ready to clench and rip away the front of his skull or pull his head from his neck. Astartes bone was powerfully made – did the primarch have the power for that in just one of his hands? Khârn thought he did.

But the hand did not strike. Instead Angron leaned forwards, the snarling gargoyle-mask of his face closing, closing, until his mouth was by Khârn's ear.

'Why?' And his whisper was like the grate of tank-treads on stone. 'I can see what you're made for. You're made to spill blood, just as I am. You're not born normal men, any more than I was.' A long, savage growl. 'So why? Why no triumph rope? Why no weapon in your hand? Why do you all walk down here so meek? Don't you know whose blood I really – eh?'

They were close enough that he had felt Khârn's smile against his cheek, and now he pulled back to see it. Angron's eyes squeezed shut for a moment, then flashed open again as he twitched Khârn away from the wall and slammed him back again. It seemed to Khârn that he could feel the fingers of the hand that held him thrumming with checked violence.

'What's this? Showing your teeth?' Another slam against the wall. 'Why are you smiling?' By the end of the question the voice was once again at that shattering roar, and even Khârn's hearing, more resilient than human, rang for whole seconds before it cleared. And in those few seconds, he realised that the question had not been rhetorical. Angron was waiting for an answer.

'I am…' His voice, when he found it, was hoarse and brittle. 'I am proud of my Legion brothers.' He swallowed to try and soothe his dry throat so that he could speak again, but before he could take another breath he was pulled from the wall and dropped. Angron's kick lofted him into the air in a long curve that fetched him up against a cold, torn corpse. When Khârn dragged in a breath it was full of the reek of blood and offal. There was no way to tell whose the body had been.

Bare feet thumped along the stone floor, counter-pointing growling heaves of breath as Angron closed the distance. He leapt and landed in a crouch beside Khârn as he tried to make his body move. The grip clamped around him again, around his jaw and face this time, and he was dragged half-upright to stare into the primarch's eyes again.

'Proud.' Angron's lips worked as though he were chewing on the word. 'Your brothers. No warriors. None of you will fight. Why… are… you…' He was shaping his words with difficulty, and one hand had risen to clutch at his head. "How, uh, how can, nnn…' And then he lifted Khârn by the front of his tunic and slammed him back down. The ragged remains on the floor gave a bloody squelch as Khârn's back came down across them.

'No pride!' roared Angron, in a voice that Khârn thought dizzily could finish the job of bone-breaking that his fists had started. 'No pride in brothers who stand there with their wits slack! Dull-eyed as a steer on a slaughter-chute! None of you fight! My brothers, my brothers and sisters, oh…' The grip on Khârn's tunic lifted, and he blinked his vision clear and looked up. Angron was not looking at him any more. The primarch had sunk back onto his haunches, one great hand over his eyes. His voice was still a powerful rumble, but barely formed and harsh with accent. Khârn had to concentrate to make out the words. 'My poor warriors,' Angron was murmuring, 'my lost ones.'

And then he dropped his hand and looked into Khârn's eyes. The fury was still in his stare, but it had been banked like a furnace, glowing a dull vermilion rather than roaring crimson.

'Your brothers,' he said in a drained voice, 'are not like my brothers, whoever you are.'

Whoever you are. It took a moment for the words to sink in, and the next thought was, He doesn't know. How can he not know? Still flat on the floor, Khârn took a shuddering breath.

'My name is Khârn. I am a warrior–'

'*No!*' Angron's fist shattered the floor beside Khârn's head. Stone chips stung his skin. 'No warrior! No!'

'–of the Legiones Astartes, the great league of battle-brothers in service to our–'

'No! Dead!' screamed Angron, his head back, muscles corded in his neck. 'Uhhh, my warriors are dead, my brothers, my sisters–'

'–beloved Emperor,' said Khârn, fighting to keep his voice cool and level, facing down the urge to gabble and plead, 'humanity's master, our commander and general, by whose–'

At the mention of the Emperor Angron had begun to shudder and now he threw his head back again, baying like a beast up into the dark, shocking Khârn into silence. Then, snake-fast, his hand closed around Khârn's ankle and with a single wrench of his body he threw him spinning through the air.

There was no time to twist in the air or curl. Khârn managed to get his arms around his head before he crashed into a chamber wall and dropped limp to the floor. Through the red-grey mist in his head he could hear Angron's voice, still filling the chamber with deafening, wordless howls. Within his own body he could feel twitching and roiling as his implanted organs worked on his system: somewhere in there Angron had damaged something badly. Something for the Apothecarion to study, he thought. If they're up to the challenge of identifying which scraps are mine after all this, he found himself adding, and the grim little mental chuckle from that thought was what gave him the strength to push himself, groaning, up onto his elbows and knees.

Angron's foot landed like a forge-hammer between his shoulder blades and flattened him back to the floor, cracked sternum sending out ripping bursts of pain, feeling the fused shell of his ribcage creaking as he fought for breath.

'You don't injure easily, do you, you meek little paperskins?' came Angron's voice from above him, the words bitten out in curt growls. 'Who makes warriors who won't make war? Your murdering bastard commander, that's who.'

More shifts in him as Khârn's metabolism noted the dwindling breath in his lungs and changed its pace to use its oxygen more efficiently. He felt the tickle of pressure as his third lung shifted to higher functioning to take up the shortfall, and a warm sensation in his abdomen as his oolitic kidney worked on the heightened toxins in his blood.

'Sends his cowardly little paperskins to die for him, oh yes, I know his sort.' Angron's words were running together into an almost continuous growl. 'Hands that've never felt the heat of blood. Skin that's never parted. Brain-pan that's never been kissed by the Butcher's Nails. Tongue that's never… huh.'

The weight had shifted on Khârn's back. Angron didn't have the leverage to keep the crushing pressure with his foot, and his other foot had started to come up off the floor. Then suddenly the pressure was gone, and Khârn whooped for air with all three lungs as Angron kicked him over onto his back.

'You're not dying the way I've seen men and women die.' Angron stood over Khârn for a moment, head high like a ceremonial statue, then began to circle where he lay, back bent and head thrust forward, a great hunting cat scenting prey. 'You take wounds the way… hnnn…' He dug the fingers of one hand into scalp for a moment, and Khârn could see his fingers tracing the lines of deep, runnelled scars. '…the way I do. Your blood crisps itself like mine, it… smells…' His hands balled into fists, and Khârn saw the tension roll up the forearms, into the shoulders, into the neck and finally once again pulling the primarch's features into the rage-mask. Slowly, clumsily, Khârn managed to sit up and onto one knee, braced for a new strike, but Angron kept circling him.

'You carry yourselves like men used to iron in their hands, not air. If I were killing you on the hot dust, I'd know your names, because you'd have paid me the proper salute and we'd have turned the rope together.' Around and around him the padding footsteps. Khârn could feel the primarch's gaze on him like heavy chain draped over his shoulders. 'Does it bother you, dying to one who will never know your names?'

Did it bother him, Khârn wondered? But of course that wasn't the question. He was an emissary, here to deliver a message, not to debate.

'We are your Legion, Primarch Angron. We are your instrument and yours to command. The deaths of our enemies are yours to command, and so are our own.'

Not a punch or a kick or a grip, this time, but a ringing, open-handed clout to the side of his head that pitched him sideways.

'Mock me again and I'll crumble your skull in my fingers before your mouth has finished the words.' Angron's voice was shaking with a precarious restraint that was more frightening than a bellow. 'My warriors. My brothers and sisters. Oh my brave ones, my brothers, my...' For several seconds Angron simply paced, his jaw opening and working soundlessly, his head twisting from side to side. 'Gone they are, gone without me, I...'

Angron's fists began to move. He beat them against his thighs and chest, brought one fist and then the other around in long looping motions to smash into his mouth and cheeks. In the new quiet of the chamber the sounds of his flesh splitting and his grunting breaths seemed magnified, textured. Khârn watched, unable to speak, as Angron dropped to his knees, fists doubled in front of his face, muscles locked taut and body shaking.

There was a silence. Finally, Khârn broke it.

'We are your Legion. Made from your blood and genes, crafted in your image. We have fought our way from the world where you, my lord, were conceived. We have spilt blood and burned worlds, we have shattered empires and hounded species into oblivion. Searching for you.'

Just let me speak, lord, he thought as he felt the strength coming back into his voice. Just let me bring our petition to you and then my mission is fulfilled and I am content. Do as you will.

'We do not fight you because you are our primarch. Not just our commander, but our bloodsire, our fountainhead. No matter what, I will not raise a hand to you. Nor will any of my battle-brothers. We are ambassadors to you now. We are here for our Legion and our... our Emperor.' Khârn tensed, but this time Angron did not respond to the word. 'We are coming before you to plead with you to take up the rightful place that was set for you at your creation.'

He began moving, wanting to shuffle closer to where Angron knelt and hunched and shook, but

even now the violence that the primarch exuded like
heat made him pause. Khârn took an unsteady
breath. Pain from his wounds kept sawing at the
bottom of his consciousness, nagging at him. He
squeezed shut his eyes for a moment, pushed himself through the battlefield exercises that had been
hypnoconditioned into him on the mountainsides
of Bodt, smothered the pain with will.

That gave him a moment to think, and with the
respite he brought his mind to bear on this task the
way he would a battlefield, a fortification, an
enemy's swordwork. He thought about his own mission, about the reports he had heard from the
Emperor's own flagship before and after the disas-
trous visit to the planet's surface, about the
primarch's own words. There had been battle down
there, they all knew that. Khârn felt a flicker of envy.
The rebels now lying as corpses down there had
already had the glory of their primarch, their primarch, leading them in–

Understanding came in a flash, given a weird focus
by the pain.

'I envy them,' he said quietly. 'Those ones who
fought with you. I wish I had known them. They followed you to battle. That is all any of my brothers
and I ask of you, sire. The chance to fight with you
as they did.'

Slowly the primarch's hands lowered from his
face. He was kneeling with his back to the nearest
unbroken light, looming over Khârn in silhouette,
but Khârn's vision took in enough infrared to let
him see the bitter little smile on the giant face.

'You? No nails, no rope. Hope you've got a good head for mockery, Khârn of the so-called Legion. We'd have had sport with you in the camps. Jochura would have been merciless. Sharp-tongued, that boy was.' The smile lost a trace of its bitterness. 'I'd watch him bait the others. In the cells at first and then after, when we were roaming. He'd mock, they'd laugh, and he and the one he mocked would laugh harder than all the rest of them. It... was... good. Good to watch. Jochura always swore he would die laughing at his killer.' The smile vanished and Angron's mouth took a brutal downwards twist. 'I told him... told him... uuh,' and Khârn felt the impact up into his body as the great fists smashed into the floor again. He made to speak but the words were cut off as Angron's arm shot out, quicker than sight, and then his hand was locked around Khârn's neck and jaw, dragging him in.

'I don't know how they died!' Angron's shout was so loud that the words seemed to fuzz into white noise in Khârn's ears. The hand shook him like a sack. 'We swore! Swore!' Khârn was being yanked backwards and forwards, and Angron's other hand beat the floor in time. Amid all the clamour a sharp new scent imprinted itself on his senses, and Khârn realised it was the primarch's blood, freshly shed. Angron had battered his hands bloody against the stone.

'We swore an oath,' Angron went on, his voice dropping to a groan like wrenching steel. 'On the road to Desh'ea I had each of them cut a new scar for my rope, and I cut theirs. And we swore an oath that

by the end of all of our lives we'd cut the high-riders
a scar that would bleed for a hundred years!' Despite
himself, Khârn's hands came up as Angron's grip
tightened around his neck and he fought the urge to
try and grapple free. 'A wound their great-
grandwhelps would still cry from! A wound to haunt
any of them who dared look on the hot dust again!'
Angron's grip shifted, and air flooded back into
Khârn's lungs. He hung half-kneeling with one of
the primarch's hands pressed into each side of his
head. 'All this,' Angron said softly, 'and even my
sworn oath wasn't enough.' He parted his hands and
let Khârn crumple to the floor. 'Because I don't even
know how they died.'

When Khârn opened his eyes Angron was sitting
cross-legged a little way from his feet, elbows on
knees, head thrust out in front of his shoulders,
watching him. He could no longer smell the primarch's blood as fresh as he had – had he lost
consciousness for a time? Or had he just lain disori-
entated in the gloom? Or did Angron's blood clot
and seal even faster than his own? He thought it
probably did. He took a breath, torso flickering with
pain, and pushed himself up on his elbows.

'And so how do you meet death, paperskin?' The
coolness in Angron's voice was startling after the rav-
ing daemon that had battered and flung him like a
puppet. 'Do you make your salutes when you're on
the dust? Declaim your lineage like the high-riders?
Declaim your kills like us? Tell me what you do
while you're waiting for the iron in your hand to
warm up to blood-heat.'

'We—' Khârn began, but the unbecoming sprawl was cramping his chest. He pushed himself the rest of the way up and knelt, sitting back on his heels, keeping his breathing steady and composing himself through the pain. Even slumped over as he was, Angron was taller than Khârn by half a head.

'The oath of moment,' he said. 'Our last act before we embark for combat. Each of us prepares our vow to our brothers in the Legion. What we will do for our, our Emperor,' Angron snarled at the word, 'our Legion and ourselves. We witness the oaths. Some Legions write them and then decorate themselves with the written oaths.'

'Did you take one of these oaths before you came in to see me?' Angron asked.

'No, primarch,' replied Khârn, slightly wrong-footed by the question. 'I did not come in here to fight you. I say again, not one in the Legion will raise a hand to you. Oaths of moment are for battle.'

'No challenge,' rumbled the looming shape. 'You do not ask their names when you walk the dust, and you don't give yours. No salutes and no showing of ropes. This is how they fight who say they are my blood-cousins?'

'This is how we fight, sire. We exist to make the Emperor's enemies extinct. We've no need of anything that does not serve that end. And we rarely fight enemies who have names worth knowing, let alone saluting. What the rope is, forgive me, primarch, I do not know.'

'How do you show your warriorship, then?' The puzzlement in the primarch's voice seemed genuine, but when Khârn hesitated over his answer, Angron lunged forwards and punched him over onto his back.

'Answer me! You little grave-grubber, you sit there and smirk at me again like some high-rid... uhhh...' The primarch had sprung to his feet and now he picked Khârn up by the throat, yanked him into the air and dropped him flat on his back again. By the time Khârn had shakily pushed himself back up, Angron had walked away to stand under one of the lights. He turned to make sure Khârn was watching, then turned and spread his arms.

The primarch's torso was bare, packed with inhuman musculature on the Emperor's design, broad, heavy and angular to accommodate the thickened bones and the strange organs and tissues that Astartes legend said the Emperor had grown from his own flesh and blood, modified twenty different ways for his children. Khârn found himself wondering for a moment if Angron had grown up with the slightest idea of what he truly was, before he realised what the primarch was showing him.

A ridge of scar tissue began at the base of Angron's spine. It travelled up his backbone, then veered to the left and around his body, riding over his hip and curv ing around to his front. Angron began to turn in place underneath the light and Khârn saw how the scar seemed to expand and thin again, ploughing and gouging the skin, in some places vanishing entirely where the primarch's healing powers had overcome it. The scar looped around and around Angron's body, spiralling up over his belly, around his ribs, towards his chest. A little past the right of his sternum, it abruptly stopped.

'The Triumph Rope,' Angron said. His hand moved to indicate the upper lengths of the scar, where it was smoother, more continuous, less ugly. There were no healed patches in its upper reaches. Khârn jumped as Angron thumped a fist against his chest with a report like a gun.

'Red twists! Nothing but red on my rope, Khârn! Of all of us, I was the only one. No black twists.' Angron was shaking with rage again, and Khârn bowed his head. His thoughts were bleak: I've started this now, and I wish to finish it, but primarch, I don't know how many more of your rages I can withstand. Then Angron's hands had gripped his shoulders, cruelly grating the bones in the broken one, and the muscles in Khârn's neck and jaw locked rigid as he worked to stop himself crying out.

'I can't go back!' came Angron's voice through the pain, and the note in his voice was not fury now but an anguish far greater than the pain of Khârn's injuries. 'I can't go back to Desh'ea. I can't pick up the soil to make a black twist.' Angron flung Khârn away and dropped to his knees. 'I can't... uhh... I need to wear my failure and I can't. Your Emperor! Your Emperor! I couldn't fight with them and now I can't commemorate them!'

'Sire, I, we...' Khârn could feel little stings and blooms of heat inside his abdomen as his healing systems worked on wounds inside him. 'Your Legion wants to learn your ways. You are our primarch. But we haven't learned them yet. I don't know...'

'No. Grave-grub Khârn doesn't know. No Triumph
Rope on Khârn.' Khârn kept his eyes on the floor but
the sneer was all too audible in Angron's voice. 'For
every battle you live through, a cut to lengthen the
rope. For a triumph, let it scar clean. A red twist. For
a defeat you survive, work some dust from where
you fought into the cut to scar it dark. A black twist.
Nothing but red on me, Khârn,' said Angron, spreading his arms again, 'but I don't deserve it.'

'I understand you, sire,' Khârn answered, and he
found that he did. 'Your brothers, your brothers and
sisters,' he corrected himself, 'they were defeated.'

'They died, Khârn,' said Angron. 'They all died. We
swore to each other that we'd stand together against
the high-riders' armies. The cliffs of Desh'ea would
see the end of it. No more twists in the rope. For any
of us.' His voice had softened to a whisper, heavy
with grief. 'I shouldn't be here. I shouldn't be drawing breath. But I am. And I can't even pick up the
dust from Desh'ea to make a black twist to remember them by. Why did your Emperor do this to me,
Khârn?'

There was silence after the question. Angron, still
standing, had let his head fall forwards and was digging his knuckles into his forehead and face. The
lights made strange shadows across his skull, lumpy
with metal and scars.

Khârn got to his feet. He swayed, but his balance
held.

'It isn't my place to know, sire, what the Emperor
said to you. But we–' Angron wheeled, and Khârn
flinched. The primarch's eyes were alight, and his

teeth were bare, but it wasn't a snarl now, it was a broad, vicious grin.

'Didn't say much to me, no he did not. Think I let him? Think I did?' Angron was in motion again, prowling to and fro under the light, his head snaking from side to side. 'I knew what was happening. I'd stood there and seen the high-riders' killers coming up for my brothers and sisters at Desh'ea, I knew, I knew. Ahhh!' His hands shot out and blurred as they clawed the air in front of him. 'Had his own brothers, didn't he, his kin-guard. All gold-plated, fancying themselves high-riders even though their feet were in the dirt like mine. Pointing their little blades at me!' Angron spun, leapt, hurtled at Khârn and slammed him backwards with an open palm. 'They drew weapons on me! Me! They... they...' Angron threw his head back, palms pressed to the sides of his skull as though sheer physical pressure could keep his boiling thoughts on track. For a moment he was frozen like that, and then he wrenched his body forwards and drove his fist into the stone by Khârn's head. Stinging grains of rock flew out from the impact.

'Killed one, though,' spat Angron, rearing up and starting to prowl again. 'Couldn't put my hands on that Emperor of yours. Ahh, his voice in my ears, worse than the Butcher's Nails...' Angron's fingers swiped and rubbed across the metal in his skull. His gaze was transfixing Khârn again. 'Took one apart though. One of those gold-wrapped bastards. No stomach for it, your Emperor, paper-skinned like you. Pushed me back, into that... place... the place he took me from Desh'ea...' The shadows over Angron's face seemed to deepen at the recollection and his body hunched and folded inwards.

'Teleport,' said Khârn, understanding. 'He teleported you. First to his own ship, and then to here.'

'Something you understand, maybe.' Angron was still moving, further away now, harder for Khârn to pick out except as a smoke-warm shape in infrared. He had his head back and his arms out, as though he were addressing an audience in a high gallery. 'My sisters and brothers and I, owned by the high-riders, floating over us with their crow-cloaks. Their maggot-eyes buzzing around us while we drew each others' blood instead of theirs.' He growled, punching and clawing the air above his head. 'And you, Khârn, owned by the Emperor who draws your blood and puts his gold-shiny puppets into the fights he won't...'

Khârn was shaking his head, and Angron had seen him.

'Well now,' his voice rumbled out of the shadow, and all the menace was back in it. The sound reminded Khârn how weak he was, how wounded, how unarmed. 'Khârn calls me liar. Khârn thinks he will question his primarch for the sake of his Emperor.' Once again Angron came out of the darkness in a leap, landing in front of Khârn with one hand cocked back for a pulverising punch.

'Admit it, Khârn,' he snarled. 'Why won't you say it?' The cocked fist shook but did not swing. Angron pushed his face forwards as though he were about to bite Khârn's flesh. 'Say it! Say it!'

'I saw him once,' was what Khârn said instead. 'I saw him on Nove Shendak. World Eight-Two-Seventeen. A world of worms. Giant creatures, intelligent. Hateful. Their weapons were filaments, metal feathers that they embedded in themselves to conduct energies out of their bodies. I remember we saw the surface roil with the filaments before the worms broke out of it almost at our feet. Thick as a man, longer than you, sire, are tall. Three mouths in their faces, a dozen teeth in their mouths. They spoke through the mud in sonic screams and witch-whispers.

'We had found three systems under their thrall, burned them out of their colony nests and chased them home. But on their cradle-world we found humans. Humans lost to humanity for who knows how long, crawling on the land while the worms slithered in the marsh seas. Hunting the humans, farming them. Killing them.'

Angron's eyes were still narrowed and his fist still raised, but he no longer shook. Khârn's eyes had half-closed. He remembered how the War Hounds' blue and white armour glimmered in the worm-world's twilight, remembered the endless, nerve-sapping sucking sounds as the lunar tides dragged the mud oceans to and fro across the jagged stone continents.

'The Iron Warriors were with us too, and Perturabo landed with the assault pioneers after our lances scoured our drop-zone bare and dry. He worked out how to dredge and shape the ground. The earth there, well, there barely was earth. Just muddy slops, full of trace toxins, the bedrock deep enough that a man'd drown if he planted his feet on it.'

'How did you stop them?' demanded Angron. 'If you couldn't stand on the ground?'

'Sentries with high-powered lasguns, sire, devices to read the movements of the mud to hear them moving through it towards us, explosives we seeded around the earthworks and allowed to sink to where the worms burrowed.

'Perturabo's earthworks were a miracle. He built trenches and dykes, penned in the mud seas and drained them, drove the worms back, reclaimed land these wretched humans could build on. And when the worms came out to fight us, they met the Emperor and his War Hounds.'

'You're speaking of yourself,' said Angron. 'Yourselves.' Khârn nodded.

'The War Hounds. XII Legion Astartes. Made in your image, as your warriors, primarch. He saw us fight in the Cephic hive-sprawls and named us for the white hounds the Yeshk warriors in the north used. He did us an honour with the name, primarch. We are proud of it, and we hope you will be too.'

Angron gave a growl, but he did not speak. The hand that had been a fist had opened again.

'The southern anchor of Perturabo's earthworks was a rock, the closest thing that place had to a mountain, the only one the sludge tides hadn't been able to wear down. When the worms saw the Mechanicum begin to change the world's face they mustered to break us under the peak.

'They buried themselves in the sludge beyond our range and came forwards under it to meet us.' Khârn's voice was speeding up as his memory filled with the sharp reek of the poisoned ground and the warning cries from the Imperial Army artillerists as the mud ocean heaved. Angron had backed away, his head pushed forwards and his eyes were full of concentration.

'They first came in a wave,' Khârn said. 'They had skulked around the fringes of the earthworks, carried off some of the crews working the pumps and dredgers. We had not fought a decisive action against them for months. But now Gheer and Perturabo had read the patterns of their attacks and placed us for the counter-assault. We formed up among Perturabo's aqueduct walls, only half-built they were and still blocked half the sky. We took our oaths of moment and primed our bolters.'

'Bolters?'

'A firearm. A powerful one. The weapon of the Astartes.'

'Ehh. Get on with it. The worms came for the earthworks.' Angron was staring over Khârn's head, yanking his hands back and forth, shuffling his feet. It was a moment before Khârn realised the Primarch was playing the defence out in his mind, ordering the lines, mapping out the ground. 'So they came up like chaer-dogs at a spike-line? Stupid to rush a shield wall. Tell me what you did.' Khârn closed his eyes, focusing past his injured body to run the conditioned routines that ordered his memories.

'The first line of them broke the mud with their jaws and filaments,' he said, 'and they came at us behind a wall of their power-arcs. The mud steamed in front of them and where the arcs converged they shattered rock. They sent a rolling bombardment ahead of them. We worked to break it with thudd guns, dropping shells behind their blast-front, and we broke up the rock in front of them with grenades. We thought we had their measure when the counter-bombardment made their front lines shiver, but they were simply filling up our attention, measuring where our own line was wavering. When their blasts dropped away they came in force to the weak points. Drove wedges into our front. To flank and envelop we'd have had to go out onto the mud where we could barely walk, and where the mud was shallow enough for us to try it, they had second and third lines ready to drag the flankers under or cook them in their armour. To break the assaults we had to get them onto rock, where we could manoeuvre better than they. Perturabo had built traps into his earthworks. False outer walls, double emplacements, killing zones along the drainage canals.' Angron nodded approvingly, looking up and down the dark chamber as though he could see the great rough walls, lit by orange bolter-flare and the blue-white power-arcs of the worms.

'But still we had to bring them inside our lines to break them. Hold them back and then fall to second positions, one formation at a time, through the Army lines to where we were waiting to drop

the axe. There were a lot of worms, primarch.'
Khârn grinned. His wounds throbbed as the vivid-
ness of the memory prompted his metabolism to
begin glanding combat stimms. 'Our axes weren't
dry for a month.' In answer Angron growled again,
making a quick double motion of his arm as
though swinging a blade forwards and backwards
at something below his own height. Barely thinking about it, Khârn's warrior brain filed away the
Primarch's footing and balance, his arm and shoulder motions, noted where a riposte might land
home. Then, still in his combat stance, Angron
pinned Khârn with his gaze again.

'The Emperor. You talk about fighting down there
in the mud but you don't talk about the Emperor.
High-rode, did he? Hung above you, did he?'
Angron's voice was rising, turning ugly and ragged.
'Laughed at you, did he? Called your blood-spills,
did he? Admit it, Khârn!' In a blur he crossed the
distance and knocked Khârn to one knee with a
looping, glancing arm-sweep.

'The Emperor,' Khârn said, and couldn't stop
himself from smiling at the memory. 'The Emperor
was a golden storm descending onto Nove Shendak's filth. When the worms were in amongst us he
came down from the peak and it was as if he had
brought a fragment of the sun down for us in
amends for the sun we couldn't see through those
filthy fogs. He shone out over the battle lines like a
beacon. His custodians were like living banners,
the troopers rallied to them, but he...' Khârn closed
his eyes, looking for the words.

'Imagine, sire, did they fight in your home with grenades? Explosive weapons, small enough to hold in the hand and throw?'

'High-rider weapons,' snarled Angron. 'Not fit for a warrior on the hot dust.'

'But imagine, primarch, some,' he searched for the word Angron had used, 'some paperskin who takes a grenade and simply grips it in his fist until it explodes. Imagine how it would destroy the hand, shatter the arm, ruin the body! Wherever the Emperor met one of their columns head on it shattered like that. He didn't repel them, sire. Didn't defeat them. He ruined them. Assault after assault, not even Perturabo when he came down to the lines for the final–'

'You've said that name already,' boomed Angron from behind him. 'Who is he?'

'Forgive me, sire. Another primarch. One of the first we found. I was new to the War Hounds when the message went through the fleets, and I almost didn't understand what it meant. Not until I saw the Iron Warriors and how they reacted. The very air seemed to change around them. They and we and the Ultramarines, we were travelling together. We envied them. They had found their blood-sire and their general. Now we have found ours.'

'Another. Another one.' Khârn risked a look around and up. Angron was standing still, hands pressed to his face again, teeth grinding as he concentrated. 'Another one of me?'

'Not like you, primarch. A brother to you. Made for conquest and kingship as you are. The Iron Warriors, they're his Legion now.'

'Brave fighters?'

'Brave enough,' Khârn answered, 'with a wall to sit on or a trench to stand in.'

'Walls.' Angron growled the word. 'Walls can be broken.'

'So we tell them, sire. Perhaps you can–'

'Walls,' Angron cut him off. 'When we first broke out of the caves and walked on stone, not dust, we were nearly trapped within walls. We had the weapons we'd drawn one another's blood with and they were ready for a change of flavour. The high-riders laughed, the way they always laughed as they looked down on us on the dust, and they called out taunts the way they goaded us when we fought.' Angron whipped his fists through the air as though he were batting at insects. 'Sent their voices through the maggot-eyes they watched us with. Voices, voices. "Oh, do oblige, wonderful Angron!"' Angron's voice was suddenly, eerily imitating a higher, softly accented, singsong voice. '"We wagered you'd take a wound from a dozen enemies, surely a single wound, won't you oblige and bleed for us?"' His tone shifted and he imitated another. '"My son is watching with me, Angron, what's wrong with you? Fight harder, give him something to cheer!" The eyes, the voices. The Butcher's Nails in my head… hot… smoke… in my thoughts…' A wolfish look stole over Angron's face. 'It was good to fight without the eyes and the voices. They tried to trap us but we wouldn't stop for them. Every line they formed we rushed before they were in formation. They were everywhere but we were fast.'

408   MATTHEW FARRER

Angron was suiting actions to words, loping back and forth, smashing and lunging and ripping at imaginary enemies.

'Jochura with his laugh and his chains. Cromach, he fought with a brazier-glaive. Hah! I gave him the first black twist in his rope, and he and I burned the watchtowers at Hozzean together. Klester riding her shriekspear through the air, you should have seen her, Khârn, so fast, and ohh…' Angron was clutching at the metal tracery poking out through his mane. 'Fast we moved, fast, not hanging between walls, entrapment is death, fast, trust and discipline… Never rest, always forwards, hunger for the enemy, that's what they taught us… Uhh, my brothers and sisters, oh, if we had known how it would end, we didn't know!' Angron fell to his knees and howled. 'All that valour! The eaters of cities, they called us! All the mountain fastnesses, burning like beacons! All the Great Coast painted in blood! We devoured Hozzean with flames! Meahor! Ull-Chaim!' Weeping and roaring, he leapt to his feet, oblivious to Khârn looking on. 'We broke them at the river before Ull-Chaim! Hung half a thousand high-riders and kin-guard from the vine bridges! The princelings' heads floating on the river, down to the lowlands as our heralds! The silver lace from their skulls, ahh, ripped from their skulls, wrapped on my fists!'

The furnace rage was back. Khârn thought to shuffle away, and dismissed the idea. He would not hide from Angron any more than he would fight him. And Angron would find him anywhere in this room anyway. And no sooner had he finished that thought than he had been wrenched from the ground by each arm and swung over the primarch's head to be slammed into the floor. Stone cracked under him.

'They paid! They paid! We made them pay!' Angron kicked Khârn across the floor, bellowing. 'Paid for my brothers and sisters! Who will pay?'

Dizzy, fainting, Khârn felt himself picked up and slammed down again, kicked again, grabbed by the neck.

'Pay, War Hound! Pay! Fight me!' Something – fist? Foot? – crashed into his chest and Khârn sprawled on the floor, choking. 'Get up and fight!'

The end of it, then, Khârn thought. Well, I carried my embassy as well as a War Hound could. He tried to rise and couldn't, so he lay full-length on his back and spoke weakly into the air.

'You are my primarch and my general, Lord Angron. I swore that I would seek you out and follow you, and I will not fight you. And if I must die, then yours is the hand I will die by. I am Khârn and I am loyal to your will.'

While he waited, he faded from consciousness then jerked back as his system shifted itself to rouse him and the pain of his injuries sharpened. He could not see or hear Angron, but he could feel the stone floor underneath him and the cool air in his lungs. When it came, Angron's voice was frighteningly close, almost by his ear.

'You are warriors, Khârn,' the primarch said. 'I know warriors when I see them.' Khârn tried to answer but pain rippled through his neck and chest when he tried to speak.

'This... Emperor,' Angron said, palpably struggling to keep his voice level. 'He is the one you swore to?'

'We swore to each other,' Khârn managed to get out, 'in his name and on his banner.' His breath took a long time to come. 'That we would not... raise a hand against you.'

Angron said nothing for a time. Khârn's consciousness had begun to flicker again by the time he spoke.

'Such devotion... from such warriors...' His voice tailed off, faded and returned. His hands were pressed to his head again. 'A man who can... a man... to whom... your oaths... for him you would...'

Minutes passed. Angron's voice came again.

'This room. I can leave it?' It took Khârn a moment to work out how to answer.

'This is the flagship of the War Hounds. Our greatest vessel. It is the instrument of your will and yours to command, primarch, as are we.'

For a long time there was no answer, just quiet and dark, and just as Khârn was starting to feel his consciousness go again he felt himself lifted, slowly and gently now, and carried through the dark.

THEY HAD LOOKED at one another when the booming knock came on the doors, unsure of what to do, but only for a moment. Then Dreagher worked the openers, and when the locks clanked and the portals groaned open he was there. The War Hounds gasped and moved back as the giant shadow on the steps grew, advanced, came into the light. With his right hand the primarch supported Khârn, battered and hanging barely conscious.

Angron stood, wary, wound tight as a bowstring, his free hand opening and closing. His breath rumbled in his throat. For long minutes each War Hound in turn blanched under the primarch's gaze, until Khârn managed to lift his head and speak.

'Salute your primarch, War Hounds. Salute he who shed blood on the hot dust and made the high-riders pay for their arrogance. Salute your blood-sire and the general of the XII. Salute the one whose soldiers were named the Eaters of Cities. Salute him, Astartes!'

And the War Hounds answered him. Hands and voices lifted in salute and axe-heads were crashed against the floor. Gathering around Angron, he towering silently at their centre, they shouted and saluted again, and again, and Khârn found the strength and voice to stagger to join the circle and add his shouts to theirs.

'Primarch,' said Angron. His voice was a murmur, but it cut the War Hounds' voices straight to silence. 'I am a general again.'

'Primarch!' shouted Dreagher in response, 'General! Your warriors were the eaters of cities, lord, but with you to command us the War Hounds will be the eaters of worlds!'

For a moment Angron swayed, his eyes and fists closed. But then he looked at Dreagher, from there to Khârn. And he smiled.

'World Eaters,' he said, slowly, tasting the sounds. 'World Eaters. So you shall be, then, little brothers.

You'll learn to cut the rope. We shall bleed, and be brothers.' This time they all met his eyes. Slowly, one of Angron's great fists came up to return their salutes.

'Come with me, then, World Eaters. Come down into my chamber and we will speak.' Angron turned on his heel and walked back into his chamber.

Silently, supporting Khârn in their midst, the World Eaters followed their primarch down into that darkness that stank of blood.

ABOUT THE AUTHORS

DAN ABNETT

Dan Abnett is a novelist and award-winning comic book writer. He has written twenty-five novels for the Black Library, including the acclaimed Gaunt's Ghosts series and the Eisenhorn and Ravenor trilogies, and, with Mike Lee, the Darkblade cycle. His Black Library novel *Horus Rising* and was a bestseller. He lives and works in Maidstone, Kent.

Dan's website can be found at *www.DanAbnett.com*

MIKE LEE

Together with Dan Abnett, Mike Lee wrote the five-volume Malus Darkblade series. He also wrote the acclaimed *Nagash the Sorcerer* for Warhammer Time of Legends. Mike was the principal creator and developer for White Wolf Game Studio's Demon: The Fallen, and he has contributed to almost two dozen role-playing games and supplements over the years. An avid wargamer and devoted fan of pulp adventure, Mike lives in the United States.

ANTHONY REYNOLDS

After finishing university, Anthony Reynolds set sail from his homeland and ventured forth to foreign climes. He ended up settling in the UK, and managed to blag his way into Games Workshop's hallowed Design Studio. There he worked for four years as a Games Developer and two years as part of the Management team. He now resides back in his hometown of Sydney, overlooking the beach and enjoying the sun and the surf, though he finds that to capture the true darkness and horror of Warhammer and Warhammer 40,000 he has taken to writing in what could be described as a darkened cave.

JAMES SWALLOW

James Swallow's stories from the dark worlds of Warhammer 40,000 include the Horus Heresy novel *The Flight of the Eisenstein*, *Faith & Fire*, the Blood Angels books *Deus Encarmine*, *Deus Sanguinius* and *Red Fury*, as well as short fiction for *Inferno!* and *What Price Victory*. Swallow's other credits include writing for *Star Trek Voyager*, scripts for videogames and audio dramas.
He lives in London.

GAV THORPE

Prior to becoming a freelance writer, Gav Thorpe worked for Games Workshop as lead background designer, overseeing and contributing to the Warhammer and Warhammer 40,000 worlds. He has written numerous novels and short stories set in the fictional worlds of Games Workshop, including the Time of Legends 'The Sundering' series, the seminal Dark Angels novel *Descent of Angels*, and the *Last Chancers* omnibus. He lives in Nottingham, UK, with his mechanical hamster, Dennis.

GRAHAM McNEILL

Hailing from Scotland, Graham McNeill worked for over six years as a Games Developer in Games Workshop's Design Studio before taking the plunge to become a full-time writer. In addition to many previous novels, including bestsellers *False Gods* and *Fulgrim*, Graham has written a host of SF and Fantasy stories and comics. Graham lives and works in Nottingham and you can keep up to date with where he'll be and what he's working on by visiting his website.

Join the ranks of the 4th Company at
www.graham-mcneill.com

MATTHEW FARRER

Matthew Farrer lives in Australia, and is a member of the Canberra Speculative Fiction Guild. He has been writing since his teens, and has a number of novels and short stories to his name, including the popular Shira Calpurnia novels for the Black Library.